Everyone loves the ladies of Covington!

"A pure charmer, a rich Southern tale about love and loyalty."

—Bookpage

"As cozy as a cup of tea and a favorite cat, the latest in the Covington series will delight fans. . . . Fans of Jan Karon and Ann Ross will enjoy these gentle novels."

—Booklist

"A must-read for women of all ages."

—The Tampa Tribune

"Genuinely inspiring. . . . The reader can't help but be moved by the 'ladies' and their progress."

—Library Journal

"Ms. Medlicott is attuned to the nuances of Southern life, and draws her characters with affectionate understanding and an inspiring message of self-acceptance, courage, and survival."

—The Dallas Morning News

"A winner. . . . The three ladies inspire by forming a community in which they thrive and find new careers and loves, all with dignity and autonomy."

—Publishers Weekly

"A heartwarming adventure."

—San Jose Mercury News

Promises of Change

JOAN MEDLICOTT

POCKET BOOKS

NEW YORK LONDON TORONTO SYDNEY

Pocket Books
A Division of Simon & Schuster, Inc.
1230 Avenue of the Americas
New York, NY 10020

First Pocket Books trade paperback edition January 2009

POCKET and colophon are registered trademarks of Simon & Schuster, Inc.

For information about special discounts for bulk purchases, please contact Simon & Schuster Special Sales at 1-800-456-6798 or business@simonandschuster.com.

Designed by Carla Jayne Little

Manufactured in the United States of America

10 9 8 7 6 5 4 3 2 1

Library of Congress Cataloging-in-Publication Data

Medlicott, Joan A. (Joan Avna)
    Promises of change / Joan Medlicott.— 1st Pocket Books trade paperback ed.
      p. cm.
    ISBN 978-1-4165-2458-8
    1. Older women—Fiction. 2. Retired women—Fiction. 3. Widows—Fiction.
4. Female friendship—Fiction. 5. North Carolina—Fiction. 6. Domestic fiction. I. Title.
    PS3563.E246P76 2009
    813'.54—dc22   2008029348

ISBN-13: 978-1-4165-2458-8
ISBN-10:   1-4165-2458-4

To my daughter, Paula, in appreciation
for her kindness and patience

Acknowledgments

My deepest thanks to Attorney Marsha Shortell, formerly victims' advocate for the Asheville Police Department, for the significant information she provided on recognizing and avoiding scams and scammers.

My heartfelt appreciation to John Cowart, LCSW, Post-Traumatic Stress Disorder Center at the Asheville Veterans' Hospital in Asheville, NC. He opened my eyes to a very important and heart-wrenching issue that will affect an entire generation of veterans and their families.

1

The Homecoming

Amelia Declose settled into her rocking chair on the front porch of the farmhouse she shared with Hannah Parrish and Grace Singleton. Gathering her shawl about her, she knotted the ends across her chest. It was early morning. A glorious sunrise wove its magic across the mountains, slashing the sky with flaming orange. The celery green of new leaves on shrubs and trees and the chirp of a baby bird in a nest artfully camouflaged in a shrub near the porch filled her heart with pure joy. *There are days when one feels glad to be alive, and today is one of those days.*

Amelia's mind drifted back years ago to when she, Hannah, and Grace had met in a dreary boardinghouse in Pennsylvania where the owner, the dour Olive Pruitt, restricted the use of the kitchen and refused to allow a wonderful cook like Grace to bake a cake or make a pot of soup.

They had taken a risk, trusted one another, pooled their emotional and financial resources, and moved to a run-down farmhouse in rural North Carolina that Amelia had unexpectedly inherited, and in so doing had revitalized their lives. Here, Amelia had discovered a talent for photography. Hannah's skills and love for gardening had resurfaced, and Grace's kindness and wisdom found their outlet in volunteer work with children and in creating a community of friends and family.

Amelia's finger traced the rim of the delicate china teacup. *The human spirit takes comfort and solace from quite ordinary things: cows milling about in a pasture, a comfortable chair like this, the tinkle of wind chimes.*

A cup of tea with her friends on this porch and Sunday dinners with their ever-increasing surrogate family were now among the happy routines in her life. Even winter, her least favorite season, had become more bearable, with its hot cocoa topped with tiny marshmallows, long hot baths, and snuggling beneath her down comforter. And best of all, Miriam and Sadie were a part of her life—her unexpected family.

Her attention was drawn to a taxi that entered Cove Road, slowed, turned into Max's driveway across the street, and pulled up to his farmhouse. The short, heavy woman and bearded man who disembarked and plodded up onto the front porch reminded Amelia of Russian immigrants in a movie she had seen recently on late-night television. Several large suitcases were deposited on Max's front porch, then the taxi rolled away.

The man helped the woman to a porch chair, then walked briskly to the front door. Something about him seemed vaguely familiar. She watched as the man carried the luggage into Max and Hannah's house, then assisted the woman from the chair, and Amelia realized that the woman was very pregnant, not fat. The front door closed behind them and light flooded the downstairs windows.

Max's son and his wife?

Could it be Max's son and his wife? No, they live in India. Hannah would have said something, would have been there to greet them. After all, she is Max's wife, even if she lives with Grace and me most of the time.

Shadows moved across Max's downstairs windows. Who were they? It was Saturday, Hannah and Max's private day. Max would never invite anyone to visit on Saturday.

Hannah usually stayed at Max's on Friday nights, but she had been here last night. Grace's companion, Bob, and Max had come for dinner, and they had all played Trivial Pursuit and talked about getting a dog. Grace had wandered into a shop in Asheville and seen a puppy she'd fallen in love with and been sorely tempted to bring home.

"Why would you want the mess of raising a puppy? Get an older, house-trained dog from a shelter," Hannah had said.

"Oh, don't do that. Get a dog from the Compassionate Animal Network. Their members raise the dogs from puppies," Bob said. "I think you'd find they're well socialized, too. When you get a dog from a shelter you have no idea what you're bringing home."

There had been much talk, but nothing had been decided.

Now Amelia's mind returned to Max's guests. Max and Hannah's Saturdays were sacrosanct. Either they drove into Asheville for brunch and to the farmers' market for fresh fruit and vegetables for both their households, or they sequestered themselves at Max's house.

"What do you do all day?" Grace had once asked Hannah.

"We turn off the phones and just hang out." Hannah had given Grace a shy smile. "We eat leftovers and ice cream, read, watch old movies, things like that. Once, we sat all day and sorted through old photos that we'd been meaning to put into an album. One thing we do *not* do is discuss our work at Bella's Park."

Across the road, the lights in Max's downstairs rooms switched off. Amelia went inside, placed her teacup in the kitchen sink, then climbed the stairs and knocked on Hannah's bedroom door. "You awake, Hannah?"

"Come in, Amelia."

Hannah sat on the edge of her bed, one foot shoved into her bedroom slipper, the other foot twisted, wiggling under the bed in search of the other slipper. Amelia bent and retrieved it for her.

"Ever notice how shoes, especially slippers, are never where you put them when you go to bed? I think they walk about while we sleep," Hannah said. "It's odd."

"What's odd is that there's a strange man and a very pregnant woman at Max's. I was on the porch when a cab deposited them at his front steps. The man opened the front door and walked right in."

Hannah hastened to the window, which overlooked Cove Road. "I don't see anything or anyone, and there's no light in Max's bedroom." She reached for the buttons on her pajama top. "I'll go right over."

"I'll go with you," Amelia said. "Meet you downstairs."

At the front door, Amelia handed Hannah a mug of black coffee without sugar, and they started across Cove Road. Hannah unlocked the front door, then flipped on the foyer light. There sat three large suitcases.

Max's heavy footsteps sounded on the stairs, and seeing Hannah, he smiled. "I was just about to phone you. Guess who's here?"

Hannah shook her head. "Who?"

"My son, Zachary, and his wife, Sarina, have come home from India, and she's about to have a baby."

Hannah was uncertain that she had heard him correctly, but there he stood, beaming and happy. "Zachary, here? But . . . I thought . . . ?"

"Yes, I know. He said he hated Covington and would never come back, but life is unpredictable." Taking Hannah's arm, Max urged her toward the kitchen, Amelia following. There Max sank into a chair and ran his fingers through his hair. "Sometimes things don't work out as planned. They've been through hell, from what they've been telling me."

"What kind of hell? What's happened to them?" Hannah slid into the chair across from Max. Amelia leaned against the wall and waited for his reply.

"You know her people are Hindus. Well, it seems there was an issue about a mosque being built on what was considered a Hindu holy site, and this triggered hostilities on both sides. The mayor, a Hindu, was ambushed and killed by God knows who, which led to the looting and burning of a prominent Muslim businessman's home. After that, it degenerated into a free-for-all.

"Sarina's brother-in-law, the accountant, was shot and wounded in the leg on the way to his office. They think it was a random shooting, but it's crazy over there, Zachary says, and everyone suddenly has a gun. Sarina's entire family and all their servants have fled to their home in the south. Just as well, it seems, for after they left, one of their stores was torched. Sarina's baby is due next month, and they felt they'd be safer here until the turmoil gets straightened out— if it ever does."

"How frightening to live in a world like that," Amelia said."People shooting other people, burning property."

"After the Twin Towers going down, I wonder if we're much safer, or if safety is just an illusion." Hannah shook her head.

"I think of India as a peaceful country, and Hindus as tolerant of all religions," Amelia said.

"This Muslim/Hindu hatred has taken root in many parts of India," Max said. "No one knows where it will lead. Zachary did the right thing. Sarina will have the baby here." Satisfaction showed in his eyes.

Hannah knew Zachary had been hardheaded in expressing his dislike of Covington. He had been cruel and had rejected his father and his father's business, and had hurt Max deeply. Max had buried the hurt, and despaired of ever seeing any grandchildren. Had Max told Zachary that she and Max were married? If he had, what had been his son's reaction? Hannah did not trust or like Zachary, and she was certain that if his reaction had been positive, it was not sincere.

An uneasy feeling settled over her. Their pleasant lives were about to be cast into confusion.

Hannah looked at Max. "Have you told Zachary that we're married?"

Max shook his head. "There's been no time. Sarina was exhausted, traveling this late in her pregnancy. She collapsed when we got her upstairs. The fright and the stress of it all, leaving her family and home, the trip—it was too much for her. We got her into bed, and Zachary took her up some chicken soup. If she relaxes and falls asleep, he'll be down, I imagine."

Max reached across the table and lay his large hands over Hannah's. "You're trembling. Now, don't you worry, sweetheart. We'll tell him about us as soon as he comes down. How can their being here affect us? We'll go on with our lives just as we have been."

"Do you really think so?" Hannah asked.

"I'm sure of it. They'll stay until the baby comes, then in a few months they'll move on to a city."

"Don't be too sure of that. Things change." The knot in Hannah's stomach began to hurt.

2

A Loss of Function

Through her open windows, Grace heard the slam of a car door. She had been up most of the night worrying about her health. This particular bout of insomnia started weeks ago when her internist had advised her to see a kidney specialist.

"Your blood work indicates there may be a slight problem with your kidneys. Nothing serious, but we need to check it out," he had said in a voice that Grace considered much too casual for the information it imparted.

The nephrologist had been young, pleasant, and patient. He had taken a thorough history and drawn a crude rendition of kidneys and arteries on a notepad. He explained that high blood pressure, compounded by diabetes, could, over time, adversely affect one's kidneys. "I'm going to have my nurse set you up for a sonogram to see if there's a blockage in the arteries that go to your kidneys."

Grace's mind snapped shut. Blockages sounded ominous. "And if there's a blockage?"

"If there's a restriction of blood flow to your kidneys, we'll go in and clean out the arteries. It's a routine procedure these days," he replied and smiled, but his smile had not reassured her.

Grace remembered Bob's heart attack several years earlier and his angioplasty, a surgical procedure to clean the plaque from a blood vessel to his heart. Bob had made light of it, saying that he had felt absolutely nothing. But the prospect of a probe snaking through her arteries terrified her, and when the young doctor suggested the possible "procedure," Grace felt weak and had had to clutch the cold metal arms of her chair for support. The nurse had walked her from the office to her car.

Later, when she told him, Bob said, "Now don't you go worrying yourself silly while you wait to have that sonogram."

"How can I not worry? I'm scared out of my mind."

The more she learned about diabetes—how serious, how dangerous it was, how it could affect her eyes, feet, everything in her body—the more upset she became. These days, even after seeing the nurse-dietician at the hospital, she hardly knew what to eat or how to cook and found it increasingly hard to get a grip on a whole new way of thinking about food. And exercise! The doctor said that was very important. She walked some, but the length of Cove Road was hardly what he meant, and when she signed on at a gym, all those fit young women leading other fit young women in aerobics or yoga made her want to never return, and she had not.

"It's going to be all right." Bob ran his hand across her arm in a gesture he probably considered soothing but that, at that moment, had annoyed Grace.

The sonogram had been painless, so when her doctor said that the test revealed no arterial blockages, Grace relaxed, until she heard his next words.

"But what we found is that your kidneys are functioning at forty-four percent of capacity."

The doctor had perched on the edge of the examination table. A chart of kidneys, bright with veins and arteries, hung like a photograph on the pale gray wall behind him. The seriousness of his words bounced off Grace's consciousness. Had Bob not accompanied her to his office, Grace would have denied the truth, as she was wont to do.

"If you were twenty-seven years old," the doctor continued, "I'd be concerned, but since you're, what?"—he checked her chart—"seventy-two . . ."

"Why are my kidneys functioning at only forty-four percent?" she had asked.

"We all lose kidney function as we age. I'm not worried, so long as we keep that function at forty-four percent. Your new blood pressure medication will help protect your kidneys."

But at night, lying in bed, Grace wondered what else was silently deteriorating deep within her body. She prayed and tried unsuccessfully to meditate and visualize herself whole and perfect and wondered if her efforts were too little too late.

It was Amelia's, and then Hannah's hurried footsteps in the hall, and the closing of their front door, that roused her from self-pity and from her bed. Grace grabbed a robe and hastened downstairs, hoping to catch them, but too late. Through their kitchen window she watched her friends enter Max's house, and for a moment she considered following them.

But Grace needed breakfast and her medication. If she waited too long in the morning, her blood sugar dropped, which resulted in a weak, slightly nauseous feeling. Gone were the days of well-sugared morning tea and coffee cake. Instead, she topped a thin wheat cracker with two slices of Swiss cheese and poured a small glass of skim milk. She carried the cracker and milk into the downstairs guest bedroom, settled into the glider rocker, and flipped on television to the house and garden channel. Whenever she was alone and the room not occupied by a guest, she breakfasted in this lovely room with its large windows and view of the shady hillside behind the house. Somehow it helped compensate for the less than satisfying change in her diet.

The room faced north, which was good, for glare bothered her eyes. It always had, even in childhood, when she'd started to wear glasses. Grace had recently visited an ophthalmologist, who checked her yearly for retinopathy, another possible serious side effect of diabetes. To her great relief, he had assured her that her eyes were fine. No change in her prescription, but he had suggested darker lenses, which she had gotten.

Whatever's keeping Amelia over there? she wondered. And why is Amelia intruding on Hannah and Max's Saturday? Then Grace's attention went to *Design on a Dime*, a makeover show that never ceased to amaze her—what could be done with so little money—and she did not hear Amelia until her friend entered the room.

"Grace. Didn't you hear me call you?"

"No. I didn't. Look at that room." Grace pointed at the television. "They're showing the before-and-after pictures. Marvelous what they've done, don't you think?"

"Oh, shut that off. I have really big news for you. Guess who's come home?"

Grace clicked off the set. "Who has come home?"

Amelia's carefully plucked eyebrows arched. "Zachary

and his very, very pregnant wife, Sarina, that's who. They arrived about an hour ago. I was sitting out on the porch having a cup of tea, just enjoying this glorious spring day. They came by taxi with lots of luggage. But until we went over there, I hadn't a clue who they were."

"Didn't Zachary declare Covington anathema?"

"Sure he did, until the Muslims and Hindus over in India started shooting at each other and burning homes."

Grace's hands covered her mouth and her gasp, then fell to her lap. "That happened in India, where they were living?"

Amelia nodded. Her face was flushed, and she literally quivered with excitement. Rarely did she have the opportunity to be in the know and to break exciting news to her housemates. She told Zachary's story to a wide-eyed Grace.

"I can hardly believe this."

"Every word of it's true," Amelia said, thinking that if Hannah had imparted this information, Grace would have believed *her* right off the bat.

"It's hard to believe. How will this affect Hannah and Max, do you think?"

Amelia shrugged. "*Mon ami*, you know men. They aren't aware of the undercurrents of people's feelings beneath their noses. He says nothing is going to change." She leaned forward. "Hannah thinks that it's all going to change, and I'm sure she's right."

"It can't change the fact that they're married."

"But it can affect their lifestyle, can't it?" Amelia said.

Grace nodded. It was hard to imagine Zachary here and his wife about to have a baby. "He never sent a cable, didn't let his father know they were coming?"

"When did he ever let his father know anything about his life, except after the fact?"

"It's all been going so well for Hannah. What's going to happen." Grace's words were more comment than question.

Amelia raised an eyebrow. "Your guess is as good as mine. Well, I have to run. Mike and I are taking Miriam and Sadie to the Toe River over near Celo. You know where that is, out past Burnsville? Mike has a job there, and Miriam's bringing a picnic lunch for us."

Grace nodded.

Miriam was the daughter of Amelia's deceased husband, Thomas, with an Englishwoman. About a year ago, Miriam and her little daughter, Sadie, had arrived unannounced on their doorstep seeking refuge from an abusive husband. The shock of Thomas's betrayal and infidelity devastated Amelia, and for many weeks she had rejected both mother and daughter. Then good sense had prevailed, and Amelia placed the blame squarely where it belonged, on Thomas, and she had opened her arms and heart to Miriam and her little girl and garnered to herself a loving daughter and granddaughter, who now lived in a cottage that the ladies had built for them near Bob's cottage on Cove Road.

Miriam's ex-husband had managed to trace her to Covington, but in a drunken stupor he had driven his car headlong into the Swannanoa River and ended his life.

Now Amelia stood, smoothed back her hair, and slung her camera bag across her shoulder. "I'm off, then."

The house was suddenly too quiet, and Grace, who needed to keep busy, trudged up the stairs to her room and began rearranging her closet. She removed turtleneck shirts, sweatpants, and sweaters, folded and stored them in the drawers from which she'd removed her summer shirts and skirts. She considered getting out the ironing board, but decided instead to hang the summer clothes in the closet, hoping that the wrinkles would smooth themselves.

Walking past the mirror, she noted her unkempt hair, a clump sticking up on top of her head, another clump waving at her from the side. Grace pulled her hairbrush through her hair and fluffed it about her face. Not great, but good enough! Then she exchanged flip-flops for sturdy walking shoes. A walk, she thought, might help burn off some of her nervous energy.

On the porch, she stood for a moment staring across the street, then started down the steps and across the lawn as if she were heading for Max's place. Then Grace turned and marched back to the house. *What's the matter with me? Why is it so important what's happening over at Max's? Hannah will be home in due time.*

When Hannah finally got home, she found Grace asleep on the living room couch, *The Long Summer* open across her stomach. Hannah leaned over, picked up and closed the book, and patted Grace gently on the shoulder.

"Grace, wake up. I need to talk to you."

Startled, Grace opened her eyes. Being awakened precipitously like this caused her heart to thump in her chest. "What time is it?

"Almost noon."

"I was reading while I waited for you. I must have dozed off. What's happening at Max's?"

Hannah sank into a nearby chair. "It's been a heck of a morning."

"Amelia said Zachary and his wife are back."

"They certainly are, and Max is so delighted at the

prospect of having a grandchild born here, he can't think straight."

Grace smoothed her hair. "What does that mean, Hannah? Why are they here?"

"I'm not sure. Zachary tells an amazing story, and Max says nothing will change for us. That's a joke. For starters, I'm home and it's a Saturday."

"How long are they going to stay? What does Zachary say?"

"It's not clear. Nothing's clear. When we told him that we're married, Zachary looked as if he'd been kicked in the stomach, but he got a grip on himself, shook his dad's hand, kissed me on the cheek, and asked if he should call me Mom. I put that to rest, fast. I said, 'Just call me Hannah.'"

"Sarina, if I remember, is sort of formal. She'll find it hard to call you by your first name."

"She was wiped out and asleep upstairs, so I never saw her. Max asked him what he planned to do, but Zachary hasn't a clue what he's doing or he wants to do. He appears to be in shock from the whole experience. I assume Amelia told you what happened in India?"

Grace nodded.

"I suggested that this wasn't the time to talk about long-range plans." Hannah paused and looked out the wide, low window.

Grace drew her legs up under her. "You're almost as stunned about their arrival as Zachary is about all that's happened to him, aren't you, Hannah?"

"You've got it right. Things were going so smoothly for Max and me, so easy and happy. Seems to me, we get reprieves in life, as if we're allowed to rest and prepare for the next difficult challenge."

"It appears that way. Surely, they're not going to stay here? Why would Zachary suddenly want to stay in Covington when he hates cows and the dairy business?"

"I sometimes think that Max has held on to the dairy in the hope that Zachary would have a change of heart and return. Why would a man of seventy-seven continue to operate a dairy, with all the problems with milking machines, the health of cows, delivery trucks, and on and on? Without Jose, he couldn't do it."

"After the baby comes, Zachary will probably take his wife and child and leave," Grace replied.

"I'd hate to see Max get his hopes up again and get hurt."

"It's out of your hands, don't you think?"

Hannah's knee bounced up and down, up and down. Grace rarely saw her this agitated. "I just don't know what to do."

"Let Zachary and his wife settle down, get over the exhaustion they must feel, and gather their wits about them. Then, see what happens," Grace said.

"Can't do much else, can I?"

Grace leaned over and placed a hand on Hannah's knee. "You can be gentle with Max and give him time. He loves you very much. It'll all work out, Hannah, you'll see."

"I wonder."

"Nothing's going to change with you and Max, not the way you two love one another."

"Thanks, Grace. I needed to hear that."

3

Gossip and News

*H*annah returned to Max's house, leaving Grace as rest-less as she had been and with no plans for the day. Bob and Martin were participating in a golf tournament and had stayed the night at the Grove Park Inn in Asheville. Grace puttered about the kitchen. She wiped off a shelf in the fridge where milk had spilled, and unloaded the dishwasher from the night before. So deep in thought was she, so concerned for Hannah and Max and what the future might hold for them, that when the phone rang, she jumped.

Velma Herrill, her neighbor, was on the line. "How you doing, Grace? How's Bob?" A pause, then Grace replied, "Bob's busy with golf, eh? That's fine, just fine. You busy today?"

"No, not busy at all," Grace replied.

"How about meeting me for lunch in Weaverville?"

Grace and Velma were not bosom buddies, though they had come to know each other fairly well and liked each other, especially since the December weddings. Grace, Hannah, and Amelia had been supportive of the five Covington women as they coped with the dumbfounding news that they were not legally married, after assuming, for forty years, that they were.

This information had come to light when Grace helped young pastor Denny Ledbetter clean out the attic of the church. Letters discovered there stated that a pastor who had been hired and had served for a brief time forty years earlier had not been ordained. The man had had the temerity to marry five couples prior to being found out and dismissed.

What astounded and angered them more was the fact that the deceased chairman of the Church Board had concealed this information. Yellowed papers hidden in a box and uncovered by Grace and Pastor Denny revealed this information and wreaked havoc in the lives of the Herrills, the Craines, and three McCorkle couples. Traumatized, jolted from complacency by this wrenching news, the couples had chosen to remarry in five sequential ceremonies on Christmas Eve. In a race against time, the ladies had stepped in and spearheaded the drive to paint and clean the church, while offering emotional support to the families involved.

"I'll be happy to have lunch with you, Velma. What time?" Grace asked.

"Say, twelve-thirty. I'm in Asheville running errands. Meet me at the Chinese restaurant in Weaverville?"

"That's fine. See you there."

Dressed in casual slacks and a lavender-and-white pinstriped shirt, Velma sat in a booth sipping iced tea. Grace slipped into the seat across the table.

"It's good to see you, Grace. We live so close, and the days fly by so fast, everyone's so busy. Seems like the older one gets, the faster time goes. Remember when you were young and couldn't wait to get older? I remember being seventeen and thinking I'd never get out of high school. Lord, I just couldn't wait to get out of there." Velma's voice trailed off.

A waiter stood at their table. Grace ordered hot tea, and they indicated that they would have the buffet. For a time they ate in silence, and Grace wondered if she should tell Velma about Zachary's return. She might as well. There were no secrets in Covington. "Can you imagine . . . ," she began.

A light flared in Velma's eyes. "You know about it, then? No, I cannot imagine. Why, Grace, she's got to be at least twenty years his senior."

"What are you talking about? Who's twenty years whose senior?"

"Why, May McCorkle, of course."

"May McCorkle? What about May?"

Velma lowered her voice and leaned forward. "She never did want to remarry that awful husband of hers, Billie, you know. Her mother, Ida, and her sister, June, pressured her, so May went ahead with it, what with North Carolina not being a common law state, and all the problems with inheritance and her kids and all."

"I had no idea. May smiled her way through the wedding ceremony," Grace said.

"Not in her heart, she wasn't smiling." Then Velma asked, "May joined your red hat group, didn't she? Didn't she tell you none of this?"

"Yes, she joined our red hat group, but no, she hasn't said much of anything. We're not a therapy group. We're into having fun and enjoying life."

"Well, she's sure changed, turned into one sassy woman. First she remarries Billie and then she ups and leaves him.

I hear her divorce will be final soon. Folks say she's been talking to Pastor Ledbetter—getting counseling is what they say."

"I would think she'd need some help at a time like this," Grace replied.

Velma's eyebrows arched. "Depends *what kind* of help. Some people think it's *more* than his good counsel she's after."

"What do you mean?"

Velma leaned across the table. "I mean, of a more personal kind. Some folks who've seen them together get the feeling it's more than a pastor counseling a member of the church, and she's not been to church since she left Billie."

Grace would have expected this kind of gossip from their neighbor Alma, but coming from Velma it surprised her. "I can't imagine, if it's anything intimate, that they'd want to be seen in a public place. If there were hanky-panky going on, wouldn't they prefer privacy?"

"Maybe so. But some people deliberately go out so as folks will see 'em and think nothing of it—throw them off guard, you know." Velma's eyes narrowed and her face flushed. She set down her fork and crossed her arms over her chest.

Grace had always considered Velma to be open-minded and fair, and she had never heard Velma gossip. What was going on? Did Velma dislike May? Why was she so upset, even vitriolic, about what May did or didn't do?

"There's those who think May's gotten real standoffish since she's joined up with the red hat ladies," Velma said.

Is Velma jealous that she hasn't been asked to join the group? Why hasn't she been asked? Brenda's organized our group. "Velma. You can't be suggesting that being a member of a red hat group had anything to do with May's decision to leave Billie?" Grace shook her head. "May's never discussed her personal life or problems at any of our gatherings. Mainly, we get dressed up in purple clothes and red hats and meet in a restaurant for dinner or lunch. One of our members is a great joke teller. We laugh a lot, and eat too much, and that's about it."

Velma sat back. Her face softened, and she smiled. "Personally, I don't believe red hats and all that stuff has anything to do with what's going on with May. It's other folks that think that, but I just thought I'd throw it out, get your opinion. May was a year behind me and Brenda in high school. She's always been an odd one. Nothing she did would surprise me." She beckoned the waiter. "You want more tea, Grace?"

"No, thanks." Grace decided not to ask in what ways May had been odd in high school. At some later date, she would ask Brenda.

Velma threw back her head. "Hey, I didn't mean to ruin our lunch. We don't hardly get to see one another. Tell me, how are Amelia and her new family getting on? Amelia seems to love that little girl, Sadie, as if she were her flesh-and-blood granny. That Sadie's so pretty, and she seems right happy, always smiling and cheerful."

"Yes, Amelia feels as if she's the child's granny. She adores her and Miriam too. We're all happy for Amelia. She had no family to call her own—children, you know—until they came into her life."

"We're all glad it turned out well," Velma said. "Amelia got any new photo shows coming up? Charlie and I always go to her openings. Amelia takes such good photographs."

She didn't wait for Grace's reply. "And how's Hannah

doing? Charlie says he saw a taxi pull up to Max's door this very morning. Max got company?"

"Now, that's what I was going to tell you," Grace said. "Max's son, Zachary, and his wife came home unexpectedly. She's about to have a baby."

"And they traveled with her about to have a baby? Bet they wanted the baby to be born in the United States. They all do, those foreigners."

"It wasn't that. There were serious problems where they lived in India—fighting, people getting killed—and they thought they'd be safer here."

"In India? Fighting? How so?"

"Religious and political problems, people fighting in the streets, burning other people's property. Sarina's brother-in-law was shot in the leg, a random shooting they think, but he was shot, nevertheless."

"Why, that's just terrible, shooting people like that." Velma shook her head. "People all over the world's got such big problems these days, don't they?"

"It's a complicated world we live in," Grace replied. "I had a letter recently from Randy Banks. Remember him? He's Lucy's—the little girl I tutored at Caster Elementary—older brother. He joined the army and went to Afghanistan and was sent on to Iraq."

"I'm sorry to hear that. No, I didn't know him. What's he have to say?"

"That he's scared all the time. That the tension, the not knowing when a bomb's going to blow them to smithereens, makes them all edgy and sick to their stomachs. He speaks of the noise of war and how horrible it is, and how even when it's quiet, he can hear gunshots and explosions in his mind. He wishes he'd never joined up."

"I feel so bad for all those young fellows over there," Velma said. "I didn't approve of this war. Charlie thinks we had to do it. I never believed that stuff about us being attacked by Saddam Hussein."

"Neither did I. Say a prayer for Randy, will you, Velma? That he comes back alive and well."

"I surely will. I'll get my prayer circle to add him to our list."

"Thanks."

Driving back to Covington, Grace thought about May and weighed the potential narrowness of a small village toward one of its own against the sense of belonging provided by that village, which had come to mean so much to her. But Denny Ledbetter and May McCorkle romantically involved? Now, that was ridiculous.

Still, Velma had started her thinking about May. Where did May live since she had left her husband? Grace didn't know. Did she have a job, and if so, what kind of a job? What was her education? Grace regretted her ignorance about a woman she had spent many hours with prior to the weddings. But except for the monthly red hat luncheons, she never saw May. Who had invited May to join their red hat chapter, anyway? Had it been Amelia or Brenda Tate? Probably Brenda. As principal of Caster Elementary School, she knew all the families of Covington. She would ask Brenda about this. Brenda could be trusted to present a fair assessment. But later that afternoon, when Grace phoned Brenda, an answering machine invited her to leave a message.

4

May McCorkle

May McCorkle's hand shook as she applied lipstick. The lady at the cosmetics counter had instructed her and demonstrated how best to outline a curve above her upper lip, which she considered too thin, then fill in with lipstick. May worried that the lipstick would wear off, as lipstick will, leaving an outline, a blur of something no longer there.

The stylish bob and a light brown color had replaced her too long and graying hair. She felt attractive now in a way she never had, but also self-conscious, though her sister, June, assured her that she looked younger, livelier, happier than she had in years. Still, May felt as if she were living, or at least hiding, in someone else's skin. Turning and twisting, unsure of the jeans that hugged her hips and butt and the brightly flowered blouse tucked into the jeans, May shivered with a mingled sense of excitement and apprehension.

Her mother, Ida, who loved adages, used to say, "No sense to cry over spilled milk. Done is done."

Well, done *was* done. May had packed her old gray suitcase and walked out of the house that had been home for years, out and away from Billie McCorkle. She had found a room in a widow woman's home in West Asheville and gotten herself a job. Minimum wage, but she was frugal. And she had resisted Billie's pleas, and then his threats, when she refused to return home.

May examined herself in the full-length mirror on the back of the bathroom door. She had put on weight. Her face was fuller and smoother. She did look younger than her fifty-six years, and she certainly felt younger and happy to be independent and making her own choices and mistakes. Billie, with his volatile temper, had been a hard man to live with, disagreeable, unyielding, mean, and hell-bent on being right. A woman, he said, should walk behind her man. A woman lived to do for her husband. For the children's sake, for peace in the household, May had acquiesced to his rules and demands: when they would eat, what they would eat, how she should dress, what church they would attend, how to discipline the children, where she went, and who she could call a friend. She had been a nonperson, always scared, constantly walking on eggs.

Then, Grace, Hannah, and Amelia had arrived in Covington. She had watched them—older women with opinions of their own, taking charge of their lives and making a difference in the community. She had watched Grace befriend that hardhearted old lady Lurina Masterson and change the old woman's life. She had marveled at the way Grace had organized members of the community to paint and clean the church in time for the five weddings, one of which had been hers.

Amelia, bless her heart, had wrapped her arms around and befriended May, June, and Bernice, strangers, who hardly anyone in the uppity part of Covington spoke to. And Hannah had helped them cope with the shock that sent them reeling when they learned from the new pastor that they were not married to their supposed husbands, and that their children were, for all intents and purposes, illegitimate. In their shock they had sought for someone to blame, to hate, only to find that the then head of the church, the man who had hidden this vital information from them, was dead and buried in the churchyard. Billie had raved, ranted, and threatened to dig him up and scatter his bones, but of course he never did any such thing. Still, after all was said and done, if not for Grace and Pastor Denny cleaning out that dusty old attic, they would not have known, and she would never have had the courage, finally, to leave Billie.

Though she had dreaded remarrying their father, May had done so for the sake of her children, for their legitimacy and legal matters like inheritance, which Amelia had taken the time to explain to her. Yes, she'd done right by her children, and how had they treated her? She had been, and still was, devastated by their anger and rejection when she had told them she was leaving their father. They were grown-up people, two of them with families of their own. Couldn't they see how miserable her life had been, and still was, with their father?

Amelia had been her friend, had helped her, driven her to the lawyer's office to start the divorce papers going. Not that she hadn't been scared out of her mind, but she had held fast to the story Hannah told of fleeing her abusive husband with two small children. If Hannah could do that with small kids to raise and no more education at the time than she, May, had, then she could leave Billie, whom she hated, especially as their children were grown and gone.

Her sister, June, bless her heart, had been supportive. She had lent May the money to pay her rent for a couple of months. That wasn't easy for June, since her husband,

Eddy, was Billie's older brother, though different from Billie as peas from carrots.

Ida, her mother, had been downright hostile. "You made your bed, you lie in it" was one of her favorite sayings. Ida carried on something fierce and consoled Billie, who drank himself into a stupor and, when he was sober, had nagged June to tell him where May was. But June had held firm and claimed to know nothing about May's plans or her whereabouts.

And now, thank the Lord, Billie was cooperating with the restraining order May had taken out against him, probably because he got hisself a girlfriend over near Marshall and moved in with her. Still, Billie was unpredictable when he drank, and she hadn't stopped worrying or listening for him to come up behind her out of nowhere.

It was Amelia who, recognizing her depression and loneliness, had suggested that May see a counselor. She had suggested a service in Asheville that charged on a sliding scale, then had explained to May what that meant. "You only pay what you can."

"I can't afford no counselor," May had replied, "and besides, I wouldn't go talking my private business with no stranger."

"Would you consider talking with Pastor Denny Ledbetter?" Amelia had asked.

"I ain't got the money to pay him or no one else to listen to me."

"He doesn't want money."

May remembered being amazed. "He don't want no money?"

"Counseling parishioners is part of his job," Amelia had said.

"Since I left Billie, I don't go to his church."

"He married you in that church, remember? When I saw him the other day, he asked how you were doing. When I told him, he offered his help. I'd accept his offer if I were you."

Several sleepless nights and anguished days later, May decided to take Amelia's advice. Now her visits with Pastor Denny had become the centerpiece of her existence, and for the first time in her life she felt listened to and valued by a man.

May closed and locked the door of her small bedroom at the rear of Mrs. Bourne's yellow cottage on Mayberry Road. It was Saturday, the day she drove to Covington to be counseled by Pastor Denny. Last time she'd seen him, he'd said he was proud of her, how she'd found a job and a place to live. He was proud that she'd kept her relationships going with her grown children, even if they weren't nice to her. They needed her, he said, regardless of what they said or did. They'd get over it in time. They'd come around, see her point of view, he said, and May held on to that hope.

Today was to be their last session, but May intended to present Pastor Denny with some new problem, anything, so that she could continue to see him. He had no idea how much that—and he—meant to her.

As she drove north on the highway, May considered what this problem would be: she should have given it more thought before starting out. Now she had to make up something about Billie or her mother, Ida, or a situation at work. As a liar, May had failed many a test. June, bless her, could lie with a straight face and her eyes wide open and innocent.

But not May. Oh, no! She'd sputter and turn red-cheeked and get all teary, and she'd been the one who'd taken many a whipping from their father's belt when they were young.

She had no right to want to see and be with Denny Ledbetter. She an ignorant women and he an educated churchman. And then there was the age difference. Where did she come to think that he could be the slightest bit interested in her? Certainly not because he spoke to her in a voice as soft and gentle as lovers spoke to each other in movies. Wasn't a kind voice and gentle manner the way a pastor would speak to anyone he counseled?

May glanced down at her hand on the steering wheel, at the faded place where her wedding band had been, and her stomach lurched. The closer she got to Covington and Pastor Denny, the more May's insides quivered. She knew that when she saw him, she would, as she always did, ache to reach over and touch his hand. But she would squeeze her fingers together hard, so as not to make a perfect fool of herself.

Denny Ledbetter's office door was slightly ajar. May hung back in the shadows of the hall, feasting her eyes on his slim form, his light brown hair falling forward in his eyes, the tip of his tongue visible between his lips as he concentrated on his typing. She knocked ever so lightly.

Denny smiled at her, pushed back his chair, and rose to greet her. "How are you, May? Come in. Sit down."

May slid into one of two brown leather chairs. "This is our last time together?" she asked. *Well, I messed that up, didn't I? I couldn't even think up a reasonable lie to keep coming.*

"Unless you have something else you'd like to talk about."

"You've helped me so much, and I thank you."

"It's been my pleasure. When will your divorce be final, May?"

"Six weeks." She brightened. "I was hoping I could come see you until it's over, until I go to court for my final papers. I can hardly sleep from the worry of it."

"I don't see why not, if you think it would help."

Relief swept over her. "Oh, yes, it would help so much. Thank you." *And now I can't think of a thing to say.* "Funny. My mind's gone blank."

"What I like about you, May McCorkle, is that you don't lie. You have something on your mind, you say it right out, and if you don't, you say that, too."

"I was wondering, if you think it's proper for me, being single soon and all, to be going to the red hat group that Grace and Amelia and the others formed? Amelia invited me, and I've been to a couple of meetings."

"What do you do at the meetings?"

"Not much. We have lunch in a restaurant. We wear purple clothes and red hats. It's come from a poem a woman wrote about being old and wearing purple and red and not giving a hoot. We eat, and talk, and sometimes tell jokes."

"Do you tell jokes?"

"Goodness, no. I ain't never been one to remember jokes."

"I don't see the harm in your going for lunch with the ladies. They're fine women, and you've told me how much you admire them."

"Sometimes the jokes are what I'd call slightly . . ." May blushed.

"Do they offend or embarrass you?"

"I can't rightly say they do. They're not really off-color. A lot of folks wouldn't even think they were off-color." She stopped. She was making this sound worse than it was. "I guess it's more that I don't understand them, and I feel foolish. I laugh like I understand, but I don't."

He smiled at her, that warm and caring smile she lived for. "I am not much good at telling jokes, either, and half the time when someone else tells a joke, I don't get the punch line. If you have fun with the ladies, enjoy yourself, and don't let a few jokes you don't understand stop you from being part of the group."

"You make me feel that my life is all right. That I did the right thing leaving Billie."

"I hope that *you* feel you did the right thing, whether I think it's good or not. It's what you want for your life that matters, May, not what I want."

May rose. "I gotta go now, Pastor Denny." She stood in the doorway clutching her purse, sweat beading her upper lip. "See you next Saturday, then?"

"That's fine, next Saturday. Same time."

May drove onto Elk Road, pulled into the parking lot of Elk Plaza, and shut off the ignition. *I gotta get a grip on myself,* she told herself. *Pastor Denny sees me like he does any of his parishioners, nothing more, nothing special. I'm gonna go crazy thinking about him like this. I ain't felt so mixed up and sick to my heart since I was sixteen and had a crush on that salesman come to sell Daddy a tractor. I sure wish there was someone I could tell about this, someone who could help me get my head straightened out. Maybe I could tell Amelia what I been feeling.* She shook her head. It was a comforting thought, but not one she trusted. *Best not to tell nobody.*

5

Zachary

Once he was ensconced in his father's home, Zachary's anger, which of necessity had been contained and controlled on their journey out of India, found an outlet at the news that his father had married Hannah. Had he been less self-centered, he would have compared his father's failure to inform him of his marriage to Hannah with his failure to notify his father of his marriage to Sarina.

Max—that's how he thought of him, not Dad—had welcomed him home with open arms, and then Hannah walked into the house, *their* house now, and that changed everything, though he wasn't sure what everything was, since he hadn't formulated a concrete plan of his own.

Hannah, they explained, did not actually live with his father, though she spent a great deal of time and many nights there. What kind of a marriage was that? Was it even legal? His father must be getting senile to get into such a stupid situation.

Sarina breathed deeply and shifted in the bed they shared in his boyhood room. Her pregnancy weighted the mattress, and his body slanted toward her, making it hard for him to relax, to be comfortable, to sleep. There had been no time to think, to digest the meaning or the consequences of that terrifying night when, waving flaming flares and screeching, hostile men had surrounded his father-in-law's compound. Unwittingly, the family had reverted to their native language, further confirming Zachary's foreignness and his inability to immediately grasp what was happening and why.

"It is nothing. It will pass by morning," his father-in-law, finally speaking in English, lied, even as the women of the household wept, and servants hauled trunks and suitcases from storage, and cars with darkened windows pulled into the driveway. Zachary had stood on the sidelines while police in heavy armor materialized to push back the crowd gathering beyond the locked gate, and when they departed, at daybreak, an armed escort conducted their several cars south, away from the town.

Nor had he had any say in the decisions that followed.

"You go to America now. It is better," his father-in-law, the patriarch, had said.

There had been no discussion of what *he* wanted or how he felt. Tickets appeared and were pressed into his trembling hands. He and a weeping Sarina had been embraced, then unceremoniously shoved toward a waiting plane. Now, with the journey behind him, his mind was as exhausted as his body. Instead of privacy and time to work things out with his father, to think through and make plans, he must cope with Max's changed marital status and a strong-willed, outspoken woman like Hannah. Max would undoubtedly discuss with Hannah whatever Zachary proposed. Feeling thwarted, Zachary centered his anger on Hannah, but he resolved to be patient, to plan

carefully, and to play the role of contrite and loving prodigal son. This would not be easy for the self-willed and im-
petuous Zachary.

In the bedroom across the hall, Max tossed and turned. He
wished Hannah had stayed the night. He needed to talk with
her about his confused emotions: pleasure at seeing Zachary, joy at the prospect of this most expected grandchild,
soon to be born, and the confusion he sensed Zachary's
return could bring into his and Hannah's lives. Zachary's
departure from India had not been voluntary, and circumstances precluded returning to India, perhaps for a very long
time. What would his son do? How would he support his
family? Where would they live? How would Sarina adjust
to not having servants, to the weather, which was so much
colder, to the mostly unsophisticated people of Covington?
Max reached for his phone to call Hannah, then through
his window saw that her bedroom was dark. Of course it was
dark. It was 3 A.M.

So what! Max threw off his covers, slipped into a robe and
slippers, moved silently downstairs, and carefully opened
and closed the front door. Night-lights flared, brightening
the yard and Cove Road, exposing him to any of his neighbors across the road who might be awake at such an hour.

From the rear of the house, Jose's watchdogs began to
bark, and moments later the German shepherds, Pete and
Hero, tore around the corner and raced toward Max, to col-
lide with each other against his legs. A shotgun under his
arm, a flashlight in the other, Jose was close behind.

"Jose. It's me." Max bent to sooth the dogs. "Hush, hush,"
he whispered.

"Ah, Señor Max. Pete, Hero, stop you bark."

The dogs turned and ran to Jose, who leashed them. "Pardon, Señor Max. We wake up the whole road, yes." He nodded toward the ladies' farmhouse, where lights had come on in Hannah's room and, now, in the foyer.

The front door flew open. Hannah, in her bathrobe, stood framed in light. "Max, is that you? Jose? What's wrong? Is Sarina all right?"

Max crossed the road and took the steps two at a time to join Hannah on the porch. "I'm sorry about the dogs. I couldn't sleep. I needed to talk to you. I thought I could sneak over quietly."

"And when you got to the house, what? You think you'd have made it upstairs without waking Amelia and Grace?"

"I was willing to take my chances."

Jose turned and disappeared with the dogs.

Hannah took Max's hands. "No harm's been done. I'm glad you're here. Come on upstairs."

They lay on Hannah's bed, her head on his chest, and talked for hours.

"I think I've recovered from the shock, but I've got this feeling that my son hasn't learned much from his experiences or travels," Max said.

"Why do you say that? What did Zachary say or do?"

"It's not what he said or did. It was his face, when we told him. Didn't you notice?" Max shifted and stuffed a pillow under his head.

"He looked as if you'd threatened to shove him into a pit of snakes," Hannah said. "What's the right word for that, 'aghast'?"

"Exactly."

"Hearing about us must have been as much of a shock to

him as his arriving back here was to you, don't you think?" Hannah stroked Max's cheek.

"He's a grown man. Things change. He'll have to adjust."

"And you'll be patient, and give him time, and not push him, right?"

Max sighed, reached for her hand, and kissed her palm. "You'll put a muzzle on me if I don't."

The next morning, at Max's invitation, he and his son climbed the hill behind the dairy barn. When was it, Max wondered, that Zachary had stopped tagging along with him on his daily walks? Had he been eight or nine years old when he pleaded excessive homework?

Bella had said, "Let the boy alone, Max. Some people don't like climbing the same hill every day."

"I can take another route," Max had replied.

"Just let him know he's welcome to come with you, and let it go at that," she suggested, and Max had heeded her counsel. Zachary had never walked with him again, until today.

Max slowed his pace. His son was winded, breathing hard from exertion. "Let's sit a bit on those boulders." Max pointed to a cluster of gray granite bruising the green hillside.

Max's eyes traveled beyond the homes on Cove Road to the layers of hills rising one above the other in the morning mist. This was his favorite view, the reason he climbed the hill.

Zachary focused on dislodging, with a stick, some object stuck to the sole of one shoe.

"Phew!" He grimaced and dug a packet of antiseptic wipes from his back pocket, drew one out, and cleaned his hands. "Cow dung everywhere, same as ever."

Cow dung. Had that been the issue, the reason the boy had disliked walking with him? Why hadn't he said that? Max would have understood. Or would he? Sadly, at that time he would probably have called Zachary silly and mocked as prissy his reaction to the smell that pervaded their barn.

"The view is spectacular, don't you think, Zachary?"

"Same view as ever. And by the way, Dad, I prefer to be called Zack, and I spell that with a *k* on the end, not an *h*."

"Sure, Zack. I'll try to remember." Bella had chosen the name Zachary. He'd wanted to name their son Tom, a good, simple, solid name, his grandfather's. Max considered that a name like Zachary would be a handicap. Had the boy been teased for the name? he wondered. If he had, he'd never complained to his father; but then he'd hardly spoken to his father once he started into his teens.

"Have you ever considered another use for this land of yours besides cows?" Zack asked.

"No, I haven't. Why?"

"Just asking. You're getting older, and I wondered how long you'd go on with the dairy business."

"I'll probably die among the cows." Max laughed. "What did you have in mind for the land, Zack?"

"It crossed my mind that it might be a nice place for homes. As you said, the view is spectacular."

"I thought you didn't much care for the view."

"I don't especially. Maybe I've seen too many gorgeous views, but other people would find it charming," Zack said.

"Are you suggesting you would like to build houses up

here to sell to other people?" Max could feel his anger rising. "Is that what you would do with my land?"

Zachary held up both hands. "Wait up, now. I wasn't suggesting anything, just commenting."

But Max could not let it go. "Turn my land into a development? Have you seen Loring Valley and what they've done there, with the mud slides and the valley flooding? What used to be a pristine river is muddy now after every little rain. Well, let me tell you. There'll be no such thing on Cove Road, and if I drop dead tomorrow, Hannah will uphold my wishes."

"You actually married that woman?"

Max found it impossible now to control his anger. "Hannah is not *that woman*. She's a fine, intelligent, capable woman, and I love her."

Zack rose and started down the hill. "Well, she's a far cry from my mother," he tossed over his shoulder.

"Hannah was a good friend of your mother's. Your mother loved her." Max was shouting now.

Zack turned, slowed for a moment, and raised his eyebrows. "Really?" He laughed.

"Yes, really." Why was he even answering his son?

An uneasy silence accompanied them down the hill, and when they reached the farmhouse, Zachary disappeared upstairs. Max headed for Bella's Park, where Hannah had gone to finish paperwork.

"Calm down, Max," Hannah said when Max stormed into her office at the park, ranting about what he assumed was Zachary's grand plan for *his* land.

"Zachary doesn't control your land. Regardless of what he thinks or what he says"—and from what little Max had told her, Hannah wasn't sure what it was that Zachary had said—"he was probably talking off the top of his head. You own the land. He can't do anything with it or to it."

Hannah grasped Max's arm and led him to the couch, where she pushed him to sit, then sat beside him and slipped her arm through his. "Let me make a suggestion. Why don't you create a trust of some kind and state exactly what you'd like to have happen with the dairy and the land? That would make it easier for me if, God forbid, I should ever have to deal with Zachary."

"Good idea. I'll call my lawyer tomorrow." He punched a fist into the palm of his other hand. "His mother dies. He packs a bag and disappears. He's gone for years without a 'How are you, Dad?' Then he drops in with a wife I know nothing about, announces that he hates Covington and is going to live and work in India in her father's business. When that doesn't work out, he's back, full of ideas about what he wants to do with *my* land."

Hannah could no longer restrain Max, who jumped to his feet and paced about the office. "Well, damn him, he can go to the devil for all I care. In fact, he can take that wife of his and get out of my house."

Hannah patted the couch beside her. "Come, Max, sit down. Let me get you some coffee, or a Coke, or would you like a beer? You're angry and hurt, and justifiably so."

He nodded in agreement and joined her again on the couch. Max brought his head almost to his chest, then threw it back hard. "You're right, as usual. I'll take a cup of coffee, please. I'm sorry, carrying on like this." He ran his fingers through his hair and smiled at her. "I am sorry, honey. Why do I let him get under my skin like this?"

Hannah brought him coffee. "You cannot ask them to leave right now, Max. But Sarina's not to blame for what

Zachary says or does, and she's about to have a baby. You wouldn't ask her to leave before the baby comes, would you?"

"I'm sorely tempted, but you're right, Hannah." He sipped the coffee. "She's not to blame. Let's see what happens after the baby comes. But Zachary—by the way, he wants to be called Zack, with a *k* not an *h*—had better stay out of my way."

"Come, let's not dwell on Zachary. Let's take a walk up the hill and see what Laura and Molly have added to the Covington Homesteads. Those girls really took you at your word, that they'd better get all the furnishings—everything—authentic, down to the last needle." She patted his hand, then slipped her arm through his and led him from the office out into the lovely spring day.

Two Covington brothers and their families had been the first to settle in this cove. They had wandered in with their covered wagons and exhausted, pregnant wives and stayed. The re-creation of their original homesteads represented a slice of history. Carefully researched, and constructed from the oldest, most weathered lumber available, the cabins and outbuildings were now open to the public, though they hadn't attracted a rush of visitors.

Working closely with school boards and chambers of commerce, Laura and Molly were attempting to remedy that by arranging for bus trips from schools in Madison, Yancey, and Buncombe Counties. Once the road was paved from Cove Road up the hill to the homesteads, busloads of retirees and other visitors would surely come.

Max slowed his stride to Hannah's amble, and they

crossed the meadow and meandered up a path to the first cabin, where they sat on the wood bench to the side of the entrance.

"Look at all you've accomplished here," Hannah said. "You can be very proud."

"So how come people aren't rushing to see it? I would have thought the locals would want to see how their ancestors lived."

"It'll take time, Max. Maybe locals won't be our primary visitors. Maybe they don't want to see how hard life was for their great-great-grandparents. And they aren't accustomed to visiting historic sites."

"But the younger generation should know what it was like for those who came before them."

"And they will, through the schools. They'll come in buses. It's going to be all right. Laura has a reporter coming from *Living History* magazine and they're working on getting *Historical Journal* to do a story. Then you'll be complaining about traffic on Cove Road. You'll see."

They sat for a time, their thighs touching, holding hands, lost in their own thoughts. Hannah remembered how she had tried and despaired of being able to protect this land from developers, and how Max had stepped in and bought the property. Now here they were, leading productive, creative lives, developing the land in ways they considered important. She was happy, happier than she had ever been. At a time of life when some people felt unappreciated and useless, she and Max had been privileged to create gardens and the Homesteads on this marvelous land.

She thought of Wayne Reynolds, Lurina's stepgrandson, who had, with her encouragement and support, graduated from the horticulture program at a community college.

Recently he had replaced her foreman, Tom, and almost immediately springs surfaced, gushing from the earth in the oddest locations. It had become essential to relocate and redesign the Oriental garden. Wayne had supervised the heavy machinery that arrived to dig ditches, reroute water, and put in culverts. What a mess that had been, especially with the early spring rains. Hardly a day had passed when she had not scraped mud from a half dozen pair of shoes. Thank God, the rains had stopped and the earth dried out.

And so it went, always something new or something challenging for her and for Max, and now Zachary and his family had arrived and, it seemed, were about to complicate their lives. Hannah felt drawn to the young woman, so far from her home and family. She must reach out to the girl, introduce her to women her own age, like Molly and Laura and Miriam, and bring Sarina into contact with Grace and Amelia.

Amelia's habits might annoy Hannah, but she knew that both of her friends had insights and skills to bring to any situation, and she would appreciate any kindness shown to Sarina, anything that might help to make the young woman feel safe and welcome in Covington.

"Well," Max said, standing and helping Hannah to her feet, "let's go on back to the office. I want to make some notes before I talk to my lawyer about that trust."

6

Sarina

They parted at the office. With determined strides Hannah walked the long block back to Max's house.

"Señora Hannah, I glad to see you." Anna, Max's housekeeper, opened the kitchen door.

Hannah sensed that something wasn't right. Anna wasn't singing, and a heavy silence hung in the air. "Is Zachary here?"

"No. He take truck and gone."

"Gone where?"

Anna shrugged. "I no know where."

"How's Sarina doing?"

Anna shook her head. "She no like company. Señora Grace come by earlier, and she"—Anna nodded toward the stairs—"she no would see her."

Bread, mayonnaise, and sliced chicken lay on the kitchen table. Anna smeared mayonnaise on the bread. "I make lunch. Maybe she eat something. She no eat, she gonna get sick."

"When it's ready, I'll take it up. I assume Zachary won't be back soon."

"He no happy when he come from walk with Señor Max this morning. When Señor Max go to work, he tell Jose to bring the pickup, and he drive off very fast, like how you say, 'bat from the hell'?" She closed and opened her fists rapidly to indicate speed.

"A bat out of hell." Hannah took the tray, to which Anna had added a bud vase with a spray of yellow forsythia, and climbed the stairs. The door across the hall from Max's and her bedroom was ajar. Hannah widened the opening with her foot and entered. The window shades had been lowered as if to hide the limpid bulge that lay beneath the bedspread.

"Good day, Sarina. I've brought you something to eat. Here, I'll rest it on this table. It's nearly noon. May I open the shades and let the light in?"

The form did not move or speak. Hannah set the tray down, walked to the windows, and opened the shades. Light flooded the room. Too much light all at once, she thought, and let the shades fall halfway down. "Everything in moderation," she said to herself.

It was then that the small round head, dark hair straggling about her face, emerged from the covers. Tears stained her cheeks, and Hannah was moved to pity.

"Let me get you a damp washcloth to wipe your face and hands."

The young woman's lips parted, though no words came. A half smile pulled at the corners of her mouth, and she accepted the washcloth and wiped her face and eyes. "Thank you," she whispered. "I am hungry."

"Good." Hannah spoke softly. "Do you want to get out of bed, or shall I bring the tray to you?"

"I'll get up. I need to use the bathroom, thank you." Laboriously, Sarina swung her legs to the floor, eased from the bed, and with great effort, her hands holding her arched back, stood. Then came short little gasps. "I am a big, fat, ugly sow."

Hannah did not respond, but turned away and listened as Sarina's slippers shuffled across the wood floor, listened to the small grunts of discomfort as she moved across the room, heard the bathroom door open and close, and water being turned on in the sink. How frightened and alone she must feel, Hannah thought. And Lord only knows what kind of comfort Zachary provides. Then the bathroom door opened and the slippers shuffled back across the room. Hannah turned as Sarina carefully, slowly lowered herself into the armchair that Max and Zachary had carried upstairs from the living room. With her glossy dark hair brushed off her face and tied back with a ribbon, Sarina seemed a frightened child.

"I am hungry," she said and bit into the sandwich, then held it away and looked at it with curiosity. "What is this, red jelly in a sandwich?"

Hannah looked closer. From the corner of her eye she had seen the can of cranberry sauce on the kitchen table, but she had not connected it with a chicken sandwich, but why not? Chicken was dry.

"It's the cranberry we use at Thanksgiving with turkey. If you don't care for it, I'll run down and make you a fresh sandwich."

Sarina took another bite. For the first time, she smiled. "I like it. It's sweet, and it moistens the chicken. I only wanted to know what it was, and I thank you for bringing me lunch."

"Anna made the sandwich for you. I just carried it up."

"I thank you both, then."

Belly protruding, legs jutting before her, Sarina ate with gusto and drank the iced tea that Anna sent.

"I thought, if you feel well enough, we might sit out on the porch, if you can manage the stairs. It's a glorious, warm day. The forsythia is in full blossom. Maybe you would like to talk about a doctor, the hospital. You must have questions. When is the baby due?"

Sarina's arms circled her belly. Her hands caressed it. "She is a girl. We had the test."

A smile spread across Hannah's face. She clapped her hands. "A girl, how wonderful. Max will be thrilled. I'm thrilled. Have you picked a name? When is she due?"

"In May, but the way I feel, my back and all, I think it will be sooner. I'm frightened and with no doctor to talk to . . ."

"My daughter, Laura, had a baby boy, Andrew. Andy. He's two and a half now. She used a woman doctor in Asheville."

Sarina's eyes brightened. "A lady doctor. Yes. You will call her, make an appointment for me please?"

"If you'd like me to, I will. Zachary can take you, or I'll be happy to."

"You will come with me, please?" Sarina dipped her head and looked at Hannah from behind long lashes. Her English was British with singsong inflections. "Men are not good with such things."

In that instant, the two women bridged both generational and cultural differences. Hannah felt as if she had known Sarina for a very long time. They spoke, then, about whether the baby would sleep in their bedroom or have her own room next door, and who would shop for the crib and other items that an infant would need.

Sarina asked Hannah if she would take her to a store to choose the crib. "I can't stand for long," she said, "but a little while. Will we have to send a truck to pick it up, like we do in India?"

"No, they'll deliver it."

"And how long will it take before they deliver our purchases?"

"They'll give us a delivery date." Hannah's heart smiled. *What a softy I'm turning into. How long has it been since I cared about such things?* "A few days, I imagine. Would you mind if I asked Grace to come along with us? Grace is very gentle and kind. You'll like her. She's a good friend to have."

"I remember Mistress Grace. She is the short plump lady, yes, and not the one with the scarf?"

"That's right, the short plump one. She's very loving."

"I am sorry I would not see her earlier. I was a mess, crying. I could barely think about getting out of the bed. I thank you for helping me, and I will trust your judgment about your friend Grace. Shall I call her that? What shall I call all of you? Miss or Mrs.?"

"Call us by our first names, Grace, Amelia, Hannah."

"Will that not be taken for rudeness?" Sarina asked.

"Goodness no. Would you like to go downstairs?"

"I would like that, yes. I believe, if I hold the railing with both hands, I can get down the steps. Being big like this, well, you know how that is."

Hannah helped Sarina to her feet. Slowly and carefully they descended the stairs and stepped out onto the front porch. "But the air is so fresh and nice, and the flowers are so pretty," Sarina said.

When Max came home he found them chatting softly and rocking on the front porch. "Well, well, it's good to see you up and out getting some sunshine." Max sank into the rocker next to Hannah. He leaned around Hannah to see Sarina. "How are you feeling, my dear? You look rested."

"I am very well, thank you. Hannah brought me some food, and she has agreed to go with me to buy a crib for the baby and others things we might need. Clothes, diapers."

"Tell Max the sex of the baby," Hannah said.

"You know what it's to be?" He rubbed his hands together.

"A girl, a little girl." She hesitated a moment, then added, "Max." She and her father-in-law had determined the night before that she would call him Max and not struggle with Dad or Father. Another informality! One more thing about America she would have to get used to.

Max could not have been more delighted. His face glowed. His smile lit and softened his craggy face. "That's splendid. A little girl. That's just splendid. Have you a name for her?"

Sarina was not listening. She was remembering home and plans for her delivery and the room prepared for the baby. But everything had changed. She was alone now and far from all that was familiar, and there was no comfort to be had from her husband. And then, today, Hannah had come. Sarina smiled at Max. "Hannah is going to take me to the doctor of her daughter, a lady doctor like I had at home."

"That's good. She's a fine doctor. You'll be in good hands with Hannah and with the doctor."

They shared iced tea that Anna brought on a tray, and when Anna called them inside for dinner, Sarina sat with them at the table and ate and felt sad that her husband had not returned. Why, she wondered, was he making life so hard for himself, for them both?

A few days later, at the baby superstore with Hannah and Grace, Sarina clapped her hands when she saw a cream-colored French Provincial crib and dresser/changing table, which Hannah insisted that they order. They shopped for diapers, sleepwear, undershirts, socks, and sweet little dresses, everything the mother of a baby girl could possibly desire.

Finally, exhausted, they headed for the food court to sit among other weary people, whose children, some happy and smiling, some cranky and crying, some running helter-skelter, seemed to be everywhere.

"I remember when Roger, my son, was little and we took him Christmas shopping," Grace said. "He climbed into a display window in the store and hid. The saleswoman, the store manager, Ted, and I were frantic. We were about to report him missing when he stuck his head out from under a mannequin's long evening coat."

"If I had done such a thing, my father would have reddened my bottom," Sarina said.

"His father scolded Roger and sent him to bed without dinner. Tell you the truth, I was so relieved that he hadn't been kidnapped or wandered off and gotten lost that I cried and coddled him. I shouldn't have, I know, but I couldn't help myself."

"It's not easy to raise a child," Sarina said. "I think Zachary is afraid to be a father. The closer it comes to my time, the more he is gone. It was so even at home in India. Some days I hardly saw him, but I didn't notice so much, as my mother and sisters were always about." Her eyes grew sad.

She threw her hand wide. "But here, I do not want to even ask him where he goes. He is always angry."

They fell silent. Neither of the older women, though furious with him, wanted to express their concerns about Zachary's daily absences, his obvious immaturity, and his complete lack of sensitivity to his wife's needs.

Later, at home, Grace asked Hannah, "Zachary leaves the house so early in the day. Where does he go, do you think?"

Hannah had just unlaced her sturdy SAS shoes and kicked them off in the living room, and listened to the *clunk, clunk,* hardly caring where they landed. Grace retrieved them and set them neatly beside the couch, where Hannah sprawled.

"I'm pooped," Hannah said. "It's been a long day. I have no idea where Zachary goes. All I know is that Max is furious with him. Zachary, it seems, hinted at how nice homes would be up on Max's hillside. Max assumes he'd like to cover the hill with houses. Not that he can, after all. The land will never go to Zachary."

"But I can see why Max is upset, the way he feels about land."

"He's livid. I don't know, Grace. Why can't Zachary just sit down and talk about his future, his possibilities, with his father? I believe Max would help him get settled somewhere in some business."

"Zachary's not without resources, is he?" Grace asked. "He has a trust fund from his mother."

"Bella must have known something she wasn't telling. That trust fund is doled out to him at so much a year, enough to live on carefully, but he can't get his hands on the lump sum. I guess she didn't take into consideration that one day he might have a family to support."

"Now that he's got a family, I wish he'd spend more time with Sarina. She's a fine person, too good for Zachary." Grace paused. "I have an idea. Let's you and I follow Zachary and see where he goes and what he does."

"Bad idea." Hannah dismissed it from her mind.

Later that evening, Grace found herself alone with Amelia. She explained the situation and her suggestion to Hannah, and Amelia responded with enthusiasm. "Just tell me when, and I'm ready. We could be regular Agatha Christies, you and I."

Several days later, Grace called Amelia at Mike's photo studio in Weaverville. "He's leaving the house, and I'm going to follow him. I'll call you on my cell phone. You meet me when I get to wherever he goes, okay?"

Within fifteen minutes, the phone rang in Mike's studio. Amelia grabbed it. "Where?" She scribbled on a pad. "Okay, be there in five minutes. If he leaves, call me. I'll take Mike's cell." She gave Grace the number.

"What's going on?" Mike's apron was wet from emulsions he'd been mixing. "I'll be tied up here for another hour. I have wedding photos to develop. The Meyers are coming over at two to select their portraits."

"Grace and I are going to follow Zachary. I told you, he disappears every day and no one knows where he goes or why." Amelia raised an eyebrow.

"Aren't you and Grace playing with fire? What if you find out something his wife would rather not know?"

"We won't tell her. We'll tell Max, and he can deal with his son."

Amelia grabbed her purse and camera, and headed for the door, then turned around. "Mike, Miriam's on a field trip with her class. I said I'd pick up Sadie at Caster Elementary at two this afternoon. Will you do it for me?"

"Sure. What classroom?"

"Second grade. Mrs. Becker. Try to get there about a quarter of two."

"Be careful, Amelia, please."

She came to him and kissed him lightly on the cheek. "Thanks, Mike, for worrying about me. You're a good friend."

Amelia's palms were clammy. Her heart raced. Grace had said, "Meet me on the corner of Sunset Street and Old Sycamore Road." Amelia did not know where that was but she followed Grace's directions and was surprised when, turning off Main Street in Weaverville, she saw *Sunset Street* on a green post on the right. The road curved down and around and dead-ended at Old Sycamore Road, a quiet, pleasant, tree-lined street of older, well kept-up homes.

Grace, hardly a sleuth, crouched behind a dogwood hedge, her arm raised high, motioning Amelia to move her car farther down the street.

Feeling ridiculous, Amelia parked and joined Grace behind the bushes.

"He went in there, 488 Sunset Street. Several men have gone in, and no one's come out."

The house was a two-story, light gray clapboard with dark gray shutters and a porch that ran the length of the front, with wide steps going up to it.

"Do you think it's a house of ill repute?" Amelia asked.

"That's an old-fashioned way of putting it," Grace replied. "I hardly think this is the neighborhood for that kind of thing. Let's go up on the porch and have a peek in a window."

Amelia held back, pulling at Grace's arm. "We can't do that, can we?"

Grace turned to Amelia, exasperation in her eyes. "Look. You stay here if you want to. I'm going to have a look." Grace slipped from behind the shrubs.

"I'm not staying here alone. What if someone comes by? What if the cops come along and see us?"

"Amelia. Stop it. You've been to too many police movies. Let's go. Stay close."

Crouching, as if somehow she would be less rather than more conspicuous if seen, Grace headed for the house and reached the steps, with Amelia trailing behind her. She hesitated a moment, looked to right and left, then marched up onto the porch and headed for the first window. The window shade, though lowered, did not completely hide the room, · and by stooping low, Grace could see inside. She beckoned to Amelia. "Come on over here. You've got to see this."

Amelia hunkered down on the wooden porch floor beside Grace and peeked inside. Game tables seating five or six men filled a spacious living room. Men, intent on their game, never raised their eyes from the cards. Cigar smoke colored the air gray.

"They're gambling, poker or black jack maybe," Amelia whispered. She nearly burst out laughing and covered her mouth. "Zachary and those five guys. They're gambling, aren't they, Grace? Is that illegal?"

"I don't think so, but what do I know? At least he's not in

a bar or with some woman." She sidled away from the window. "Come on. Let's get out of here."

Nervously, looking in both directions, they descended the steps, crossed the yard, and hastened to Grace's car.

"What do we do now?" Amelia leaned against the car and fanned her face with her hands. She was breathing hard.

"You okay?" Grace asked.

"I'll be fine in a minute. What next?"

"I'll tell Hannah and let her pass the information on to Max."

"I hate Zachary, shirking his responsibilities like this. Do you think he's addicted to gambling?" Amelia pushed away from the car.

Grace was getting into it. "Let me take you to your car. I don't know if he's addicted. It's hardly what I expected to find."

"Me neither. I'm rather disappointed. I'd anticipated a more exotic ending to this sleuthing."

7

How Much Is That Doggie in the Window?

The Perfect Pet Shop was small and crammed with vari-eties of canned, bagged, and boxed cat and dog food, leashes and collars, animal beds, vitamins, doggie beds, and other paraphernalia that drew dog lovers. Grace hesitated before entering the shop, deliberating with herself as to the wisdom of bringing home a puppy. Everyone had been ada-mant about getting an older dog from the shelter or from a foster family.

It's no different than a child, Grace assured herself. A dog can be scarred by the way it's treated as a puppy, just as a child who's been mistreated can be scarred. Her dog would know only love and good care. These sweet little pup-pies had already suffered the trauma of separation from their mothers and confinement in a cage. Poor little tykes, she thought, living in a cage.

Grace pulled open the door of the shop and headed to where the cage stood, and two puppies yapped their heads off and clawed at the wire siding. With relief she noted that the puppy that had first captured her attention was still there, along with a smaller, black-and-white puppy. The puppy she liked seemed shier, yapped less, and as she approached, it scooted to the rear of the cage and huddled as if afraid. *Poor little thing!*

"I would like to have that puppy." Grace pointed to the curly-haired brown-and-white female. "And that one." *When did I decide on two puppies?* "I'll take them both." *How can I leave that dear little black-and-white puppy alone in a cage?* "What kind of dogs are they, anyway?"

"A mix, probably cocker spaniel and terrier. The little fellow's going to have shorter hair and look more like a terrier. He won't shed as much."

"Where did they come from?" Not that she cared, but her housemates and the men might ask.

"The mother belongs to one of the girls who works here. We don't usually sell puppies, but her dog had seven pups and she needed help getting rid of them."

"How much are they?"

"Twenty dollars each. That okay? They've been wormed and have had their first shots."

Grace nodded.

"I'm so glad you'll take them both. The black-and-white's the runt of the litter, but he's a dear little fellow." The salesgirl reached inside the cage, handed Grace the brown-and-white puppy, which Grace had already named Carole, and pulled out the second puppy. "He's cute, isn't he? Sweet little white face, except for these few black spots. If the cage fits in your car, take them home in it. You can always bring it back, or I can let you have it real cheap, say ten dollars. They're used to it and can sleep in it at night, at least until you get them housebroken." She picked up the cage and started toward the cash register. "You'll have to take them in for follow-up shots. Any vet will do. Just show him these papers."

Grace paid and she received in exchange puppies, cage, tags, and papers. She drove home with puppies yapping, a supply of food that would last a month, a book the salesgirl recommended called *Raising Your Dog Right*, and a headache she knew stemmed from anxiety. Would Hannah and Amelia tolerate not one but two puppies? Blessedly, lulled by the motion of the car, halfway home Carole and her brother fell asleep.

Bob was outside mowing his lawn when Grace pulled into his driveway and beckoned to him. He laughed at her cargo. "You're gonna have your hands full."

"Come and help me get them inside," Grace said. Hannah's and Amelia's cars were in the driveway. "I need moral support and protection if Hannah starts throwing things at me."

Bob carried the cage into the house, and Grace released the puppies in the kitchen. Immediately, Amelia knelt to pet and hug the puppies, who climbed all over her and licked her face. "They like me already," she said.

"The brown-and-white one is Carole," Grace said.

"Do let's name this little fellow Benji," Amelia said.

Hannah stood in the doorway to the kitchen, her arms crossed. "Benji's just peed on the floor. Did you get something to clean dog pee and poop with, Grace? I'll not have this house stinking."

Later, Grace sat with Amelia on the grass in their front yard and enjoyed watching the puppies romp, tackle, and tumble headfirst over each other. Puppy growls issued from their throats. Grace was thrilled when she called Carole and the puppy came over to her, with Benji hard on her heels. Amelia scooped him up. Carole, Grace thought, is the alpha dog here.

"What is it about this little fellow that I love so much already?" Amelia asked.

"He's easy to love," Grace replied. "He looks at you with those big dark eyes and your heart melts. Sadie's going to adore them. Next thing, she'll be nagging Miriam to get them a dog."

The puppy licked Amelia's face, and Amelia, fastidious about her makeup, seemed not to care. "Hannah thinks you're nuts bringing home two puppies."

"I think so too, but I'm glad I did. There were only the two of them, and I couldn't leave Benji alone in that cage."

"Speaking of cages, are you sure it's good for them to stay in the cage, even when one of us is in the house?"

Grace eased Carole from her shoulder to her lap and continued to pet the curly fur. The puppy snuggled, sighed, and closed her eyes. "From what I've read, they feel safe in a small space. The book said to put them in and take them out of the cage frequently at first, so they get used to the fact that we'll always be back to take them out. When they're in there, they'll settle right down and go to sleep. If they were underfoot all the time, Hannah would be demanding we get rid of them."

"That's true. She doesn't seem to like them, does she?"

"I don't believe that for a minute." Grace stroked the puppy gently. "It's Hannah's way to act gruff and then warm up to new things slowly. Wait and see, a couple of weeks and she'll be vying with us for their attention."

Carole lifted her head, then shook and raced away to throw herself at the smaller Benji. She brought him to the ground, where they rolled and growled, then licked each other's face. "They've been together from birth. Carole would have been lonely without him," Grace said.

Unseen by them, Hannah peeked from the kitchen window, a smile on her face, and wondered how it was that they had not gotten a dog years ago. She had had dogs, and had loved and lost them. Over time, she hardened her heart to yet another loss. But it was safe now. At her age a puppy would surely outlive her.

8

Randy Banks Returns

*I*t was Amelia, sitting in an ice cream parlor in Asheville, who was the first of the ladies to welcome Randy Banks home from Iraq. The brusque young man with the cane, who let the door slam behind him, looked familiar. He limped to her table and indicated he wished to sit. She nodded and gestured to the chair opposite her, still uncertain who he was.

"Howdy, Miss Amelia."

His eyes were hollow, empty, and lacked warmth. It took a few more moments before she recognized Randy Banks and realized that his wounds extended way past his physical injuries, to his spirit.

"Randy Banks. How good to see you. How are you?" *Stupid question. What is he to say to that?* "Please, sit down. Can I buy you an ice cream sundae, an ice cream soda, a cone, anything? Does Grace know you're home?"

He slumped into the chair across from her, stretched his leg to the side, and rubbed his thigh. "I haven't called her yet. She worried more than my ma did about my going. She sure was right. Everything Mrs. Grace said was right." He stopped and looked away. His eyes clouded, but no tears came. It was as if, needing to eliminate a scene that only he could see, he lowered a shade.

They sat in silence for a time eating ice cream cones. Amelia wanted to cry when he licked his lips and repeated several times, "Nothing ever tasted this good."

From the parking lot, a car horn blew. Randy rose. His eyes went to his leg, and he eased up from the table. "That's my ride home. Can't drive with this confounded leg. Thanks a lot for the treat. Tell Mrs. Grace I'll be along to see her right soon."

Amelia watched him go, leaning heavily on his cane, watched as he rested a moment against the car before turning and easing into the passenger seat. Then he reached down, lifted his leg, and carefully brought it into the vehicle. She heard the car door slam hard and felt his anger and frustration. The ice cream, so delicious a moment ago, lost its flavor and felt like leather on her tongue. She did not finish it. If I were young and a photojournalist, she thought, I might be in Iraq photographing these young men. I'd show the American people just how unglamorous war really is. But would they let me—whoever they are—or would they confiscate my film? Digital. She would learn digital and send her photos back in a flash without anyone's by-your-leave.

Amelia found Grace trying to keep a sudsy Carole from flinging herself from a large washbasin in the yard outside the kitchen.

"I saw Randy Banks. Randy says he'll be over to see you soon, Grace."

"He's back?" Grace lunged for Carole, who used the momentary slackening of Grace's hold to place her paws on the edge of the pan and struggle to escape. Grace grabbed her hard. "You stay right here." She held the dog firmly now, and looked up at Amelia. "Why didn't he let me know he was home?"

Amelia explained about his injury and the cane. "I don't know what happened, how he was wounded or how badly. He seemed highly agitated—no, more like depressed."

Grace's heart sank. Randy was injured. Grace had heard and read about the number of suicides of young men and women after coming home from this war, or who had killed themselves while still overseas.

"I wouldn't wait for him to visit you. I'd go to him," Amelia said.

"Thanks for telling me. I'll go later, when I'm done with this puppy."

Carole shook herself hard, splattering suds on Grace and Amelia.

"I'll dry her for you," Amelia offered. "Where's Benji?"

"Safe. In his cage."

Later, distracted and unaware, Grace drove faster than the speed limit and never heard the police car siren until it pulled alongside her and the policeman waved her over.

"Officer," she said, feeling confused, "I am so sorry. Whatever I did, I'm sorry." He towered above her car. "What did I do?"

"I clocked you going twenty miles above the speed limit, ma'am." His hand shot out. "Your license and registration."

Grace fumbled in her purse and extracted the license, which vanished into his huge palm. His fingers closed about it. She rummaged in the glove compartment for the registration. "I am really sorry. I was thinking about Randy Banks. He's home from Iraq and he's been injured."

"Even more reason to watch your speed, ma'am, so *you* don't end up injured." He strode to his car, leaving her flustered, embarrassed, and angry at him and at herself.

After what seemed a very long time, the policeman returned and busied himself writing her ticket. At one point he looked down at her. "I know Randy Banks. Poor guy got shot up pretty bad, I heard. He's been at Walter Reed Hospital."

It was worse than she imagined. She accepted the ticket, which would cost her $125, folded it, and slipped it, her license, and the registration into her purse. "Thank you," she murmured, but her mind was on the Banks family. Why hadn't Randy's mother or his sister Lucy or any one of those children called or come by to let her know? "I'm very fond of Randy, of the whole family. I'm on my way over there now."

"You don't recognize me, but I was one of the policemen who went to the motel that night and arrested that bum Jerry McCorkle before he could hurt Randy's sister. I followed his case in court. He got his just deserts, I'm glad to say."

"I'm sorry. I didn't recognize you." *I don't want to stay here and talk to you. You've just cost me a lot of money.*

"How is the girl? What was her name, Lucille?"

"Lucy. She's fine, doing well in school."

"Glad to hear that. They don't all end up okay." He paused a moment and looked away, then back at her. "I'm sorry about the ticket, but you were speeding at quite a clip."

"I'm sorry, too. Well, I'm off now."

He bent and tipped his hat. His badge read *Sergeant*

Dick O'Neal. "Take care of yourself, Sergeant Dick O'Neal, and thanks for helping Lucy." Grace drove away slowly, her stomach quivering.

Randy sat in a lounge chair, his leg stretched stiffly before him, his cane close at hand. His head was thrown back, his eyes closed, and a book lay open on his lap. Grace's car door closed harder than she had anticipated, and from inside the house a dog barked. Randy's body jerked and came erect. He looked around, his eyes wild and frightened, and his hand reached for a gun no longer at his side.

"It's me, Randy. Mrs. Grace. I am so sorry I startled you. I didn't realize I closed my car door so hard."

Randy ran his arm across his brow, then covered his eyes for a moment with both hands. He took a long, deep breath. "It sounded like . . . like a gunshot."

"Forgive me." She walked toward him, then hesitated, unsure if his spirit had returned to the here and now. He smiled, which reassured her, but she approached him cautiously. Then the front door of the house flew open, and the youngest Banks daughter, Audra, who had once informed Grace that she preferred the name Teresa Marie, rushed up to them and threw her arms about Grace.

"Mrs. Grace. You came. I was hoping you'd come. He'll listen to you, for sure. You tell him it's okay. He's home. No one's gonna shoot him no more."

"You hush up, Audra." Randy turned to Grace. "It's nothing. Sometimes loud noises startle me, that's all."

"I'm not Audra, remember?" The child looked at Grace, who nodded. Then she turned back to her brother. "So what about the nightmares and screaming at night, waking us all up?" Audra hung behind Grace. "You sure do scare me, Randy."

"I'd never hurt you, Audra, uh, Teresa Marie. You got no cause to be scared. They was just bad dreams, things I remember from the war. They'll stop coming after a time. That's what they told me at the hospital, before they sent me home. 'Just give it time, soldier. Keep a stiff upper lip and it's gonna be all right.' That's what they said."

Randy's eyes filled with tears. He looked at Grace. "Only, it ain't no better and not getting no better. That's why I haven't been round to see you, Mrs. Grace. I didn't want to come until I was all right again, 'cept now I think I ain't never gonna be all right no more."

Her heart aching, Grace approached and hugged him. "It sounds to me like what you've got, Randy, is a case of what they call post-traumatic stress. I read an article about it in *Newsweek* magazine. From what I've read, you're not alone. Lots of soldiers are coming home with post-traumatic stress. They can help you with counseling and medicine. It's not like when the Vietnam vets came home and no one knew what was happening to them. Did they suggest you get help from the veterans hospital in Asheville? Did they give you a name of someone to see?"

"No, ma'am, they didn't. They said it'll pass in time."

"Well, it might pass in time, but why should you suffer while you wait for that to happen, when there's help out there?"

"It would be wrong to go running for help, taking up someone's time when there are guys coming home in worse shape than me," he said.

Anger stirred in Grace. "No, Randy. It would be right,

not wrong, for you to get all the help that you need. You're as important as anyone else and deserve all the help that's available."

"Listen to Mrs. Grace, please, Randy," his sister said.

He shook his head. "I appreciate your coming over here, Mrs. Grace, but I got to do this by myself, show I ain't weak and got no guts."

Grace's hands flew to her head. "This is all wrong. Whoever told you getting help was wrong, after you've given so much to your country?" She turned away, arms crossed. "I hate this war. Hate this whole horrible war." Struggling not to break into tears, she walked to her car. "I'll go now, but I'm coming back with all the information you need. Then you can decide."

"Leave it be, Mrs. Grace. Just leave it be," Randy said quietly, firmly, his voice so cold it scared her.

"Maybe you should listen to him and leave it be," Hannah said, after Grace related her visit with Randy. "Maybe it's a matter of time. Someone professional must have evaluated Randy and decided he could handle it by himself."

"Or some fool made him feel he didn't deserve help. There are more men and women coming home with psychological problems than anyone anticipated, only how the generals and the people at the State Department wouldn't know this would happen and plan for it after what happened to the Vietnam vets, I don't know."

"And all the suicides," Amelia said. "I read somewhere that many soldiers are committing suicide."

"How does anyone win a war like this against—what, guerrillas in a civil war? You only have to study history to see that guerrillas know every nook and cranny of their own country and have the advantage."

Amelia didn't like where this was going. They would all end up with splitting headaches, and they couldn't do a thing about the war in Iraq. She'd stopped watching the news weeks ago. It actually made her so tense her stomach hurt. "So what's the answer?" Amelia asked.

"Leave Iraq," Grace said. "You wait and see. That's what we're going to have to do, or keep losing men and bringing home badly injured men and boys." *I've got to stop talking and thinking about this. My blood pressure must be sky high.* "I have to do something," Grace said. "Tomorrow I'm going to the VA hospital in Oteen, talk to someone about post-traumatic stress, and find out what's available for Randy."

"I'd go with you." Amelia wondered if Grace had told Hannah yet about Zachary's gambling and decided that this was not the time to ask. Then she slapped the side of her head lightly. "Heck, I'm sorry, Grace. I can't go with you. Mike and I signed up for a four-day photo field trip in Cades Cove."

Amelia left the house then and did not see Hannah's raised eyebrows or the look she cast at Grace that said, Well, you can't depend on Amelia now, can you?

Grace needed to think and talk about something other than Randy Banks and his problems. Time to tell Hannah about Zachary. "I think you should sit down, Hannah. I have something to tell you about Zachary. Amelia and I followed him. We know where he goes."

"You followed him?" Then she smiled and leaned forward. "Tell me, where does the no good son of a gun go?"

"You won't believe it."

Hannah crossed her arms. "Try me."

"He goes to Weaverville to a private home. Guess what he does there?"

"Stop playing with me. If you're going to tell me, tell me."

"He gambles. We saw him sitting in a smoky room filled with tables and men playing cards," Grace said.

"Well, my goodness. Who would have guessed? Zachary a gambling man. Wait until I tell Max. How did you know where to go?"

"I followed him. Amelia and I parked behind some bushes, sneaked up to the house, and peeked in a window."

Hannah covered her mouth with her hands. "My Lord, Grace, what if you'd been seen? What if a police car had driven by and seen you?"

"Well, none did. And now you know." She handed Hannah a folded piece of paper. "Here's the address. Do what you want with it."

"And you went with Amelia."

"Yes. You weren't around when Anna called to say he was leaving, and I didn't want to go alone."

Hannah studied the address. "Well, I'll be darned. Zachary gambling." She slapped her palms against her knees. "Well, that's not as bad as I suspected. I thought much worse of him. Thanks, Grace. I'll tell Max, and he can do what he wants about it."

9

Rivalries

*Y*ears earlier, when the ladies committed to sharing a home and to being there for one another as they grew older, they had done so in good faith. But now, Grace worried that these intentions were eroding because of the bickering between Hannah and Amelia, too often expressed in sharp words, snide remarks, and withering looks. Why, she wondered, couldn't Hannah smile rather than scowl at Amelia's flippancy? And why couldn't Amelia accept the fact that Hannah took things too seriously at times, and not crack jokes at those moments when Hannah's mouth tightened and her eyes clouded with displeasure? Lately Grace felt caught in the middle, and she was determined not to take sides.

"I don't know why you don't read them the riot act," Bob said as they raised their arms to spread the voluminous sheet across his king-size bed. "You gals have been together for years. You've weathered some pretty major things. You'd think the personality kinks would be worked out by now, or Amelia and Hannah might be more tolerant of one another."

The sheet lay flat on the bed now, and they began to tuck it in. "You're improving at turning under the corners just right. You want the bedspread on?"

"I think not. It's heavy to handle, and too hot to use."

Grace fluffed his pillows and set them against the head-board. "If you'd gotten a queen-size bed, like I suggested, you could make it up by yourself."

"What, and miss the pleasure of domesticity from this king-size bed? When we make it up, I think of us as an old married couple, don't you?"

"You never give up, do you, old man?" She laughed and kissed him, and they walked into the living room.

"Hannah and Amelia still have issues. After Amelia came back from Maine last year, they decided that what we three share is top priority, and worth overlooking each other's foibles. But gradually, their ability to tolerate one another slips away. It worries me. I'd prefer perfect harmony."

"When you're all angels with harps flying around in heaven, you'll have perfect harmony," Bob said. "Maybe, when one of them comes under stress, she takes it out on the other."

"Could be, but why not on me?"

Bob laughed. "You're the oil that keeps the wheels turning. They need your level head and calm manner to smooth things over. They can't risk angering you or having you decide to walk out on them." He nodded toward the bedroom. "They know, I'm right over here, ready and eager to welcome you." Bob winked at her. "Can I interest you in moving in with me?"

"No. I like things just as they are, and so do you. You just won't admit it." Grace snuggled next to him on the couch. "But I think you're right. Hannah is especially stressed since Zachary came home."

"He's a disgrace, that Zachary."

"Hannah's rather amazing the way she's taken Sarina under her wing. She's made an appointment for her with

Laura's obstetrician, and she's helping with the arrangements for the birth. Hannah's hired a nurse to be with Sarina and the baby for several weeks after the baby comes."

"Hannah's doing all that, eh?"

"Someone had to step in and help," Grace replied. "The poor girl's alone in a strange country."

"This isn't some strange country. It's America." Bob's army background surfaced. "She should be glad she's here and not over there getting shot at."

"Spoken like a true man." Grace smiled at him. "Well, I'm off now."

"Hey, not so fast. Aren't we going to cuddle a bit?"

"And muss that bed we just fixed so nicely?" Grace kissed the top of his head and departed.

Back at the farmhouse she found a message from Brenda returning her call of several days ago.

"Brenda," Grace asked when she phoned back, "you going to be home awhile?"

"I am. Come on over. I just made a wonderful marble cake. Oh, I forgot, you don't eat cake."

"Thanks. I love cake, but it's best if I forgo that pleasure. I just had coffee with Bob, and I'm not hungry."

"You just come on along whenever you like," Brenda said. "I'll be here."

Fifteen minutes later, Grace and Brenda sat on Brenda's porch swing.

"I keep intending to ask Bob and Max to put up a swing like this on our porch," Grace said. "Every time I sit here, I love it."

"It's relaxing to swing. Takes one back to being a kid, I

guess. You're up high. You can see over the railing, see everyone passing by."

For a time they exchanged pleasantries: how things were at Caster Elementary School, where Brenda was the principal; that they were glad winter was behind them; news of children and grandchildren. Grace had learned that here in the South one did not rush things; one relaxed and allowed conversation to unfold.

Finally, Brenda asked, "So what's on your mind, Grace?"

"I'm almost embarrassed to say."

"Well, you just go ahead and say it anyway."

Grace hesitated a moment. "I had lunch with Velma last week—"

Brenda waved her hand. "Say no more. Velma's been all over the place chatting about May with anyone who will listen."

"That's not like Velma."

"No, it's not," Brenda said.

"Then you know what people are saying about May and Pastor Denny?"

"I've heard things."

"I got the sense that Velma doesn't like May. She mentioned that May was odd back in high school. What did she mean by that, do you know?" Grace asked.

Brenda kicked the porch floor and sent them swinging higher. "I was in class with May and June. June got all A's, if I remember right, and May, well, May was a dreamer. Not odd, just a dreamer. She'd stare out the window. She wrote poetry she wouldn't show to anyone. Besides her sister, she didn't seem to have any friends. People called her stuck-up, but I think she was just real shy.

"When we were busy snickering and making eyes at boys, May was sitting in the library reading Romantic

poetry: Shelley, Keats, Wordsworth. I know this because one
of her kids got in trouble one time, some silly thing, and she
had to come to my office.

"'He's a good boy,' she told me. 'Shy, and quiet, and likes
to read, like I do.' May went on to tell me that she'd de-
voured books of poetry when she was in high school, but her
son was fascinated by pirates of the Caribbean.'"

"A gentle boy, Edward, not bombastic like Billie, and May
loved him the most of her kids. I think he went on to work
in medicine, a lab technician or a radiology technician, and
lives in Georgia somewhere." Brenda shook her head. "May
should have gone to college and made something of herself,
become a librarian or a teacher. Instead she walked right out
of high school to the tune of the wedding march. Ida loved
the idea that her twins were marrying brothers. June got a
fairly decent, hardworking man. Billie was a bum from day
one. I never liked him. I don't think May did either."

"She married him."

"Or she was pressured into it. Ida's still a force to reckon
with. Imagine what she was like when her daughters were
young. She ruled that house and everyone in it with an iron
will." Brenda paused, waved her hand to brush away a flying
insect, and continued.

"I don't think there's anything going on between May
and Pastor Denny. But if there were, would you give a hoot
if they were having an affair?"

"Personally, no. I like May, though I hardly know her. She
wasn't much of a talker when we were getting ready for the weddings," Grace said. "I don't even know where she lives now."

"Lord, but I hope nothing's going on between her and
Pastor Denny. I'd sure hate to see her get hurt and be humiliated on top of that."

"Would Denny be so foolish as to overstep his bounds as pastor and counselor?" Grace asked. "He's a dedicated pastor, and honest."

Brenda's feet kicked the porch deck hard again and they fell silent while the swing went up-down, up-down in a narrowing arc. "Bunch of narrow-minded harpies are what they are, Alma and the rest of the gossips. I just hope this doesn't get back to Pastor Denny. He might just up and leave this congregation, and I'd hate to see that happen. He's so well liked."

"I wouldn't have thought that Velma would be in on this kind of gossip," Grace said.

"Lord, Grace, everyone around here's got memories like an elephant. Back in high school, Charlie Herrill had a big-time crush on May. Everyone knew. He followed her around like he was a dog. He'd sit and stare at her in the cafeteria, and he moped around outside the classes she was in and the library. Only time he ever voluntarily went into the library was following May. Anyway, May never gave him a second glance. But Velma wanted Charlie, so she hated May." Brenda shrugged. "Velma got him like she wanted, and I doubt he's looked at another woman since. But Velma has that old memory stuck inside of her, and now May's gonna be single. Maybe she's worried about that."

"Charlie's crazy about Velma. Of all the couples who got married, I'd say they are the happiest," Grace said.

Brenda shook her head. "Personally, I don't think there's an inkling of truth in all of this. May will move on with her life. The counseling will end, and people will gossip about someone or something else. It's started already. They're talking about how strange that Banks boy, Randy, is since he came home from the war."

"I hate to hear that. I'm very fond of Randy. Randy Banks is suffering from post-traumatic stress disorder. It's classified as a mental disorder that requires treatment. I'm going to the veterans hospital next week to talk to one of the counselors. I hope we can convince Randy to see someone over there."

"I wish you good luck with that."

Later, as Grace walked home, her mind picked up on her conversation with Bob regarding Amelia and Hannah. She understood Hannah better than Amelia. Hannah had greater depth and staying power, she thought, but Amelia's charm and creativity amazed Grace, and she treasured Amelia's humor and whimsical nature. Unfortunately, Amelia was jealous of Hannah and preferred being alone with Grace. But there were times when Hannah's intolerance and expectations of Amelia seemed unreasonable.

As she turned into their driveway, Grace thought of her mother's advice in difficult situations: "Wait and see." Her mother's counsel had often irritated her, yet it had proven wise. Left alone for a time, tempers cooled, reason prevailed, and new or additional information could help resolve disputes. She had considered confronting Hannah and Amelia. Now she wasn't sure.

"I'll wait and see," Grace said aloud. As she exited her car and started up the driveway, she stepped into a depression in the gravel and nearly fell. As she checked her knee and back she felt suddenly old; like an old car her parts were wearing out. *Good Lord, getting old is a drag.* She shrugged and continued up the driveway. *But better than the alternative.*

10

Grace Gathers Information

$\mathcal{T}$he following Monday, Grace met with a counselor at the veterans hospital in Oteen, just east of Asheville, in his office in a small building just to the side of the main hospital. She introduced herself as a close friend of the family and shared with the counselor all that had transpired when she visited Randy, and her fears for his well-being.

"Randy was always optimistic and kind, a loving son and brother, before going off to war. He'd been enrolled in the technical college in a computer program."

The counselor, whose long career had focused on such cases, was soft-spoken and kind. He explained that the sights and sounds of war led to the damage of the soldiers' minds — post-traumatic stress disorder, or PTSD.

"In the process of becoming a soldier, one's trained to kill," he said. "And killing, seeing your friends killed, changes a person." His eyes were sad. His voice and demeanor expressed deep caring. "War, with its killing and destruction, sets the stage for a loss of morality and values and turns many soldiers into savages. Acts are committed that don't fit the range of one's normal values or behaviors. Our boys change. This protracted war, the extended tours of duty, only make it worse."

The details were more than Grace had bargained for, and at one point she put her hands over her ears. "Please, don't tell me any more. If mothers heard what you've told me, there'd be no wars, because mothers would rise up in protest."

He returned to being technical, providing information that did not touch Grace in the same way as the details of war.

"New evidence indicates that PTSD results from subtle changes in the brain that occur under severe stress. These changes actually alter the way memories are stored."

He used medical terms that she would not remember.

"Don't they ever completely recover?" Grace asked, her hand on her heart.

He shook his head. "I have vets from World War Two, Korea, and Vietnam that I've been seeing in groups weekly for years. Oh, they learn to manage, to cope, to get on with their lives, but sometimes out of the blue something triggers a recall, and the reaction isn't pleasant. In these groups, they help one another in ways I can't help them." He sat back in his chair. "Unfortunately, not everyone who needs counseling comes in. Some vets feel getting help's an admission of weakness."

That sounded like Randy. "How does someone get to you for help?"

"A doctor's referral; a family member convinces their son, brother, or husband to come in; or the person recognizes he or she needs help." Then he added a caveat. "We're finding we can't just put the vets returning from Afghanistan and Iraq in with the older groups. What they have to say's so brutal it retraumatizes the older fellows, so we have to see them individually, which isn't as helpful as in a group, as I told you."

Does Randy have a doctor? Grace wondered as she drove home. If not, could she convince him to go to one, and which one? And how would she know if that doctor would suggest that he get help, if Randy made light of his problems?

Grace's head ached. What she had heard today was more than she ever wanted to know, more than she could speak about to others, and much more than she would share with Myrtle Banks. Why, she asked herself, did she take other people's problems so to heart? Was she a busybody, intrusive and presumptuous? Grace lifted her foot from the gas and slowed the car. She was going seventy miles an hour on the bypass around Asheville. The speed limit sign she'd just passed said fifty-five. Moments later, a police car pulled up behind a station wagon ahead of her. Grace breathed a sigh of relief that this ticket stop did not involve her.

At home, to distract herself, Grace began to prepare a tuna salad with apple chopped into small pieces, celery, and almonds, and she was surprised when Hannah stepped into the kitchen, her hair rumpled, as if she'd been lying down.

"You're home. I thought you were at work or at Max's." Grace pulled out a chair for Hannah.

"I needed time alone," Hannah said. She strode to the fridge, took down the cookie jar, and set it with a thump on the kitchen table. "I'm craving something sweet."

Hannah usually said "no" to cookies. "Is something wrong?"

Hannah settled into a chair, lifted the lid from the jar, drew out a cookie, and waved it like a baton. "Yes. Something's wrong. I gave Max that address where Zachary plays cards, and he tore it up. Said he wasn't about to interfere in whatever Zachary's doing, which pretty much leaves things as they are."

Hannah replaced the lid on the jar. "Max and Zachary barely talk. Sarina's depressed, and who can blame the girl? Fate's handed her a sorry situation. Max and I have lost our wonderful Saturdays alone, and I'm feeling down. I'm going to eat away my depression, and I'm fed up to my ears with Amelia."

Grace covered the bowl of salad, placed it in the fridge, and joined Hannah at the table. "Look at me. What's Amelia got to do with this?"

Hannah shrugged, finished a cookie, and took another. "Amelia left her umbrella open on the porch again. If I've asked her once, I've asked her a thousand times to shake it off good and put it in the umbrella stand."

"Hannah, really. How important can that be?"

"It'll blow away in a strong wind. She's so irresponsible."

"I don't believe Amelia's umbrella and whether it blows away or not matters a wit to you."

Hannah dropped her head into her hands for a moment before looking deeply into Grace's eyes. "You're right, it doesn't. I'm on edge these days. I want Max to take action, to bring whatever is going on with Zachary to a head. Everything bothers me. Our lives, Max's and mine, have been turned upside down."

"Did you ever consider that Max is afraid to confront his son, afraid that Zachary will drag that poor wife of his off to God knows where? It seems to me Max is thrilled to have the baby born here."

"Too thrilled."

Compared to the things Grace had just heard at the counselor's office, this seemed petty, but she said, "Hannah, my dear friend, Sarina will have the baby, and Zachary will have to face reality. Things will change. Wait and see. It's only a few weeks now until the baby comes."

"If I live that long." Hannah crossed her hands on the table. "I have such an uneasy feeling about Zachary, about what he's capable of doing. I don't trust him. I think he's going to hurt his father, and Sarina, and me in the process."

Grace rose, stood behind Hannah's chair, and placed her hands gently on her friend's shoulders. "Hannah. It's going to be all right."

Reaching for Grace's hands, Hannah squeezed them gently. "I pray you're right."

11

Why Me?

There had been times when Amelia had felt close to Hannah, especially after that dreadful episode of Amelia's involvement with that awful man Lance Lundquist, and the time when they'd been drawn close by the catastrophe of their home burning to the ground. But then there was their Caribbean cruise, and Hannah's irritation and constant criticism of her. Perhaps sharing a suite had made for too close quarters. Amelia had been hurt and angry, and justifiably so. After that trip she considered moving out, and had escaped to Maine on a photo trip to think things over.

Reconciliation and what seemed to be a greater acceptance of each other followed, and Hannah could not have been kinder than when Miriam and Sadie arrived, and Amelia had summarily rejected them for many weeks while she worked out her anger at Thomas. Hannah and Max had given them a place to live and been so very kind to them. So, why had Hannah's and her relationship deteriorated again?

Amelia admitted to being jealous of Hannah and Grace's friendship, jealous that Hannah, who she considered less attractive than herself, had found love and marriage with Max. *Wait a minute. Didn't I reject Simon the art critic from*

New York's proposal last year to move to New York and share his glamorous life?

Well, anyway, enough was enough. The constant bickering had to end. It upset her, poisoned her day, and was driving Grace out of the house. If Grace decided to move to Bob's cottage, what then? Amelia's stomach dipped. She ought to be more accepting of Hannah, and not react to the comments Hannah made. Hannah was, after all, under a lot of stress since Zachary's arrival. Max and Hannah's Saturdays, which were so important to them, had flown out the window.

When the phone rang, Amelia considered not answering it, and when she did, she was surprised to hear May's voice.

"Amelia, this is May McCorkle. How you doing?"

"Pretty good, thanks, and yourself?"

"Sometimes good, sometimes not so good."

"When is your divorce final?"

"Two more weeks. But it's not the divorce I want to talk about." May hesitated. She wanted to cry. *Please Lord*, she thought, *don't let me cry*. But she needed to talk to someone, and not anyone in her family. "I wonder if you'd be willing to meet me somewhere. I got a problem I'd like to talk about."

"Of course."

"Today maybe? I'd come wherever you want."

"How about Weaverville at the new coffee shop, what's-its-name?

"The bakery on Main Street."

"That's the one," Amelia replied. "On the corner where the drugstore used to be."

"What time?"

"In an hour?"

"I'll be there." For a moment, May regretted calling Amelia. She ought to be able to handle life without needing to run to anyone for help. But this was an extraordinary circumstance, unlike any she had ever experienced. She couldn't eat or sleep for thinking about Pastor Denny Ledbetter, wondering how he felt, worrying about the age difference. No, she had to talk with someone older and more experienced, and she liked and trusted Amelia. May hung up, reached for a box of tissues, and blew her nose. Anticipating that she might need them later, she stuffed a handful in her purse.

May showered and applied makeup, which always made her feel better, and dressed. She stood in the center of the small bedroom and looked about her. Jammed into the closet and shoved beneath her bed were boxes and bags, her life in a nutshell, hastily thrown together when she left her home. She hadn't opened box or bag and couldn't remember their contents. A short while ago, she had had a home and furniture, bedspreads to choose from, television sets in several rooms, and June living a half block down the road. Where would she end up? What would her life be like? Where and when would her possessions ever again see the light of day?

Returning to McCorkle Creek was out of the question. Ida was furious with her for divorcing Billie and blamed her for the failure of the marriage. Ida would kill her if she knew about the pastor. May leaned her head against a wall. Lord, what was she going to do?

Sunlight flooded the room. Thank the Lord this bedroom faced south and could be counted on to be bright on a sunny day. Rainy or overcast days depressed May. They always had, but more so now with no home, no garden, no children she could turn to for support, especially James. She had loved James. After Edward, she loved James the most. She tried not to, but she still, in her heart, blamed his brother Vince for the accident that killed James. Vince had been driving drunk. When the policeman came to the door with the news, she'd prayed it was Vince who had been killed, not James, and she'd gone just about out of her mind when they told her it was her James, her Jamie.

Vince always drank too much, and Billie encouraged him, shared beer with him when the boy was only four years old. She had warned him, but what did her warnings, or anything she had ever said, count with Billie? James's death was as much Billie's fault as Vince's. Even now, thinking about it, May doubled over and clutched her stomach. *Oh, God, forgive me. Who am I to decide who lives or dies? But why my James, my dear good boy?* Tears flooded her eyes. *Stop this. Stop right this minute.*

May grabbed her bag and headed for the car, but her thoughts lingered with her children. Her daughters were decent young women, married too young, with kids. *I wish I'd been closer to them. I never was. Never could find what to say to them.* And yet she missed them. She'd be lying if she said she didn't. James had been unplanned and unwanted until they laid him in her arms. *Don't start that again. I gotta meet Amelia with a smile on my face and not red puffy eyes.*

At the coffee shop, Amelia's eyes feasted on exotic cakes and pastries displayed behind the slanted-glass wall of the high counter. She decided on a Danish pastry and a café au lait as May arrived and came to stand beside her.

"It all looks so yummy, doesn't it?" Amelia said.

May hardly saw the shelves of goodies. "Sure does. I'm gonna have a plain coffee with some cream and lots of sugar."

They found a table close to the window. The coffee shop hummed with chatter. Two women pushed strollers into the shop, selected food and drink, and settled into a table at the back. Laughter spiraled up from a table of four well-groomed older women, and May envied their casual interaction and the implied intimacy of friendship.

"Well, May, what's on your mind?" Amelia's soft voice drew May back to the business at hand. May's heart raced, and her face grew warm. The coffee shop seemed suddenly inappropriate and way too noisy for what she wanted to say.

"Could we take our coffees and go sit over there?" May pointed across the street to benches in a small grassy area near the parking lot.

"Or we can drive to Lake Louise. It's not far. Take our coffees. There are lots of private places we can sit and talk." Amelia crumpled the paper plate and napkin. "Come on, let's go."

Relieved, May followed Amelia to her car and in less than five minutes they were seated near the lake, where a family of ducks scrambled from the water and hastened toward them, anticipating treats. These not forthcoming, the ducks waddled back to the lake and swam away.

"May. What was it you wanted to talk about?"

The bench was hard. May crossed and uncrossed her legs. She stared past the lake at cars dimly seen through shrubbery and sighed. "Where shall I begin?"

"Anywhere," Amelia replied. "Just start, and whatever it is, it'll get easier."

"You know, I've been seeing Pastor Denny for several months."

Amelia remembered seeing them at the diner one day, May leaning forward, her eyes fastened on Denny, and Denny waving his hand, seemingly pontificating about something or other. She'd thought nothing of it. "Yes, and . . . ?"

"He's been very kind, very helpful," May said.

"I expect he would be. He's a kind man."

May's brows puckered. "Why do you think Pastor Denny isn't married?"

Amelia finished her coffee, rose to dispose of the cup in a trash bin close at hand, then settled on the warm, thick grass. She looked up at May. "Maybe he never found the right person."

"You'd think he'd have married long ago. He's an attractive and caring person."

"You considering matchmaking? Both your daughters are married, aren't they?"

May said, "Oh no, not that. Yes, they're both married. Not my daughters. Oh, no." She blushed and felt utterly foolish.

Amelia waited.

May sank down beside Amelia and plucked bits of grass, discarded them, plucked more bits of grass, and discarded them. Finally, Amelia reached for one of May's hands and cradled it in hers. "What is it, May? What's troubling you?"

May's slacks were green, almost the color of the grass. "It's about Pastor Denny." Her voice dropped and Amelia leaned closer. "And me."

"About Pastor Denny and you?"

"I think I've gone and fallen in love with him." *There, I've said it*. A heavy weight shifted from May's shoulders to the pit of her belly. Already she regretted her admission.

Amelia looked out at the lake. Ducks were everywhere, swimming in line or in circles. "You think you're in love with Pastor Denny?"

The floodgates opened; May could not stop. "It's making me crazy. I can't sleep nights for thinking about him."

"Oh, May, my dear. Did he lead you on, encourage you?"

"No. He's not done nothing like that." May leaned forward, pain and embarrassment in her face.

Amelia gathered her thoughts. What would Grace say? She wished May had invited Grace to this meeting instead of her. She thought back to her own therapy after Thomas died in the auto crash. She'd done a bit of transference, developed a crush on one of her therapists, but she'd had the good sense to realize what was happening, and so had the therapist. Had Denny missed May's growing infatuation? Amelia drew a deep breath,

"When a person goes to a counselor, they're vulnerable and in emotional pain. The counselor cares about us, listens in a way that maybe no one has ever listened. It's easy for any of us to project or feel love or anger on our therapist."

How am I going to get out of this now? Oh why did I ever open my stupid mouth? May's hunched shoulders straightened. Her face lifted and brightened. *She's given me a way out*. "That sounds like it might be what's happened. Yes, that's probably what's happened. Like you said, no one's ever listened to me before. Thanks, Amelia, for helping me understand. I needed to talk to somebody, and you've been right kind. I thank you for listening and helping me understand about these things." *I have got to get out of here before I say more, betray myself, and really mess things up.* Anxiety filled May's eyes. "You won't tell anyone about this, please."

"I promise. I won't say a word."

May considered her lack of education and age, both barriers to Denny Ledbetter. The bleakness of her life struck her; she wanted to curl into a ball and die.

Amelia felt sorry for May. What would this woman do? Maybe she'd been too hasty leaving her husband. Amelia wasn't going to get into that. They stood, brushed the grass and bits of soil from their clothing, and drove back to town. When they parted at May's car near the flower shop, May waited until Amelia disappeared into the shop, then headed back to Covington.

12

May Persists

As she drove past Elk Plaza and McCorkle Creek, May looked neither to the right nor to the left. She didn't care if the gossips on Cove Road saw her, or what they might say. But when she parked directly in front of Cove Road Church, her determination flagged, and her energy whooshed away like a leaf on a swift stream. She sat there arguing with herself whether to follow through on her plan or turn and go home. Go home, a part of her screamed. Go home! May turned the key in the ignition.

As the engine sprang to life, a shadow fell across her windshield and a knock sounded on the window. Turning her head, May gasped at Pastor Denny Ledbetter standing at the window, making signals with his hand indicating that she should roll down the glass.

He wore a gray short-sleeved shirt with crisscrossed golf clubs embroidered in white across the pocket, and he was smiling. "Come to see me, May?"

Unwittingly, May nodded. Her throat was dry. Words fled.

"Well then, open your door, and let's go on up to the office."

Where the strength came from, she did not know, but she managed to slide from the car and walk alongside Denny up the paved pathway beside the church. The afternoon sun behind tall pines in the nearby cemetery cast long shadows across the concrete walkway. Ahead she could see Denny's cottage, where he had lived with Pastor Johnson before the old pastor passed away several years ago. May had been inside that cottage once to pay respects to the ailing Pastor Johnson, and her mind filled with the memory of wood-paneled walls, a redbrick fireplace, plaid throws cast casually over the arms of chairs, and the welcoming, cozy feel of the place.

Pastor Denny opened the door to his office and stepped back to allow her inside. "What a gorgeous day, eh?" He flipped the light switch and turned on the window air conditioner. He waved his hand. "It's more than a bit stuffy in here. I had a christening earlier in the church. Then I rushed off for a round of golf with Grace's Bob and his friend Martin. If you'd gotten here five minutes earlier, you'd have missed me. I just got back." He looked at her and smiled. "You look very nice today. What can I do for you, May?"

Encouraged, May sank into the armchair in front of his teak desk, a gift from the women's auxiliary last Christmas. The desk replaced the old army-issue gray-metal desk that had served Pastor Johnson for so many years. The auxiliary had also painted the office a pleasant shade of yellow, not too bright, not too saturated or mustard colored. Pastor Johnson's prints of local waterfalls remained on the walls, and on many a day, when the question put to her by Denny required deep consideration, May had focused on these prints. They helped her relax.

Denny pulled out his green leather chair, sat, and looked at her. "Well. What's on your mind?"

May felt the urge to use the ladies' room. She needed time, and words that would not come. She reached for a Kleenex from a box on his desk, blew her nose, and concentrated on a waterfall. "You've never married?" May asked. *What a stupid thing to ask, and so rude. If he gets up and walks out, I deserve it.*

"Why no. I never have been married. I came close to becoming engaged once, to a woman in my last parish."

May continued. "Have you never met anyone else you felt you couldn't live your life without?"

"No. I haven't." Denny shifted and leaned back in the chair. "I'm of the opinion that there are any number of people any one of us could marry and be quite content with."

"You don't believe in one great love, then?"

"I guess not. Maybe I'm just jaded. I've seen so many couples marry with high expectations and hopes, and a couple of years later they're divorced. Fifty percent of marriages end in divorce. Discouraging, don't you think?"

I'm one of those fifty percent, one of those parishioners that helped turn him off of marriage. Her stomach tightened. Here she was a fifty-six-year-old, miserable, divorcing woman who felt as if she were fifteen and in love. Worst of all, the object of her passion sat across from her discussing marriage and divorce as if they were just old friends hashing over some church issue that neither of them cared much about.

Denny picked up a pencil and tapped its eraser end on the desktop.

Next thing he'll shove back his chair, and that will be the end of it. I've never been very brave. I've let people push me around. I've done things I didn't want to do to please others or to keep from hurting anyone. May leaned forward, rested her arms on his desk, and looked into his eyes. *Say it right out. Get this off your chest, once and for all.*

"I believe, Pastor Denny, that I have gone and got myself a big, old silly crush on you."

13

Things Not Meant to Be

The air-conditioning unit shifted gears, its hum falling to almost inaudible. Denny's eyes went blank, then left her face and fastened for a moment on something behind her. He shut his eyes and when he opened them, May read concern, not love. She had been too quick, too ill prepared. She had made a perfect fool of herself, humiliated herself. May wanted to sink into the ground, disappear from the face of the earth, and die. Tears sprang to her eyes.

"Denny, you back there?" a male voice called. Footsteps sounded in the hallway and moments later Charlie Herrill stood in the doorway. "Oh. May. How are you? Did I interrupt something? Sorry. I'll call you later, Denny."

The pastor was on his feet heading for the door. He clasped Charlie's hand and drew him into the room. "Not at all. Come in."

May felt as if she'd been kicked in the stomach.

"May and I are finished, wouldn't you say, May?"

Smile. Nod. Get out of here fast. "That's right. We're finished." She picked up her purse and started for the door, her legs acting on their own volition. "Thanks for your time, Pastor."

"Certainly," he replied.

May started down the hall, veered right, and barely made it to the restroom. She kneeled by the toilet and heaved until she thought she would die. Hugging her stomach, she rolled onto her side and lay on the cold tile floor for what seemed an eternity, until suddenly she realized that the men might leave the church, might have already left the church and locked the doors, unwittingly trapping her inside.

May hauled herself to her feet. Leaning against the sink, she dashed water on her face and rinsed her mouth. In the glare of fluorescent lights, she looked frightful, her hair mussed, her face paste white, her jaw trembling, her mouth pursed to cry. She ran a comb through her hair, opened the door, and peered down the hall. Light from the office fell across the narrow hallway. Low male voices, a cough, a laugh issued from the office she would never enter again. She couldn't let them see her.

Removing her shoes, May sneaked into the church sanctuary. Light spilled through stained-glass windows. Holding her breath, May hastened down the aisle and stepped into the foyer.

Dear Lord, let the front door be unlocked.

The knob turned easily. The front door of the church swung wide. After a furtive look in both directions, May dashed across the grass to her car.

From her kitchen window, Alma Craine across the road noted May's departure from the church. Alma's eyes narrowed. "She's been with the pastor and Charlie," Alma muttered. "What were the three of them doing in there? I bet Charlie caught them red-handed, and he stepped in to put a stop to it." That is what Alma presented two days later to the ladies at the beauty parlor.

14

Under Wraps

For several days, May remained in her room. When she did not leave the house, and no one called or came to see her, Mrs. Bourne, always concerned that a boarder might take ill and die under her roof, tainting her home forever, broke her own rule and used her key to enter May's room.

The shade was drawn. She yanked open the curtains and raised the bamboo shade. In one corner May huddled in a large leather armchair, clutching her knees to her chest, head on her knees, her hair straggling over her face and shoulders.

May had been a good tenant all these months—quiet, pleasant, paid her rent on time. Mrs. Bourne hastened to the chair. "May, are you sick? Shall I call someone in your family?" Then, she remembered that May had given her not a family name but a funny name, Amelia Declose, as the person to call in case of emergency. Why would a McCorkle not provide the name of someone in her family, when there was a whole peck of 'em living over in Madison County? Something was fishy. May remained frighteningly immobile and said not a word. Whatever trouble the woman was in, Mrs. Bourne didn't want to know. She minded her own business, never got involved with tenants. Still, she asked, "May. You sick?"

When May did not respond, Mrs. Bourne left the room. She got the number May had given her from a book on her desk and walked straight to the phone.

Amelia checked her camera bag for sufficient film and batteries. Mike had nagged her to get with it, to move into the twenty-first century with digital, and she had purchased an expensive five-pixel digital camera. Though it was lighter and easier to carry, she preferred her old Pentax. Today she would be working in Pisgah Forest in dim light and she wanted all the control a manual camera afforded. Picking up her tripod, she started for the front door.

The phone rang. Amelia let the machine take it and stopped in her tracks when she heard a woman's high-strung, alarmed voice.

"I'm looking for somebody name of Amelia Declose. May McCorkle here rents a room from me, and she's looking sick like a dog. Won't talk or nothing. You get this message, call me back, or come quick as you can." The woman gave her phone number, plus sketchy directions from Patton Avenue, and hung up before Amelia had time to set down her equipment and reach the kitchen phone.

What had happened to May? Was she sick, or was this related to their conversation about Denny Ledbetter? Amelia went cold. May had said that she had a crush on Denny Ledbetter. Amelia had made light of it. Should she call Denny and see if he would go into Asheville with her? What was she thinking? No! Where was Grace? At the school, tutoring kids? With Bob, and if so, where? Grace would handle this or any situation better than she could. But Grace was not here. Amelia phoned Miriam, who had planned on going with her today.

"Miriam, dear, I have a friend in Asheville. Her landlady called. My friend is ill. I have to cancel our photo jaunt. No, dear, I think I best go alone, but thank you for offering to go with me. Yes, let's plan on shooting tomorrow. I don't think there's any rain in the forecast."

Mortified by her landlady's intrusion, May hunched in the chair, afraid to unclasp her legs, afraid to stand for fear she might fall. Except for a half dozen candy bars, she had not eaten in two days, had not wanted to eat, wanted to die. Now, suddenly, she was terrified that she might die.

She had rehashed, relived, and chastised herself for every moment spent in Denny's office and for every word spoken. What a crazy thing to assume he might care, to open herself like that. His rejection had been wordless, and his relief when Charlie Herrill appeared was too painful, too humiliating. If only, if only she could turn back the clock.

Anger flared. *How dare Mrs. Bourne open my door and walk in? What will I say to her, that I presumed too much and got what I deserved? Mrs. Bourne has been kind to me. She cared enough to check on me. I could be dead in here, and who would know? But darn, she left the window shade open, and the light hurts my eyes.*

May rocked back and forth. "Oh, God," she moaned. "What am I going to do? Help me. Please, help me."

How long she huddled in the chair wallowing in misery, May did not know, before footsteps sounded outside her room and Amelia opened the door and entered. For an instant, May wondered how Amelia knew, and the next moment Amelia's soft arms were about her shoulders. Wracking tears came then, and shakes so bad that Amelia must hold her tight for a long time. When May finally gained a measure of control, they sat on the floor, Amelia holding her as if she were a child.

"Talk to me, May. What happened?"

May shook her head and buried her face in her hands. "Don't want to talk about it."

"When you left me, did you go to Pastor Denny? Did you tell him what you told me?"

May groaned and nodded.

Amelia smoothed May's hair. "What did he say?"

Exhausted, May looked at Amelia with eyes bereft of light and hope. "I might as well be dead. If I was to see him ever again, I'd just die. How could I have been so stupid? And the worst of it, when I told him, before he had a chance to say anything to me, in walked Charlie Herrill on some church business." May smeared her tears across her cheeks with the backs of her hands. "You should have seen his face, Amelia. He was so relieved to see Charlie, he jumped right up outta his chair and rushed to the door to pull him in. You know what he said?"

"No, I don't. What did he say?"

"That he and I were finished, as if we were finished with a counseling session, when he really meant that he'd never see or talk to me again. It was awful. I couldn't wait to get out of there."

"You must have been devastated. You poor darling. I'm so sorry."

"Not so sorry as me. I should have listened to what you said instead of going off like a crazy woman."

"Let me get you a wet washcloth to wipe your face and eyes," Amelia said.

"I'd appreciate that right much." May felt better. Embarrassing things happened to people and they survived. She recalled a time when she had stood to speak at a PTA meeting at Caster Elementary School and her mind went blank. She had stood there like she was frozen, feeling the perfect fool, until someone snickered. She'd sunk into her seat, wanting to shrivel up and die. But she'd survived that and more, and she'd survive this, sure as the sun would come up. She'd never gone to another PTA meeting, and she'd make sure she'd go no place near Pastor Denny.

"I never called in to my job to say I was sick," May said. "Maybe I haven't got a job no more." She shrugged. "Who cares? I hate assembly line work. That's what I was doing."

"There's money for women who've been divorced, so they can go to school," Amelia said.

May laughed. "Go back to school? Me?"

"Yes you. You're very bright, May. You should get some training so you can get a decent job."

"Where have I got to go?"

"A-B Tech and talk to somebody."

"Maybe I could train to work in a hospital. I always did like caring for sick people," May said.

"That sounds like a wonderful idea."

May's shoulders slumped. She was not nearly as brave as she pretended to be. She was afraid of the future, afraid of going to college, an impossible dream until this very minute. "How am I gonna live and pay the rent until I get me the money to go to school?" She accepted another wet washcloth from Amelia and ran it along her arms. "This feels so good. Guess I could use a shower about now."

Amelia left her then, but not before she impulsively invited May to stay with the ladies at their farmhouse until she worked out new arrangements and her money for the tech school came through. It was a gesture, that was all, and it was inconceivable to Amelia that May would accept her invitation. Hadn't May just declared that she never wanted to set foot in Covington, or anyplace where she might run into Denny Ledbetter? Inviting her made Amelia feel gracious and generous of spirit.

It came as a shock several days later, after she and Sadie returned from walking the puppies on Cove Road, when Amelia found a message from May on their answering machine. The puppies, still on their leashes, raced around her feet while Sadie chased, caught them, and tickled their tummies.

Amelia listened to the message in shocked silence a second and third time as May's voice said, "I thank you for inviting me to stay awhile with you ladies. I went to A-B Tech and the money's easy to pay for schooling, but I ain't got nowhere to live. The training's eight weeks." Pride filled her voice. "I'm gonna be a nurse's aide. When would be the best time for me to bring my things over?"

Amelia plopped into the closest chair. What had happened to never seeing Denny? He lived nearly across the road from them. Benji had tangled himself around a leg of the chair and she bent to help Sadie unleash him.

"Can we let him run about the house for a bit?" Sadie asked.

Amelia nodded.

"Won't Hannah be angry if she comes in and catches Benji out of his cage?" Sadie asked.

Amelia put her arm about the little girl, whom she

absolutely adored. "We'll let him run about the house for a little while, but you watch him, and don't let him chew on anything."

"Oh, goodie good." Sadie raced toward the living room with Benji at her heels.

What to do? Amelia hadn't mentioned May or Denny to Grace and Hannah, and Hannah wasn't in the best of moods these days.

15

Change and Confusion

Across the road at Max's, Hannah, furious with Max, pounded one fist into the palm of her other hand. "Why can't you understand that Zachary's up to no good? I am warning you. He'll do whatever he can to undermine our relationship."

"Aren't you overreacting? So, he gambles to pass the time. He could do worse. You thought he was seeing a woman or maybe involved in drugs. Better he should gamble."

"This isn't about his gambling, Max. A few days ago you were furious with him for the way he spoke so rudely to Anna."

"I won't tolerate rudeness in this house. It's Anna today, Sarina or you tomorrow."

"But you never said that to him, did you? Why? Can't you see that his being here has changed everything for us? It's subtle, as if he's determined to somehow undermine what we have together. Look at us. Here we are, arguing. We never did that, did we?"

"Why would Zachary being here matter to what we do or when or where? We have our own lives to live. What's stopping us from going on just as we did before they came?"

"I'm not here as much as I used to be, am I?"

"Hannah, I consider this your home as much as it is mine. Your choosing not to come over as often, or to stay overnight, isn't what I want, you know that."

"Things aren't the same, Max. They just aren't. Going on as we were before they came no longer seems feasible."

Max replied, "How is it different from my spending nights with you at your place?"

"There's no hostility in the air at my place. I don't get the feeling the walls have ears and eyes."

They had had this discussion, or argument, several times of late. Max was for biding their time. He brushed aside the idea of confronting Zachary about his attitude toward Hannah, his future plans, and his treatment of Sarina. Hannah was dumbfounded at his seeming indifference. "You're burying your head in the sand," Hannah had said. "Can't you see that Sarina's miserable?"

But Max did not. From his point of view, Sarina should be happy not to be living in a place where there was fighting in the streets.

To Hannah, Zachary's look clearly said, What the devil are you doing here?

Max refused to see what was happening all around him, and this drove Hannah to distraction.

"I'm going home," Hannah said. "See you at work."

Grace's car slipped into their driveway just as Hannah crossed Cove Road, and they walked up the steps onto the front porch together.

Hannah said, "I am fit to be tied."

The strain around her friend's eyes and mouth troubled

Grace. "What's going on? Sit down and talk to me." They walked to the rockers and sat.

"I'm totally frustrated. It's no longer pleasant to be at Max's place. Nothing's the same anymore. I'm concerned for Sarina, who's obviously depressed. Mostly, I don't like or trust Zachary."

"It'll be better for Sarina once she has the baby," Grace said.

"You keep saying that, while things keep getting worse. What if she has the baby and slides into postpartum depression like Laura did after Andy was born?"

"We'll watch for that," Grace said. "We know what to look for now. We can't replace Sarina's family, and her customs are very different. We don't even know what they are around the issues of childbirth and child rearing. I do know that she trusts you, Hannah, and depends on you."

Hannah grasped the arm of her rocker. "So, I should form an attachment to the baby and have it break my heart when Zachary snatches his wife and child away? He'd like nothing better than to do that to me—to his father. That young man's consumed with anger and resentment. I just wish I understood why."

They could hear the puppies barking inside. Hannah's eyes hardened. "Let's go in and see what those animals of yours are doing in the house."

When Hannah yanked opened the front door two puppies dashed between her legs, ran out onto the porch, and down the steps. Amelia and Sadie followed close behind, waving their leashes.

"Benji, Carole, come back here," Amelia yelled.

The puppies raced around the yard, getting closer to the

road by the second. Grace took the steps two at a time, and she and Amelia finally collected the wriggling bundles of fur and transported them to the pen behind the kitchen. Sadie trailed behind with the leashes.

Hannah turned and shook her head, but said nothing. The last thing she needed to concern herself with now was puppies, but it was clear they must install a fence out back so the puppies could be outside and safe.

With the puppies tucked and settled in their cage, and Sadie settled before the television in the guest bedroom, Amelia beckoned Grace to the kitchen. "I must talk to you."

Grace pulled out a chair at the kitchen table and sat. "Why the conspiratorial tone?"

"A cup of tea?" Amelia nodded toward the boiling teapot on the stove.

"Sure. Why not?"

Amelia made them each a cup of tea and set the box of Splenda on the table near Grace, who opened two packets and poured their contents into her cup. "At least this doesn't have an aftertaste, and I can enjoy a cup of tea." She looked at Amelia. "What's the matter? You look like you've seen a ghost."

Amelia collapsed in the chair across the table, told Grace about her meeting with May at Lake Louise, about May's confessing her feelings to Denny, about Charlie arriving, and May's landlady calling her to May's room. "May's been through the wringer, and she's trying to pull herself together. She's taking an eight-week nurse's aide course at A-B Tech. She lost her job at the factory. Awful work, assembly line, minimum wage."

"I'm very sorry for May. She must have felt humiliated

when she went to Denny Ledbetter and that happened. I feel sorry for him, too. What could he say? She's way older than he is."

Amelia nodded and folded her arms across her chest. She tossed her head and laughed lightly. "And fool that I am, I invited May, in the most offhand, casual manner, believe me, to stay awhile with us until she got settled."

Grace pictured the shy, silent May telling Denny that she was in love with him. Amazingly, Alma had been right when she said that something was going on, though she assumed it was a mutual caring between Denny and May. "Doesn't it strike you as ludicrous that May would want to live here with us, almost across the road from Denny, if she's so humiliated? It's unavoidable, if she stays here, that she'll run into him. What can May be thinking?"

"I doubt that she's thinking at all right now. She's miserable and grasping at straws," Amelia said. "In a million years I never dreamed she'd take me up on my invitation. It was so off-the-cuff, so casual."

"Hannah know about any of this?"

"No. I hoped we could tell her together. Hannah's in such a bad place lately. She'll have my head. Will you be there when I tell her, please? May called. She asked when she could bring her things over."

"She can't come unless Hannah agrees, you know that?"

Amelia turned from Grace and stared out of the kitchen window at a forsythia branch decked with yellow flowers. The branches of the shrub grew taller and wider each year and more strikingly lovely when it bloomed, even as they obscured the view from the window. Hannah will trim it soon, Amelia thought. Or she will move it farther from the house, for if she cuts it, it'll be boxy, and square, and lose its

willowy quality. She started then, for she could hear footsteps on the stairs, and moments later, Hannah joined them
in the kitchen.

When Amelia explained what had happened to May, and
her invitation that May be their houseguest, Hannah's jaw
dropped. This she did not need, a scatterbrained woman in
crisis parked in their guest room, sitting at their table, hog-
ging their living room, talking about her problems. Hannah
had enough problems of her own. How like Amelia to be so
inconsiderate! At that moment, if she could have, she would
have ignited a rocket under Amelia and sent her flying into
space.

Hannah felt Grace's hand on her arm. The tightness in
her shoulders and jaw slackened, and she took a deep breath.
It was amazing, Grace's ability to calm her. Foolish Amelia
had invited the woman. It was done, and Hannah would be
the ogre if she objected. "Well, this is a pickle, isn't it? It's
not what I would have chosen, but what the heck, I guess
we're going to have a houseguest."

Amelia stared at Hannah. She had anticipated Hannah
yelling, demanding to know how she had dared do this without consulting Grace and herself. Amelia was speechless.

Hannah folded her arms across her chest. "I depend on
you to occupy May and keep her from under my feet. I'm
in no mood to babysit or listen to anyone's problems. I have
my own problems."

One week later, May arrived, her old Chevy spewing
puffs of white smoke from its exhaust. May parked as close
to the steps of the porch as possible, then looking left, right,
and across the road, and seeing no one, carried several boxes

and suitcases up onto the porch. Amelia helped May bring in two more suitcases, and May followed Amelia to the downstairs guest bedroom.

May gasped with pleasure. "It's so beautiful. This is the loveliest room I have ever had the privilege to stay in. Thank you so much, Amelia." Dropping a suitcase, she turned to hug Amelia. "How can I ever thank you? You've saved my life."

"Don't thank me. I couldn't have asked you without Hannah and Grace's okay. May, sit a minute." Amelia waved May toward the bed and took a seat in Grace's glider rocker. Grace would have to give up her special breakfast place, but she would smile and act as if it didn't matter. Guilt for inconveniencing Grace assailed Amelia.

"I want to warn you," Amelia said. "Hannah's going through a very hard time right now, so if she's distant and unfriendly, it's not your being here."

"Oh, I am sorry. Is she not well?"

"She's well enough. Zachary, Max's prodigal son, has returned from India with his very pregnant wife. The baby's due anyday now, and Max and his son don't have a good relationship. Their being here has put a strain on everyone."

May's face grew sad. "I know how hard that is when family relations are strained, like my mother and me. I'll stay out of Hannah's way. Just tell me what time she gets up, and I won't be in the kitchen or anywhere around."

"Hannah's an early riser and out of here by eight in the morning. I've cleared a shelf for you in the kitchen." Amelia rose from the glider. "Well, let's get the rest of your things from the porch."

Soon May's boxes, shopping bags, and suitcases sat randomly on the floor of the guest bedroom. "This is it," she said. "I'll shove these boxes under the bed and in the closet, get everything out of the way."

"Another thing. Feel free to use the kitchen. We ladies used to take most of our meals together, but these days we don't sit and eat together very often. Grace sometimes has lunch or dinner or both with her companion, Bob, who lives in the little cottage next door. I spend a lot of time with my granddaughter, Sadie, and her mother, Miriam. They just moved into the other cottage past Bob's, and Hannah's often at Max's. Much of the time, you'll be on your own."

"I'll be glad to grab a bite in town," May said. "I usually have an Egg McMuffin in the mornings with coffee. I won't put you to any trouble. Thank you for everything, Amelia. I just have to pay attention to Pastor Denny's going and comings so as not to meet up with him."

Amelia smoothed her slacks. "I have a photo shoot this morning. You make yourself at home, unpack, and settle in."

May nodded, then reached for a loose-bulging knitting bag, drew out a ball of yellow yarn and needles, sank into the glider her savior had vacated, and began to knit, the needles flying. For a moment, Amelia stood in the doorway watching her and remembered a spinster lady who had lived next door to her grandmother. Mostly she sat in a rocker on her porch knitting as if her very life depended on it, never lifting her head, even in response to nine-year-old Amelia's cheery "Hello" as she roller-skated past the woman's house.

"Knitting," her grandmother had said. "Mrs. Paine has lots of worries, and knitting helps to relax her."

Amelia watched May's head bent in concentration over

the needles. A wise lady, Mrs. Paine. Bless May. "I'm off now." Softly, Amelia closed the door behind her.

A few days later, Hannah complained to Grace. "I can't abide May living here."

"Has she done something to offend you?"

Hannah brought her hand down hard on the kitchen counter. "No, she hasn't. In fact, she's quiet as a mouse. It's not normal to be that quiet. What does she do when she's here? I feel as if she's studying us." Hannah scratched the side of her cheek. "Notice how she acts around Amelia? May hangs on every word Amelia says, as if Amelia's some kind of oracle." She grunted and raised her eyebrows. "Some oracle."

Grace clasped Hannah's arm and guided her to a chair. "Now, you sit right down and let's talk about this." Grace brought them each a cup of freshly brewed tea. "A good hot cup of tea will help you calm down." Two packets of Splenda were emptied into her cup and she stirred, the spoon tinkling against the porcelain. "May's not going to be here long. You can't let her upset you like this."

"I hate myself for being upset," Hannah muttered. "I should feel sorry for her and be more generous of spirit, like you are."

"You are generous of spirit, Hannah. Never think otherwise. I've seen how you are with Sarina. Her own mother couldn't be kinder or more caring of her."

Hannah sighed and sipped her tea. "How could I not care, the poor little thing? She's so far from home. Imagine what that must feel like."

"Right now, May also has no home."

Hannah said, "Of course, you're right. May hasn't a home either. What will she do with her life, anyway?"

"May has plans. She's studying to be a nurse's aide or assistant."

Hannah wrinkled her nose. "A nurse assistant. Someone who empties bedpans?"

"I'm not sure what they do, but it's important work in a hospital. And for May, it's a start. She's bright. Who knows where she'll go from there? She's quiet, because she doesn't want to bother us. She'd pack and leave, even if she had to live on the street, if she thought she were upsetting you."

"You're right, Grace. I'll try to see her as you do and remind myself it's not forever." She gave Grace a piercing look. "It's not forever, right?"

"Certainly not."

"Truth is, I'm angry that Amelia moved her in here without asking either of us," Hannah said.

Reaching over, Grace rested her hand on Hannah's arm. "I had a moment or two of being annoyed about that, but I think it all happened so fast. Amelia made an offhand remark, and May took her up on it. Not the end of the world, right? Not the end of the world, and you're helping a woman without many resources and in need, right?"

"Right. But I still don't like it," Hannah said.

"I understand that."

This is what's so incredible about Grace. She's so good and so generous of spirit. I always feel better, feel like a better person, when I talk to her. Hannah leaned across the table. "I'll just accept that May's here and concentrate on her finding a better place to live soon."

"That sounds like a good idea. I'll do the same," Grace replied.

16

A Baby Girl Is Born

Sarina's baby arrived two weeks past her due date. On May 12, Hannah, in her bedroom across the street, awakened to the sound of Max's pickup reversing, heard the screech of tires, and from her window watched it turn left onto Elk Road. The baby was coming. Why hadn't Max called and wakened her?

"You need a cell phone so I can call you when it happens," he had said.

"I hate those things," she had replied.

"They're so easy to use."

"I'm glad you think so," she replied. "It's not easy for me."

Like so many electronic items, she found a cell phone annoyingly complicated. Cell phones were designed for midgets with tiny fingers. Her wide fingers hit the wrong buttons and she must use the tip of a fingernail (and hers were short) or a pencil tip to punch the numbers. On a scale of one to ten, with ten being "I hate this," she rated cell phones a ten.

How many times had they gone round and round this issue? How many times had she agreed and done nothing about it? Hannah slapped her forehead. And when she finally did get one, where was it? Tucked away in the glove compartment of her station wagon. Now she must drive alone to Memorial Mission Hospital.

Zachary's hostility reached Hannah the moment she stepped into the waiting room. And Max's huge grin as he rose to greet and embrace her did nothing to relieve her irritation.

"What's she doing here?" Zachary had said in a stage whisper designed, Hannah was certain, to be heard by her.

"She's dilating fast. The baby should be here soon. This is gonna be an easy birth, thank God." Max ignored his son and guided Hannah toward two empty seats across the room from Zachary.

"That's a blessing." Hannah remembered the anxious hours waiting for Laura to give birth to Andy. Laura had been over forty, and the hours of her labor had dragged on and on. Hannah worried about complications, but thank God, there had been none. Sarina was younger. She'd be fine. Sarina was who mattered now, not her husband.

Suddenly Zachary stood near them. Hannah looked up. "Well, Zachary, are you excited? You'll be a father soon."

Children, Hannah believed, grew to appreciate their parents when they became parents. She wasn't sure about Zachary. His anger seemed rooted in events she had no knowledge of. Still, she hoped parenthood would soften him and serve as a bridge between him and his father. For Max's sake, she wanted to like Zachary, but his abrasive and discourteous manner toward her and his unbridled rancor toward his father chilled her, and she distrusted and disliked him.

"Just want to get it over with. Damn nine months have been as long for me as for her," Zachary muttered.

Hannah swallowed her anger. The fool! How could he compare the discomfort and stress of Sarina's pregnancy to his petty moods? Sarina's home, her family, her way of life had been swept away as if by a flood, and Zachary's behavior had been insensitive, inconsiderate, and downright mean. Never had Hannah seen him comfort his wife or reassure her. Instead, he had abrogated his responsibility for her well-being.

"A little girl," Hannah said as he moved past them. "We're delighted it will be a little girl."

Zachary's pacing stopped. He glared at Hannah. "We are not your family."

"Hannah is my family." Max glared at him.

Hannah regretted coming. She turned to Max to say that she would go, when a volunteer appeared in the doorway and announced the birth of a baby girl, six pounds and twelve ounces. "Follow me, and I'll take you to them," she said.

Zachary filled the exit door, barring Hannah's way.

Max stepped between them and put a protective arm about Hannah. They followed the volunteer, then, with Zachary trailing them and grumbling.

"You were certainly right about Zachary," Max said. "I apologize for not paying closer attention to his behavior. Forgive me for making light of your concerns."

"Right now, it's all about that young woman and her baby," Hannah said.

Max slowed to match Hannah's amble, then realized it was designed to allow Zachary to pass them, to be the first one into Sarina's room, the first to see his baby. Marvelous Hannah, Max thought, strong and often tough, yet capable of such kindness, such thoughtfulness.

Bella had seen that in Hannah and spoken of it, but back then he had been miserable about his wife's illness and then her death. Bella had been right in her appraisal of this woman. Hannah had seemed to him at first merely strong and tough-minded. Later, as they worked together, he began to see how trustworthy and capable she was and he had fallen in love with her. Hannah was his love, and what a woman, warm and sensual, wise and kind.

Zachary quickened his pace and entered his wife's room. Hannah slowed even more, and Max stopped. "Yes, my love, we'll let them have time together."

A small pink bundle nestled in Sarina's arms. The young woman's face glowed with happiness as she looked up at her husband. "Come, see your daughter."

Zachary approached the bed. The anxiety and fear that had inhabited his wife's eyes for many weeks were gone. She reached toward him and placed the baby in his arms.

Zachary cushioned the infant in his arms. She whimpered. He looked down at her and his heart softened. He felt something he had never anticipated, a deep and tender love. His child was the most beautiful little person he had ever seen.

"She's wonderful, beautiful, and she looks like you," he said as he returned her to Sarina, who smiled up at him.

In the doorway, his father and Hannah looked at each other and beamed approval. Then, to their astonishment, Zachary beckoned them. "Come see my daughter." He smiled. "My wife has given me a beautiful daughter."

"She's beautiful," Hannah said. "She has such lovely

silky hair. My babies were born bald. I never found that very attractive."

"Would you like to hold her?" Sarina asked.

Hannah hesitated, preferring not to provoke Zachary's ire. But he nodded. Hannah's eyes filled with tears when she took the infant from her mother. "Look, Max, isn't she beautiful? So sweet, so precious." With a stab of pain, Hannah remembered that she had felt nothing like this tender love for her own daughters when they were born. Bill Parrish had made it very clear that he would welcome boys and only boys, and she had given him not one, but two girls. His disappointment had manifested itself in stamping feet, swearing, ignoring her and the babies when she came home from the hospital. And fool that she had been, she had felt guilty, even knowing that it was his sperm, his male chromosome, that determined the sex of a child.

Max was saying, "She certainly is a beautiful baby."

Hannah held the infant to Max, who cooed over her. Then Hannah returned her to her mother, and Max and Hannah took their leave.

"They left so soon," Sarina said. Her eyes searched Zachary's face. "Hannah was so good to me, Zack. She's been like a mother to me, so kind and gentle, always saying the right thing. Try to see her as I do. Please be kind to her. Hannah is a good woman and your father is very happy with her."

He sat in a chair by her bed and stroked the baby's silky hair. He had shaved his beard and looked like a boy, his dark, curly hair falling forward into his eyes.

For all our sakes, I wish he were more of a man, more like his father or my father, someone I could depend on. I wish he knew what he wanted out of life, what he wanted to do or be. His immaturity frightens me, especially as I am so far away from home. There was no one to blame but herself. Sarina knew this. She had sensed his weakness before marrying him, and chose to believe that he would change, would lose his wanderlust, settle down, and find a place in her father's business. And he had tried, first this and then that aspect of the multinational export-import business. When that failed, he had shown little interest in her father's vast land holdings or in the management of her family's properties. Who was this boy-man she had married? Why would he not share his thoughts and feelings with her?

She had had much time to think of late, and had come to accept that as the saying went, "What you see is what you get." Zachary was who he was. She could not change him. Her hope that he would change had been an illusion born of love's insanity. She rationalized: So what if he were not or would never be strong as her father or his own father? She was strong enough for both of them, and if he would agree, with the help of his family and her new friends, they could make a good life in Covington or, if he must live in a city, in Asheville.

One thing, however, nagged at her, one unanswered question. Where had he gone every day while she sat miserable in his father's house? She refused to think that he might be seeing a woman. This was the one sin she could not, would not, forgive.

At that moment, a nurse entered and gathered up the baby. "You rest now. I'll bring her back in an hour so you can feed her."

Zack stood. "Like she said, you need to rest. I'll go now, and I'll be back this evening."

She reached for his hand, and he held hers, then bent and kissed her. "I love you," he said.

"And I love you." She looked up at him, her eyes hopeful. "What will we name her?"

"What would you like to name her?"

"I thought perhaps Shalina for my grandmother. But we live in America now, and I assume we will for quite a while. Am I correct in that assumption?"

He nodded, but his heart plummeted. Zachary Maxwell had no clue as to what he would do, what he wanted to do, where or how, and his confusion, the muddle in his brain, frustrated and angered him. He detested his father-in-law for so precipitously, and without their input, changing their lives. How dare the man shove tickets at them and wave good-bye? The fact that he had not protested or even asked a question, that he might have some responsibility in the matter, never crossed Zachary Maxwell's mind.

The news from India, from Sarina's eldest sister, the informal family spokesperson, told of continued raids and killings in the province from which they had fled. Several of their father's fields and crops had been burned. Although the family had had no part in the argument about the site of the mosque, they represented the *haves*, and it appeared that the *have-nots* were determined to change the status quo. There were, she reported, no plans to return to their home in the north, and although her sister wrote that they were missed, there was never a mention of Zachary and Sarina returning to the bosom of her family. Crap. He never liked India anyway. Too damned hot.

Sarina's voice broke into his musing. "I don't want her

burdened with a name over which children in school will tease her. So, something American and simple will be fine."

"My mother's name was Arabella. She hated it and changed it to Bella, but I don't want to name her for my mother. I couldn't bear calling 'Bella' all the time. It would seem as if I were calling my mother." He fell silent, then said, "How about Sarah? Sarah has the *s* letter of your grandmother's name, but it's pure American."

"Sarah. Yes. That is fine. I do indeed like that very much. Sarah, an American girl."

An American girl with the face and soul of India, Zachary thought as he bent again to kiss his wife.

Sarina wound her arms about his neck and held him. Her heart ached that her mother and her sisters were not here to celebrate with her the birth of her child.

Nightmares of the night and day when they had fled their home drove her from sleep. They were nightmares of screaming, torch-bearing, angry mobs chasing them, of being separated from her family, falling, houses burning. She never woke her husband, never shared her terror, but lay there, her heart racing, drenched in perspiration, taking deep breaths to quiet and comfort herself. Then anger would come—at her father. He hadn't dispatched her sisters and their husbands to England.

And in the daytime, sitting alone, her thoughts had been haunted by the memory of looking back before boarding the plane that day, to see her family huddled together, her mother wiping tears from her eyes, her sisters waving, her father's jaw set in a hard line. They would never return, of that Sarina was certain. She would never be welcome in her parents' home again so long as she was married to Zachary Maxwell.

So, then, she had consoled herself, it was better that they were in America. Perhaps it was where they should have lived from the beginning. It had been hard for her grandparents and parents to accept a Westerner, a Christian, as her husband. Although Zachary practiced no religion, marriage to an outsider was frowned upon by the culture in which she lived. Her sisters married Indians of their own class. Although they were a Westernized family—her father, she herself, and her sisters and brother had all been educated in England, and the family had lived abroad for many years— once they returned to India, there was always the pressure to conform. And her mother, educated in India, had always been more comfortable with the old ways.

Her brother said that he had met Zachary on a hiking trip in the Himalayas and invited him home. From the moment she laid eyes on Zachary, Sarina wanted to lean against him, to press her body close to his, to kiss and hold him. The intensity of these feelings frightened and embarrassed her. These were not feelings one shared with anyone, not sisters, friends, mother, an old nurse, no one. Her mother's arguments, her grandmother's admonishments, her father's concerns had fallen as ashes before her desire for this handsome American.

"I am telling you, Sarina," her father said, "people about here don't take well to strangers, and an American will never fit into our culture. You will see that I am correct."

Unfortunately for her, he had been correct. Zachary spoke openly and too often about how much better and easier things were in America. He had no concept of how to treat the help in the fields or in the household, and he too often made inappropriate comments about things or people that upset her father and especially her mother.

All those months before her baby's birth, Sarina had lain awake missing home, wondering if in the chaos of that evening, her father had grasped the opportunity to rid himself of her husband, whom he considered a boil on the body of the family. Painful as it was, Sarina believed that dispatching them to America had served her father's deeper purpose. If only he had not done so in such a draconian manner.

Sarina sank against the pillows and closed her eyes. She should be angry with her husband for failing her these last months; but then, on that chaotic day in India, with everyone rushing to sort and pack things, with concern that at any moment the house might come under attack, Zachary sat in their quarters and moped. He helped no one to do anything; he did not even pack his own clothes and books. Later, when they were alone and she was frightened, when her sisters' husbands comforted them with a hug, a reassuring smile, he distanced himself from her, offering neither support nor reassurance. Crisis immobilized him! Shocked and mortified at his indifference, his ineffectiveness, she had lowered her eyes in front of her parents.

Sarina squeezed her eyes tight to hold back tears. Zachary had been neither kind nor supportive of her, nor had he expressed gratitude or appreciation to his father for welcoming them with open arms. Zachary had not hugged her or dried her tears when she wept for home and family. Instead, he exhibited hostility toward those who stepped forward to offer support: Hannah, Grace, Amelia, his father, and Anna. Without them, how would she have survived?

So, why wasn't she angry with him? Because, she told

herself, this is not the time or the place for anger. We have a child. It is a time for gladness and celebration, for patience and understanding. Her capacity for forgiving ran deep, and she worried that she would be called upon, repeatedly, to draw from that reservoir. But for today, for now, joy must prevail. She opened her eyes and smiled at Zachary.

Feeling disoriented, Zachary walked slowly across the hospital parking lot searching for his white Camry among the plethora of white Toyotas. Finally, his handheld clicker made contact and lights flashed. When he unlocked the door and slipped into the front seat, a wave of heat wrapped about him. Zachary started the engine and waited for relief from the air-conditioning. He thought of his baby, his little girl, and brushed away tears of joy.

Holding the baby had nearly overwhelmed him, nearly brought him to his knees. He ached to beg Sarina's forgiveness for bringing her to Covington and abandoning her. "I wasn't myself," he wanted to whisper. "It was terrifying—the mobs, the noise, the fires, the gunshots, all that happened in India—and we have never even talked about it."

But words failed him, as they so often did with his father and on various jobs when he encountered highly competent men who reminded him of his father. In his father's presence, Zachary felt insignificant. The ability to make simple, everyday conversation failed, leaving him tongue-tied.

He never expected to come home penniless except for his mother's trust, and he could hardly support a family on that the way it came to him in drips and dribbles. Fear squeezed his heart, and his throat tightened. He wasn't prepared to be a father. He hardly knew how to be a husband.

I can do this. I can take care of my family, he thought. But it sure would be easier if Dad hadn't married Hannah. That land of his is the key to my freedom. What do they need all that land for? If I had some of it I could build rental houses for income that would free me to travel. Zachary leaned forward and lay his head against the steering wheel. *I've got to figure out a way to get my hands on a chunk of that land.* Then he shifted gears and drove from the parking lot.

Sarina's sadness vanished with the birth of her child. No one spoke of the young family moving out of Max's farmhouse, especially as Zachary's attitude and behavior softened. Hannah came and went with almost the ease and lightheartedness she had enjoyed prior to their arrival. Zachary no longer disappeared, and when Sarina spoke to her about her fears that Zachary might have had another woman, Hannah told her about Grace playing detective and Zachary's gambling.

Some days Zachary sat in Anna's kitchen with a mug of coffee in his hand relating tales of his life in India. One afternoon, Hannah eavesdropped as Zachary told Anna of his travels, about the ship he crewed on being locked by ice floes in the Bering Strait and about the tropical beauty of the east coast of Tanzania. He spoke of mountain climbing and the beauty of Nepal.

"I'm a good climber. Not the best, maybe, but good enough," he said. "Up there on that mountain, I felt close to my mother."

"She was a special woman, a good woman, your mother," Anna said softly.

Hannah tiptoed away, but in the kitchen Anna listened,

smiled, nodded, and patted Zachary's shoulder. Unsure that she understood everything he said, Anna was certain that he was different, happy, since the baby came. After all, he smiled and was attentive to his family, and pleasant to Señora Hannah.

Saturdays returned to a satisfactory pattern for Max and Hannah. Many Saturday nights they checked into a motel suite in Asheville and shopped for fresh produce at the farmers' market on Sunday mornings. Hannah found Amelia less annoying, and May, moving quietly in and out of the house, was easier to ignore. Even the puppies, twice their size now and sometimes careening through the house, no longer irritated Hannah, and she found moments to pet and cuddle them, especially Benji. She had been instrumental in having a chain-link fence put up in the backyard, so the dogs could be safe.

Then, over dinner one Saturday evening, Hannah urged Max to sit down with Zachary and talk about his future. "Perhaps there's a role for him at Bella's Park."

"And what might that be?" he asked. "I have no idea what his skills are or what he wants to do."

"He enjoys climbing mountains. I heard him tell Anna. Maybe he could hike those seven hundred acres of Bella's Park and see what we have up there. We don't know if there are old hardwood forests, waterfalls, caves, or what up the hillside. Don't you want to know what's up there?"

"I'll think about it."

As the days passed, Hannah persisted. "Why do you keep putting off talking to Zachary? He's your only child."

Max shook his head and his brows furrowed. "Perhaps I'm afraid that if we try to talk, we'll end up arguing as we always have."

Remembering the conversation between Zachary and Anna that she had eavesdropped on, Hannah said, "Give it a try. He loves Sarina and the baby. They both understand that things have changed in India. Naming the baby Sarah says a lot." She paused a moment and tapped her forehead. "I have an idea. Why not ask Bob to have lunch with you and Zachary? Let Bob ask the questions. He'll be a good buffer and keep you both on the straight and narrow."

"Especially after you've coached him?"

She shrugged and raised an eyebrow. "Come on, Max. Give it a try."

"Okay, honey. I'll set something up."

"Wait too long, and I'll be back to nag you," she said.

17

May and Denny

*I*t was not until she moved in with the ladies that May realized how lonely she had been living in a room in a stranger's home, and she was grateful for their generosity and kindness. May tried to be unobtrusive. She moved with silent steps, rarely entered the kitchen when the women were there, and avoided coming or leaving through the front porch if they sat outside.

"When I finish my program at A-B Tech, there's a job and further training waiting for me at Pardee Hospital," she told Amelia.

Good Lord, Amelia thought, she's planning to stay until she graduates from this program.

From behind closed shades in the living room, May studied Pastor Denny's goings and comings. Mornings she remained inside until Denny began his run, rounded the corner, and turned left onto Elk Road. Then May dashed to her car and headed in the opposite direction, driving a mile to the right on Elk Road before turning onto a dirt side road that circumvented Denny's exercise route.

Amelia wondered when the inevitable confrontation between them would occur. She understood that a lack of closure could haunt a person, and she wondered if May had chosen to stay with them for that reason, closure.

And then, several weeks after May moved in, Amelia responded to his knock and opened the front door to Denny Ledbetter.

He stood there, moving his hat round and round in his hands. "May I see May McCorkle?"

"Certainly. Come right in." Slightly amused, Amelia led him into the living room. "Make yourself at home. I'll get May."

When Amelia announced that the pastor was here, May's hand fastened about the bedpost. Her legs went weak and her stomach tightened. "I'm not going out there. I'm not going to let him humiliate me again. I hate him."

"You don't hate him. You're hurt and disappointed, and you need to bring closure to this and get on with your life."

"Maybe so, but I still hate him."

"May, be sensible. Think about it. You told me at Mrs. Bourne's place that you never wanted to see him or Covington again, and yet you came to stay with us. He lives across the road. It was inevitable that you would run into him. Maybe you wanted it to happen. Here's your chance to clear the air, settle this once and for all, and stop asking yourself why this and why that."

May's expression changed from anxious and fearful to curious and interested. She sank into the glider and looked up at Amelia. "You think that's why I came here?"

"Yes, I do. I ran into June in Asheville the other day. She told me that your aunt Lil, the one who lost her husband last year, asked you to stay with her, and she's much closer to A-B Tech than we are."

May's hand rose to her mouth. "You knew that and you let me stay?"

"For a while, yes. I figured you'd have to confront the pastor, and the sooner the better. And since he's made the overture . . ."

"All right. I'll do it. I'll see him." She ran a comb through her hair, patted her cheeks with color, and put on lipstick. "I look okay?"

"You look lovely," Amelia said and opened the bedroom door.

When May entered the living room, Denny rose to his feet. His hat hit the floor and, embarrassed, he bent and picked it up. "May, you look very well. How are you?"

"How do you think I am?"

"Well, I don't know. Charlie came in and, well, we never had a chance to finish our conversation."

Arms crossed, she stared at him. "Struck me, you were glad enough to see him and mighty glad to be rid of me."

"I was shocked and flustered. I wasn't very professional, I admit, but all I could think of was what might I have done or said to make you, well, you know."

"To make me think you cared for me more than just as a person you counseled?" May's shoulders sagged, and her jaw quivered. She lowered herself into the closest chair. Her hands gripped the arms. Lord help me, she thought. This is a thousand times worse than the PTA goof-up.

"You didn't do anything but be kind to me. I hadn't much kindness from any man. You were different, and I got, well, carried off by it."

"I do like you, May, just not the way, well . . ."

"I don't no more."

"I can see that."

May's eyes grew sad. "I'm too old for you anyways and too country for a man of your education."

He stood by the window, holding the hat in front of him. May wanted to yell, "Put that old hat down. I'm not going to come near you."

"I don't know what to say that will make you feel better. I'm very sorry. I handled it badly, very badly, and I hurt you. I am so sorry."

"You waited a mighty long while to tell me. I been here weeks now," May muttered. Leaning forward in the chair, she focused on her clasped hands. *It ain't so bad seeing him, talking like this. At least he don't hate me. He looks so young. He is awful young, young as my youngest daughter. I been addle-headed as a calf in a hailstorm.*

Even now, he talked to her gently, kindly, not yelling like Pa or Billie would have done. And it struck May that it was this kindness she had responded to by fancying herself in love with someone as young as her daughter. Lord, what had she been thinking? She felt embarrassed and foolish.

"I made a fool of myself," she said. "Put us both in a bad position. I built it all out of place."

"And I am sorry for anything I may have said or done to encourage your feelings. I should have realized. I'm sorry not to have been more insightful. I ought to have been aware of what was happening and discussed it with you long ago."

"I guess we're two big old fools, then. Leastways, one old one." May looked at him as if seeing him for the first time and saw a trim young man with sandy hair and kind brown eyes, a man perhaps too young to be counseling a woman her age. But he *had* helped her. She had come to see herself as a worthwhile person, worthwhile enough to have the courage to enroll at A-B Tech to learn a trade and make something of her life.

It hadn't been easy those first days at A-B Tech with all those bright young people, and everyone talking fast and moving fast. She had wanted to drop her new books and run as if from the devil. But she hadn't. Instead, she had tightened her grip on her books, lifted her head, pasted a smile on her face, and walked into that first classroom, where, to her amazement, everyone had been kind and welcoming.

Denny walked over to May and extended his hand. "Can we be friends, then?"

It seemed to her that there was more that should be said. A sense of loss swept through her, loss for the way she had felt, so young and gay, and then she felt sad to think that someone she could talk to, someone who listened to her, was gone. It was as if she were leaving a part of herself behind with Pastor Denny Ledbetter.

May searched his eyes—friendly, yes, but guarded—and shook his hand. "We can be friends." She watched him walk away then, thinking how strange it all had been and that she would miss him. But the terrible ache for him and the humiliation she had felt were gone.

The following week, May, after repeatedly thanking the ladies, piled her bags and boxes into her car and departed for Aunt Lil's home in South Asheville.

The evening May's car rolled out of the driveway, the ladies ordered a mushroom, onion, green pepper, and pepperoni pizza from the diner on Elk Road and ate dinner on the porch.

"I feel lighter and free," Amelia said. "I hadn't realized quite how taxing this whole thing with May has been."

Grace set her glass on the porch rail. "I felt all at loose ends for a while having a stranger living in the house for so long. I hated losing the use of our guest room. I like to have my breakfast there. Funny how you get used to something like that, sitting in a certain room, in a specific chair, looking out a certain window. I'm going to enjoy breakfast tomorrow."

Amelia said, "As I watched Denny leaving the house today, it occurred to me that we should have him and Miriam for dinner one evening, maybe with Hank and Laura."

"Are you matchmaking?" Hannah laughed. "And why not? All anyone can ever do is introduce two people. After that, they either like one another or they don't."

But when, a week later, Denny came for dinner, most of his conversation was directed to Bob and Max, and Miriam seemed totally indifferent to the fact that an eligible male sat at the table.

As they cleared the dishes, Hannah said to Amelia, "Well, as I said, you can do the introductions. What happens after that is out of your hands."

Amelia placed the glass that she was about to insert into the dishwasher on the table and absentmindedly ran her finger across its rim. "I'm disappointed. I do so want Miriam and Sadie to stay in Covington or somewhere close. I don't want to lose them when I've just found them." She looked at Hannah. "I know Miriam's young, and she deserves to meet someone and remarry. I just pray it's someone who lives and works in this area."

"Maybe Miriam's had a bellyful of marriage for a while. When you've lived with an abusive man, it's not easy to trust another one of them," Hannah said.

"Of course, you're right. Well, I'll just put this out of my mind and stop trying to be a matchmaker." Amelia added the glass to the dishwasher.

18

Randy Banks

Grace felt guilty. She had neglected the Bankses, had not sought out Myrtle Banks to share the information she garnered at the veterans hospital or been back to see Randy. Nor had she asked Hannah about Lucy. In fact, she had neglected all the young people in her life for what seemed like ages, including Tyler and his sister, Melissa. She had not spoken to her son, Roger, in South Carolina, but he hadn't phoned her either, which indicated that he was busy and happy.

What was she to do? She couldn't force Randy to go to the VA hospital and talk to the counselor. Grace waited and prayed for direction. When the phone rang early the next morning and a tearful Myrtle Banks asked if she could talk to her, Grace agreed immediately.

"I got me the day off. Could you meet me at the diner on Elk Road, so as we could be alone?" Myrtle asked.

"I'll be happy to meet you," Grace replied, certain this was about Randy.

Myrtle waited for Grace at the chrome-and-red diner. Black-and-white tiles covered the wall behind the eating counter. They slid into the red vinyl seats of a booth.

"I hope this ain't put you to too much trouble," Myrtle said.

Grace reached across the table and rested her hand on Myrtle's. "Now don't you worry. It's no trouble at all. I'm glad you called. How are you? How are Randy and the rest of the family?"

"Randy's worrying me something fierce. He's waking up screaming more and more nights, and he frightens the children. But worse than that, he's talking about shooting himself. He keeps saying there ain't no point in his living no more." She bit her chapped lower lip, and her eyes were pools of worry. "I dunno what to do, Mrs. Grace." Myrtle lowered her face into her hands, and for a moment, as the waitress approached their booth, her shoulders shook.

The young waitress stood there, her pad in her hand, and looked quizzically at Grace, who smiled briefly and gestured her away. "Come back in a couple of minutes, will you, please?"

The waitress turned her attention to clearing a nearby table, and the clatter of plate on plate seemed louder than need be, which annoyed Grace, but Myrtle seemed not to notice.

Grace leaned across the table and took Myrtle's hands. "There is help for Randy," she said. "There's help at the veterans hospital over in East Asheville. I took the liberty of going there. I talked to the nicest man, a counselor, who works with soldiers who've come home from war. Randy's not the first, and he's not the last soldier to have what's known as post-traumatic stress syndrome."

"They got a name for what ails my boy?" Myrtle's eyes went wide.

"They do, and Randy has all the symptoms: depression, rages, starting up at the slightest noise, being suspicious of things and people, having nightmares."

As she listened to Grace, Myrtle nodded.

"Soldiers come home from the war and keep remembering all the terrible things they saw and heard, and there are plenty of them. Sometimes, at war, they do things that make them feel as if they've lost their own humanity." She was being too specific, frightening Myrtle, and she hadn't intended to do that. "These memories get burned into their minds. It's like they're watching a movie, only to them it's as real as if they're still over there and whatever it is, is still happening to them."

"Like, what's happening to them?" Myrtle asked.

"Whatever they saw, whatever they heard, the noise of war, and the awful horror of war. Maybe they saw their best buddy get killed, or they saw a child blown up before their eyes. I cannot even begin to imagine the kinds of things these young men experienced and what they had to do to survive. Whatever it is, they bring it home in their minds. To them, every door that slams shut, a car door, the bathroom door, all doors, sound like a gun going off."

Myrtle's hands covered her cheeks. Her mouth hung open. After a moment, she asked, "What can we do?"

"We can convince Randy to talk to the counselor at the veterans hospital. That would be a good start."

"What's the counselor man going to do to Randy? Give him an injection of something to calm him down?"

Grace drew a deep breath. "No, he's not going to inject anything into Randy. He would talk to him privately and let Randy talk about whatever happened to him."

"But won't talking about it make it worse?"

"That's not what will happen. You and I and his family and friends haven't been to war or know what Randy's been through and is still going through. But the counselor has heard it all. He can encourage and help Randy pick up the pieces of his life." It bothered Grace, as she talked, that there were no groups for Randy, not enough men home from this awful war for him to speak with, men who shared his experience.

"I hadn't thought about it like that, but you're sure right, Mrs. Grace." Myrtle shook her head. "None of us knows what my boy's goin' through." Her face brightened, and she looked deep into Grace's eyes. "And they can fix him back like he was?"

"Life changes us. You know that as well as I do. Maybe Randy will never be exactly like he was, but maybe he'll stop having horrific dreams or thinking of suicide. Hopefully, Randy can take his life back, find work he enjoys, meet someone, and fall in love one day and get married."

"I want my boy back like he was before he gone to war." Myrtle rocked, holding her shoulders with her hands.

"I know you do. And it can be much better than it is. What is ever the same, Myrtle? Are you the same woman you were when you married your husband? After he died were you the same woman, or today compared to when you first started your job? Haven't you changed?"

She nodded agreement. "I surely have. Had to. You're right, Mrs. Grace. I used to hie me away from people. Now I joke and carry on with the best of 'em. Tell me what I gotta do to help my boy, and I'll do it."

Grace looked at Myrtle in her homemade magenta-and-white-striped shirtwaist dress. The color was wrong for the woman, with her graying hair, thin, pale face, and large, dark eyes dulled by poverty and loss. Grace's heart went out to Myrtle.

"Talk to Randy and urge him to get some help. I'll talk to him also, if you think it will help. I'd be happy to set up the appointment and to drive him there, whatever it takes. Deep inside, I believe that he knows he needs help, so let's see that he gets it."

"I'll do whatever you say for me to do."

Grace picked up her menu and handed one to Myrtle. "I'm hungry. You must be also. Let's have something to eat."

That evening, the ladies sat on the porch and watched the sky turn to flame and the glow of evening spread across the landscape. Grace was glad to turn her mind from Randy and post-traumatic stress disorder to the affairs and concerns of her friends.

Amelia related having argued with Mike and refused to fly to New York for another show of her work. "I told Mike that that's not what I want to do, not how I want to live. I'm not forty, and I'd rather use my energy to shoot photographs, not travel. I just don't have the driving ambition for fame and recognition any longer. You understand, don't you?" She looked from Grace to Hannah, and both nodded. "It's enough that I've published two coffee-table books that sell well in the Carolinas. I don't want to sleep in hotel beds or be harassed at airports. They always pat me down. I detest that. Why do they do that? What do I look like, a criminal?

"I'm satisfied with my life and my work. Look at the book of the Inman family photographs. I had misgivings about doing that book after the flood washed away almost all they owned, but they urged me to, and we all love the way that came out. They show it off wherever they go. The oldest Inman girl invited me to her school to talk about the flood and how I took the pictures." Amelia stared into space for a moment, then changed the subject.

"I wish Mike would shoot more. He's so talented. His black-and-white photos are magnificent. He should teach less and do less studio work. He's so darn good, and no one sees his work. He won't even join the local photo club, F32, and he won't show his work at local galleries."

"Maybe," Hannah said, "you'll have to take a portfolio of his work to a gallery."

"He'd be furious."

"Not if you land him a show," Hannah replied. "He might pretend to be annoyed, but how could he not love that?"

"That's a really great idea, Amelia. Do it," Grace urged.

"I'll think about it. But I am not going back to New York."

"That decision have anything to do with Simon, the art critic?" Hannah asked.

Amelia turned to Hannah. "Honestly, I don't think so, although I'd hate to think what he might say about my work after the way I treated him."

"How badly did you treat him, anyway?" Grace asked.

"I think I let him off easily. I hardly knew the man, and there he was asking me to live with him in New York. I said no, graciously. I can hardly remember our conversation, exactly what he said or what I said but it seemed natural that he left as soon as he did. We hadn't any more to discuss." She slapped her hands on the arms of her rocker. "No, it's not about Simon. It's about me. I hate making small talk with strangers, and sitting for hours signing photos tires me. I'd feel this way if I'd never met Simon."

"I believe you." Grace raised her hands, indicating no argument. "You didn't want to have a New York show before you ever met Simon."

Amelia slowed her rocker and smiled at Grace. "Thanks for remembering that. Tell it to Mike, so he'll understand how I feel about this."

They rocked in silence then, until Hannah said, "I've asked Max to have lunch with Bob and Zachary. And I asked Bob to try to get information out of Zachary, like what his interests are and what he thinks he might enjoy doing. Max thinks if *he* broaches the subjects, he and Zachary will end up arguing."

"Bob's the right person to do that. He can be very tactful," Grace said. "His last work when he was in the army was with a SWAT team, talking down a hostage crisis, and that was way before we heard about hostage taking."

19

It Never Rains—It Pours

The well-appointed Southern Meadows Country Club occupied a rise above the golf course. Max, Bob, and Zachary were escorted to a table near the huge expanse of glass overlooking the green. Once settled, they engaged in small talk about the weather—not too hot yet, too much rain for this time of year—and the quality of the golf course below, which Zachary knew nothing about and found boring. They studied the menu and ordered.

"Have you ever played golf, Zack?" Max had warned Bob about Zachary's name change.

"It's never appealed to me," Zack said. "Seems silly chasing a ball."

"It's quite relaxing and pleasant out there on the course. What are your hobbies or interests?"

"They're certainly not golf."

Bob pressed on. "So what are they, may I ask? I'd be interested to know."

Zack crossed his arms over his chest. "I ski, and I enjoy hiking and mountain climbing. I used to scuba dive, did that a couple of times when I worked on a cruise ship that traveled through the Red Sea." He uncrossed his arms and leaned forward, his face suddenly animated. "Great coral reefs there, an incredible world, quiet, colorful. Most people don't know it, but the Red Sea offers some of the world's best diving."

"I admire anyone who's not afraid to dive. You must be very knowledgeable about tanks and all that," Bob said. "I tried scuba diving once on a Key West holiday, but I'm afraid it wasn't for me."

"I prefer mountain climbing. That's where I really get a high, no pun intended."

"Your father tells me you've traveled a great part of the world by freighter. What was that like?"

Zack placed his elbows on the table. "I was one dumb kid when they first hired me and apprenticed me to the ship's mechanic. Boy, was I scared out of my mind, the noise down there, the size of those engines."

"So you're a mechanic," Bob said.

"Nope. I was all thumbs, and they got rid of me darn quick. I went up top to load freight. Not a glamorous job, but at least I could see the sky." He glanced at his father. "And I didn't stay long on any one ship. We'd hit a city, say Singapore, and I'd sling my knapsack over my shoulder and find work on shore for a while."

"What kind of work?"

"Loading ships, busing in restaurants, things like that, enough to get by for a time while I explored the area. I'd hike and sightsee, enjoy the food, the music, the girls, then hop another freighter and on to the next port. I pretty much traveled the world that way, except for Norway. For some reason, I never did get to Norway, but I hear the fjords are beautiful. And I never really explored Morocco. Sick as a dog when I hit that port. I always wanted to go back."

"Sounds exciting. Lots of adventures." Bob beckoned the waiter for another beer.

"Yes, it was great adventure, lots of excitement." Zack nodded. "Excitement can get into your blood like a drug. You grow to crave it."

"I can imagine. Travel, as in the army, can do the same. Once you're out, you feel odd staying in one place for a long time. But if you wait it out, you can get over it, just like you can beat the drug habit." They were silent for a few moments. Then he asked, "What would you say you learned from all that travel?"

"That the world is one hell of a magnificent place, and most of us live our lives in one small corner of it, and like old Mr. Thoreau said, 'lead lives of quiet desperation.' Also, although people look and act differently, underneath we're all the same."

From Max's point of view this was going nowhere. His son liked to hike, climb mountains, and meet new people. "Given your choice, son, what is it you'd like to do now that you're back in the States?"

Zack studied his father. His throat went dry. He could converse like a normal human being with Bob, but not with his father. He reached for his iced tea and emptied the glass. That was better. "I honestly don't know, Dad. I got a bachelor's degree in history by correspondence from an accredited university in Illinois. But you need a master's to teach. I was going to continue, had a program lined up, but that went by the boards when I met Sanjay, Sarina's brother." *Whew! That wasn't so hard now, was it?*

"Where did you meet Sanjay?" Bob asked.

"Believe it or not, at a base camp in the Himalayas. We climbed a ways up that mountain. I can't even remember its name. We climbed with a Dane, a German, two Frenchmen, and our guide, an amazing fellow, fluent in all but Danish. Luckily the Dane spoke French. Sanjay and I shared English but with different pronunciations. He'd been educated in England." Zack laughed. "That, and the fact that we were the least experienced members of the group. Anyway, he and I never did make it even halfway up. He invited me to meet his family and his in-laws when and if I got to India."

"And of course you got to India," Max said.

Zack directed his reply to Bob. "Why not? I liked Sanjay. I hadn't visited northern India, which is near Nepal and lush and beautiful. The rest is history." He turned his gaze to the window, to several men followed by caddies dragging golf bags down the steps of the club, headed for golf carts. The golfers piled into carts and drove toward the first tee. The caddies walked. Zack shook his head. "Golf. I just don't get."

Max was impressed that his son had had the fortitude to study and obtain a degree. As he listened to Zachary, Hannah's idea seemed more feasible, a long shot maybe, but he decided to chance it.

"Zack, we haven't a clue what's up on those seven hundred acres behind Bella's Park. We're working the bottom twenty or so acres, but the rest, well, who knows? Would you be interested in going on up there and sort of informally mapping its assets and liabilities? I'd like to know if there's water. Are there flat areas for pasture? How much timber have we got in that old growth? How steep's the terrain? Are there caves or waterfalls?"

Zack considered this. Seven hundred acres. All he'd need was twenty. Surely he could convince his father to part with a mere twenty acres of his precious land. He'd be somewhat the hero, returning with a report of timber stands, and who knew what else. He looked at Max. "I could do that. That's a lot of land not to know what's there and how you might use it."

"A deal, then?" Max extended his hand, which Zack shook.

Max left Zack and Bob at the club. He had other matters on his mind. Earlier, Jose had approached him about retiring from the dairy and opening a small restaurant at Bella's Park. Jose would run it with the help of Anna's cousin Irena, a mature woman who currently lived in Charlotte.

"*Mama mia!* Irena *muy buena* cook." Jose had smacked his lips and rolled his eyes. Irena had recently lost her husband. If Señor Max did not object, Jose proposed building, with Señor Max's permission, a small addition for Irena at the back of their house, which was located to the side and back of the barn. Max had promised to discuss this with Señora Hannah and get back to him.

Jose's announcement stupefied Max. How would he run the dairy without Jose? Could he handle the dairy and Bella's Park alone? Maybe Hannah could run the park, and he could devote himself to the dairy. He could hire a new foreman and train him. Heck! The thought depressed him. Jose knew what he was thinking before he said a word. They'd been a team for many years.

Creating Bella's Park had changed his life and his thinking. He loved working with Hannah. His days were shaped by the hours they spent together, and at the end of the day he relaxed by walking through the gardens with her, beautiful gardens that flourished under her green thumb. Now he must return, find Hannah, and discuss Jose's proposal with her.

Max found Hannah at home and asked her to walk with him on the hillside behind the barn. He could think best up there away from phones and interruptions. They walked awhile, then stood where the land flattened and ran in a wide shelf. Below them in the valley a light mist settled, blurring trees and houses, creating a fairy-tale landscape.

"Look, Max, the valley's been transformed by the mist and this marvelous afternoon light. Amelia would be thrilled. She should be here to photograph this."

"I guess she should be," he replied. "But right now, I've got several things we need to talk about, and I don't need Amelia hanging around."

"All right then, talk."

As his words spilled out, Hannah turned to face him. "Hold on Max, slow down. You've asked Zachary to explore the seven hundred acres and do an informal survey. Fine, but he's not a surveyor. I'd figured he'd take a hike and make a few notes."

"Of course he's not a surveyor. Whatever he does, we'll have more information than we have now. It was your idea, remember?"

"I guess it was." She rubbed her cheek, which stung from the bite of some small creature. "And Jose wants to leave the dairy and open a restaurant at the park, and you're thinking of closing the dairy? That's a lot to digest. What kind of a restaurant? Where at the park? When did you start thinking of closing the dairy? My head's spinning."

"So was mine when Jose first came to me about this. As far as I can tell, it's to be a Mexican restaurant—tacos, tortillas, burritos, things like that are very popular these days—

and as for where, I imagine that storeroom off the entrance across from the reception desk might do just fine. It's a good-size room, and we hardly utilize it. Add some good lighting, maybe a window or two."

He stopped and laughed. "It all seems like too much these days. My mind feels jumbled sometimes, and other times it's clear as a bell. But yes, that's right. It's a lot to lay on you. Let me tell you my thoughts about the dairy."

They walked on, Max speaking slowly, trying to see into their future even as he spoke. "The other day I was standing next to a cow that I raised from a calf and I couldn't for the life of me remember her name. I named that cow. It came back to me, of course, but that bothered me. It's not the first incident of forgetting."

"I forget. I walk around with a list I make every morning, or I wouldn't remember what I need to accomplish on any given day," Hannah said. "Grace complains of the same thing. It's normal at our age to sometimes forget names or things."

"I've always had a sterling memory," he replied. "But it's more than that. I've had the feeling for a while now that the cows and the dairy are too much for Jose. He has arthritis, and since he can't take Vioxx any longer, it's really flared up. Aleve works, but not as well, he says, and cold, damp, or rainy days don't help. I've watched him. Sometimes he can hardly straighten up."

Max slung his arm around Hannah's shoulder. The wind was brisk, and in her long-sleeved cotton shirt and summer slacks, Hannah felt chilled. She leaned against Max's shoulder, pressing her body into his for warmth. Suddenly, aware of her discomfort, and against her protests, Max removed his leather jacket and settled it across her shoulders.

Grateful for the comfort it afforded, Hannah squeezed his hand.

"Will you really close the dairy, or just find someone to replace Jose?"

Max scowled. "Who can replace Jose? We've had a good run, Jose and I." He fell silent for a moment. "There's a time for everything. The time's come to retire from the dairy business."

Hannah agreed. The park was a full-time job, and although Jose oversaw the dairy, there were emergencies that Max must be involved in, like the flood that left cows stranded in knee-deep water and destroyed several of their new milking machines. Lately, when Max spoke of the dairy, his brow furrowed and his eyes clouded with concern, while the park and its projects revitalized him.

Yes, she thought, the time has come to let the dairy go. "How hard this must be for you. The dairy, the animals mean so much to you."

His shoulders rose and fell. "As I said, there's a time for everything, honey."

"Yes, there is, and sometimes our bodies remind us of that truism, like Jose and his arthritis."

"Me and my memory and the fact that I can't multitask the way I used to." He was silent for a long while as they ambled across the meadow.

Hannah slipped her arm through his for the support she needed on uneven ground. Her neck was cold, and she slipped her arms into his jacket and held it close about her throat. Lately, her knees ached. No, they hurt a lot. Kneeling resulted in swelling, which she iced, and she deferred seeing a doctor. He would propose surgery, probably knee replacement, and that terrified her. Surgery always had. For

years, until she moved in with Grace and Amelia, she had
put off hip replacement. They had forced her to the doctor,
to the hospital, and afterward had taken care of her. They
would be there for her again, of course, but still she avoided
the doctor and tried to hide the pain.

"You think I'm doing the right thing to sell the cows, the
whole business, machines, everything?" Max asked.

"It's a huge change, but as you say, the time has come.
You enjoy your work at the park, and there's so much more
to be done there. I know it's a hard decision."

Max sighed, then said with determination, "Yes, I think
that's exactly what I need to do. There's a dairy in Georgia's
been after me for a couple of years now to sell them the
cows, equipment, everything."

They walked on. Without gloves her hands ached from
cold, and she dug them into his jacket pockets. "A restaurant would be a nice thing at the park, especially if the food's
good and the decor's pleasant. Jose have the funds for this
restaurant?" she asked.

"It seems that he does. He and Anna have been saving
for years, hoping for this, he tells me. Anna and Jose have a
cousin, Irena, who they say is an incredible cook. They want
to bring her up from Charlotte. She was widowed recently,
and they want to build her a place to live at their house, if
we don't object."

"What would they do, add a room?"

"A room and bath, I believe." Max increased his stride,
and Hannah grasped his arm, held tight, and gritted her
teeth as she tried to match his pace. Lord, but she would be
miserable when she got home.

She could feel him straighten his shoulders. "It's settled,
then. I'll tell Jose my plans for the dairy and that we think

it's a fine idea about the restaurant, and that he can bring Irena up from Charlotte and so forth. We'll work out the details later."

"That was fast."

"Not really. I think deep inside I knew this day was coming."

Ahead of them a granite outcropping came into view. "Let's sit over there and you can tell me about your lunch with Bob and Zachary," Hannah suggested. "I take it it went well, if you've asked your son to climb the mountain."

"The boy's got a degree in history." Pride filled his voice. "Imagine that. Studied as he traveled and did one of those correspondence courses from an accredited university. Now, that takes initiative and determination."

"Is he expecting to teach history?"

"I don't think so, but you never know. He'd need to go back and get a master's degree, he says. Meanwhile, let him find out all he can about those seven hundred acres."

They sat for a while on the warm, flat boulder. "Bob questioned Zachary, and Zachary actually opened up about his life and travels, told us how he met Sarina."

Max talked, and Hannah leaned against him trying not to think about her aching knees and cold hands.

"It boils down to this. Zachary loves to explore new places, and we haven't a clue what's up that mountain. Getting him up there to informally survey the area would be a great way to find out, keep him busy, and maybe give us something to talk about."

"Back when we were trying to stop Anson from selling to that developer, didn't Wayne go up that mountain hunting for ruins or rare species of plants, so we could make a case against a housing development?" Hannah asked.

"He made it up several hundred feet, but the brush thick-ened and he stopped. I doubt he even knew what the heck to look for."

"What's going to keep Zachary from stopping when he gets to that same area?"

"Jose has a man we'll send along with him, someone with a mean machete arm. He'll tackle any underbrush they run into. I don't want Zachary up there alone. You never know what's there, sudden drop-offs, snakes, waterfalls, caves."

"It sounds like it might work, and who knows what could come of it?" Hannah shivered under Max's jacket.

"I'm hot and you're shivering. Let's get back down." Ris-ing, Max helped her to her feet.

The sun slipped below the far hill, taking the mist and fairyland with it. They descended slowly. Hannah's knees hurt now and she clung to Max, worrying that he would ques-tion the difficulty she had walking, but his mind brimmed with plans, and he did not comment on her slowed gait.

Hoping no one would see her, Hannah limped into the ladies' farmhouse. From the kitchen doorway, Grace gri-maced as she watched her friend laboriously climb the stairs using both hands for support on the railing. She had seen Hannah favoring one leg, but had been waiting for Hannah to explain or complain, which Hannah never did.

Grace filled two plastic bags with ice, wrapped them in slightly damp towels, and carried them up to Hannah, who lay on her bed, shoes on, eyes closed.

Hannah said, "Grace, thank you. I thought about ice packs after I got upstairs, and Lord knows, I couldn't go back down for them."

Grace held the ice packs up. "Both knees or one?"

"Both. Thank you."

"So what do you plan to do about your knees?"

"Put off going to the doctor as long as I can."

"Sooner would be better. Whatever it is, it's getting worse."

"You're right, of course." Hannah shifted.

The ice pack on her left knee slipped, and Grace reset it. Grace untied Hannah's shoelaces and removed her shoes.

"I'm such a baby when it comes to surgery. You know that."

"When you had hip replacement surgery, it went well. You recovered fast, and your hip's been great ever since." Grace wagged a finger at Hannah.

"Thanks to you and Amelia. You took such good care of me, but I'm that many years older."

"And we'll be there for you same as before. Look, Hannah, none of us is made of steel. We're all aging, and sometimes one or another of our parts wears out. Thank God, we live in a time when medicine offers so many new and successful treatments."

"I know that. It's an old fear of going under the knife, I guess." Hannah lifted her head and looked intently at Grace. Then she changed the subject. "While we were up on the pasture, a soft mist settled over everything on Cove Road. I thought about Amelia and remembered her talking about how ethereal and enchanting pictures taken in the mist could be. I actually said to Max that I wished Amelia were there with her camera, and it surprised me that I would care."

"You care more about Amelia than you let on. It would mean a lot to her to know that you thought about her," Grace said.

"You think so?"

"I do. Amelia sees you as someone who does everything right, knows what she's about, and has it all figured out."

"You really think so? She's so creative. I admire that about her, and her wit and humor. Look at what she's accomplished since we've been in Covington, and she'd never owned a camera. I think she's remarkable."

"You two ought to tell one another how you see each other. It might get you past the small things that irritate you," Grace replied.

"One of these days maybe we will." They were quiet for a time. "You know, Grace, I've been thinking. Maybe I've taken my frustration about Max and Zachary out on Amelia. Not that she doesn't annoy me at times, but not to that extent, really."

"So, do something about it. Start a dialogue with Amelia. Have a good heart-to-heart. Now, I'd like to know about that lunch Bob had with Zachary and Max."

"Bob didn't tell you?"

"I haven't seen Bob."

Hannah updated Grace about Zachary, Jose, and the restaurant, and Max's plan to sell the animals and equipment and close the dairy.

"Now, that's almost too much news. When things start happening, they happen fast." Grace set the ice pack straight on Hannah's left knee. "I like the idea of the restaurant, and anything that'll give Max and Zachary a point of common interest can't be bad. But sell the dairy?" She made a clicking sound with her tongue. "Won't that be like cutting off Max's right arm?"

"He's ready for a change, or so he says. I admit, though, it'll seem odd with the dairy gone. I can't say I'm fond of the

smell, but I do enjoy watching cows graze on the hillside."
She smiled at Grace. "It's time, he says. There's a time for
everything."

Grace nodded and pointed to Hannah's knees.

Hannah ignored that. "Max says he's given it a lot of
thought. He's got plenty to wrap his arms about: me, the
park, and now a grandchild." Hannah was suddenly very
tired. "Grace, my knees feel better, thanks to you. I need to
rest, sleep perhaps. Can we talk about this later?"

"You bet. Rest. Is the ice still cold? Shall I get you fresh
packs?"

"They're cold enough. Thanks. I just need to rest."

The lines on Hannah's face seemed deeper, the wrinkles
about her eyes longer, her hair grayer, almost white. Grace
looked at her friend and thought, *She's tired, that's all, and
in pain. She overdid it today, like we all do sometimes. Do
we think we're impervious to aging, that we're still fifty? We
all have more lines and wrinkles than we did five years ago.
She'll be fine. She'll be her usual self after a good rest.*

Hannah's eyes were closed. Grace bent and kissed her
forehead. "Sleep well, dear friend."

Hannah smiled but did not stir or open her eyes, and
Grace tiptoed from the room.

20

Exploring the Mountain

His father did not trust him. The idea that someone needed to accompany him, to clear a path up the hillside, angered Zachary. Well, he would show them all. His long stride soon outpaced Jose's cousin, Fortino, and within half an hour the man lost sight of Zachary. Confused and upset, he scrambled down to Bella's Park to report to Señor Max the impossibility of keeping up with Señor Zachary.

"He go like an *hombre* on fire," Fortino said.

Max sighed. He should have expected this from his irascible son. "Don't worry about it." Max patted Fortino on the back. "Go on back to the dairy and help Jose."

Max found Hannah in the rose garden. "Zachary can't cooperate in anything."

She dropped her hand clippers into a basket and motioned him to a nearby bench. "What's he done now?"

"Took off at a tear so Fortino couldn't keep up. They hadn't gone four hundred yards when Fortino lost sight of Zachary."

"Zachary's had lots of experience, hasn't he? Isn't that what he said?"

"That's what I thought he said."

"But you're not sure?"

He shrugged. "If he's hiked in the Himalayas, this hillside of ours ought to be a snap, wouldn't you think?" Max looked away. "Sometimes, though, I wish he'd get lost permanently."

With a guide, she thought—Zachary had always hiked with a guide—but she did not say that to Max. "I thought since the baby came you two were getting on better."

"One minute I think so too, and the next minute he's cold and withdrawn, and I feel shut out," Max said.

"He's having a hard time. He'll be all right after a while. He's a thousand times more affectionate with Sarina, and he certainly loves that baby," Hannah replied.

"It's too complicated for me. I never understood him and I don't now."

"We don't have to understand our kids in order to love or accept them. Wait and see what he comes back and reports."

"I'm not sure I'll believe whatever he says." Max stood. "I've got to get back to the office. I expect a call from the guy in Georgia about the dairy. I think we have a deal."

Hannah sat for a time wondering how this alienation between father and son had begun and how or if it could be healed.

Unconcerned about the man he had outpaced, Zachary climbed higher, and with every step his exhilaration increased. He loved solitude and the quiet of the forest, yet longed to tear out twenty acres of trees and replace them with roads and houses. Rental income would free him to travel, to live the unfettered lifestyle he desired.

At times like this, it was easy to brush aside thoughts of

his wife and daughter. Easy to forget marriage and having responsibilities. His life plan had not included marriage. Sarina had sent his blood racing, and a girl like Sarina you did not love and leave. He should have vanished from their home the next day, moved on, picked up a woman along the way, someone who expected no commitment. But he hadn't.

Did he love Sarina? There were times he was sure he did, like the day Sarah was born. In that moment he had loved them fiercely. But now? He brushed those questions aside. He must concentrate on the task at hand.

Zachary pushed on until he reached a sun-filled glade abundant with wildflowers. Then he sank to the earth, leaned against a gnarled oak trunk, and closed his eyes. As he often did before falling asleep at night, Zachary imagined himself perched on a camel's back, heading east away from Marrakech, in Morocco, toward the Atlas Mountains. Desert sands stretched before him; snow-capped peaks loomed on the horizon. He had visited friends in Marrakech, and from their porch watched the sunrise turn the snow-capped mountains golden. As that dream faded another came; he rode on horseback along the shores of Lake Baikal in southeastern Siberia.

As a boy he had discovered a nineteenth-century book, *Siberia and the Exile System,* by American engineer and explorer George Kennan. Kennan's eloquent descriptions of Baikal—its depth and clarity, the pristine quality of the lake, the immense, breathtaking beauty of the surrounding forests and mountains, and the varied and abundant mammal and fish populations—had enthralled him and still did.

Sarina's and the baby's sweet faces floated into his mind, banishing daydreams. Guilt replaced wild longings. He loved his wife, and little Sarah touched his heart. He heard his mother's gentle voice telling an impatient boy, "There's a time for everything, my son."

But for him, it seemed that there was never enough time. It was a lesson he must learn: patience. Zachary rose, brushed off bits of dirt, leaves, and bark, and continued upward. As he climbed, he stopped to check his compass. He was heading due north. Increasingly, the land revealed its secrets. A magnificent waterfall plunged into a ravine. He estimated the drop of the water to be seventy feet or more. He encountered streams, some no wider than the span of his jump, others too wide to leap across. Large areas of hardwood forest, a fortune in lumber, rose above him, and wide swaths of mixed hardwood and pines.

Zachary stumbled across rock outcroppings and past the gaping, ominous mouths of caves. He had always hated caves and caverns, dark, narrow spaces. A middle school trip to Linville Caverns found him rooted in fear, unable to step into the hole in the hillside. No assurances that it was well lit and paved, or that hundreds of people visited the cave, could entice him to take a single step in its direction.

He pushed on. A dense forest unfolded before him. Zachary jotted notations in a notebook and estimated the number of feet from one point to the next. He banded trees with different colors of surveyor tape, to indicate this or that feature. But would he, he wondered, knowing his lack of surveying skills, ever be able to locate these trees again?

Not the beauty of this land, the breath and depth of the forest, the thundering waterfalls, abated his lust for land, which grew only stronger. He must convince his father to deed him twenty or thirty acres, out of sight of the buildings at Bella's Park. A dozen rental houses would provide him the income to support Sarina and Sarah and leave him free to satisfy his lust for change, adventure, and travel. He avoided considering the consequences of this plan: bulldozers leveling trees and tearing at the earth, roads and erosion, washouts, streams of water trickling or pouring down the hillside.

His father would say no. Why? Meanness. Plain old meanness. What was this distrust that lay like a pall between them? They had never been able to communicate. Their relationship, as far back as he could recall, had been suffused with a lack of ease. Why? His father had never raised a hand to him. What had happened between them, then, to create such distance and ill will that had persisted into adulthood?

As he circumvented rock outcroppings and used a stick to push aside the prickly branches of bushes, Zachary searched his memory for clues. He had been, perhaps, inordinately attached to his mother. He had adored her and followed her about like a puppy. He remembered weeping as if his heart would break—he thought it surely would—those first few days when she left him at kindergarten.

Had his father been jealous of the many hours his mother spent with her son, reading to him, taking walks with him, putting him to bed at night? Even when he was thirteen, she would sit and talk with him at bedtime. They had both disliked the smells of the dairy, and they gave silly names to cows his father prized: Dumbbell, Stinky, Miss Disgusting. His mother taught him how to draw, although he could never get the colors right to paint, and he remembered with pleasure the many times they had laughed together.

One incident stood out in his memory. Their laughter had drawn his father's attention, but when Max entered the room, they stopped and sat silent, staring at him. What had they been laughing about? He couldn't remember. Max had stood a moment, then turned and left the room. Had Zachary filled some place in his mother's life that his father failed to fill? Sadly, he could no longer ask his mother this or many other questions.

Because their relationship so often excluded his father, Zachary felt responsible for his mother's happiness and had tried in every way to please her, suppressing his adventurous and more reckless nature so as not to cause her worry. Her illness and her death devastated him, but it freed him. He felt no guilt then about packing and leaving Covington less than a week after her passing. He ought, perhaps, to have explained to his father where he was going, what he planned to do. Instead, he had opened the door early one Sunday morning and vanished for a very long time. Reprehensible behavior, yes, but he remembered his delight in being free and far from cows, Covington, and Max.

The sun sank low. The air chilled him. Damn it, he'd paid no attention to the time. He must make his way down the mountain before nightfall. Zachary moved downhill as fast as he dared. The steep ground propelled him forward almost at a run from tree to tree. Suddenly a twist and a sharp pain speared his ankle and he hit the ground hard and doubled over.

Nausea born of pain brought tears to his eyes. He assessed the situation. His palms were bruised, his left elbow scraped and bleeding. When he touched the elbow, tiny bits of stone clinging to the cut fell to the earth. Blood stained his fingers. Gritting his teeth, he struggled unsuccessfully to stand. He knew, then, that he had either torn a ligament or broken his ankle.

Through the cobweb of broken glass that had been his watch, he could barely see that it was 8 P.M. Soon the light would vanish.

Max checked the time. It was almost eight and growing dark. "Zachary's not back. I'm worried." He waved his hand in a dismissive gesture. "I'm being paranoid," he told Hannah. "He'll pop in here any minute. After all, he's climbed mountains."

Hannah shook her head. "I'm worried. Zachary should have been back an hour ago. What kind of supplies did he take with him, do you know?"

Max's eyes clouded. "A compass, a walking stick, and lunch, and no flashlight. I distinctly recall offering him one, but he laughed and said he'd be back way before it got dark. My God, what if something . . ." Max reached for the phone and called the house. "Anna, get Jose and call Bob, get all the men you can round up. Zachary isn't back. We're going up the mountain and look for him. Tell Jose we'll need the largest flashlights we've got and something to carry the boy down on, if he's been hurt."

Zachary gathered his wits and shifted to a less uncomfortable position. He studied the terrain. The stream he thought he heard was perhaps his imagination, for there had been no sign of water close at hand as he descended, and he craved water. All about him the land fell off steeply. The earth he rested on was peppered with rocks of various sizes and degrees of sharpness. Removing his torn shirt was painful and seemed to take forever. Once it was off, he managed to remove his undershirt, which he tore into strips. Small stiff branches of a nearby bush provided what he needed for a splint for his leg. His ankle throbbed as if struck repeatedly by a hammer. *Stupid! Stupid! Stupid!* What had he been thinking? What kind of a big shot had he tried to be, starting out without first-aid supplies and a flashlight?

Back on Cove Road, men gathered: Charlie Herrill, Frank Craine and two of his sons, Jose, Fortino, Bob and his son Russell arrived with flashlights, blankets, ropes, and knapsacks filled with water and food. After a short period of indecision about which direction to strike out in and whether to remain as one group or to split into two, they decided on two parties. Taking divergent routes, they started up the hillside. Through an old foghorn, which sent eerie echoes bouncing off of the hills, Max repeatedly called his son's name.

The moment the men departed, Hannah dialed 911. The mountain behind them was steep and dark; they would need all the help they could get. She identified herself and the address, and said, "We've got a man lost on Anson's Mountain on Cove Road in Covington. There's a search party out—two parties of four—but it's seven hundred acres, and they're gonna need all the help they can get."

"I'll pass this to Search and Rescue," the operator said.

Relieved, Hannah sank into a chair. That was the name, Search and Rescue, that for the life of her she couldn't remember when she had picked up the phone.

Zachary tried to calculate how far down the mountain he had come before his injury. Mustering every ounce of strength and gasping with pain, he grasped the tree closest to him, placed pressure on his good leg, and hauled himself to a standing position. His heart sank. In all directions, a jungle of underbrush and small trees blocked his view. With the increasing darkness and underbrush, visibility ended in a few yards. Resigned to his plight, uncertain that a rescue party could locate him tonight, Zachary lowered himself to the ground. Tears stung his eyes. *Think*, he told himself. *Stop feeling sorry for yourself and think*. His hands burned from bruises; still he scraped together leaves and mounded them to cushion his foot and ankle.

Zachary gathered twigs and small branches within arm's reach. Stones were more available, and calling on old Boy Scout skills he fashioned a ring of stones into which he placed the wood. Out of habit, he carried a cigarette lighter, though since the birth of Sarah he no longer smoked. Soon, a small fire offered a measure of comfort and the hope that it would ward off animals attracted to the scent of his blood.

How long had it been since he prayed? How long had it been since he had stepped into a church? Was God available to people who ignored him until they were in deep trouble? Zachary lowered his head, closed his eyes, and bargained with God for protection and rescue; he would change his attitude, change his ways, treasure his wife and child, and be kind to his father and Hannah. He could hardly believe it when he heard the hum of an engine overhead and saw the lights of the helicopter bob and weave between the canopy of leaves.

"That a fire down there?" the pilot asked his copilot.

"Where?"

"There it is. Look. Over to the east."

"I read you."

The helicopter dropped lower. "There it is. It's a fire, all right." The copilot pointed.

"Well, at least we know he's alive. Probably injured. When are these people gonna learn not to hike solo? Go ahead, drop a flare." A moment later, light filled the night sky.

Farther down the mountain, Bob heard the roar of the helicopter.

"Max! See the light? It's a helicopter, Search and Rescue. Hannah must have called them. Thank God. Look, Max, they've dropped a flare. There goes another one. They must have spotted him."

The mountain blazed with light.

"Please God, they've found him." Max grabbed Bob's arm. "You think the helicopter found him?"

"Your son probably built a fire, and they saw it," Bob said. "Otherwise they couldn't have spotted him in the dark."

Relief swept over Max. Images of Zachary injured or dead at the foot of a waterfall and gut-wrenching regret for their years of alienation vanished. There was still time! Back at the office, Max had prayed for Zachary's safety, and he, like his son, wondered if God, whom he had pretty much ignored, would hear him.

"Should we continue up?" Max could hardly think straight.

"They know what they're doing. They'll find him and bring him down. Let's start back. I bet they'll have him at the office before we get there," Bob said.

When the search team reached Zachary, they checked him over and medicated him, then placed him on a stretcher dropped by the helicopter and fastened the straps, securing him inside the frame. At that moment, the wind picked up, and fears of the stretcher slapping into a tree and further injuring Zachary or the man traveling up with him precluded an air rescue.

"We gotta take him down on foot," the medic informed the pilot. "Keep the flares coming."

It was an arduous task conveying Zachary down the mountain over steep, rocky ground and around thickets of thorny branches, and when, an hour later, they cleared the forest and started across the meadow, Max, Bob, and the others were waiting.

Max watched in silence as the medics and their patient emerged from the woods. To him they represented a band of angels, and he scrambled from the rock on which he had been sitting and staggered toward them. "Zachary, my son."

"He can't hear you," the medic said. "His ankle's broken in several places and badly swollen. He was in a lot of pain, and we sedated him."

"Is it only his ankle? Is that what you said?" Max asked. "No internal injuries? No head injuries?"

"Not that we can tell, but they'll check him over at the hospital once we get him to Asheville."

"Thank God you found him. Thank God he's alive. How can I ever thank you?" Max moved from man to man, blocking their way, shaking any available hand, patting the men on their backs. Tears lined his face. And then his legs trembled and gave way, and Max sank to the earth.

Minutes later, he lay on the stretcher Jose had brought and was being carried downhill at a precipitous angle. A younger, macho Max would have protested. Instead, acknowledging that he, too, had a breaking point, and grateful for their help, he closed his eyes. *Here we are, father and son, helpless as babes.*

The news that her husband was missing on the mountain reached Sarina when Anna began to weep and Jose gathered up equipment preparing to hurry off to Bella's Park. Sarina collapsed in a chair in the kitchen. Zachary was lost, maybe dead, and they had been fighting before he started out, arguing about their life together and his restlessness.

"I am who I am" were his last words to her before slamming the door behind him. "If you can't take me as I am, then leave."

And go where? Sarina never cursed, but she had raged inside and the words spewed from her mouth. "You go to your devil in the hell you believe in."

"Señora Sarina, come, lie down on the couch. I bring you tea. You drink, you feel better. You no worry. No cry. The men gonna find him. My Jose, he gonna find him."

How could they find one man at night, in the dark, on a thickly forested mountain? Zachary could be lying facedown in a cold river or might have fallen over a cliff and lie crushed or injured on the rocks below. Sarina's anger faded. She loved him. The thought of losing him terrified her. The huge loneliness she felt in their relationship was preferable to living without him.

"Come," Anna said. "No use to sit here and cry. We go to Señora Hannah at the office." Anna wrapped the baby in a blanket and handed her to Sarina, who stared down at her child with blank eyes. Anna took the baby from her mother. "We go. Come."

They crossed the porch, went down the steps, and hurried onto Cove Road. At the church Anna stopped, walked up the path, and tried the handle. The front door opened, and they entered the cool dim interior. Anna kneeled and crossed herself.

Sarina, a Hindu, followed suit. She kneeled, crossed herself as Anna had done, bowed her head, and prayed. "Krishna," she whispered, "hear the cry for help from sincere hearts like Anna's and my own. Bring my husband home safe to me."

They stood and left the church, closing the door behind them, and moments later reached Bella's Park. Anna handed the baby to Amelia and went out into the night.

Sarina curled her small body into Hannah's embrace. "My dear child," Hannah said. "It'll be all right. Search and Rescue will find him."

"What are Search and Rescue?" Sarina blinked back tears.

The roar of a helicopter drew the ladies to the office windows. "What does it mean?" Sarina asked.

"It's the helicopter they sent to find your husband, and it looks as if they've found him. I see men coming down the hillside." There was alarm in Grace's voice. "They have not one but two stretchers."

"Dear God, something's happened to Max." Hannah pressed her hand to her chest.

"Why Max?" Amelia asked. "It could be anyone."

Sarina poked her head out an open window. "I must go to him."

If there were no God, Grace thought, man would have to

invent him, for we are too small and helpless to go it alone. "You might be in the way if you run to meet them," Grace said to Sarina. "They'll be here in a few moments. They'll try to put the chopper down on Cove Road or there will be an ambulance along any minute."

Bob offered his arm to help Max from his stretcher, then waited while the medic checked Max's pulse and heart. "You're fine," he said. "The shock, your son and all, was a bit too much."

The helicopter circled and settled on the wide swath of grass in front of the office. A medic intercepted Sarina, who rushed to her husband's side. "He's out cold. Sedated. He's got a broken ankle, but otherwise he seems fine. We'll go ahead and chopper him in to Mission Hospital."

"Can I go with you?"

"No, ma'am, sorry. He's fine. Sleeping like a baby." He pried her fingers off the rim of the stretcher and eased Sarina toward Grace, whose arms circled her shoulders. "You just take your time getting there, and don't you worry. He's gonna be all right."

Zack had always prided himself on being a man of action, a man not given to wasting time in contemplation. Restlessness was inherent to his nature. He had never wondered why. When he was little, his mother had laughed, referring to his fidgeting and inability to sit still as his having ants in his pants. When he was an adult, the grass appeared greener around every bend, over every hill, in the next town or city. But now, with a wife and child, his restlessness was no longer a laughing matter.

As the pain and swelling in his leg and ankle subsided

and they sent him home, Zack's mind fastened on his ordeal in the forest, on his fears and prayers, and his promise to change his behavior and his life. Easier said than done. Although pampered and fussed over by everyone, he resented the enforced rest.

Somewhere in the back of his mind, Zack had always felt he had been born too late. Ah, to have been among those stalwart men blazing trails west with Lewis and Clark or riding hard across the desert with Lawrence of Arabia. Perhaps, as they believed in Sarina's India, he had lived those lives or had lived in those eras, and he ached to live them again.

The door to the bedroom opened and closed, and he heard the baby's soft whimper as his wife slid into the chair by his bed. How to reconcile the dichotomy, his desire to be with Sarina and baby Sarah versus his longing, his desperate longing to flee Covington and be free? *Am I crazy? When Sarah was born, I felt at peace. I believed that my hunger for adventure could be tempered and even replaced by my family.*

"Zack." Sarina's voice ended his musing. "Are you hungry? Shall I get you a little snack? Shall I get more pillows to raise your leg? They said it should be raised, did they not?"

"No. Leave me alone, will you? I don't need anything to eat, and my leg feels fine." It was all he could do to refrain from asking her to leave him alone. "I'm fine."

He had not talked about his ordeal with anyone. He had climbed higher and more difficult mountains and had never fallen or been seriously injured. But he had prepared for those climbs and not headed off precipitously, as he had done on Anson's Mountain. What he felt when the shock wore off was anger at himself and humiliation. He detested that he had whimpered like a baby and begged for medication.

It hadn't helped that his rescuers treated him as if he were an amateur, someone who had never hiked a trail. Assuming that the medication had knocked him out before it actually had, they had joked about "stupid Yankees" with their know-it-all attitude, who wandered off marked trails.

"There are no marked trails up in this forest, and you know it," he wanted to yell, but his throat was thick and his mouth dry, and he had floated away to awaken, nauseous and confused, in a pristine hospital room, surrounded by hovering family.

The chair creaked. Sarina rose. "Sarah's asleep. I'm going to lay her in her crib. Are you sure I cannot get you anything?"

Just go and leave me alone. "Yes, please, will you make me an omelet with fresh eggs? It tastes so much better when the eggs are fresh." He hoped that her search for fresh eggs would take her to the Herrills, who kept chickens, and that it would occupy her for a good long time. Assailed by guilt, he hated himself for wanting her gone.

Sarina deserved better. She deserved much more than he could give her. And now that his father had married Hannah, Hannah would inherit his mother's home and the land. It struck him, then, that no one owned him. That when he was well and strong again, he could pack a bag and leave. The thought comforted him. He felt in control of his life again.

What of Sarina? She'll be fine. Her family in India did

not want him, but she could return to her parents or stay in
Covington. They loved her here and the baby too; let his
father and Hannah support them.

Zachary had mastered easing from his bed into the
wheelchair, and now he wheeled across the hall and into
the unused bedroom from which his mother's rose bed was
visible. Huge pink and red roses were in full bloom. Hannah had preserved his mother's roses, trimmed them and
cultivated the earth around their roots. Much as he hated to
admit it, his mother would be pleased.

According to Anna, Hannah and his mother had been
good friends. That struck him as ludicrous. Aloof Hannah
and his warm and loving mother? And now Hannah had
stepped into the role of Sarina's surrogate mother.

Hannah wielded a great deal of influence with his father.
It struck Zachary, then, that if he stayed awhile and cultivated Hannah, he could use her to obtain the land he so
urgently wanted, land that would buy his freedom. Perhaps
it would be expeditious to bide his time.

Sarina returned with the omelet and coffee to find him in
bed as she had left him, but now he smiled at her and accepted the tray with thanks. "She's sleeping, our baby?" he
asked.

"Like a little angel." Sarina's eyes clouded. "I wish my
mother could see her."

"It's a shame she can't." He caught hold of her hand. "I
sure wouldn't mind getting out for a bit. If you could help
me downstairs, or call Jose and ask him to help me to the
car, you could drive me to Weaverville. I'd like to get a video

camera and film to take pictures of Sarah and you to send to your family."

She bent and hugged him. "Oh, thank you, Zack. They will be so happy to get pictures of us all." *He's changed. The shock of his experience has changed him to the Zachary I hoped he would be.*

21

Ida and the Charming Scammer

June and May's mother, Ida, never failed to inform a stranger that June had been born two minutes prior to May, and that she had gotten the months mixed up, which had been the fault of the medication, otherwise June would be named May and May would be named June.

"Why do you do that, Mama?" June had asked again and again. "I wish you wouldn't." It embarrassed her, and in her eyes made Ida appear confused and hardly the strong-willed matriarch of the family she was.

Ida did it again this afternoon, relating the birth story and the naming of her girls to a pleasant-looking young man in overalls, who leaned against the porch post and looked as if he had all the time in the world. In fact, he made Ida feel that everything she said was of great interest to him.

When June rolled into her mother's driveway and stopped her car, the man removed his cap and nodded in her direction. She was dropping off groceries, as she did every week, and the stranger took the steps two at a time and offered to carry the bags.

"I can manage quite well," June said.

"It would be my pleasure, ma'am." His eyes were clear and brown and disarmingly friendly.

"Who are you?" June asked.

"Ray Wilson," he replied. "I've been working in the neighborhood over there." He waved his hand in the direction of Elk Road or Loring Valley, but offered no further information about the job he had been working on, for whom, or why he was leaning so casually against a post on her mother's porch.

Brushing him aside, June settled one bag snuggly in the crook of each arm and climbed the stairs. He was ahead of her and held the front door open. Two empty glasses on the table by Ida's chair indicated to June that Ida had offered the man a drink of iced tea. Ida kept a pitcher of tea ready at hand in the fridge, a habit dating back to the days when her children were in and out of the house. She had encouraged them to drink tea rather than Cokes, without realizing that tea had caffeine just as Cokes did. With all the sugar Ida used to sweeten the tea, Cokes would have served as well.

"Cokes got too much of that there caffeine," she'd say, shaking her head, her eyes serious.

"Well," Ray said to Ida, once June was out of earshot, "you made the right decision to get these things fixed. I'll be back tomorrow morning and get that driveway done for you."

"I'll be watching out for you," Ida said.

Ray bowed slightly, sauntered down the steps, hands shoved deep in his overall pockets, and strode away from the house, Ida's home for thirty-two years.

June rejoined her mother on the porch. "What was he saying to you?"

"Nothing. We was just chatting about things."

"What things?"

"Now, don't you question me like I was a child, girl. I

wasn't born yesterday. Get on home. It's past five, and your
husband's waiting on his supper."

June had her problems; it was easy to forget Ray. June's
youngest boy, Bryan, was in jail again, picked up for the
sixth time for driving without a license. What did they want
from the boy, anyway? He had to drive to get to work. He
had to work to pay his rent and support Marlene and the
baby, even if they weren't married. June believed in marriage, and her son refused to marry Marlene.

"I ain't marryin' nobody till I'm sure she's here to stay,"
Bryan said when his mother pressed him about a wedding.

"How long's it gonna take to be sure?" June had asked.

Bryan shrugged. "You never know about folks from way
up there in West Virginia. I'll know when I know, and I'll
let you know."

Pastor Johnson had talked to Bryan a year ago, way before
the baby came, and Pastor Ledbetter, her sister May's friend,
had talked to him more recently, but Bryan wouldn't budge.
He wouldn't baptize the child, either, and that really upset
June. How could he condemn the child, her grandchild, a
baby with no will of her own, to hell's fire? Maybe, she told
herself when she lay in bed at night, if the baby died in sin,
God would have mercy on her, and June prayed that would
be the case. After all, she'd remind God, it ain't the child's
fault she ain't baptized.

June had decided long ago not to become attached to
her granddaughter. Marlene and Bryan fought a lot, and
that girl could just pick herself and that baby up and walk
out anyday. She had a mama to go home to. June had never
been to West Virginia, but Bryan seemed to think it was a

place she wouldn't want to go. June was certain that if Marlene left, she'd never see hide nor hair of either of them ever again.

Her mind fastened on Bryan. Who was gonna bail him outta jail this time? His father said he sure wasn't going to. They wanted $1,000 bail, and June hadn't seen that kind of money in one place in all her born days. As she drove home, she wondered if Ida had $1,000 set away in savings, and if so, could she be convinced to part with it? June shook her head. Probably not. Ida was no fan of Bryan's.

"It's the sixth time they've locked him up. He ought to stay in jail and learn his lesson," Ida said when she heard. "He's a grown man, over twenty-two years old, and he ought to know better than to go speeding in the first place."

What did Ida know about how hard it was making a living today? June wondered. Ida had never worked a day outside her home. Pa had raised and sold livestock—pigs, goats, cows—and he'd farmed some, and mowed lawns for the government over at the women's prison in Swannanoa. And Pa had left her mother pretty well off, far as June could tell. Ida was closemouthed about money. June knew that Ida had the house clear of a mortgage, and Pa had had a life insurance policy with the government, plus Social Security. Ida should be well off.

After Pa died, they'd sold off most of the animals because of all kinds of new environmental laws about animal waste and runoff in streams, but Ida had kept a few goats penned in the pasture away from the stream. Mama sure loved those old goats like someone would love a kitten, or a puppy, or even a child. She was up there every day, rain or shine, heat or cold, tending those goats, and one time when they'd had a blizzard, Mama brought those confounded goats right on into the house. June resented the goats. Mama paid them more attention and gave them more affection than she's ever done June or May or any of her children.

June pulled into a driveway and stopped. Where was she? She slapped the side of her head with her hand. Lord, if she hadn't turned into May's old driveway. Billie rented out the place when he took up with that girl from Mars Hill. May was asking for half the house in the divorce, but how was she ever gonna get that Billie to part with that house? It had been in his family for Lord only knew how many years.

"He could take a mortgage," May said.

"How do you know about mortgages?" June asked.

"I got me a lawyer, and that's what he told me Billie could do, and I could have my half the money, and he could keep his stupid old house."

June shrugged. It wasn't her business. This was one time she was going to listen to her husband, who said, "Mind your own business, June. Don't you go getting in the middle of this."

Lord, but she missed May. All the years past, they'd never let a day go by without talking in person or on the phone, except for the time May lived with the ladies on Cove Road. She'd told June not to phone her there. Something about Miss Hannah being out of sorts and May not wanting to upset anyone. What was gonna happen to May? She was a woman in her fifties going back to school. May said hospitals needed all kinds of help, but her sister wasn't so sure they'd hire someone May's age. June shook her head. She had enough to worry about with Mama getting older and Bryan in jail without worrying about May.

June reversed the car and drove another block to her own

home, an old, rambling two-story farmhouse with a long, wide porch that was much in need of paint. And those old chairs on the porch with their worn-out cushions ought to be dumped. Every time she suggested that to Eddy, he'd agree, give her a hug, and say he'd get to it soon. He was well intentioned, but he didn't get to things right off. Well, she couldn't stress about that now. One of these days she'd get someone, maybe Bryan when he got out of jail, when he got his license back, to bring his pickup and carry them old chairs to the city dump.

When June drove away, Ida went inside, locked the doors back and front. Then she heated up some bean soup left from the night before and swallowed several Aleve tablets to ease the arthritic ache that tortured her back and shoulders at the end of the day. After finishing the soup, she brewed a cup of tea, doused it with hot milk and plenty of sugar to sweeten it up good, for it served as dessert. Ida carried the cup to the living room and turned on *Wheel of Fortune*, which she watched daily with religious fervor. Phone could ring, people could knock on her door; when Ida watched *Wheel*, she ignored everyone and everything. There was Vanna's smiling, pretty face. My Lord, Ida wondered, what does that girl do with all them dresses? She never wears none of 'em more than once.

Sometimes after *Wheel of Fortune*, Ida phoned June, and they'd chat about the day, and she'd ask about May. She wouldn't talk to May, hadn't since May left Billie, but she wanted news of her, some of which she'd pass on to Billie, though lately he wasn't much interested in what May said or did. That's how things changed. Billie used to be a right good son-in-law, but since he took up with that lowlife girl from Mars Hill, she hardly saw or heard from him. It'd sure be nice to have a young man like Ray Wilson for a grandson-in-law, she thought; shame all my granddaughters are married.

Ida was quite pleased with herself. Ray had given her a lot to consider today, and she needed to stay quiet this evening and do some thinking. She wouldn't have to nag Eddy or listen to June tell her she needed to get three estimates for any work she wanted done if she wouldn't wait for Eddy to get to it. That nice young man was gonna fill in the ruts and pave her driveway and replace that gutter out back by the kitchen, which he said was rusted and had a lot of little holes in it. Funny, she'd never noticed it leaking, but then, she didn't go out back when it rained and stand there and look up at it. It was sagging too, he'd said, and looking to fall down any minute, and when they did, with no gutter up there, the rain would get under her house and lead to Lord knows what kind of trouble with the foundation.

She had handled it all herself, had made the decision, and paid him half his fee in cash for the paving and the gutter. He'd said that she reminded him of his granny out west in Ohio, and 'cause of that he'd given her rock-bottom prices for everything. The asphalt for the driveway, he'd explained, was leftover from a driveway he was paving, and he'd fill in the ruts and make hers smooth and beautiful for just about nothing. She had given him $650—cheap, she thought, for all he was gonna do.

Ida smiled. Ray was such a nice young fellow. He'd noticed how worn the carpet was on her front porch and offered to bring her a new one that wouldn't rot from rain getting on it. She'd given him another $100, her grocery money, so he could get the carpet and install it tomorrow. Her porch was gonna look brand-new when he got done.

Ida relaxed, sat back, and gave her full attention to *Wheel of Fortune*. The man standing in the middle position behind the wheel spun the wheel real hard. Round and round it went, and finally stopped on *Bankrupt*. The woman next to him landed on $3,000 twice, solved the puzzle, and won close to $15,000. The woman screamed, yelled, and jumped up and down. Ida wished she'd settle down and let the show continue. Ida prided herself at solving the puzzles from her armchair. If she had a chance to be on that show, she knew she could win a lot of money.

June served her husband the fried chicken, mashed potatoes, and corn she had picked up at KFC on the way home. One thing about Eddy, whatever she put on the table he ate, so long as it was hot and there was plenty of it. As usual, after a meal, he retreated to his chair in front of the TV, and turned on a sport station full-blast.

"Eddy, turn that thing down," June yelled.

"Whatcha say?" Eddy yelled back.

She marched into the living room. "Eddy, if I've asked you once, I've asked you a hundred times to keep the sound down. I live here too, and it hurts my ears, all that shouting and screaming." June walked to the set and turned it off. She stood in front of it blocking his view.

"Ah, June, move. Whatcha do that for?"

" 'Cause I got something troubling my mind, and I need to talk to you, Eddy."

"Make it fast, then. Clemson Tigers are up against Duke. It ain't about Bryan, is it?" He fingered the remote.

"Not this time, it ain't. It's about Mama. When I dropped off her groceries today, there was this guy named Ray leaning against a post on her porch."

"What kinda guy? Someone courtin' old Ida?" He laughed and slapped the arm of his chair.

"A young man. Good-looking enough fellow and pleasant, too. Mama wouldn't say what he was doing there, but when he left, she went on and on about how she liked him and how nice he was."

The smile vanished from Eddy's face. "Don't make no sense. Why'd a young man want to be hanging around Ida for?" He slapped the arm of his chair again. "I heard some talk at work about a bunch of travel trailers parked over by the river near that park where we used to take the kids to when they was small. Could be the fellow stopped by to ask directions or something like that." He waved the remote, dismissing June. A moment later the game, with all its noise, was back on the set.

June stood in front of the screen and flipped her dish towel in his direction. "How come that doesn't sit right with me? No. It's something else, and I aim to find out just what's going on."

Eddy turned the sound to where it hurt her ears, and June hurried from the room, slamming the door behind her.

Being as she was the receptionist at the beauty parlor on Elk Road, June was privy to all kinds of gossip, some true, some false. She'd heard that four Winnebagos had come busting into Covington and parked themselves at the campground by the river. Someone said there were lots of kids running around instead of being in school, clotheslines strung from trees, and women washing clothes in the river.

"Is that permitted, the soap and all going in the water?" someone had asked.

No one knew for sure. June hadn't given it another thought, until now. She'd check with Mama, of course. Eddy was probably right. She had a tendency to overreact. If someone stopped by to ask directions and Mama offered him a glass of tea, nothing wrong with that, and he seemed like a decent sort of fellow.

Ida waited all morning for Ray Wilson to return. Had he been injured on his job? Had he taken sick? He must be sick. Colds that settled into the chest were going around. Her cousin Betty Austin was so bad she had to go to the hospital and get treated for pneumonia. They'd nearly lost her, and it was weeks until her cough finally went away.

June had been high and mighty when she'd stopped by at noon and heard that Ray hadn't returned as promised. "If he's so nice like you say and he's sick, surely he'd a found a way to send a message, have someone make a phone call. I bet you'll never see him again."

Chills passed right through Ida. Her stomach knotted so hard it hurt. She'd given Ray $650, plus $100, just about all her Social Security check. The check had just been deposited in her bank, and she'd drawn out the money. She should have written him a check. Then she could have run to the bank and canceled it. But he'd said he needed cash for supplies now, and she'd felt she couldn't pass up the chance to spruce the place up a bit, replace the gutter, and save the roof from a tree he'd said he'd trim as a special favor to her.

It had seemed like a lot for not too much money. June and even Eddy, she had thought, would be proud of her when it was done.

The hours ticked by; three o' clock slipped into four o'clock, and Ida wanted to weep. By five o'clock, when June stopped in again, she was in tears.

"What's wrong, Mama? You not feeling good?"

"Ray never came back. He was gonna do so many things for me, and cheap, too."

"Like what things, Mama?"

"He was gonna pave the driveway, make it real pretty, and change the gutter out back that's rusted bad and got holes, and there's a limb on that tree over yonder to the side of the house that's gonna break and crash my roof come a high wind."

"Nonsense." June stomped out back, followed by Ida. She shaded her eyes and squinted up at the gutter. "Eddy checked your gutters when he cleaned out all the leaves from the oaks this spring. He never said there was anything wrong with them."

Ida stood there wringing her hands. "It's full of holes where the tin's worn through, and it's sagging, can't you see?"

June whipped out her cell phone and tapped her foot, waiting for Eddy to pick up. He was home. She'd just left him there. "Eddy, get over here to Mama's right away. I think we got us a problem."

Ida made a resolution. Upsetting as this was, she sure wouldn't tell them about the money. June would be at her forever, fussing about how she could throw away money when she could have used it to pay bail for Bryan.

June walked the length of the back of the house. She

studied the gutter again. "I tell you, Mama, I don't see no rust, or sag, or holes nowhere, but Eddy'll get out your ladder and climb up, and he can tell better."

It struck Ida, then, that Ray Wilson hadn't used a ladder, just shaded his eyes and looked up. Were his eyes so much better than June's? He had used the short ladder she kept on the porch for changing lightbulbs when he told her there was a split in the limb of the tree in front. She had believed him and handed over her money like she was a money tree.

Ida considered herself luckier than some women her age who lived alone, many only on Social Security. She had Social Security and her husband's government pension. He'd worked for the state around and about the prison in Swannanoa, and his life insurance money was safe in a CD at the bank. She had a paid-up house, but even with a paid-up house, costs never stopped. Insurance and taxes kept going up. The government, Ida thought, should pass a law against increasing taxes on the homes of older folks. She'd written a letter to her congressman and told him so. She had gotten a long letter back that went on and on about all he'd done for folks. Well, he sure hadn't done anything about her taxes or insurance.

And there was always something in an old house that needed fixing, replacing, or changing. Last winter, her wood-burning fireplace smoked so bad she'd gone and gotten herself one of those pretty self-vented gas fireplaces. You couldn't be without heat in case a bad storm came and the electric went, like it had in 1993. Mother of all storms they'd called it, and folks up in the mountains died of cold before help could reach them. That weren't gonna happen to Ida.

*   *   *

Eddy's big truck roared down the road, sending dust flying. He pulled into Ida's driveway, turned off the engine, got out, and slammed the truck's door behind him. He was a big man, tall and heavyset, and had a way of making his presence known. Now his footsteps on the front steps and through the house to the backyard sounded to Ida like those of a giant. *Thump. Thump. Thump.*

Arms folded cross his chest, Eddy towered over the women. "What's the problem over here?"

June explained.

"There weren't no holes two months ago," he said, but at June's insistence Eddy went into the shed they'd bought at Lowe's last summer and set up out back for Ida, dragged out the extension ladder, and stationed it against the wall of the house.

"You get a good hold on this here ladder," he said to his wife. Then he began to climb, the ladder trembling with every step. He called down to them, "Far as I can see, no sagging anywhere, no rust, and no holes. The gutter's clean as a whistle and in good shape." The ladder shook as he climbed back down. He rubbed his hands together. "You got me over here for this?"

"And that fellow told Mama that a tree limb's about to fall on the roof and make a hole."

"How'd he know that?" Eddy asked.

"He climbed up my short ladder. He leaned it against the tree," Ida said. Her throat felt dry and grainy, as if she'd inhaled a mouthful of dust still floating in the air from Eddy's big old truck tires.

Ida trailed June and Eddy around the side of the house to the oak, which had been growing out front for as long as she could remember. Eddy set the short ladder against the trunk, and soon his head and shoulders vanished among the branches and leaves. When he descended, he said, "This tree ain't got no split branches. Any chance a limb might get blown off by a high wind and land on the roof is mighty small, and if it did, it wouldn't do a lick of damage. So, you got nothing to worry about, Ida." He laughed a hearty laugh. "That fellow was gonna make him a pile of money off of you. Good thing he never came back."

June whirled to face her mother, her eyes accusing. "I hope you didn't give him any money in advance. Did you, Mama?"

"Oh no, I'd never do a thing like that." Ida hated herself for lying. She could feel all her insides quivering.

Eddy slapped his hands together. "No harm's done, then. Maybe the cops got wind of him and run him off."

"Thanks for checking it out, Eddy." Ida felt small as a snail and wished she had a shell to crawl into.

"Well, Mama, no harm's done. We'll be on our way, then. I got to go into Asheville to the mall. You wanna come? I got to get a present for Sandy. Her birthday's coming up."

Ida shook her head. "Lord, I sure did forget my own granddaughter's birthday. So many birthdays these days, I can't keep track no more. Pick me up something for her, will you, June? I feel a little meager today. I'll just rest and watch TV."

Ida stood on the porch and waited for June to leave.

When June reached her car she turned to her mother. "You gonna come over at seven and eat supper with us tonight?"

"Probably." The way Ida's stomach felt, she couldn't eat a thing, but she needed to keep things as normal as possible.

"Okay. See you tonight."

Ida waved and June was on her way. With heavy steps and an even heavier heart, Ida shuffled to a rocker chair on the porch and sank into it. Slowly she rocked, unable at first to think. Then her mind cleared, and she relived her visit with Ray Wilson.

He'd come to the door, hat in hand, so polite like, and asked for water. She'd offered him iced tea. They'd sat awhile on the porch, and he'd told her how hot it was working out in the sun and how he was in the building trades and had been replacing a roof and doing some driveway paving over in Loring Valley. She'd told him about the storm that had flooded Loring Valley a couple of years ago, and how much repair work there had been then, and he'd said how he'd wished he'd known about it.

She'd asked him where he was from, 'cause he didn't talk like he was from these parts.

"Ohio," he'd said. "From Hinckley, Ohio." And he'd told her about the buzzards that came every spring to a field in Hinckley, and how the town folk all turned out to see them.

"Mightly ugly, buzzards are," she'd said.

He'd laughed. "You're right. They're mighty ugly. But it's our town's claim to fame and it brings in a lot of tourists."

He'd been so easy to talk to, so friendly. He had a wife back home and three kids, he said, but the work had dried up in that area, and that's why he was on the road. She'd been on the verge of inviting him to stay awhile with her and save his money at that motel he said he was living in down south by Fletcher. She'd thought of June, then, and what she'd say about that, and bitten her tongue. And now it turned out, she'd been taken in, made a perfect fool of.

The grit, and Ida was known for her grit, oozed out of

her. Stupid. How had she ever let this happen? Feeling sick to her stomach, and old, and bereft of good sense, Ida eased up from the rocker, shuffled inside, crossed the living room to her bedroom, and threw herself on her bed. She'd rest awhile, and then she'd figure out what to do.

22

Amelia's Suspicions

The day Ray Wilson visited Ida, Amelia was alone in the house when someone knocked on their front door. Amelia did not open the door to strangers, but peeped instead through the living room window. A pleasant-looking young man, with his hands shoved into his overalls and a cap pushed back on his forehead, rocked back and forth on his heels. As she watched him, his eyes narrowed. He seemed to be inspecting the walls, the ceiling of the porch, the steps up to the porch. Walking to the steps, he craned his neck up—looking at what? A bird? The gutters? Then, returning to the front door, he knocked again.

Amelia's car sat in the driveway. He would assume someone was at home. He looked nice enough, but one never knew, one could never be too careful. Amelia had read an article in a magazine she'd picked up in the beauty parlor the other day warning about scams. A *don't* list included *Do not open your door to anyone you do not know or anyone posing as a repair person that you have not called.*

Tiptoeing, Amelia sneaked up the stairs, closed her bedroom door, and locked it. Phone in hand, she was about to call for help or guidance, but her mind went blank. Who should she call? She dialed 911 and hung up. Surely this was not a 911 call. Who, then? Velma and Charlie Herrill. Their phone rang and rang. Max and Hannah weren't at Bella's Park; the answering machine in Hannah's office said that they'd gone into Asheville for supplies. She couldn't recall where Grace was, and earlier she'd seen Bob load his golf bag in his car and drive away.

From her bedroom window, Amelia watched the man walk across the street toward Max's house. Amelia dialed Max's number and thank God, Anna answered.

"Señor Max's house."

"Anna. This is Amelia. There's a stranger, a man, coming over to your door. He knocked here, but I didn't let him in."

"No to worry, Señora Amelia. Señor Max, he tell me never open door to anyone I not know. I no let him in, and I get Jose to go round and chase him away."

"I don't know what he wants. He may just be asking for directions or something." Was she making too much of this, making a mountain out of a molehill? The man had reached Max's front door. Amelia could see his feet; the roof of Max's porch hid his head. "He's at your door now, Anna."

"I call Jose. He take care of everything. You no worry." And Anna hung up.

Amelia watched from her window as Jose strode around the corner of the house. He carried a pitchfork in one hand, and in the other led one of the dogs on a leash. The dog, Hero, barked and jumped toward the man, but Jose restrained him. The stranger descended the steps and, keeping his distance, stood for a few moments talking with Jose before shoving his hands in his pockets and strolling from the yard. When he turned left and headed for Elk Road, Amelia breathed a sigh of relief and wondered what she had made such a fuss about. Then the phone rang.

Anna said, "He say to Jose he lost, and Jose tell him how to go, and he go. Jose say he no like the look of the *hombre*. He too pretty."

Too pretty? An interesting way to describe someone you didn't like the looks of. "Thanks, Anna. I'm leery of any strange man going door to door."

"It no problem, Señora Amelia."

"Well, thank Jose for me."

"*Sí.* I tell Jose. *Adios.*"

He was gone, thank goodness, and that was that. She might as well go downstairs to the dining room and lay out the dozen black-and-white photographs Mike had asked her to critique. She had been flattered by his request. Mike routinely critiqued her work and rarely asked her to reciprocate with his.

She laid the photographs side by side, stood back, and studied them carefully. With black-and-white you worked to capture a range of shades from white through gray to solid black, which was not always easy. Your eyes could trick you; you could miss either end of this spectrum and end up with a too-gray and murky look. Amelia examined each photograph seeking the kind of clutter the human eyes could overlook: an electric wire, a twig or leaf. And then there was the matter of balance and composition.

Amelia circled the table. Something wasn't right with the photo of children playing on a wooden bridge. It was a wonderfully composed shot but a hot spot, a too bright area, captured her attention. It detracted from the picture, drawing her eyes from the center of attention within the photograph. Why had Mike missed this flaw? Of course, if he liked the photo a great deal he could always retouch it in the darkroom, burn in and darken the hot spot.

Therein lay the advantage of black-and-white film. In the darkroom, you retained control of the final product. This was also true of digital photographs. People did remarkable things with them using Photoshop or Paint Shop, neither of which Amelia understood or was prepared to master.

Amelia scrutinized the remaining photographs. They appeared flawless. She gathered them up carefully and returned them to Mike's container. Then she sat for a moment, intensely aware of the silence around her.

Since May left to live with her aunt in South Asheville, the house seemed inordinately quiet. May studied at home, and her presence had given Amelia a sense of safety at times when the other women were out of the house. Amelia missed her. When she was alone in the house, she always struggled to control her anxiety. She would never tell them, but she would pull back the shower curtains and pound her hand against clothes in the closet, to assure herself that no one was there. What if someone was there? What if, one day as she ran her hand across the clothes, she saw a man's shoes? What would she do? Thinking like this frightened her. Amelia grabbed her purse, whipped a scarf around her neck, tucked the box of photographs beneath her arm, and headed for the door.

On the porch, she stopped and perused the neighborhood. Was that man really gone? He could have doubled back. Satisfied that he was nowhere in sight, she hastened to her car, drove onto Elk Road, and headed for Mars Hill.

Traffic on the road to Mars Hill seemed unusually heavy and slowed considerably as she neared the park by the river. What was going on? In the near distance, lights atop a police car flashed. A policeman stood in the middle of the road directing traffic into one lane, where another policeman raised his hand, stopped each car, and asked for driver's licenses. Amelia slowed, stopped, produced her license, and was waved on. If not for all the excitement and the comings and goings in the park, she would have thought this was a routine traffic check. It was not!

The park amazed her. Never had she seen this many police cars in one location around here or policemen running about waving to one another, calling to one another. In the park, laundry flapped on lines strung between trees. Scattered about were towers of black trash bags, and policemen were talking to people outside the travel trailers. Then cars, including hers, were directed back into two lanes and traffic speeded up. What in the name of heaven was going on?

For the past seven months, Bob had volunteered at the local police department. Although his job would eventually be registering visitors who came to pay the bail of new prisoners, he had been through a varied training. Several nights each month, he had ridden in a police vehicle with an on-duty policeman and had been amazed at the action, most of it suspicious if not downright dangerous, out there on the streets. He had participated, his heart in his mouth, in a car chase and arrest. Now, as he returned from a day of golf, here he was inching along Elk Road in a single lane. Recognizing Terry Slater, the policeman he had accompanied on the car chase, Bob slowed even more.

"Hey, Terry," he called. "What's going on?"

Terry walked over to his car. "Hi, Bob. We had us a regular caravan of con artists scamming little old ladies around these parts. They hightailed outta here before we got here." He lifted his cap and ran his arm across his forehead. "That's par for the course. Somehow they get wind we're onto them, and they're gone like a puff of smoke. The boys are looking for leads, names, whatever they can find out."

"Good luck," Bob said. He stepped on the pedal. Grace. Where was she, anyway? Had she been targeted by some con man? By the time he reached Cove Road, Bob's agitation showed on his flushed face. Grace's car was not in her driveway. Maybe Hannah would know if there had been any problems on Cove Road. But Hannah's phone at Bella's Park rang and her answering machine came on.

"We will be out of the office today. Please call back."

Where was Amelia? He tried but got no answer from Mike's studio. A glass of beer and some pretzels would hit the spot. Bob poured himself a cold glass of beer, went out onto the porch, and settled into a wicker armchair. He drank slowly, savoring each mouthful. Grace was fine. She would have told him had there been anyone snooping about trying to sell them anything or trying to fix something, and she wasn't home today. He just couldn't for the life of him recall her telling him where she was off to. Was she meeting Tyler in Asheville? Had she mentioned that, or was it just that Tyler had been to see her? Those two had a special relationship. He smiled. But damn, why couldn't he remember?

The neighborhood was quiet. No cars came or went on Cove Road. No one was out walking a dog or jogging. He watched the sun sink behind Snowman's Cap and the sky darken, and gray clouds appeared out of nowhere and tumbled across the mountain. In the distance, thunder clapped. He rubbed his arms. The temperature was falling. And then the heavens exploded; rain pelted the earth. The wind whistled past the corner of the porch. Why didn't he recall hearing the weatherman predict a storm today? Lately he just didn't remember things, and he used to have a sterling memory. That troubled him. There were moments, at sunset and late at night, when he thought about dying. The obituary in his former army battalion newsletter listed the names of men with whom he had served: Tom Fredricks, a bright young fellow, a lawyer, who left the service to go home to Albany, New York, and his family's law firm. Bradley Wells, a farmer, who preferred farming in Iowa to soldiering and got out fast as he could. They were younger than he was and they had both passed away. He could see their faces. Bob closed his eyes and repeated the lines spoken after Hamlet's death, "And flights of angels sing thee to thy rest." It was all he remembered of a play he had hated and from which he had been required to memorize long speeches when he was in high school. Then he reminded himself how lucky he was to have met Grace and fallen in love at a time when he'd given up any thought of such a thing happening. They had had several very good years together. But the very thought of not being, of not existing as flesh and blood, of not being able to touch anyone ever again or be touched, made him extremely sad. It made him want to weep for himself.

Bob began to relax; the beer did that for him. Beer and thinking of Grace. He pulled a hassock closer, stretched out his feet, rested his head on the back of the chair, and closed his eyes. For as long as he lived, he would try to live fully, to love well, and to tell those he loved that he loved them.

Suddenly, something was pulling on his leg, punching him in the stomach. Reflexively, he flailed his arms, shoving the "thing" away.

23

This Kind of Thing Doesn't
Happen to Me

*B*ob awakened to Melissa's screams. The little girl clung to her father and wept while Russell tried to quiet her and to explain that she must never pounce on Grandpa or anyone when they were sleeping.

"It scares them. It scared Grandpa, and he woke up too fast. He didn't even know it was you."

"He pushed me away," Melissa said between sobs. "He hurt my arm." She rubbed her arm.

Bob scrambled from the chair and scooped her into his arms. "My darling, baby, I'm so sorry. I was sleeping like a rock. You know how rocks sleep, don't you?"

She shook her head.

"They sleep very quietly and very deeply. You startled me, and I'm so sorry that I scared you. Give me a big hug and a kiss, honey."

The child wound her arms about his neck. Her cheek against his cheek was wet, and he dried her tears with his big handkerchief.

"A rock can sleep?" she asked.

He nodded solemnly. "Everything sleeps, animals, people, even rocks." He winked at Tyler, who leaned against the wall of the house, his hands crossed, disbelief on his face.

Tyler was at that age when his father's and his grandfather's clay feet were becoming apparent. He rolled his eyes. "Where's Granny Grace?"

"I was going to ask you that very question. I haven't the foggiest idea where she is, but I imagine she'll be home soon."

"You people need cell phones so you can contact one another. Suppose one of you got sick, or had a car crash, or something?" Tyler asked.

"You're right. You're right, of course. We do indeed. We've been talking about getting cell phones, again," Bob replied.

"Don't harangue your grandfather." Russell put his arm about his son's shoulders, but Tyler moved away. Unfazed, Russell said, "Tell you what, we'll drag your grandparents kicking and screaming into the twenty-first century. We'll get them new cell phones, and this time we'll teach them how to use them. What do you say to that?"

Tyler grunted something that sounded like yes.

Melissa, always needy of attention, pinched Bob's ears. "Grandpa, Grandpa, look at me. I can wiggle my nose like Samantha the good witch on television. She's pretty, Grandpa. Do you like her? I love her."

"Tyler, run inside and bring that box of toys Granny Grace put together for Melissa to play with, will you?" Russell said.

Tyler stepped inside, letting the door slam behind him.

"Tyler's a bad boy, slamming the door," Melissa said.

Melissa had been nearly incorrigible since before her parents divorced, before her mother, Emily, gave custody of her to Russell and moved away to Florida. She had been seeing a child therapist ever since and thankfully was calmer and more manageable, though she still had her moments.

Tyler returned and set the box on the porch. He crouched beside it. "Come over here, Melissa. Let's check this stuff out. Let's see what's new in this box." Grace replenished it regularly. Melissa squirmed to be set down and raced over to her brother, leaving the men to chat.

Russell lowered his voice. "You heard about the scam artists that targeted Covington, Marshall, and Mars Hill?"

"Heard about it briefly on the way home. Terry, that cop I rode with, was directing traffic over at the park. He told me a little, but no details. Who were these people? Who'd they con? Do you know?"

"A couple of older women up McCorkle Creek: Betty McCorkle, and a woman named Lucille Delbert and her sister, who's a Carter, and a couple of women in Loring Valley. Can you believe that?"

"No, I can't. It's hard to believe anyone would be that gullible. They paid in advance, I assume, and lost their money?"

"That's the story," Russell said. "From what I heard, the scammers had their pitch down pat and were very persuasive. Seems they roll into town, canvas an area, and target widows whose houses look a bit frayed and who drive older-model cars."

"Why older-model cars?"

"I have no idea," Russell replied.

"They lived in those trailers that rolled in a week or so ago. Terry said they were gone when the cops got there."

"There sure were a lot of cops in that park," Russell said. "I heard they were Gypsies."

"There aren't any Gypsies around here that I know of."

"That's the local gossip," Russell said.

A shrill yell from Melissa drew their attention.

"Play nice, or I won't play with you," Tyler said.

"I hate you." The child threw a handful of small blocks at Tyler, who stood and walked away. "I like Sadie better. She plays good."

"Sadie lets you cheat." He looked at his grandfather. "She's as mean as ever. She's never going to change." He took the porch steps two at a time, walked to the car, and climbed inside. Headphones plastered to his ears, Tyler's body swayed to sounds they could not imagine.

Grace turned her car into Cove Road and into Bob's drive. She got out, stopped to pull a weed making its home in the driveway, and all smiles, strolled up to the cottage.

Tyler rushed to meet her, his eyes wide with excitement. "You oughta hear what's happened, Granny Grace. Big stuff. People got scammed. I guess that means they gave away their money to someone who said they'd do something for them and didn't."

"Scammed? What are you talking about, Tyler? Who got scammed? Someone I know? When did all this happen? I've only been gone for a couple of hours."

"Didn't you see them? The cops stopped all the cars by the park and asked for our driver's licenses. I showed them my learner's permit."

"It must be over. There are no cops or anyone by the park now," Grace said.

"Of course, they waved us right on. What does a scammer look like anyway?" Tyler asked as he followed her up the steps.

Grace kissed Bob's cheek, hugged Russell, and submitted to Melissa's loud and vigorous demonstrations of affection. With the child on her lap, Grace settled into a rocker beside Bob. "What was Tyler telling me about people being scammed? Which people got scammed and by whom?"

Bob and Russell shared their experiences.

Grace shook her head. "I hope no one was seriously hurt financially."

The saga continued when Amelia and Hannah returned home and hastened across the yard to join them. Amelia looked agitated and related her experience with the stranger at their door.

"My instinct warned me. He just didn't look honest, and I never will open the door to anyone I don't know. But, my Lord, it was very upsetting. Think of those poor people who were conned out of their money. Who are they? I wonder if we know any of them."

"You hear about things like this and read about it, but to have it happen in our neighborhood is definitely sobering. One would hardly expect scammers to pick Covington," Grace said.

Hannah reported that Velma's cousin over on Rector's Corner Road in Marshall had been promised a new roof and had parted with $800 in cash. Betty Austin, her beautician had told Amelia, handed a man $300 in cash to lay a coat of macadam on her driveway. "He told her he was getting it for her dirt cheap, as it was left over from a paving job he'd just finished. They say lots of money was given in advance for new roofs, gutters repaired, trees trimmed, porch steps to be replaced and painted, as well as exterior house painting. And the thieves just vanished.

Amelia continued. "Ida's name was mentioned, but only

that she had been visited by someone she described as 'very pleasant,' but she had the good sense not to hand over a penny. In fact, she had her son-in-law come over and check everything the man said needed fixing, and it was all a lie."

The hubbub continued for days as report after report came in. Men discussed it over coffee at the diner; women chatted while pushing shopping carts at the market. Pastor Denny invited an attorney from the police department in Asheville to visit the church on Sunday afternoon to educate everyone concerning scams and to provide information that would arm them against future scammers. "Scammed" and "scammer," words hardly included in anyone's vocabulary in Covington, became household words.

"Are you going to go to the meeting?" Grace asked her housemates.

Amelia shook her head. "I'm not. I bet nobody comes."

"I think a lot of folks will come to the meeting. I'm going to go. I want to hear what the speaker has to say. The more we know about this kind of thing, the better off we are," Grace said. "Hannah and Max are going. I ran into Miriam and she said she wanted to go."

Amelia again shook her head. "You can tell me about it. I'm taking Sadie to the nature center Sunday afternoon, and I won't break my date with Sadie." She adored the child. This was the grandchild she had never had, and a day did not pass that Amelia did not offer a prayer of thanks for Miriam and Sadie coming to Covington.

24

The Meeting

The turnout for the meeting exceeded Denny Ledbetter's expectations. People walked across the street and down the road from their homes on Cove Road, their condos in Loring Valley, their farmhouses and bungalows in McCorkle Creek. They drove from Barnardsville, Marshall, Hot Springs, and Wolf Laurel, and their cars, pickups, and SUVs lined Cove Road and spilled onto lawns and into anyone's unoccupied driveway. They crammed into pews and occupied folding chairs set up in side aisles and at the rear of the church. The vestibule doors were secured open and the vestibule crammed with chairs, and still there were more attendees than seats.

Marsha Shortell, attorney and victims' advocate for the Asheville Police Department, was tall and attractive. She stood behind a long table piled with stacks of papers. After introductions, she wasted no time, and speaking in a clear, firm voice, launched into her talk.

"What has happened in Covington is happening all over this country. In a typical scenario, there's a knock on your door and usually it's a pleasant man who informs you that he's just completed a roof or a paint job, or some other job, down the road. Passing your home, he happened to notice that your roof is badly in need of repair. The shingles are dry and curling and ready to pop off, or he'll tell you that your tin roof is in need of renailing to keep the rain out. He might mention that heavy rains are predicted for your area, and you could sustain thousands of dollars of damage to the attic and ceiling if you don't take care of your roof immediately. He tells you that the water damage won't show inside the house until sections of your roof have rotted, and he paints a frightening picture of soggy insulation attracting mold in your attic. Lucky for you, he says, he has materials left over from a job he's just finished, and he can fix your roof cheap for x amount of dollars.

"He seems honest, real, and sincere, and you're frightened at the prospect of a leaking roof. He seems to be offering you a really good deal, and he looks so clean-cut and honest. You agree and hand over cash, and off he goes to collect his tools or the lumber he says he'll need, and that's the last you see of him or your money."

Heads nod. People shift in their seats. Attorney Shortell quotes statistics.

"Our senior population accounts for way too large a percentage of consumer fraud. As many as thirty percent of all seniors fall victim to a scam, whether it be home repairs, the lottery, travel, or something else."

"Why is that, do you think?" a man in the second row asked.

"Many of you grew up at a time when business was conducted with a handshake. You trusted the person whose hands people were shaking and you prefer to believe it's still that way. Also, many older people live alone, and they're glad to have a caller, especially someone as pleasant as these scammers usually are. From the scammers' point of view, whether it's true or not, older widows have been left well-off by their husbands and have money in the bank."

A woman raised her hand and was acknowledged. Grace recognized the woman from the beauty parlor but could not put a name to the face.

"I got a call once from a real nice lady wanting me to donate to some charity in Africa. I told her I was fixin' to cook me up a mess of beans and hung up." Satisfied, she crossed her arms over her chest. "I donate to my church and nothing else. If there's a worthwhile charity needs givin' to in Africa, they'll take care of it."

"You were smart to hang up," Marsha Shortell replied. "There are plenty of fake charities out there, and these people are skilled at playing on our sympathy."

"Yeh, like an e-mail I got the other day from some guy with a name I couldn't pronounce with a sob story about some child," a man in the middle row said. "I deleted that one fast."

"I had a whole heap of e-mails one time claiming to be from a bank, a credit card company, and a phone company I never did hear of," a man in overalls said. "I'd read somewhere that legitimate companies don't ask for personal information in an e-mail, and these folks did, so I deleted 'em."

"Very wise of you. How many of you use computers?" the attorney asked.

More than half of the people in the room raised their hands.

"We all have to be so careful. If an e-mail arrives from someplace or someone that you aren't familiar with, it's best to delete it. I know that's hard. It's tempting to open it, but don't. I can't stress this too strongly. Never open an e-mail you can't identify. Even opening one of them and immediately deleting it could expose you to a computer virus or get your name and e-mail on a long list other scammers would use. When you delete enough times, chances are those particular scammers or annoying salesmen will move on to someone else."

"Except those guys who want to sell dish television," someone said, and everyone laughed.

The attorney continued. "And those door-to-door encyclopedia salespeople. You need to resist their sales pitch. Every school and library has encyclopedias. Many of your grandkids have computers, and there are encyclopedias on-line for them to use."

Before she could continue, someone muttered to her neighbor, "I done that. I bought me a fancy set of encyclopedias and Jamie, my granddaughter, never did open not one of those books. I paid on them for three years."

"You're not alone. It's hard to resist something we think will help our children or grandchildren, isn't it?" the attorney said.

Heads nodded.

"And that's exactly what those scammers and salespeople rely on." Marsha Shortell picked up an armful of papers from the table and walked down the center aisle, handing stacks to be passed along, until Denny took the papers and continued to distribute them.

She returned to the table and picked up a single sheet of paper with a list typed in large, very dark print, which she held high. "Here's a list of scams to watch out for. I'll pass them out, and I will leave more of this information with your pastor.

"There are people offering lower-interest-rate mortgages and schemes for consolidating your debts. Watch for them, especially in January, and don't say yes to any of them. If you need a loan, go to a bank. And watch out for people offering you what is known as reverse mortgages. That's where, if you've paid off your home, you can collect a monthly payment against the appraised price of that home. You could end up without a home or income. For some reason, the month of May seems to bring out that type of scammer. If you think you need one, be sure you discuss a reverse mortgage with your bank or the bank of someone you know and trust." She waved the paper.

"On the sheet that the good pastor was kind enough to hand out for me, there is a list of do's and don'ts. It's very important that you *do not* give your Social Security, credit card, or bank account numbers, your mother's maiden name, or your date of birth to anyone unless you know the person or institution asking for it, and there is a legitimate reason why they need that information.

"Once a scammer has your Social Security number, for example, he or she can open a bank account, take out a loan, and much more in your name, and it will take a very long time to get it all straightened out, plus the aggravation, which you do not need."

She handed Denny another stack of pages, at the top of which was the phone number for the Do Not Call Registry, 888-382-1222, and the Web site www.donotcall.gov if anyone preferred to use the Internet.

"Just phone and tell them you want to be on the do-not-call list. It's that simple. And I urge you not to wait, but to get on that list as soon as possible. Are there any questions?"

Many people spoke up, women especially, saying that they considered it impolite not to open the door when someone came to call.

"Resist the temptation, please. I cannot urge you strongly enough, no matter how rude you think it is. Do not open your door to anyone you do not know or anyone you did not ask to come to your home. Don't, under any circumstances, get involved with strangers at the market who ask you what kind of mayonnaise you buy and why, or how to tell if a melon's ripe, or anyone trying to casually strike up a conversation with you. Just move on, and don't talk to them. If they persist, walk your cart to the register and complain or ask for the manager and let him know that a stranger is bothering you. There are times when it does not pay to be nice, and that is one of them.

"Also, there are organizations available to help you check out a product or a business trying to sell you something. You can contact the Better Business Bureau for help, and you can locate the nearest office in your phone book or on the Web at www.bbb.org. It's all on the pages I gave you."

People studied the sheets she had provided.

"The Federal Trade Commission's job is to protect you. Call them at 877-382-4357. You can file a complaint at the National Fraud Information Center. That number is 800-876-7060. These names and numbers are all on that second sheet I handed out. And if you belong to AARP, the American Association of Retired Persons has lots of good information about how to avoid becoming the victim of fraud."

She set her palms on the table and leaned forward. "Just remember, if it sounds too good to be true, it really, truly is too good to be true. If you get hooked into talking to a salesperson, tell them you'll think about it, and you'll get back to them. They'll hate that, and believe me the pressure will come on, but don't buy on impulse or let them guilt you into anything. If you ask to see their credentials or business card, they'll often make an excuse and leave."

Someone laughed. "I got a call one time telling me I won the lottery, and all I needed to collect the money was send in a fee for the taxes."

"How'd you handle that?" the attorney asked.

"I laughed in his face and slammed down the phone, that's what I done."

"Well done, I'd say."

Everyone laughed. People relaxed, and the questions kept coming.

"I got a letter one time that said the FBI wanted my Social Security and other information. I started to write it and send the letter in, but my wife here"—the man poked the arm of a women seated beside him—"she said no, not before we checked with our lawyer. He said that no legitimate agency like the FBI would send me a letter asking for that kind of information. Correct?"

"That is correct." The lawyer picked up a sheet of paper.

"What about people trying to fix your house for you?" someone asked. "When did you say scammers target people about home repairs?"

"Home repair scams are most prevalent in the spring. Some of you know that from recent personal experience."

A cough. A nervous giggle. A laugh. Many heads nodded.

A few more questions and the meeting came to an end. For those people, mainly women, in and about Covington who had been victims, the scammers had cashed their checks or pocketed their cash immediately and vanished.

Fortified with information and lists of do's, don'ts, and phone numbers, all that their unwitting victims could do now was return to their homes and try not to dwell too much on the mistakes they had made.

Ida, hiding her gullibility and monetary loss from her family and friends, acted smug and felt guilty. A few days after the meeting at the church, she fell ill. It began with a cold that settled in her chest. When June failed to hear from her mother, who phoned her every morning and sometimes at night, June stopped by.

The shades were drawn throughout the downstairs of the house, and except for a floor fan, the air hung as still as swamp air on a late-summer day. Ida lay on the couch in the living room shivering and covered with a blanket. June touched her hand to her mother's forehead.

"Mama, you've got you a fever. Why didn't you call me?"

"I figured it would pass," Ida murmured. "And it will, if you'll go away and leave me be. I'll lie here and sweat it out." Her rasping cough belied her protestations.

June pulled the blanket off her mother, and Ida turned away and covered her chest with her arms. "Don't do that, June. I'm right chilly, can't you see?"

"I see, all right, and we're going to Doc Johnson right this minute, Mama. I'll go upstairs and get you some fresh clothes, and we'll brush your hair and put some powder on you."

"Bring the Johnson's baby powder. I fancy that better than the sweet-smelling stuff May got me for my last birthday. Used it once. I wouldn't be surprised if that's what gave me this cough."

June rolled her eyes. "It's more like your cold's dropped

into your chest, and you know you're given to bronchitis, Mama."

Doc Johnson had been Ida's doctor for more years than she could remember. He reprimanded her and wagged a long bony finger in her face.

"You know better than to let this go like this. You've got you a mighty big infection going on in that chest of yours, Ida. I'd put you in the hospital, but I know what a stubborn old woman you are. So, I'm gonna give you a shot." He looked at June. "You get these antibiotics right away. See that she takes them every four hours and call me in the morning. Let me know how she is. If she's not better in two days, she's going into the hospital.

"Now don't you start with me, Ida," he said in response to her open mouth and raised hand. "Not a word out of you." He turned to June. "That's how it's gonna be, so you see that she doesn't miss taking a pill, not one of them, or so help me, I'll send the ambulance to carry her off."

"See me here?" Ida poked her chest. "I'm sitting right here. Why are you talkin' to June like I'm not here?" She doubled over with a bout of coughing.

"Well, I'm telling you to your face now, Ida," the doctor said. "You take these pills to the very last one and don't be saving none of them for one of your goats. Goats don't use people medicine. It won't help them not one little bit. You got a sick goat, you take it to the vet."

Ida waved a hand at him. "That was just that one time. You gonna keep reminding me?"

Doc Johnson laughed, put his arm about Ida's shoulders, and led her to the door. "You go on home now and rest, Ida.

Let yourself get better. It would probably be best if you took her home with you, June, so she gets looked after properly. Better get someone reliable to see to her goats or she won't stay still."

It was guilt made her sick, Ida knew that. Guilt for losing good money, like flushing it right down the toilet. She longed to tell someone, but how could she? She'd acted high and mighty when her neighbors were feeling real bad. She'd acted uppity and said, right out there in front of them all, that she'd been too smart to get taken in by a scammer. She thought about this as she coughed until she thought she'd die. The bronchitis was God's punishment, and she'd have to bear it.

He was older now, almost a man, nearly fifteen, and he'd been shaving dark fuzz from above his lip for weeks. Still, when he had a problem like the one troubling him now, it was to Granny Grace he turned.

Thinking about love nearly stopped his heart. It was embarrassing how Alicia, his chemistry lab partner, caused his heart to thud and his palms to sweat. She was the most beautiful girl in school, and he had a big, big crush on her. But did she reciprocate those feelings? One day she'd smile at him and say or do something that set his heart racing and his knees wobbling, and the next day she'd brush him off as if she didn't give a hoot. It was driving him nuts.

Delighted to see Tyler, Grace shut off the ignition and sat for a moment thinking how tall he'd grown and how his features were changing; his nose was longer and his jaw wider.

The gangly teenager rose from the steps and came to greet her with open arms. "Granny Grace, you're as pretty as ever." He hugged her. "How about you be my date at the prom this year?" Not that he was a senior or even a junior, but the prom was open to sophomores, and the band was usually terrific. Most of his friends planned on going. He had no date for the prom, and it hurt remembering Alicia boasting in class to Sue Ellen, her girlfriend, that Roger Tiffton, a senior, had asked her to the prom. He'd wondered then if she had raised her voice just so that he would hear this news. He had heard it, all right. If she had plunged a knife into his heart, it would not have hurt more. It was his own fault. He had never had the guts to ask her out.

25

Teenage Angst

Several days after the meeting at the church, Grace returned home to find Tyler perched on the top step of her front porch, twiddling a twig between his fingers. His long legs, stretched out in the warm spring sunshine, reached almost to the bottom step.

He had been waiting for fifteen minutes when Grace's car turned into the driveway. She always drove slowly, and it frustrated him when he was her passenger. But she really listened to him, and had given him good advice since they met, when he was in the third grade. His mother, Amy, had just been killed in an auto crash and he had lost all interest in school until Granny Grace had been assigned to tutor him. She had done more than tutor him. His heart warmed thinking of it. She had loved him and helped him through those awful months and she met and just about married Grandpa Bob, only they never really got married. Dad had said that at their age, what did it matter? They weren't going to have babies or anything, the very idea of which had cracked him up laughing. Grace was as much his granny today as if she were married to Grandpa, and she'd taught him that you could create a family by bringing together the people whom you loved.

"Hey," he said, "you and Grandpa could both come to our prom. We've got a great jazz band this year."

Grace laughed. "That might be fun, and it's a lot closer than going into Asheville to a hotel to dance." She hooked her arm through his and they climbed the steps, entered the house, and walked into the kitchen.

"How come," he asked, "you always take people straight into the kitchen, and Aunt Amelia takes them into the living room?"

Grace set her purse and a small bag, from which she removed a bottle of vitamins, on the counter. "I was just about out of my multivitamins," she said. Then she turned and looked at him. "I don't know, Tyler. I guess it's a habit. I enjoy sitting at the kitchen table and having a chat over a cup of tea or milk and cookies. Amelia's more formal than I am. She prefers to chat with her guests in the living room. It doesn't matter, does it? Guests who come here are happy either way." She reached for an apron and fastened it about her waist. "What would you like, cocoa, tea, juice, milk?"

As far as Tyler could recall, his own mother had never worn an apron, nor had Emily, his former stepmother. The apron suited Granny Grace in a way it would not have suited his mom or Emily. Granny Grace was a very special person, and he felt happy knowing that she loved him and was always there for him.

"Milk," he said. "Milk will be just fine."

"And cookies." Grace set an old-fashioned tin box decorated with flowers on the table. "Help yourself. I bought these. Didn't have time this week to bake."

He pulled the box against his chest, pried the lid off, and removed several oatmeal cookies dark with raisins. No need to beat around the bush, to hem and haw, before getting to the point as he did with Dad. With Granny Grace you got right to the point.

"I got a girlfriend problem."

"What kind of a girlfriend problem?"

When you talked to Granny Grace it was eyeball to eyeball, no studying your feet or shifting your gaze about. "Her name's Alicia Hibbs. She lives over near where we used to live before Emily left and we moved closer to you and Grandpa." He paused for a moment. "We're in several classes together. In chemistry lab we work on the same assignments at the same table."

"So what's the problem, my boy?" She loved calling him her boy and thinking of him as her boy. She noted the flush on his cheeks. "Well, you just say whatever you want, Tyler. Get it off your chest."

"She's awfully pretty. She's got long, dark hair and green eyes. But she's a flirt. She flirts with me, and she flirts with other guys, too. Sometimes I think she likes me a lot. I like her a lot. And then she does something that makes me think she hates me."

"And what would that be? What does she do that makes you think she dislikes you?" Grace asked softly.

"One thing I don't like is that whenever I start to tell her anything about myself, what I like to read, or do, she changes the subject and talks about herself."

"She sounds like a very self-centered young lady."

"Maybe she is. She sure treats me with contempt in lab, as if I don't know what I'm doing. And I *do* know. Only I get flustered standing next to her, and I make mistakes. I could kick myself. No wonder she thinks I'm an idiot."

Grace realized how serious he was, how upset. "Is this affecting your grades, Tyler?"

He nodded.

"That's not good, is it?"

"It sure isn't."

"Does this Alicia know how you feel about her?"

He shrugged and averted his eyes for a moment. "Sometimes I think she does. Sometimes I think she doesn't care enough to want to know."

"So you haven't indicated to her how you feel, is that right?"

He pulled back from the table. "Heck no, I haven't told her." He shook his head. "I'd feel like a fool if she laughed in my face."

Grace rubbed her forehead. "Lord, it's been so long since I was in high school. How do young people today behave when they like someone?" She fell silent. Then she said, "Well, I can see where this is a problem, not to be sure how someone feels about you. Can you request a different lab partner? Is there another lab you could transfer to?"

"What's that gonna solve?"

"Your chemistry grade, for one thing," she replied.

When he did not answer, she said, "You don't want to do that, do you? You want to be near her. Well, then, you're part of the problem, aren't you?"

He leaned toward her, his face flushed, his eyes anxious. "I guess I am, but Granny Grace, I never felt like this about a girl before. I like her a lot. Very much."

"It won't do a bit of good, then, for me to tell you that she may be the first but not the last girl you'll fall in love with and be rejected by, or that you can't make a person care for you because you care for them, or make them behave the way you want them to behave, so, I won't say those things."

Tyler laughed. "You just said all of those things, Granny Grace."

"Did I, now?" She leaned forward and reached for his hands. "Listen, my boy, I can promise you, there will come a time when you'll meet a girl, and you'll both feel the same way about each other, and that will. be wonderful. Truth is, you can't make this Alicia change her ways or be something or someone she isn't. You can come right out and tell her how you feel, and if she rejects or embarrasses you, then so be it, or you can let it go and forget about her, or you can just stay silent and go on pining and letting your grades slip."

"But she makes me feel—"

"You own your feelings, Tyler." He started to speak, but she raised her hand to stop him. "Let me finish, dear boy. I'll tell it to you plain as day. You have choices. You can pine for a girl who isn't available, a girl who toys with your affections, who, in plain words, is a self-centered, mean-spirited stinker who flirts with other boys. You can torment yourself over her, or you can get a grip on the situation and on yourself. You can accept reality and move on. In time, you'll find a girl worthy of you. In matters of the heart, in matters of love, Tyler, if it's this hard and this painful, it's just not right, and that means that Alicia isn't the girl for you."

He sat there, tears stinging his eyes, not wanting to hear her hard words, for that is what they were to him. He had hoped for reassurance about Alicia, or some gimmick or trick to win her over, but Granny Grace had handed him a bitter dose of realism, and he was angry. Across the table he saw that her eyes were anxious, worried. Perhaps she knew how he was feeling. Tyler wished he had never told her about

Alicia. He loved Alicia! But he knew that Granny Grace was right. Alicia was a selfish, mean-spirited flirt. She did know how he felt about her even if he hadn't told her right out, and she toyed with his affections. Alicia Hibbs didn't give a hoot about him.

With Granny Grace it was safe to express his emotions. Tyler crossed his arms on the table and lowered his head onto his arms.

Grace sat, hands folded in her lap, and waited. Finally she said, "I know this is hard to accept and it hurts. I am sorry."

Tyler raised his head. Her eyes were teary. "It's not what I wanted to hear, you know. It does hurt. It's so hard."

"It's very hard," she said. "Very hard."

"Like for Romeo and Juliet?"

She smoothed his hair. "No, not like Romeo and Juliet. They loved each other. It was their parents who made all the trouble, who wanted to keep them apart."

"Were you ever rejected by someone you loved, Granny Grace?"

She thought a moment. "Yes, I was. In high school. In my senior year I fell in love with a boy who was new to our town and to the school. Imagine having to start your senior year in a new school. He looked so lonely, and I fell head over heels for him." She stopped. "My goodness, Tyler, you've got me going now. I haven't thought about Hank Hessler in years."

"What happened, Granny Grace? Tell me." He leaned forward, distracted from his own unhappiness and eager for every word.

Grace nodded. "Hank Hessler. Why, Tyler, I must confess, he quite took my breath away. We had several classes together." She smiled at Tyler and raised her brows. "I nearly flunked history and math. All I could do in class was look at him. In math class he sat catty-corner from me, so I could see his profile. I doted on his profile. He looked so lonely and so noble. I offered to help him with math—he wasn't good with numbers—or to show him around town. He was polite but indifferent, and I built every simple hello, every smile, into something that simply wasn't there."

Her cheeks flushed, and she covered them with her hands. Then Grace laughed and slapped the end of the table with her palm. "What a silly goof I was. By Thanksgiving, he was holding hands and going steady with a girl in our history class. He just about broke my heart, and all that stuff about his caring for me was all in my head. But then your grandfather—goodness me, Tyler, I mean Ted Singleton—asked me to the senior prom." She laughed again and smoothed her hair. "We started dating, Ted that is, and I married him and lived happily ever after." It was worth stretching the truth here.

"Thank you for telling me, Granny Grace. I feel better. I think you're right. I have built a whole fantasy in my head about Alicia. It ought not to be so hard and so hurtful. A person ought not to lie in bed at night and suffer, wondering if someone cares for them. When it's right, you know it. They show you they care, like Grandpa Ted did with you. I feel he's my grandpa, too, even if I never knew him."

"He would have loved you, Tyler. Being honest with another person you care about is very important. No game playing. There doesn't have to be. Your grandpa Bob and I were honest with one another from the start. We let each other know how we felt. That's how it ought to be. Now you remember that. Your heart feels happy, and you feel secure about the person's affection for you."

He stood, circled the table, and hugged her.

Grace thought, This boy—loving him and being loved by him and by his grandfather—this and the other dear people are what make my life worth living.

26

One Crisis After Another

With all the talk about scams, Amelia almost forgot that Mike had admitted to her that he had been to see her eye doctor and had gotten a diagnosis of fast-growing cataracts. He was terrified of surgery.

"I knew someone, once, whose cataract surgery was botched. His sight was worse afterward. It was terrible. I'm not taking that chance," Mike said.

"So you're going to go blind, Mike? You're a photographer. You need your eyesight to create, to make a living. My ophthalmologist is a wonderful surgeon. Let me make an appointment for you. I'll drive you and go into the examining room with you. If you decide to go ahead, you'll stay with us while you recuperate. Years ago, my Thomas had cataracts removed from both eyes, and he was just fine. His sight came back perfect. It's a safe procedure these days."

Mike remained adamant, until one afternoon, alone in his lab, he stumbled and fell, spilling a pan of chemicals onto the floor. The liquid splattered onto his arms, hands, and face. It stung his skin and powerful fumes saturated the small, closed room and caused his eyes to burn. Scrambling to his feet, Mike made his way to the sink. Again and again, he splashed cold water on his hands, face, and eyes, and lay wet towels on his arms and across his eyes. Then, groping his way along the wall, he reached the phone and dialed Amelia.

"My God, Amelia, I've had an awful accident. Please, come quickly. I need to get to the eye doctor as fast as possible." His voice rose hysterically and Mike broke into tears. "It's an emergency. Will they see me without an appointment? Oh, God, hurry, hurry, Amelia."

"I'm sure someone in his office will see you, Mike. I'm on my way. Keep washing your skin and eyes with fresh water. Don't go back into that darkroom. Don't try to clean up the mess, you hear me? Stay out of there. I'm on my way."

"Amelia, you think I'm crazy? I wouldn't put my foot in there for love or money. Hurry, please."

Amelia left a note on the fridge and ran out to her car. It took all her self-control, and the knowledge that a ticket would delay her, to stay within the speed limit. At sixty miles an hour, she felt as if she were crawling. Twenty minutes later she arrived at Mike's workshop.

Mike was a wreck. His clothes, bleached white in spots where the solution had touched them, smelled of the strong solution. His arms dripped water, and he had wedged a wet cotton pad between his left eye and his glasses. The other eye, when Amelia looked at it carefully, appeared to be more clouded than she remembered. Amelia did not call the doctor's office but hurried Mike to the car.

"Everything's a blur," he said as they drove to Asheville. He was trembling. "I can't make out individual trees. They're all lumped together, a blur of trees. Oh, my God, I'm going blind, Amelia. What am I going to do? Why didn't I listen to you? Oh, God, don't let me go blind." He clutched her arm and began to sob.

"Take a deep breath, Mike. It's going to be all right. Let go of my arm. I'm driving. You won't go blind. My doctor is excellent. You'll be fine. Take a deep breath. Sit back. Try to relax. Keep that wet cloth over your eyes. It's going to be all right."

"How can it be all right? I'm going blind. I can't see a thing with my left eye."

"Your left eye has a wet patch over it."

"And now I'm losing my mind. I didn't remember putting that on there. Ah, yes, now I remember. The light hurt. You told me to keep it wet. Was that the right thing to do, do you think? Should we stop at a drugstore and get some kind of eye drops? The pharmacist would know what to do, wouldn't he?"

"Mike. We're almost at the doctor's office. That's the best place for you to be. They'll know exactly what to do."

"But they might not take me right away. I might have to sit for hours." Mike hugged himself, rocked, and moaned.

"You're working yourself into a frenzy. Now, just calm down. See, we're here." Amelia pulled into the parking lot of her doctor's office. "Okay, now, take a deep breath."

Mike did as instructed.

"Good! You ready? Let's go in."

A nurse hustled Mike into an examining room. A few minutes later, the doctor walked in. "Let's see what we have here," he said.

"Am I going to go blind, doctor?" Mike spoke in a whisper.

"Let me have a look."

The examination took perhaps seven minutes, and then the doctor shoved back his stool. "Lucky for you, that solution didn't actually get into your eyes. It burned your arms.

The fumes must have been potent." He lifted Mike's left arm. "See the spots? It must have splattered, and wherever it hit you, it burned your skin. I'll give you a prescription for an ointment to reduce the swelling and ease the pain. The burns aren't third degree. You may have some discoloration of the skin, but nothing requiring plastic surgery. They'll heal. Now, about your eyes."

Mike leaned forward. He gave Amelia a quick, anxious look. "Am I going to be blind?"

"Certainly not. You've got advanced cataracts that need to be removed. Another few weeks and all you'll see is a blur. Tell the desk to set you up for surgery, first opening I have." The doctor stood and shook Mike's hand. "And don't worry. I guarantee you, afterward you'll marvel at how bright everything is, the sky, colors, everything." He nodded at Amelia and left the room.

"You see," Amelia said as they walked to the checkout desk. "I told you. It's a nothing operation. You're going to have the surgery, right?"

Mike tossed his head. "Do I have a choice? Tell me, do I?"

When they left the building, Mike had scheduled a pre-op appointment for one week from today, with surgery the following morning.

"I won't have to go to the hospital, thank heaven. They have their own outpatient clinic." He smiled at Amelia and squeezed her hand. "I simply can't tell you how relieved I am. I detest hospitals. People get sick in hospitals. I know someone who got an infection in a hospital and died." He turned to her. "Thank you for everything. I've been such a crybaby, and you've been so patient and good to me."

"Isn't that what a friend is for? I'm glad you're going to have the surgery."

"Look what it took to get me there. I could have spilled that stuff into my eyes and really messed myself up."

"But you didn't, and it will all come out just fine."

Mike fumed and fussed all that week. In the wee hours of the morning, he paced his living room. Each day he picked up his cell phone to call and cancel his surgery, but reason prevailed, and he snapped the phone shut and shoved it back into his pocket. He could not work and avoided going to his workshop, even though Amelia had a cleaning company come in and give the place a thorough scrubbing.

When Amelia arrived to drive Mike to the clinic, he was in his pajamas and robe. They entered a charade in which she followed him about his living room with his clothes draped over her arm.

"Please, Mike, get dressed, and let's go." She tapped her wristwatch. "We only have ten minutes before we must get on the road."

"I'm canceling." He handed her his cell phone. "Call and tell them I'm not coming."

"I most certainly will not. Listen, Mike, you cancel and it could take weeks to reschedule."

"I'm not going under the knife. I absolutely will not have anyone cutting at my eye."

"It's laser they use, not a knife."

He stopped circling the couch and stared at her. "Really?"

"Really." She dumped his clothes on a chair. His shirt slid onto the floor. "You do what you want. Go blind. I'm out of here."

Before she reached the front door, he grabbed her arm. "No, wait. I'll get ready. It won't take a minute. Please, don't go."

After his surgery, Mike stayed at the ladies' home. In a few days, when he felt better, he made light of the surgery and told everyone who visited—the neighbors, Pastor Denny, everyone who came—"It was nothing at all; it went fabulously."

As the days passed and his eyes healed, the world did indeed grow brighter and more beautiful, and Mike felt as if he had climbed a mountain. Still, he hesitated to go outside or back to work.

"We want you to come to the christening party we're having for baby Sarah tomorrow." Grace stood at the foot of his bed where he lay resting. The sound had been turned off the television and the commercial flashed and blinked.

"Oh, I couldn't," Mike said. "It's too soon for me to go anywhere."

"Too soon for you to walk from this bedroom, this cave you're living in, to the living room to sit in a chair with your back to the window?" Grace asked. "Nonsense. The party's at two in the afternoon. You be there, or I'll come in here and drag you out."

Prior to Zack's accident on the mountain, Sarina had asked Pastor Denny to christen Sarah in the little church on Cove Road. When Hannah questioned her decision, Sarina asked, "It's what you do in this country, isn't it?"

"Many people do, but you're Hindu. Why would you want to christen Sarah in a church?"

"Because we live in America, and regardless of what Zachary says, I want her to be like everyone else."

"Conformity isn't always the best course of action," Hannah said, and then she decided to drop the matter. Sarina had enough on her hands with Zachary, who still wore a cast, pouted, and complained all day. Since his accident he was more deeply self-involved and distant, and Hannah was concerned.

"The stairs are too much for me to cope with," he had said, insisting that he sleep downstairs on the couch. "It's just for now."

Hannah wondered if he was bipolar, the way his moods shifted from sunny and pleasant to gray and sulking. Whatever he was or was not, he made them all nervous.

"I feel as if I have to walk on eggs around Zack," Sarina said. "I had such hopes for us, but now I do not know my husband any longer." Tears welled in her eyes.

Hannah remembered feeling that way with Bill Parrish. She worried about Sarina and wished that Zachary would simply disappear.

Grace stretched the christening from a nice little affair attended by the extended family and a few friends into a party that included their neighbors on Cove Road. In preparation for the event, she cleaned for days, baked cakes, and made egg and tuna salad, ham and chicken finger sandwiches, and spreads.

Amelia, Miriam, and Sadie decorated the house with pink balloons.

"Aren't you all going a bit overboard?" Bob asked.

"Sarina's had little enough joy since she came here. I want this to be the nicest day for her, a very special occasion," Grace replied.

On the day of the christening, Max helped his son into the ladies' living room, settled him in the armchair, and pulled up the hassock to support his leg. Grace seated the reluctant Mike near Zachary, but with his back to the window. *They can sit together and commiserate with each other.*

"How are you doing, Zachary?" Mike asked.

"It's Zack, not Zachary," a sullen Zachary replied.

"Sorry."

An uncomfortable silence followed. Then Mike said, "Sorry about your accident. Thank goodness it wasn't your back. That would have been—"

"Hey, I know, worse, right? Well, this is bad enough, and who knows when I'll be able to climb again."

"These things heal. At one time or another, I've broken my leg and my arm and, see"—Mike stretched out and wiggled his left leg and right arm—"they're good as new."

The arrival of their neighbors saved Mike from pursuing further conversation with Zachary. When Amelia sat beside him, he whispered that she must find him another place out of the glare and *away* from Zachary, or he'd go back to his room. Amelia helped Mike change to a seat closer to Bob, by the fireplace.

Zack's voice rose higher and higher. "Damn steep, that hill," he said to Charlie, who took Mike's seat. "Anyone could take a spill up there."

"Right. It's a darn steep mountain. Anyone could have

taken a spill, " Charlie replied. "I used to do a bit of hiking when I was young, and that old hill of Anson's was
always a challenge. The higher you get, the steeper it
gets."

"Why the hell didn't you tell that to my father?"

Charlie frowned. "It never came up. I had no idea you
were going on up there, or I would have."

"Yeh, I just bet you would," Zack muttered.

Charlie changed the subject. "That's one cute baby you
have there. Quite a head of hair she's got on her. Our kids'
heads were as bald as their bottoms." He laughed.

"Are you suggesting that my child's got something wrong
with her because she's got plenty of dark hair?" His eyes narrowed and his voice grew more strident. "What the devil are
you saying? That my child's not good enough for you people
'cause her skin's darker than yours?"

Silence filled the room, and everyone turned to look at
Zack, who shrugged. "Well, everyone comments on Sarah's
hair being dark and thick. What's so cute about bald babies?
They're ugly as pigs. Who wants a kid that looks like a pig?"
His laugh was more of a snort.

Sarina half rose from her chair. Hannah, standing nearby,
slipped an arm about her. "Let it go, Sarina."

Charlie's fists clenched. He stood and glared down at
Zachary, then stepped away. "Your wife is a lovely woman.
Everyone likes Sarina and welcomes your child." His voice
filled with contempt. "We can't say the same about you."
Charlie turned, took Velma's arm, and moments later the
front door slammed behind them.

Amelia raised her glass. "This is Sarah's day, and I propose a toast to her. Good health and long life."

They drank, then Alma hugged Sarina, and she and

Frank left and others drifted away until only the ladies, Sarina, Bob, Max, and Zack remained.

Max glowered at his son. "What in heaven's name is wrong with you? How dare you insult these good people, my neighbors?"

Hannah came to stand beside him. "Not now, Max, for Sarina's sake."

"How could you?" Sarina was a small woman and slightly built. Now she stood, threw back her shoulders, and seemed to grow in stature as she turned to her husband. "How could you be so rude? Those people have been kind to me and to our baby. If they had prejudice against me in their hearts, I would know it. I'm the one who's been around them. You're never around. You don't care about me or about our daughter. I am sickened by what you have done today, Zachary. I am sick to death of you."

"Don't call me Zachary. I hate that name. I'm Zack," he screamed at her. His face grew red. The hair on his arms bristled; his fists clenched as if preparing to strike whoever approached him.

Sarina stood her ground. "I met you as Zachary. I fell in love with Zachary. Zack is a cold name, associated with changes in you that are unbearable. I hate the name Zack, and I will call you Zachary."

If someone doesn't intervene, someone is going to say or do something so below the belt, they'll regret it forever. Grace intervened. "Anyone want a cup of coffee? Cake in the kitchen, anyone?"

No one moved. Then Hannah led Sarina from the room, and the others followed, crowding into the kitchen and leaving Zachary alone in the chair by the window.

The baby awakened and fussed. Immediately, Sarina brushed away tears and took the infant from Miriam, who had been holding her. "I'll take her upstairs and nurse her."

"You don't have to leave," Hannah said. "You can nurse her here."

"It's better I go upstairs," Sarina said. "I need to be alone and calm myself."

Max broke the silence in the kitchen. "That was quite an exhibition. I apologize for my son. His mother must be turning over in her grave."

"You don't own his behavior," Hannah said. "He needs a therapist before he really goes off the deep end."

"I agree with Hannah. The boy's deeply troubled," Bob said.

"How do you make someone go for therapy?" Amelia asked.

No one replied.

Max's face was grim. "In a small town like Covington, we need one another. Zachary knows that. How many times has he seen me plow Frank and Charlie's driveways after a major snowstorm? How many times has Frank been over, any time of the day or night, to fix plumbing in the dairy or the house? If there's a barn to build, we help one another. If someone's ill, we pitch in and get the chores done.

"Charlie's been my friend from my earliest days in Covington. It was Velma's kindness that helped persuade Bella to stay in Covington, when all she wanted was to run back to Atlanta. Velma, bless her, was Bella's friend. She visited Bella frequently during her illness." He brought his fist down on the kitchen table. "Zachary's behavior is unwarranted and unacceptable."

They ate then, trying to comfort themselves with cake and coffee or tea. Suddenly, a heavy thud and the sound of a pot shattering came from the foyer, accompanied by a shout for help.

27

When Will It End?

Zachary was sprawled across the foyer, eyes closed, a leg twisted, an arm outstretched, the other at an odd angle.

Max kneeled beside his son. "Hannah, call nine-one-one."

Hannah picked up the phone in the kitchen.

Sarina started down the stairs. She handed the baby to Miriam and kneeled beside her husband. "Zachary, speak to me. Are you hurt? Talk to me." She clutched her father-in-law's arm and shook it. "Max, he won't open his eyes." Her voice rose. "Is he dead? Tell me, is he dead."

Max felt for Zachary's pulse. "No, he's not dead. He's been knocked out by the fall. He didn't bring a cane, insisted he didn't need it. The fool must have decided to walk without support. Big shot!"

Sarina wrung her hands. "Why is his arm off from his body like that?"

"It appears to be broken. He must have hit the table when he fell. The vase smashed to the floor, and so did he." Bob was on his knees beside Max.

"Get him up. Get him up off of the floor." Sarina's shrill tone surprised everyone. Wild-eyed, she looked from one to the other. "Someone do something. Do something."

Bob put his arm about Sarina.

Zachary shifted slightly and moaned.

Sarina huddled against Bob. "He's been like a crazy man since we left India." Her shoulders shook, and she buried her face in Bob's chest.

"It's best not to move him," Bob said. "The ambulance is on the way."

Grace leaned against the foyer wall and observed the unfolding scene. Amelia had taken Sarah from Miriam and she paced, Sarah crying in her arms. Bob tried to comfort Sarina. Hannah appeared with a blanket and covered Zachary, then walked away.

Sadie huddled against her mother, who stroked her hair, comforting the child. Everyone spoke in whispers.

Grace wondered if Zachary had let go and fallen deliberately, a ploy for sympathy. Even he wouldn't be that stupid, her mind said, but her instincts suggested that Zachary Maxwell was capable of just about anything. Poor Sarina, she thought. My heart goes out to her.

The doorbell rang, and Hannah opened it to the medics carrying black bags, a collapsed gurney, and blankets. They revived Zachary, splinted his arm, and lifted him onto the stretcher. One of the medics spoke to Max, then moved the gurney out, down the steps, and into the ambulance. Sirens wailed as they drove off to the hospital in Asheville.

"Hannah and I will take Sarina to the hospital," Max said.

"Can I leave Sarah? There are bottles in the fridge at home. Can I leave her with you?" She looked from Grace to Amelia.

"Certainly," Grace said. "You go, and don't worry about Sarah."

Zachary had broken his arm. He had dislodged the pins that held his ankle together and sustained a concussion. The emergency room doctor wanted to admit him for observation. It was then Max learned that his son was uninsured, the bill for Sarina's delivery was unpaid.

"Damn him," Max said to Hannah. "I'd have put him on the dairy's medical, if he'd said something." An embarrassed Max assumed responsibility for his son's emergency room treatment and the orthopedist's services, but refused to pay for hospitalization.

"That would cost me two thousand dollars a day for him to lie in bed and be pampered by nurses. He can darn well recover at home," he told Hannah.

"You'll have to sign him out," the doctor said. "He's going to wake up in a lot of pain. He'll need care. He'll have to use a bedpan. It would help if you hired a private nurse for a couple of days." He scribbled instructions on a sheet of paper. "Follow this routine and bring him to my office in ten days, unless the swelling in that ankle doesn't go down, or he has memory lapses, or blurred vision."

Max did not care. He was indifferent to this son of his. If anyone deserved to suffer and hopefully learn something from it, it was Zachary.

It was dark when an ambulance transported Zachary back to Cove Road. Hannah had phoned Anna, and she, Jose, and their cousin Irena, newly arrived from Charlotte, had prepared the dining room, moved out the table and chairs and brought down a bed from upstairs. A pot of Anna's chicken and rice sat on the stove waiting for them.

Although medicated, Zachary moaned and groaned all night. Sarina paced, frantic that he was suffering.

"I had a cousin moaned like that even if he got a little splinter in his finger. He say it make him feel better," Anna said. "Don't worry so much. They fix his ankle again, and his arm, too. He gonna be fine after a while." She looked into Sarina's troubled eyes. "He's tough, Señora. Nobody travel around the world like he done and not be tough."

Sarina sat in Max's oversized recliner. Tears ran down her cheeks and dripped from her chin. She covered the baby's head and felt the hot tears on her hand. *Ironic, water was dripped on Sarah's head at her christening, and my tears are christening her with my pain. Please, Krishna, God, whoever is listening, do not give my child an unhappy life with unhappy parents.*

She would not raise Sarah in a strife-ridden home. Divorce in America was not a disgrace. Her family would not bear witness to her shame. Twice during the long night, she nursed and changed Sarah, and took comfort from the baby's softness and her sweet helplessness. She reminded herself that she was loved by many in Covington, even if not by Zachary, and that once she was divorced, Hannah, the ladies, and Max would surely help her find a job and a place to live.

Sarah's small body grew heavy on her chest, and Sarina sank deeper into the big chair and closed her eyes. Her mind wandered through her childhood home, seeing her mother in traditional Indian clothing standing in the kitchen instructing the cook, who chopped onions on a dark wood table. Her father sat behind his huge mahogany desk in his office, mulling over a ledger, his glasses low on his long, narrow nose.

In her mind, she wandered down the hall and entered the room she had shared as a child with her two sisters. The room was large. Tall windows offered a view of the garden and lotus pond. Pink lotuses were in full bloom.

The smell of curry filled her nostrils, and she heard the house servant, Fatima, call them all to dinner. Home! Familiar food! Rice rather than potatoes. Mangos and fragrant spices. Dear Krishna, how she missed it all.

Upstairs, Hannah lay in bed and worried. Zachary was hostile and mean-spirited. His manner of speaking to Sarina bordered on verbal abuse. Dark circles ringed the young woman's eyes, and Sarina was increasingly impatient with Sarah, who had been the light of her life and source of joy.

"Zachary's behavior is intolerable for Sarina," she told Max. "I think she won't stay with him much longer if he continues his crude behavior."

"Aren't you overreacting? He isn't any worse than he was."

"Which is bad enough, and he *is* worse. You don't see it. You're busy with the sale of the dairy. It's all happening so fast. You're off to Asheville talking to lawyers, having the cows checked by the vet, and preparing everything for shipping. There's the emotional aspect of it, too, giving up the dairy. You're exhausted every night. Your heart is heavy with the loss of it."

The next morning, carrying Sarah upstairs, Sarina slipped and fell on the stairs. She lay there weeping, sheltering the baby with her body, until Hannah heard her and rushed to help.

"Are you hurt?"

Sarina shook her head. "Just so tired, I think I cannot take another step."

"I'll help you up. Go and lie down. I'll have Anna bring you up breakfast." Hannah found Max out back. "We've got to do something, Max. Zachary must go into therapy." She told about Sarina falling. "That girl's going to collapse."

"I'm sorry, Hannah. You're right. I didn't realize. What shall we do?"

"Let me think about this."

Hannah went directly to the end of the hall, to the baby's nursery, and knocked.

A soft voice answered. "Come in." Sarina rocked, her head thrown back, her eyes closed. The baby seemed to be sleeping on her shoulder. "She finished nursing! I have been sitting here looking at her. She has grown so fast, has she not, Hannah? I think when she grows, she will not be small as I am."

"She's beautiful, and you're a good mother, Sarina."

"She cannot count on affection from her father."

"Zachary doesn't spend much time with her, does he?"

The corners of Sarina's mouth turned down. "Hardly at all, and he is very demanding and unpleasant. If she cries, he puts her on the bed, in a chair, even on the floor, and walks out."

"You're very tired, my dear," Hannah said.

Sarina sighed. "I am weary to the marrow of my bones."

"Max and I have been talking about how things are with Zachary. Would you like to go home and visit your family, let them see the baby?"

Sarina's eyes brightened, and then the light in them faded. She shook her head. "I cannot. They will say to me, 'Where is your husband?' and I will cry, and they will know how bad things are, and I will be shamed. My mother will say, 'I told you to marry your own kind, like your sisters did.' " She shook her head vigorously. "My father will demand that I never return to America. The servants will speak about me behind my back, and my sisters will pity me. I cannot go home without my husband, even for a visit."

For a time, the soft squish of the rocker was the only sound in the room. "I understand," Hannah said. "We were wondering if you think your husband would benefit from counseling."

"I do not know much about counseling, but from what I have heard, it can be helpful. He would never go. He is too stubborn and arrogant."

"What if he thought you would leave him? Would he consent to go, then?"

A long silence followed. Sarina rose and placed the sleeping baby in her crib. "Maybe he would. I do not know. Once, I could have said yes, he would do anything for me, but now I do not know. I do not think he would. May I speak to you freely, Hannah?"

"Of course."

"We lived in India for two years, and he was never like this. He was very considerate, not only of me but also of my mother and aunts. Why has coming back to his home affected him so badly? What is between him and his father? Why does he not feel joy? What does he want?"

"I believe it stems back to his childhood, but what it was, what happened between him and his father or even his mother, I don't know."

"I have thought I will leave him, get a divorce. I can do that without his consent, yes?"

"I believe you can. Maybe then he would get some help, and maybe that would make things better."

"Maybe. I do not know what to do anymore." Sarina lowered her head.

Hannah had heard intervention mentioned regarding someone with a drinking problem. Family and close friends, his minister, and a counselor had gotten together with the person involved and confronted him, each person speaking from his or her heart regarding their relationship with the person, and it sometimes worked. The person involved in that matter had agreed to get help. Hannah needed more information and the name of a counselor who knew about such things. She would talk to Denny Ledbetter.

"Nothing can be decided today. Stay here and rest. Anna and Jose will see to Zachary's needs."

"Thank you, Hannah. I will do as you say."

28

Denny Ledbetter

After church on Sunday, Ida McCorkle dawdled while June waited impatiently by her car. When the last hand had been shaken and the last parishioner walked away from the church, Ida approached Pastor Denny. She leaned close and whispered, "Pastor, I gotta talk with you."

Ida's simple cotton dress with its white collar, her tan straw hat tipped ever so slightly to one side, and the manner in which she clasped her simple brown faux leather purse with both hands reminded him of a woman in a Norman Rockwell calendar tacked to his kitchen wall.

"Are you free tomorrow?" he whispered back, wondering why they were whispering.

Ida nodded. "Eleven in the morning?"

He nodded, attempting to appear casual rather than conspiratorial, which is how he felt with June standing by her car, tapping her foot, one hand on her hip and staring at them.

"Mama, will you *please* hurry up?" A faint smile crossed her lips. "Sorry, Pastor Denny. Eddy's waiting on us for lunch."

"I'm coming, June. I'm coming." Clutching her hat

against a sudden brisk wind, Ida hurried toward her daughter.

"What were you and the pastor talking about?" June asked as they drove home.

"I was telling him how much I liked his sermon."

"That sermon about Job? I was bored out of my mind. I've had enough of those old Bible tales. I like it when he talks about what's going on in the world and refers it to Jesus' teachings." She checked her watch. "Lord, we're late. I stuck that pork roast in the oven before we left and told Eddy to take it out at noon. I hope it isn't dry as cardboard."

"It'll be fine. You're a right good cook," Ida said, hoping to mollify her daughter. She wanted to ask about May. May had been on her mind of late, and she missed her. She'd about decided the time had come to make it up with her daughter. But May was living with Lil, and from the day she'd met her sister-in-law those many years ago, something hadn't sat right between them. She had never trusted Lil, though she couldn't rightly say why. Their babies were born the same year. They'd cooked for and cleaned up after family picnics, and one fall she and Lil spent the good part of a week weeding the family cemetery, getting it ready for the annual family gathering.

Fact was, Lil hadn't never done her nothing. Still, there was something about Lil, the way she kept her nose in the air, like she was better than anyone else. Ida had never told anyone how she felt about Lil, but she sure didn't want to feel beholden to her just 'cause she took May in to live with her.

"How's May doing?" Ida asked.

"May's doing fine. She's going to finish up her course next month. They have a ceremony at the technical college. I'm going to see her get her certificate. You want to go with me? Eddy won't go. He says graduations bore him. May would sure like it if you were there."

"I'll think on it."

Don't think so long that the day comes before you give me some excuse why you're not going to go, June thought. "I know you're fond of Billie, Mama, but Billie's got him a new girl and new life, and May's kids are all busy with their families. They're glad enough their ma's getting on with her life, but none of them are going to see her get her paper. That's a shame. I wish you'd stop being mad at May. She's got her a job waiting for her at Pardee Hospital. She's making something of her life. We all ought to be happy for her."

"Lil going to the graduation?" Ida leaned against the car door, her body turned away from June.

Exasperation crept into June's voice. "Tell me the Lord's truth, Mama. What's Aunt Lil done you're so against her? She's been right good to May, and you should be glad for that."

"I'm too old to be beholding to Lil."

"Aunt Lil is mighty lonely since Uncle Jimmy passed, and May's been good company. There's no question of you being beholding to her."

"Well, then, that's different. I'll go with you. I'm not gonna let her be the one to see my daughter finish her classes and me not there."

June rolled her eyes and turned the car into her driveway.

Ida approached Denny's office with trepidation. Nervous as a cat, she'd visited the bathroom a dozen times before leaving the house and now her mouth was so dry, she wondered if she'd be able to say a word.

Pastor Denny greeted her warmly, offered a seat, and settled into a chair across from her. "How have you been, Ida?"

"Same as Sunday," she replied, avoiding his eyes. "Fine, I guess."

Denny waited. Counseling parishioners made him uncomfortable. His training consisted of several courses in pastoral counseling followed by two months of practice, during which he never felt adequate to the task. It seemed like he could never fill Pastor Johnson's shoes. Lately he was called to do more listening and counseling, and he sure could use some reassurance that he was doing it right.

"Your job as a pastoral counselor is to listen," an impatient instructor had once told him. "And if that's not enough, quote scripture. The answer to every man's problem lies in the scriptures."

People and their problems were complicated, and spouting scripture at them had never seemed like an appropriate response to Denny. Pastor Johnson had advised patience and listening.

"They solve their own problems," he had said. "You act as a sounding board, and in time they'll figure it out for themselves."

Desperate for further education on the subject, Denny invested in a library of counseling and psychology texts, which further confused him, for they presented a wide range of theories and techniques. With the questioning of Freud's theories in the seventies, the field had been blown wide open, and there were models from passive to direct intervention to active confrontation. There were so many techniques and approaches to counseling these days, it would take years to explore all the possibilities.

Ida's presence reminded him that he had made a mess of it with May McCorkle. Never mind. She had said that without his help she would never have had the courage to go to A-B Tech. That was good, wasn't it? But what else would she say? All he remembered was the look on her face that day when Charlie arrived and saved his hide. What should he have said to May that day? How does any counselor handle a direct approach from a client? He hated that he had taken the coward's way out. Denny assumed, incorrectly, that it was concern for May that brought Ida to his office.

Ida twisted her handkerchief into a knot, untwisted it, and twisted it again.

Perspiration coated Denny's upper lip and dampened his armpits. He waited. Lord, but waiting for someone to speak was hard.

"I done gone and done a terrible thing," Ida said.

Denny leaned forward. "I'm listening."

"I done lied. I boldface lied in God's church."

"You lied? What did you lie about?"

"I didn't tell no one that I was scammed good as the next one. That scammer fellow talked me out of a lot of money, too." Her face vanished behind a large, plaid handkerchief, and she blew her nose. "I been sick regular with first one thing and then another. It's gonna kill me if I don't confess." She crossed her arms over her chest. "Now, I done said it."

"Did anyone in church ask you directly if you had been scammed, Ida?"

"Well no, they didn't." He knew nothing of her conversation with June and Eddy, and she wasn't about to tell him.

"You didn't lie, then," he said.

Her expression changed. The lines about her mouth softened. "Well, ain't that right, Pastor? I never did tell no lie to no one in that church, now, did I? I never did tell June and Eddy what happened. They would have gone on about my being a foolish old woman, getting soft in my head. I seen what Margaret Hank's children done to her, when she started getting forgetful." Ida's eyes grew wide. "She's living in one of them old-age homes in Enka. I been there to see her." She tapped her temple. "If anything will make a person soft in the head, it's living in one of them old-age homes. Seems to me they sit around waiting to die."

Denny nodded. He ought to ask her if her daughter and son-in-law had asked her directly if she had been scammed. He did not. *Lord, forgive me. Sometimes it's better not to know certain things.*

Ida smiled, folded the plaid handkerchief, and tucked it into her purse. "I heard tell you been a good help to people around here." She stood, smoothed her dress, and ran her palms across her hair, pushing it back from her face. "I didn't tell June and Eddy, and I don't intend to tell them. I'm hoping confessing to you is gonna quiet my mind."

"You won't tell them?"

She shook her head so hard it dislodged a bit of hair from the bun at the back of her neck. She tucked it away. "No sir, I ain't gonna tell them nothing. It weren't their money, and they don't need to know. Done is done!" She rubbed her hands together as if she were washing them.

Ida was right, Denny thought, in her appraisal of how they would treat her. He felt sorry for her. She was elderly and didn't need this stress. It was enough, what she must be going through with May.

"You've confessed to me, and I don't think telling them

about it now matters much. Why don't we sit here a minute and pray about this? Ask God's forgiveness and his
blessing."

They bowed their heads and prayed silently. Then he
said, "Amen, Lord, and thank you for your blessing."

"Amen, Lord, and thank you for your blessing," Ida repeated. She opened her eyes and smiled at Denny. "Bless
you, Pastor Denny. You done helped me plenty this day."

"Ida," he asked. "How is May? Have you seen her?"

"She's going to get her certificate right soon. I'm going
with June to see her get it."

"That's good. You'll congratulate her for me?"

"Yes, Pastor, I'll tell her you sent your best."

"We're all proud of her."

She stood, plopped her hat back on her head, and left.

Denny sat in his office thinking about Ida's visit and what
she had said about his parishioners saying nice things about
him, saying that he had helped them. Which ones? he wondered, making a mental list of those he had seen recently.

Timmy Herrill and his wife had been in. Timmy was still
out of work, almost a year now, poor fellow, and the Herrill
household strained at the seams. Charlie had been in to talk
about it. He and Velma were considering taking an apartment in Weaverville and giving over the house to the young
family. If they moved, he would miss them. He hoped they'd
still come to church.

Molly and her husband had dropped in to talk about one
of their boys, Alfred, recently diagnosed with ADD, attention deficit disorder. Where did these names come from?
Boys were loud, and some boys were wilder and louder than
others. He himself had been a handful at the orphanage.
Today there were labels for everything. On the other hand,

Denny had seen Alfie, as they called him, tearing up and down Cove Road on his bike, popping wheelies and yelling at the top of his lungs, annoying everyone. He was rather a wild one.

Denny chewed the end of his pencil. Alfie had almost crashed his bike into Pastor Johnson one time, rest his soul. Denny had grabbed the pastor's arm and yanked him onto the grass as the boy careened past. He and Pastor Johnson had sat on the stoop of the church for a time then and talked about whether to call Alfie's mother at Bella's Park, where she worked. Denny had been gung ho to do this. Pastor Johnson restrained him.

"Kids will be kids," he said, "Let's not make a big issue of this."

He missed Pastor Johnson; the community missed him. Well, no sense sitting here commiserating with himself over the loss of his friend and surrogate father. He could never fill his shoes, but he could do his best to tend the old man's flock.

Denny pushed up from his chair, Pastor Johnson's chair. He moved slowly down the narrow hallway to the sanctuary. Light from the stained-glass windows played across the pews and aisle. Denny slipped into a pew, bowed his head, and prayed for courage and guidance. *And please, God, don't send me anyone else to counsel for a while.*

29

Photography Workshop in New Mexico

Several days later, Amelia announced her intention to sign up for a photography workshop in Santa Fe, New Mexico. "Miriam and Sadie are going with me, and I am so excited."

Across the table, Hannah looked up and raised an eyebrow.

"Oh, all right, it's not about their wanting to shoot pictures. I want to bring them with me. Miriam's never been out west, and Sadie's thrilled. Santa Fe is special, and working with Martha Dinsk is very special."

"Who's she?" Hannah asked.

"Only a world-renowned photographer, who photographs for national and international magazines. She rarely does workshops, and when she does, they're usually in places like Bangkok or Kenya, places I probably would never go. This is a great opportunity."

"You're a professional. Aren't you advanced for a workshop?" Grace asked.

"I'd think by now you'd be giving workshops," Hannah said.

"It's for advanced photographers. But there's more to it. It'll give Miriam, Sadie, and me a chance to do a family thing."

"So, when do you leave?" Grace asked.

"In ten days."

"It's a wonderful idea, Amelia. You'll have a great time," Grace said. "I'm glad Miriam and Sadie are going."

The sign read *Santa Fe City Limits.* Miriam slowed the rented car and sighed with relief. The winding drive up the mountain was finally over. What surprised Miriam was that she actually liked this high, wind-blown desert environment. The endless vistas and the deep blue sky thrilled her.

Following directions provided by Martha Dinsk, they drove past adobe houses that sat behind thick, sand-colored walls, until they came to their hotel on a main thorough-fare.

Built in traditional adobe style, the lobby of the hotel boasted low wooden beams, soft leather chairs and sofas, and oval fireplaces, which fascinated Sadie, who stood before one huge fireplace with her mouth agape.

Their room's comfortable leather chairs, tall Hopi polychrome-pot lamps, and Ganado red, black, and gray rugs charmed them. Amelia relaxed and rested. For the first time that day, Miriam relaxed, but not for long. At four that afternoon, the workshop students were scheduled to gather with Martha Dinsk in a third-floor meeting room.

"I don't want to leave Sadie our first night," Miriam said.

A knock sounded on the door and Amelia said, "I forgot, we arranged for someone to stay with Sadie. The person is probably here now. If you want to come with me, Miriam, to meet Martha Dinsk, she can take Sadie for a walk."

Sadie piped up. "You go with Grandma, Mama." She

walked toward the door and opened it. A young woman, perhaps nineteen years old, stood in their doorway, smiling.

"Sadie?" She extended her hand. "I'm Laurie Landrey."

"Mama," Sadie said, "Laurie and I will sit in front of that big fireplace in the lobby. Do you think we could do that, Laurie?"

The young woman nodded.

"Yes, we could do that, and then maybe we could walk down to the Plaza. It's pretty at night, and there's music."

Miriam nodded. "Whatever you want to do is fine. You will look after her, Laurie, and keep ahold of her hand if you go out."

"I'll do that. Sadie will be just fine. We'll have a good time."

Amelia and Miriam hurried to the meeting room, whose rounded windows set deep in thick masonry walls offered a distant view of lavender mountains. A dozen men and women had already arrived, and several turned as they entered and nodded greetings.

Dressed in casual slacks and a denim shirt, Martha Dinsk, a small, hardy-looking woman with twinkling blue eyes and a boyish haircut, welcomed them with enthusiasm.

"I'm delighted to be here with you, and to welcome each and every one of you to this workshop, especially as it will be my last in America for several years," she said. "I anticipate we shall have a glorious time. There's no place to do photography like Santa Fe with its marvelous light." She handed folders to everyone.

"All that you will need to know about this week—our

daily agenda and a few general rules to keep us on track—is here. I'll go over this with you tomorrow after you've read it and in case you have questions. Right now, we still have enough light for a shoot, and the light is perfect." She waved toward the windows. "So grab your gear and meet me in the lobby in five minutes."

Amelia and Miriam hastened to their room, gathered up camera bags and Amelia's tripod, and waited impatiently for the elevator to take them to the lobby. Moments later, led by Martha, an excited troop of photographers followed her onto the street and hastened toward the Plaza, the historic heart of Santa Fe.

A man, his name tag reading Ben Mercer, fell into step with Amelia and Miriam. "I guess everyone came with someone, except me. May I walk with you?"

Miriam nodded.

Amelia said, "When you're working at one of these workshops, you're essentially alone. You get completely absorbed in what you're doing. But you must know that."

"This is only my second workshop. I called so often and pleaded so well, Martha finally let me come. Have you been at it long—photography?" he asked.

"About six years," Amelia replied.

"And you?" he asked Miriam.

"Not very long. Everything I know, my mother, Amelia, has taught me." *It seems easier not to explain the relationship further. Sadie calls Amelia Grandma.*

Ben tapped his camera. "I haven't exhibited or had anything published. Have you?"

"Amelia has," Miriam said. "She has published several books, and her work is exhibited and sold in a gallery in New York City."

"I'm impressed," Ben said.

"We'd best hurry." Amelia picked up her pace. "Sounds like Martha's giving instructions."

Martha was saying, "Santa Fe is the oldest capital in the United States. It's seven thousand feet above sea level and surrounded by the Sangre de Cristo Mountains." She pointed to a long, low adobe building. "That was the Palace of the Governors; it's a museum now. We'll set up here. It's a perfect place to do close-up and wide-angle shots. I assume you all brought tripods?"

Everyone but Miriam carried a tripod across their shoulder.

Martha's eyes swept the semicircle of students. "My protocol is for you to shoot a minimum, but not a maximum, of two rolls of thirty-six slides every day."

Amelia pulled out the green sheet from the packet distributed to them earlier and read quickly down a list. The subjects to be photographed included landscapes, architecture, nature, which she said meant flowers or animals, and candid shots of adults and children.

Martha said, "We'll be going on two field trips. We'll go by bus to Taos Pueblo tomorrow. The bus leaves from the portico in front of the hotel at eight A.M. sharp, so breakfast will be at seven. Another day, we'll travel to the old mining town of Madrid. The remainder of the days, you'll be on your own. The assignments are on the sheets I gave you. Each night you'll turn in your film, and the following evening I'll critique the slides."

Amelia felt a twinge of regret. Bandelier National Monument, an ancient Indian site, was not a field trip. Taos was a living pueblo; Native Americans lived there; but Amelia wanted to shoot the ruins of a long-vanished civilization, and that was Bandelier. Now she set up her tripod as everyone else was doing.

On the ground, under the Palace portico, Native American women sat cross-legged beside beautiful silver and turquoise jewelry and pottery, spread out for sale on exquisitely hand-woven rugs.

Amelia had done her homework; she recognized the rosette style, Hopi bracelets and Navajo bracelets characterized by five oval stones. Stepping forward, she noticed a little girl of about four with flowing black hair and huge dark eyes, sitting close by the wares of an older woman, perhaps her grandmother. The child's legs formed a triangle, within which she stacked seven or eight small drums of different sizes and colors, sometimes placing a smaller drum on the bottom, the wider, bigger drums on top, resulting in the drums toppling over.

As she watched the child's unself-conscious play, Amelia unscrewed her camera from the tripod, squatted, and photographed the child stacking the drums. She caught the swish of little hands, and the blow that sent the drums tumbling and scattering. Head tipped back, her dark hair sweeping the richly woven blanket on which she sat, the child laughed loudly.

Amelia shifted her position: a bit to the left, higher, lower, more to the right as she snapped the shutter again and again. The girl piled the drums and sent them careening beyond the triangle formed by her chubby legs.

The moment she finished, Amelia approached the older woman, offered her card, and apologized for shooting before introducing herself. The child's name was Antonia, and her grandmother was gracious. Amelia thanked them and asked for their address so that she could send copies of the photographs.

A male voice startled her. "That was great, thanks."

Amelia stared at Ben. "Thanks for what?"

"I hope you don't mind. I took a picture of you shooting that little girl."

She moved away from him.

Ben fell into step with her. "Please," he said, "You're annoyed with me. I apologize. I ought not to have done that without asking permission. It's just that I followed your lead and photographed the child, but then I couldn't resist. You're my candid shot. I'd very much like to make amends. Someone mentioned a nice little bistro near the hotel. May I take you and Miriam there for an early dinner?"

"My granddaughter, Sadie, is back at the hotel. She's seven. We'd have to bring her along." *That ought to put an end to that.*

"That would be great," he said. "I'd love for her to come along as well."

Amelia studied his face. She noted an old scar on the side of his chin. His hair was of no particular color, yet his brown eyes were kind, and his smile turned an ordinary face into mildly good-looking. She sensed that he was interested in Miriam. "If it's okay with Miriam, it's fine with me," she said and moved away.

"I'll check with her." Ben walked over to where Miriam squatted, shooting photos of art objects.

The group moved on and turned the corner, disappearing down a side street. Amelia hurried to catch up and did so just as Martha said, "Be alert to the special quality of light in Santa Fe. This time of day the Sangre de Cristo Mountains turn blood red, a spectacular sight."

They rounded another corner and the scarlet mountains came into full view. Everyone grabbed cameras and the shooting continued until scarlet faded to purple and then to gray. Miriam stood beside Amelia and put her arm about her shoulders.

"Look at that crescent moon. It's larger and brighter than any crescent moon I've ever seen. Thank you so much for bringing us along, for giving me this opportunity to see Santa Fe and to be with you. It's very special."

How lovely she is, and how much I love her. "The pleasure is all mine," Amelia said. They turned then, and arm in arm strolled back to the hotel.

Sadie was beside herself with excitement. Laurie had taken her to the square. "Did you see the red peppers hanging from hooks? They looked like small bananas until I got close, and Laurie said they were red peppers. Imagine hanging peppers like that? They're just so funny." She doubled over giggling and tugged on Amelia's arm. "Did you take pictures of them, Grandma? Please, will you take my picture with a bunch of them hanging on either side of my head, like they're my hair?" She stuck out her tongue and panted. "Like long doggie ears." She wagged her head back and forth. "The kids at school will think that's the funniest thing they ever saw."

"Yes, of course. We'll go back there in the daytime, you, your mother, and I, and I'll take pictures of you and the peppers," Amelia said.

"Tomorrow?" Sadie asked.

"Tomorrow you'll go with us on the bus to a place called Taos. There's a pueblo there I think you might like to see."

Sadie skipped about the room and flopped on the bed. "What's a pueblo, Grandma?"

"It looks like a chocolate cake, but it's really apartments where Indians lived years ago, and some of them still live there. The pueblo slopes some, I think, and it looks like layers of chocolate cake about to topple over."

"Can I go inside?"

"I don't think so. They probably don't welcome strangers into their homes, especially people who arrive by bus for an hour or so." Amelia sat on a chair and unlaced her sturdy shoes. She rubbed her toes.

Miriam came in from the bathroom, a towel wrapped about her hair.

"I'm hungry," Sadie said.

"Good Lord," Amelia said. "I forgot we agreed to have dinner with Ben. You still up to that, Miriam? If not, I can give him a call and cancel."

"I think it might be fun, if you're up to it. I'll slip into something. Sadie, get dressed." She extracted a hair dryer from her suitcase.

"Who is Ben, and where are we going?" Sadie asked.

"Ben's a nice man who's along on the workshop. Look at you, you must change that shirt. It has a stain on it. How about your plaid shirt?"

The T-shirt Sadie wore was half off and moments later she was buttoning the front of the plaid shirt. "I like it that I'm going. Sometimes grown-ups don't want children along when they go out to eat," she said.

The waiter set a huge salad bowl and a basket of chips and salsa before them and refilled the adults' wineglasses. Miriam indicated no more Coke for Sadie, who pouted briefly.

Ben half finished his glass of wine. "What do you think of our instructor? Loading us with work, isn't she?" he asked Amelia.

"That's what we're here for," Amelia replied.

"That's true, but it seems to me there's hardly enough time to shoot all of her assignments, what with two days spent on field trips."

"Why do you keep looking at my mama?" Sadie asked.

Ben blushed. "I'm sorry. I didn't mean to be rude. Your mama reminds me of my mother, Arlene."

"Eat your salad, Sadie," Amelia said.

They were silent for a time, then Ben said, "Did you know that five hundred artists call Santa Fe home?"

Amelia nodded. "I hope we have time to visit the artists' street before we leave." She looked at Miriam. "I'd like to get something for Sarina and I want you to pick out something special for your new home."

"What fun, and thank you."

"Where do you live?" Ben asked.

"In Covington, on Cove Road, just down the road from Grandma," Sadie said.

"I plan on renting an SUV and heading down to Bandelier National Monument in Frijoles Canyon in the next few days. They tell me you can stroll right up to old ceremonial kivas." He looked at Sadie. "But if you want to see the inside of a cave dwelling, you have to climb up to it on a ladder." He turned to Amelia. "Would you like to drive out there with me, all of you, any of you? There'll be plenty of room."

"Climb up to a cave?" Sadie's eyes grew wide. "Can I go, Mama? Grandma?" She looked at Ben "If we go, can I climb up to a cave?"

"I think not," Amelia said. "Our schedule seems pretty crowded as it is."

"We could do our landscape and architecture assignments there. I just bought a zoom lens seventy millimeters to two hundred millimeters. I'd like to climb up to a cave and shoot down into a kiva. I hope the two hundred's long enough to give me the shot I want. What do you think?"

"It depends on the distance. You're not into digital, I take it?" Amelia said.

"I have a Canon, and I guess that's what I'm comfortable with. Digital mystifies me. You into digital?"

"Like you, I'm still using my old manual camera," Amelia replied. She reconsidered the Bandelier trip. It was something she and Miriam had discussed, and Ben was right, they could do their landscape, architecture, and maybe even people shots there. Still, she was uncomfortable with the idea of making a trip across the desert with someone they hardly knew. Still! "Would you like to go, Miriam dear?"

"Yes, I'd like to go, and I'd like Sadie to see as much of the area as she can."

"Oh, goody goody." Sadie clapped her hands.

The waiter brought their pizza and they set to eating. When they were done, Ben asked, "Coffee, anyone?"

"Not for me, thanks. I'm not the least bit tired," Miriam said.

"What say Sadie and I go back to the hotel? I'm very tired. It's been a long day. Sadie, you and I can snuggle in bed and I'll read you a story," Amelia said.

Sadie nodded. "Don't be too late, Mama."

"I won't." Sadie kissed Miriam on the cheek.

"Thanks for having dinner with me, and I'm glad we'll all go to Bandelier," Ben said.

For another hour, Miriam and Ben sat over coffee, discussing music and poetry, and she talked about teaching in an inner city school in New Jersey. She was a widow, she said, without giving him details, and loved Covington. She spoke about the ladies Amelia lived with and the close bond between them.

"Life is good," Miriam said.

Ben spoke of his mother, whom he had been very close to and who had died many years ago. She had been to Santa Fe once and loved it. That was why he'd wanted so much to come on this trip. He lived, he said, in Virginia, in Charlottesville, and he was an information technology consultant and building a nice business from his home. He looked deep into Miriam's eyes. "If you didn't mind, I'd very much like to drive down to North Carolina and visit with you sometime. It's not that far, no more than a long day's drive."

"That would be nice." Miriam looked at her watch. "We have a long day tomorrow, Ben. We'd best get back to the hotel."

"He's very nice," Miriam said when she returned to the room she shared with Sadie and Amelia.

"He's courting you," Amelia said.

"I guess maybe he is." Miriam laughed. "And it feels so odd having a man pay attention to me. Still, he's not pushy, thank God."

"He does seem nice," Amelia conceded, thinking for a moment how sad she would be if Miriam married Ben and moved away. Now, that's really selfish of me, she thought. Hannah would knock her on the side of her head if she could read her mind at this moment.

30

Taos Pueblo

Amelia woke at dawn and dressed, then woke the others, and they called room service and breakfasted in their room, which delighted Sadie. The early-morning air was crisp and cool as they boarded the bus for the field trip to Taos Pueblo. Sadie wiggled into the seat alongside Amelia, and Ben sat beside Miriam across the aisle.

With a squeal of hinges, the doors slammed shut and in a belch of exhaust fumes the bus wrested itself from beneath the portico and rumbled into the narrow street. The harsh rocky landscape, broken by stunted dusty-green shrubs, melancholy patches of aspen, and the occasional clump of rust and yellow wildflowers, contrasted with the lush green of North Carolina. They rolled past what the driver said were broken-down miners' cabins and swept past clusters of meandering goats. At San Juan Pueblo, they stopped to buy fresh fruit.

"If you prefer to stay on board," Ben said to Miriam, "I'd be glad to get fruit for us. What do you like?"

"Cherries," Sadie said. "I like cherries best."

A woman in the seat behind them pressed a ten-dollar bill into his hand. "Please, Ben, get some fruit for all of us on the bus, will you?"

Minutes later, Ben climbed back into the bus, and as if he were hosting this outing, he passed around bags of cherries and plums. His warmth and good cheer broke the tension natural among strangers cooped in a small space, and people began to chat easily with one another.

When they reached Taos Pueblo, Amelia and Sadie were last off the bus, and while the others milled about or fiddled with their gear, they stepped away from the group. Amelia scrutinized the famous, well-photographed pueblo.

"It appears to be an apartmentlike complex four stories high in places," she pointed out to the child beside her. She had gotten Sadie a small automatic camera and encouraged her to take pictures. When Amelia made a telescope with her finger and thumb through which she examined shadows, protrusions, setbacks, deep doorways, and high small windows, Sadie followed suit.

Kneeling beside Amelia, Sadie squinted through the frame created by her little fingers. "Grandma," she asked, "where does one apartment begin and the other end?"

"It's hard to tell, isn't it? The plastered clay walls remind me of a mocha iced cake I made for my father's birthday when I was ten."

Amelia studied the flat roofs. Round wooden rafters near the roofline poked several feet out from the walls and broke the monotony of the façade. She wondered if the life of the pueblo occurred on the bare courtyard in front, or on flat rooftops, or on interior patios.

There was, however, no time to ask questions, for as they stood on the dry dusty ground outside the bus, Martha Dinsk launched into explanations and instructions.

"Taos Pueblo is over a thousand years old, the oldest pueblo north along the Rio Grande, one of the oldest inhabited places in the United States. It's a World Heritage Site and a National Historic Site." She raised her hand and pointed. "Notice the scaffold set up along one side? See where those weathered areas are being plastered with fresh clay? They're using the same type of clay and building methods as their great-great-great-grandfathers. New units are added, when needed, and built in traditional style.

"The inhabitants don't like us getting too close or trying to get inside the pueblo itself or taking pictures of them," Martha said. "It's their home, after all, not a museum, and they welcome us to designated areas, shops and"—she waved her arm—"this open courtyard. They sell delicious bread that they bake in those beehive-shaped ovens over there."

Several members of the group began to shoot, while others, cameras dangling at their sides, tripods on their shoulders, ambled toward tables crowded with pottery, jewelry, colorful shawls, blankets, and strings of dried red peppers.

"Do let's get some of that bread. I can smell it," Sadie said.

Amelia looked around for Miriam. She and Ben were strolling toward the ovens, deep in conversation. When they reached the ovens, Ben spread his jacket on the earth, bowed to Miriam, and waved, indicating that she should sit. Miriam threw back her head, laughed, and sank to the ground onto his jacket.

The odor of fresh baking bread drew Amelia and Sadie toward the ovens. An unsmiling Native American woman with a colorful shawl about her shoulders and turquoise necklaces layered about her neck slid a long wooden spatula into the oven and retrieved several loaves of brown-crusted bread. She didn't mind being photographed, had probably done it hundreds of times for tourists and photographers.

Amelia thought that she expected a tip, though the woman did not actually say that. Amelia would have liked to linger, to chat, to ask about pueblo life, but the woman, her baking done and her sale made, turned and walked briskly away.

"I don't think they like tourists," Ben said as Amelia and Sadie joined them under a tree.

"I'm actually embarrassed to be here," Amelia said. "She wasn't very friendly when she sold us the bread."

"This is very, very good bread. Do you like it, Mama?" Sadie asked.

"It's very good bread," Miriam said.

Ben pulled off an end of a loaf. The golden crust crackled as he broke it apart, its odor spilling into the warm air. He held up a chunk. "I agree, Sadie. It's incredible bread."

Amelia's mouth watered, and she shared a small loaf with Sadie. They munched in silence. Above the hard-baked earth of the large, unpaved courtyard, dust-laden heat waves pirouetted in the air. Amelia found the clay tones of the land and buildings harsh and hostile. Her eyes scanned the area seeking a bit of color and found it in the ropes of red peppers affixed to the beams above the sheds that shaded the sale tables.

"Look, Sadie. Red peppers. Let's get some shots of you with clusters hanging on either side of your head."

They strolled over, explained to the vendor what they wanted to do. He agreed. Amelia positioned Sadie and the child preened and posed, turning her head this way and that, laughing. Amelia tipped the vendor, and they ambled back to where Miriam and Ben sat, their heads close in conversation.

Far to one side, beyond the bus, a narrow brook twisted through the crusted landscape, and Martha Dinsk kneeled in the dust to shoot, to work with a small group of students. Some of them stretched out flat on the hard-baked earth, shooting both river and pueblo, probably using a 28 millimeter or 24 millimeter lens, which Amelia knew were Martha's favored lenses. With the river prominent in the foreground of the shot and the pueblo beyond, either the twenty-four or twenty-eight lens offered a perfectly focused shot from river to pueblo.

Lying on the hard, dusty ground or squatting hardly appealed to Amelia, although with Sadie in tow, she rejoined the others by the river. Amelia set up her tripod and camera, attached her longest lens, and faced the pueblo. She adjusted the lens for a perfectly focused pueblo and let the area halfway to the pueblo go soft and blurry. She waited and waited. Her back and legs began to hurt. Most of the others followed Martha to where the Native American woman was again drawing paddles of bread from her oven.

And then it happened! Five children in bright red, green, and yellow ponchos, followed by a bent old man with a walking stick, emerged from a ground-floor doorway of the pueblo. Amelia began to take beautiful photographs and stopped only when the small troupe vanished around a corner.

At that moment Ben, Miriam, and Martha Dinsk joined her. "Yes." Martha turned to Ben. "You can meet the shooting requirements at Bandelier. The hotel will pack you a picnic lunch. Be sure you take plenty of water."

The return trip included a rest stop at a small church, the Santuario de Chimayó, that sat behind high adobe walls and was known locally as the Lourdes of the Southwest. Amelia came away with memories of the red-and-gold carved and hand-painted wooden altar and the reredos, the sacred painting rising to the ceiling behind the altar. She sat for a time in a pew in the dim interior, unwilling to defile the peace of the church by shooting photographs with a flash.

When she left the chapel, Amelia wandered into a small side chapel, whose walls were hung with crutches and written tributes that testified to miraculous healings attributed to the sand taken from a depression in the earth. This depression, she learned, was revered as the well, or El Posito.

"They say that in the year of our Lord 1810, on Good Friday, a light came out of the ground right here, and when they dug, they found pieces of a cross," a woman named Mildred said. "They say this earth heals." She kneeled, dug her hands into the shallow well, and crossed herself with muddy fingers. On the way out, Mildred purchased a vial of muddy sand at the gift shop. "For a friend," she said, blushing. "She's been ill and she believes that this will heal her."

Sadie stood on the sidelines silently observing the adults. Back at the hotel, she turned to Amelia. "Grandma, I like to take pictures. When I grow up, I want to be a photographer and make books of pictures just like you."

When Amelia and Sadie arrived at breakfast the next morning wearing matching crisp white shirts and khaki slacks, they found the others speaking with animation about their plans for their first independent day. Some were going to shoot gates in walls along small side streets. Others talked of strolling the Plaza, visiting the museum, and shooting candid people shots there.

Sadie departed with Laurie, and Amelia took Miriam aside to explain the uses of her new camera, then suggested they spend time shooting together. Leaving Ben and the others behind, they strode away, turned left on a side street, and came face-to-face with a startlingly bright, aqua-colored doorway upon which hung a red pepper wreath.

"Stand by the door, will you, Miriam? I'd like to take a shot of you against that background," Amelia said.

Across the street, a man in a large sombrero grinned and waved at them. It was Ben. "I bought a three hundred millimeter lens and this hat."

Amelia waved, smiled, took Miriam's arm, and guided her toward the Loretto Chapel, famous for its miraculous staircase. Would Ben, she wondered, grasp the idea that they wanted to work alone?

The dimly lit, simply plastered interior of the chapel offered a cool respite from the summer sun, and on a table by the front door Miriam picked up a pamphlet.

"Listen to this, Amelia. According to legend, the corkscrew stairs were built without nails or visible support beams by a carpenter who appeared mysteriously." She read on. "He's said to have completed the job using only a T square, a hammer, a saw, and a tub of water for bending the wood. And the man left without taking money or leaving his name. It's incredible."

Amelia appraised the staircase with its two full turns, no center support, and no supports from either side. "Incredible indeed," she said.

Throughout the day, members of their group came together and moved apart. Ben was ever-present, and Amelia realized that try as she would, she could not keep Ben from Miriam. Besides, it was clear to her that Miriam liked Ben, and that soon Amelia would be taking a backseat to a budding romance.

Later that afternoon, Miriam asked if Amelia minded if she went out with Ben for dinner.

"You go ahead, Mom," Sadie replied. "Grandma and I are going to order up dinner. Then we're gonna take hot baths, wash one another's hair, and curl up in bed with good books." And the matter was settled.

Early the next morning, Ben called their room to say he had rented an SUV for their trip to Bandelier and asked what time would they like to leave.

"We're up, so we might as well go down for breakfast and hit the road," Amelia said. They gathered their gear and headed downstairs.

Carefully, Ben deposited all their equipment in the back of the SUV. Everyone settled in and buckled up. "Let's go to Bandelier," he said and handed Miriam a map. "Can you read a map?"

"Of course I can read a map." Miriam exchanged her dark glasses for reading glasses and studied the map. "Bandelier National Monument. Got a pen? I'll mark it. Easier that way, and I won't have to keep changing my glasses."

He handed her the pen from his pocket. The city fell away behind them. Ben drove slowly and in time they came upon a narrow dirt road to the left.

"I wonder where that goes?" Miriam asked.

"Let's find out." Veering sharply, Ben turned onto the road. A hundred feet along, they stopped for an old man with sun-baked, furrowed skin who ambled along behind a small herd of sheep. The dust-laden wool hung thick on the backs of the sheep, and dust coated the man's hair and clothing.

Ben parked the car and they got out. The old man stopped. *"Buenos dias, señor,"* Ben said.

"What kind of sheep are they?" Amelia asked, after greeting the man.

"Just sheep, señora." The man shrugged.

"After you shear them, do you sell them to the butcher?" Ben asked.

Amelia was relieved when the old man said, "No sell sheep, señor. Sheep *mia familia.*"

Ben peppered the man with questions. Where did he graze his sheep? How many did he have? How old were they? How could you tell a sheep's age? In no time, Ben and the man were chatting like old friends, and Ben was circling the sheep, while the old man identified and named each member of his flock. Next thing they were photographing both man and sheep.

The old man, Eduardo, grinned, exposing large, overlapping teeth. He stood knee-deep in sheep, selected a lamb from the lot, and held it as tenderly as one would hold a baby. At their request, he kneeled among them. Then he leaned against a tree, the sheep clustered at his feet. When it was over, Eduardo and Ben shook hands. Ben handed him a twenty-dollar bill. "For the *familia.*" Ben nodded toward the sheep.

"Sí, señor. Muchas gracias." The man clicked his tongue and departed, the sheep stirring up dust.

"You were wonderful with him," Amelia said

"Voted most popular guy in the eleventh grade," Ben said.

"You're a born salesman."

"My father was a salesman. He traveled. Never at home." Ben shook his head. "Not for me, thank you."

They were cruising at sixty-five miles an hour. Huge mountains loomed on the horizon, yet so clear was the atmosphere that they appeared close enough to touch. Amelia pointed out to Sadie that vast spaces and clear, clean air produced a false illusion of closeness, and that the mountains were actually many miles away.

They drove in silence for a while, Amelia certain that they were lost. Then a sign appeared pointing left. *Bandelier National Monument.* The road changed and became a well-graded two-lane with signs warning of curves ahead. After a time, it straightened, and the terrain grew flat. Ben picked up the conversation where he'd left off.

The inhospitable desert mesa vanished, and they began the descent past tall canyon walls to the sign that read *Frijoles Canyon.* At the park station, they picked up maps and historic information, and within minutes strolled beneath sheer walls on a paved trail among ruins and remains of ancient ceremonial kivas where, in olden days, men had invoked the great spirits. They photographed the crumbled walls of ancient structures and strolled to the end of the canyon, where a small waterfall sent its crystal liquid trickling into a narrow stream.

Sadie took off her shoes and dangled her feet in the cold water. "Oh," she said, pulling her feet out. "It's really cold."

Back at the center of the canyon floor, Ben pointed up. "I'm going up to one of those caves and shoot the kivas. Who wants to climb the ladder?"

Amelia tipped her head up, up, up. Along the length of cliff wall, at what seemed a great height above the canyon floor, a series of solid wood ladders led to dark ragged holes. "That is definitely not for me."

"I'd like to," Miriam said, "but I can't. I'm afraid of heights."

"I'll be right behind you on the ladder," Ben said. "I'd never let you fall."

"I want to climb up and see the cave," Sadie said.

"Why?" Amelia asked. "If you're not comfortable with it, why do it, Miriam?"

Miriam studied the height, the ladder, and Ben. "For the challenge, I guess, and Sadie wants to go up so badly. It's a challenge, I guess. It's time I accepted a challenge."

"We going to climb the ladder, Mama?"

"I think so."

"Wait a minute," Ben said. He pulled a large checkered bandanna from his back pocket, folded it, and tied it across Miriam's forehead. "You can't climb with your hair falling in your eyes."

Amelia rummaged in her purse and found a rubber band. She tied Sadie's hair in a ponytail, then, her heart racing, she watched Miriam place one foot after the other on the ladder and begin a slow ascent, with Ben bringing up the rear. Once she was safely inside the cave, Ben climbed back down and helped Sadie up.

They had not progressed more than five rungs when Sadie looked up and said, "I'm scared."

"Don't look down," Ben said. "I'm right behind you. Don't be scared. You can't fall. I'm right here."

One foot after the other, holding tight to the sides of the ladder, they climbed. Occasionally, Amelia heard Ben's voice urging Sadie, "Don't look down. Take a deep breath." Then they reached the top and climbed safely into the cave to sit side by side on the rough earth, like a family, Amelia thought. They peered down and waved at her. She waved back, her heart in her throat, worried, now, about their climb back down.

Sitting next to Ben, Miriam felt on top of the world. Across the valley, cliff walls rose steeply to a tree-fringed plateau on which, the guidebooks said, a lost civilization had grown corn, sweet potatoes, and other crops.

"It's hard to imagine families living way up here in a cave. Why didn't they live below?" she asked.

"Perhaps they only slept here. I imagine they'd feel safer at night from attacks from men or animals. I know I would. Maybe they spent their day below under less permanent shelters that have long vanished."

"I cannot imagine their carrying water up these ladders," Miriam asked.

"They carried up water?" Sadie asked. "How would they do that?"

"If they did, it was probably in leather pouches," Ben replied.

They sat for a while and watched the less adventurous wander among the kivas. "Look at me, Grandma," Sadie called. "I am sitting on top of the whole world."

Amelia looked up at the trio sitting happily at the edge of the cave. Miriam and Ben might fall in love and get married. Ben might take them away from her. She felt ashamed to begrudge Miriam happiness.

Amelia gave her attention to photography and completed the architecture assignment by shooting ancient ruins. Then she watched the dearest people in her life ease onto the ladder and slowly return to the valley floor.

"I want to thank you, Ben," Miriam said. "I'm quite proud

that I climbed the ladder, and I never could have done it without you. I'd have stood down here, ached to climb up, and wouldn't have had the nerve. You gave me courage."

"Me too," Sadie said.

They left Bandelier and drove up the steep, twisting road through the canyon, and out onto the mesa. After a time Ben asked, "Are you guys hungry? I am. The hotel packed us a picnic lunch."

"I could eat a monster," Sadie said, and rubbed her stomach.

"I could eat a monster, too," Amelia said.

"How about let's park and have us a picnic in that grove of trees, in the shade, over there?" Ben suggested.

"Now that sounds like a wonderful idea," Miriam said.

Moments later, Ben parked in the shade near an old streambed. They removed the picnic basket from the rear, and Amelia spread the plaid tablecloth while Sadie set out paper plates. Miriam and Ben unpacked ham-and-cheese and turkey sandwiches, sealed containers of macaroni salad, sliced ginger pears, iced tea, plastic glasses, and utensils.

Amelia waved them to sit. "Very nice."

They ate in silence. Then Ben pointed to the dry stream-bed. "Water flowed here recently." Leaning forward, with his fingers he traced a bootprint that was firmly fixed and clearly visible in the hardened silt.

"How do you know that?" Sadie bent to look. "It's just dried-up dirt."

"Look closely. That's the print of a modern-day sneaker. This footprint was made after a rain, when the streambed was still muddy, not quite dry."

Miriam joined her daughter and examined the stiff crust. "Yes, I see it." She sat cross-legged on the hard earth and looked about her. "The dryness of this whole place mystifies me, and yet there seems to be so much life below the surface of what appears dead in this heat."

"Heat drought is what they believe drove the inhabitants from this area, from their pueblos and the land," Ben said. "Imagine what that must be like. You've been growing food for years and suddenly no rain and no food, and you have to pack up everything you own and move. I wonder how often that happened to those people?"

"We've moved a lot with just our clothes," Sadie said as if relating the most ordinary of things.

She rarely spoke of her father, a drunk, or of being awakened at night by her mother, being bundled into a car, and going off into the night, until they finally arrived in Covington. Her father had died when he drove his car headfirst into a river. To Sadie that meant she and her mother would never have to move again.

Amelia marveled at Sadie's seeming adaptability, but she wondered if someday those troubled times, with all their fears and stresses, would surface to haunt her. Amelia brushed away such thoughts, brushed off her slacks, and rose. "Do I see wildflowers growing in the grove? Come on, Sadie, let's have a look at them."

They ambled thirty feet into the poplar grove, where red, lavender, yellow, and white wildflowers, most of which Amelia did not recognize, spread in clusters. Carefully, so as not to crush the flowers, they zigzagged to the end of the grove, where harsh desert sand brought the blanket of color to an abrupt halt.

Amelia leaned against a tree trunk, closed her eyes, and felt the heaviness of her lids. It had been a long day, and she was tired. She listened to the wind whispering as it swept toward them, and opened her eyes. In the crystalline air, cloud castles loomed above shadowed, snow-peaked mountains. Happy to be here, in this place, on this day, with Miriam and Sadie and even Ben, she lifted her face to the sky.

"Sit here with me, Sadie." Amelia patted the earth beneath a tree. "Feel the wind? On old maps, the north wind is depicted as a man with plump cheeks straining to blow the winds of the world."

Solemnly, the little girl looked up at her. "Really?"

"When we get home, I'll show you in a book I have. The wind has different names in different places, and sometimes it even has different names for specific things in the same place—like in China *tiu* means to move with the wind like a tree, *yoa* means to float on the breeze, and *fung* can mean either the wind or a person's breath."

"You mean the wind, the plain old wind, has so many different names?" Sadie lifted a hand toward the breeze. "Hello, wind." She turned trusting eyes to Amelia. "You know a lot about a lot of things, Grandma."

Amelia felt a thrill every time the child called her Grandma. "And in Germany, when the wind blows in a certain way, they call it a *foehn* wind." She puffed out her cheeks, and Sadie giggled. "They say when a *foehn* wind blows, people go a little bit crazy and do silly things."

"Like what, Grandma?"

Amelia didn't want to say that the police did not welcome a *foehn* wind, that on nights when a *foehn* wind blew crime increased. "Oh, things like, well, someone might just suddenly begin to dance in the street, or sing for no reason."

Sadie laughed. "What other places call the wind funny names?"

"In Sweden *frisk vinds* are gale-level winds, and China's

first autumn breeze is called the *sz*. Can you imagine, when September comes, people wait for a weatherman to announce a breeze called *sz*?"

"'*Sz*' sounds like bees buzzing," Sadie said. "Will you teach me again about some of the winds, so I can tell about them in school? Our teacher likes it when we share different things with our class."

"I'll write the names of the winds down for you, sweetheart. My goodness." Amelia looked at her wristwatch. "It is getting late, and we have a long ride back to the hotel. We have to turn in our film."

When the workshop came to an end, Amelia moved about saying her good-byes.

Martha Dinsk said, "I've enjoyed having you in the workshop."

"I've loved being here. You've given us a memorable experience, and I appreciate it that you allowed me to bring along my daughter and granddaughter." Amelia no longer felt the need to explain that Miriam was not actually her daughter, but was the daughter of her deceased husband with another woman, a good woman, as Amelia had come to think of Stella, Miriam's mother, also deceased.

"Remember to send me a copy of your books," Martha said. "I look forward to seeing your work. You're a fine photographer. Hard to imagine you've been at it for such a short time."

Standing close together, Ben and Miriam seemed unable to part. "Will I see you again?" he asked. "Can I visit you in

Covington? Would it be all right with Amelia, do you think? I don't think she likes me."

"Amelia takes time to warm up to new people and new ideas. You're welcome to visit us, and I am sure Amelia will be glad to see you, as will Sadie and I."

"The days flew by," he said. "I loved every minute of it. Meeting you was the best part of this entire experience."

"I'm glad Amelia suggested we come along. Thanks to you it was a very special time."

Sadie tugged her mother's hand. "Come on, Mama. Grandma's waiting, and we've got a plane to catch in Albuquerque. I can't wait to get home and show my pictures to Tyler."

31

Randy Attempts Suicide

"Grace." On the other end of the phone, Myrtle Banks was crying.

"What is it? What's happened, Myrtle?" Grace's heart raced. Something terrible had happened.

Myrtle sounded desperate. "Randy. He's done gone and tried to kill himself."

It took a moment for her words to register. Weeks ago, Grace had arranged a meeting for Randy with a counselor at the veterans hospital. Randy had agreed to go and said that, no, he didn't need her to drive him. He had thanked Grace and said, yes, it was time he talked to a counselor. In the weeks that followed, she hadn't heard from Randy, Lucy, or Myrtle, and Grace assumed that he had kept that appointment and was seeing a counselor.

"He tried to kill himself? Randy attempted suicide? Dear God in heaven. When did this happen? Where is he? How is he?"

"Yes, he did try. Lucy found him in the bathtub. He had done gone and cut his wrist, Mrs. Grace. Oh my Lord, but it was too awful, Lucy finding him like that. That child's been through enough, without seeing her brother lying there in . . . in . . . well, you know, and not knowing if he was dead and gone."

For a time, Myrtle was unable to speak. "Lucy thought he was dead. She kept ahold of her senses, though, the Lord bless her, and right off she called nine-one-one and they came a-runnin' and carried my poor boy to the hospital. The men who came with the ambulance said if he'd a cut both his wrists, he'd a died for sure, what with losing so much blood and all."

"He promised to see the counselor."

"He never did go to no counselor like he promised you, Mrs. Grace. He never went nowhere, just sat in the house with the shades down and wouldn't eat nothin'. And he made us swear we wouldn't call you. He said he'd go the next week and the next week. He's right stubborn, like his pa. Lord, that man never changed his mind once he'd decided something, and I figure Randy just decided he wasn't going to go at all. You done so much for us already, we didn't have the heart to bother you, and Randy telling you one thing and doing another and acting like he would tear the place apart if we told you."

"Myrtle, I am so sorry, so very sorry. I'm glad Lucy found him in time. Which hospital did they take him to?"

"The one that the veterans go to in Oteen. They wanted to carry him off to the regular hospital, but Lord, we got no insurance to pay that, and Lucy done told them how he was just back from Iraq, and how he'd been shot up there, and how he wasn't right in his head since he got home. So they carried him off to the veterans hospital."

"When did all of this happen, Myrtle?"

"Last night, just before I got home from work. They say we can't come to see him until tomorrow. I can't even sit beside my baby and pray over him."

"Pray for him at home, Myrtle. Just pray for him." After assuring Myrtle that Randy was in good hands, and that he would be all right, and that now, finally, he would get the kind of help he needed, a trembling Grace hung up the phone. She had been leaning against the wall, and now she sank into a kitchen chair. For a long time she stared at the floor, her mind rerunning her conversation with the counselor, trying to recall every word he had said to her about post-traumatic stress, and he had said a lot. But had he mentioned suicide? Perhaps he had, but she couldn't remember.

Suicide! Randy must have been in a hole so dark and deep he could not climb out. Ending it all must have seemed the only way. Who was she to judge Randy? That was best left to powers greater than herself. How did it feel, she wondered, that moment when the decision was made and one took pills, or sat in a car in a closed garage with the engine running, or slit one's wrists? Did one regret the choice, want to stop the process, or did a person simply feel relief to end what must be total misery? Enough!

Only yesterday, Bob had said, "You're involved in too many things. You're going in a million directions and you look exhausted. You worry about the Banks family. You've tried and tried to help that boy, Randy, and now this business with Zachary is draining you. He's Hannah's family. Let her handle it.

"On top of this, you're running over to Mars Hill several times a week to see Lurina. Didn't you just tell me that Lurina's busier and happier than she ever was in that old rattletrap of a house of hers? She plays bingo every evening, and she went in a bus with a group of ladies to Roses in Weaverville and to lunch at the Chinese restaurant. Moving to Mars Hill Retirement Community was the best thing that ever happened to Lurina.

"You've got to slow down, Grace. You must start saying no, taking care of yourself. If you visit with Lurina once a week, and you bring her back here for dinner one evening a week, that's enough."

Grace had argued that that was not enough, that Lurina was like a mother to her, that she loved her and wanted to see her.

"And who looked after Mike when he had eye surgery? He stayed with you ladies, and you worried about him. Where was Amelia?"

"She was there, but she's got Miriam and Sadie now, and she was getting ready for her trip to Santa Fe. It didn't take much for me to keep an eye on Mike. If I made lunch for myself, why wouldn't I offer him a sandwich? Mike was no trouble. He was easy."

Bob had persisted. "And you're involved with our grand-kids, and you still tutor children over at Caster Elementary School. You find time to bake for everyone around here. How many people and their problems must you take on be-fore it gets to be too darn much for you? I don't want to see you collapse."

Bob had offered a fair appraisal of her life. She was going in too many directions. Some days, she started out in the morning and didn't remember where she was going. This wasn't dementia, she realized, just juggling too many plates in the air. How had she dug herself in so deeply with so many people, all at the same time?

"I know you're right. What's drives me so, do you think?" she'd asked.

Bob had rubbed his chin and gotten that look on his face

that indicated that he had something on his mind but would rather not say what it was.

"Tell me. I need you to be honest with me, Bob."

"I think you're running scared."

"Running scared of what?"

"Maybe you're just plain scared of dying." He put his arm about her shoulder. "Sometimes we're all just plain scared of dying."

"Everyone dies," she replied, but avoided looking at him.

Bob leaned across their chairs to kiss her cheek. "Of course we do. Some of us are more what I'd call people oriented than others. Some people like doing things for others, helping others. That's you, my love. Maybe you feel time is running out and you're trying to do as much as you can for the people you care about."

"You think that's it?"

"Well, I don't really know, but maybe, maybe it could be. There are some of us who think we ought to get on the stick and do something for someone else before our time runs out, and some of us, like me for instance, don't feel that's what their lives are about."

"What is your life about—I mean, when you really search your soul, Bob?"

"Loving the people I love, not knowingly harming anyone," he replied. "I feel an obligation to myself, to you, to my grandkids and my son to take care of myself, to stay in good health. It seems to me that at this time of our lives, we spend a certain percentage of time on what I call maintenance, going to doctors, having our teeth and eyes taken care of, working out, staying healthy. That's an obligation. Staying well, so we'll be there for those we love."

Grace considered this now. Bob had been right. She was indeed on a treadmill, and not a healthy treadmill. Too often she ignored her needs and wants, even her health. It would be far better for her diabetes if she took more time planning, shopping, and preparing healthy food. Grace had looked deep into Bob's eyes.

"I'm just an old busybody, aren't I?"

"No, not an old busybody. It's just that all your life you've wanted to help people, and it's easy to get carried away. Only, you're getting older, we all are, and we haven't the mental or physical energy we had when we were younger. You need to prioritize, to say 'no' more often. You used to rest in the afternoon. When did you last do that?"

"I can't remember."

"You need to start doing that again."

"You're right. I needed to hear all you've said. And I am going to make changes. I will, you'll see."

"I'm sure you will," he had said and kissed her cheek.

And here she was, berating herself and feeling guilty that she hadn't done enough for the Banks family, for Randy, when she had done her best. And now she must get up from this chair and walk over to Bob's cottage and tell him that Randy Banks had attempted suicide and was at the VA hospital, and that his mother had called, crying, seeking comfort, wanting Grace to help her and her son. Suddenly Grace felt depleted. All she wanted to do was find Bob, have him hold her and help her with Randy. She continued to sit for a while longer, gathering the energy to move from her chair.

Grace found Bob sitting on his front porch and wondered why, on such a muggy day, he preferred being out rather than inside, where it was air-conditioned. The weatherman had predicted rain for this evening. She hoped a good rainstorm would clear the haze that hung over the mountains and cool things down. Grace took the chair adjoining Bob's and fanned herself with his folded newspaper, and told him about Myrtle's phone call.

"You tried to help the boy," he said. "You can't force anyone to get help, but I'd say this suicide attempt was a desperate cry for help."

"He just about bled to death."

"But he didn't die, did he now, honey? And he's at the hospital, where he belongs, where he'll get help, and it's out of your hands."

"I'll visit Randy, of course, and try to encourage the family. Lucy could probably use a shoulder to cry on. I can't let her down."

"She's got Hannah, doesn't she? She works with herbs at the park."

"Yes, but she's always been special to me. At a time like this, she probably needs both Hannah and me."

"I think you ought to butt out of this one," Bob said.

"How can I? I promise you, I will as soon as Randy is out of the woods and things settle down." She looked at her wristwatch. She had replaced the narrow band and small rectangular face with a large, round-faced watch with dark numbers and hands.

"Life is so full of pain. I hate this rotten war, hate what's happened to Randy. He'll never be the same. That's what the counselor said. It's something he'll carry inside of him forever. He was just a kid when he went, so sweet and kind. I hate the cruelty, and horror, and bloodshed he's seen." She began to cry.

"It's the price of war," Bob said. "Old men sit around in sterile offices and make decisions, but it's the young men and women who fight and die in their stupid wars."

Grace heard the anger in his voice. They had never talked about war or about Bob's thirty years in the army. She had no idea that he felt this way, or how he felt about war in general. She had no idea what battles he had been in, what he had seen, or their effect on him. She never thought of Bob when she thought about post-traumatic stress syndrome.

"Will you go to the hospital with me to see Randy? I don't know what to say to him. You'll know what to say. Please. I know you don't like getting into other people's affairs, but this is different, and I need you to help me and help Randy. I know you can."

Bob was silent for a time. Then he slipped his arm about her. "It'll be all right, honey. Randy's in good hands now. Of course, I'll go with you, do what I can."

She leaned forward and threw her arms about him. "I love you, Bob. I always will."

"I love you, too, honey."

When they visited Randy the following day, he was in far better spirits than Grace had seen him, and she wondered if this was due to his medication. He was on antidepressants, a nurse told Bob, and was being visited daily by a therapist. At that news, Grace breathed a sigh of relief.

"I'm shamed at what I did," Randy said. He raised a bandaged hand and wrist.

"Well, son," Bob said, "you just need to be thanking God that your sister found you."

"I do, sir. Lucy saved my life. It was so stupid of me. It

was a terrible thing to do. I'm sorry I put my ma and the girls through this. I'm sorry I didn't listen to you, Mrs. Grace."

"What's done is done," Bob said. "You've got work to do to get well. I'm counting on you. All of us who've been in the armed forces, we've all seen some pretty awful things, and there comes a time to set that all behind you. It's what's ahead of you that counts."

"Your family loves you, Randy," Grace said. "And I love you. All we want is for you to get well."

Randy looked at Grace and nodded, but when he looked at Bob, respect and appreciation filled his face. Their eyes held for a long moment. Then, with his undamaged hand, Randy saluted Bob. "As you say, sir."

As Bob and Grace walked down the hospital hallway, Bob reassured Grace. "The boy's in good hands, and he's got spirit. He's gonna get through this just fine. You wait and see."

"Thanks for coming with me. The respect Randy has for you is obvious, and the encouragement and camaraderie he felt for you is exactly what he needs."

"I just might come on out here and see how he's doing next week," Bob said.

Grace squeezed his arm. "That would be wonderful." She pressed against him and squeezed his arm.

32

Catching Up

A week after Amelia returned from Santa Fe, the week after Bob and Grace visited Randy Banks at the hospital, the week after Hannah discussed with Max the possibility of gathering relatives and friends to confront Zachary with his attitude and behavior, the women freed themselves of all appointments and made time to sit together in their living room and catch up on their busy lives.

It had been a day of fitful weather. Sunshine so brilliant it stung your eyes was followed by layers of gray clouds and rain that hammered the roof of the farmhouse. By late afternoon the sky cleared and a soft, warm breeze stirred the curtains at the open windows in the living room. The aroma of Grace's freshly baked bread drifted from the kitchen.

The ladies drew their chairs in a circle. Amelia turned worried eyes to them. "There was this man at the photo workshop, Ben something or other, from Virginia. He took quite a liking to Miriam, and she appeared interested in him. Every time I turned around, he was talking to her, walking with her, helping her with this or that. He even made points with Sadie by helping her climb up to a cave high in the cliff at Bandelier Monument. My heart was in my mouth the whole time they were going up and down that ladder."

Grace said, "I would imagine so. A cave in a cliff?"

"The park ranger said no one knows who the inhabitants of the site were. They left no written or pictorial records and they simply vanished. Perhaps, he said, they were part of the Anasazi people, but no one really knows. They believe that the people used the caves to sleep in at night, or maybe they went there for protection from animals or possibly other tribes. But this Ben . . ." She shook her head.

"What are you saying, Amelia? Are you upset because Miriam seemed to like this fellow Ben?" Hannah asked.

"I don't want to lose her and Sadie. If she falls in love and marries Ben and moves away from this area, I'll be devastated." Amelia looked away. "I'd hoped that Miriam and Denny would fall in love."

"Now really, Amelia," Hannah said. "Don't you think if there were chemistry between Denny and Miriam, we'd know it by now? You can't make something like that happen."

Amelia sighed. "I know that. It's just that I finally have a family, and I love them so much I can't bear the thought of losing them." Her chin quivered.

"It's ridiculous to think you can control where your children live or who they marry," Hannah said. "My Miranda lives in Pennsylvania; Grace's Roger lives in South Carolina. They visit; we see them."

Grace felt the tension, which had eased considerably of late, mounting between Hannah and Amelia. "I can understand how Amelia feels, that she wouldn't want Miriam and Sadie to move away. It's a valid concern."

"Well," Hannah conceded, "you're right, Amelia. I wouldn't like it much if Laura and Hank up and moved and took away my grandson, Andy."

Grace looked at Amelia. "You know how things are when you meet someone on vacation. It's romantic, exciting, but in the light of reality it often pales. If Miriam stays in touch with Ben and she wants to see him again, and he comes here, I suggest that he stay with us. We'll get a sense of who he is. Maybe if he doesn't have deep roots in Virginia, he would move here." She was silent a moment.

"In a way, we live in a cocoon. We've gathered people we love about us, and we want our lives to stay the same. Does anything stay the same? We really don't have control, especially when it comes to the needs and wants of others. People do what they think they must do for themselves. Any one of the people we love could pick up tomorrow and leave Covington. They could pass away, like Harold Tate or Old Man or Charles have."

"I hate it. I hate change," Amelia said.

"But then, Amelia, there are changes that make us happy, like Miriam and Sadie coming here," Grace said.

"You're right, of course. Miriam and Sadie haven't lived here a year, but still, it would break my heart if they moved away." Her hands moved nervously, her fingers knitting into one another. "I try not to think that I deserve a family, but I feel that I do. Miriam told me just the other day how much she likes teaching at Caster Elementary, and Sadie's happy in school. She adores Tyler and Melissa. Already she thinks of them as cousins. Every night, I pray that God will keep us together."

"Well, I suggest we wait and see what happens. Ben might never contact Miriam." Hannah was eager to engage them on the topic of Zachary. "Can we talk about Zachary now?" she asked.

"Certainly. Tell us what you and Max have decided to

do," Grace asked. "But first, let me get a big plate of bread, butter, and marmalade while the bread's still warm and crusty." She rose and hurried away.

Amelia and Hannah sat silent, while from the kitchen came the sounds of a drawer opening and closing, silverware clinking, plates taken from the cabinet. Grace reappeared carrying a tray, and Hannah stood and moved a small table to the center of their circle.

Grace set the tray down. "We have orange marmalade and plum jelly and, of course, grape and strawberry."

"Orange marmalade." Amelia twisted the top of one of the jars. "My favorite."

"Mine too," Hannah said.

Amelia extended the open jar to her. "Help yourself."

"After you," Hannah replied.

Amelia bit into the bread. "This is so good. You're such a good cook, Grace."

Hannah nodded agreement.

Grace relaxed, relieved that the tension between her dearest friends had evaporated. She wished such tensions never stirred, but this was yet another matter over which she had no control.

After a time, Hannah said, "Max and I have decided that we can't just sit by and tolerate Zachary's mean-spirited, rude behavior. After Sarah was born, he softened and acted like a human being. It sure didn't take long for him to slip back into being obnoxious, and his accident on the mountain seems to have been the catalyst to unlock the meaner parts of his nature again.

"Poor Sarina's in tears more often than not about something he's said or done. Anna and I are fed up, and Max is ready to kick him out. We want to try one last thing, to confront him, get him to face up to the effects of his behavior on Sarina and everyone else."

"How do you plan to do that?" Amelia asked. Since returning from New Mexico she had been busy developing her photographs and Zachary had slipped off her radar.

"Interventions, I discovered, are used for people involved with drugs or alcohol, usually. But it could work here. The idea is that when someone is confronted by many people they care about it makes an impression and they break down and sign on for the help they need. We'd ask Sarina, Anna, Jose, you ladies, Pastor Denny, and Bob to come to Max's place one evening. We'd all tell Zachary how we see his behavior, and how it impacts us. Denny has agreed to facilitate the process. He's had some training in this. Will you participate?" she looked pointedly at Grace. "Grace, are you comfortable confronting Zachary, telling him how you see him acting and how you feel about it, without having to apologize to him?"

"I can do that. Yes, I can. I'll do whatever I need to do," Grace replied.

"Good. We'll have a meeting first and each of us will decide what we'll say to him. We have to be firm and specific but not hostile." Hannah looked at Grace again. "Max is going to invite Bob to participate."

"This is one time when I'll have no trouble saying what I think," Grace said.

"Fine. And you, Amelia, are you okay with this?"

Amelia nodded. "It will be my pleasure."

"It's settled, then." Hannah sat back and slathered butter on another slice of bread.

They were silent for a time as they drank their tea and enjoyed the warm bread. Then Amelia asked, "Anything else happen while I was gone?"

"Goodness, yes," Grace said. "The quick version is that Randy Banks attempted to commit suicide. Lucy found him in the bathtub. He was taken to the VA hospital. Bob went with me to visit Randy, and they connected with one another. Bob's going to go back by himself to visit him."

"My Lord, Grace, that's just terrible. That poor girl. What a shock that must have been for her and for his mother. I am so sorry for them," Amelia said.

Hannah nodded. "Lucy will need all the support we can give her. She's talked some to me, but the way I see it, you're the one, Grace, who she really needs right now."

"I know. Lucy's having a hard time putting it out of her mind, seeing him like that," Grace said. "But in time, I hope she'll be all right, especially since Randy's finally getting the help he needs."

Sarina had extracted a promise from Zachary to be at home on the day and time they chose for their intervention. Zachary was there, completely unaware of what he was facing, and to everyone's surprise he sat, head down, and listened to the indictments made against him from one after the other of those gathered. They spoke of his irresponsibility, his crudeness, especially the manner in which he spoke to his wife and Hannah without consideration of their feelings. His indifference to his own family. His disrespect for his father. He did not argue, defend himself, or make excuses. Suddenly, his shoulders began to shake and, kneeling before Sarina, he laid his head on her lap and sobbed.

Denny motioned them all to be quiet, to wait, and they sat there, embarrassed, uncertain what to do.

Finally Zachary quieted, raised his head, and addressed

his father. "When Mom died, I couldn't seem to work through my grief, so I walked away. When I brought Sarina here that first time, I thought maybe we could make our home in the States. But Mom was everywhere, and my sense of loss was overwhelming. Rather than talk to you about how I felt, I did what I've done so often in my life. I ran."

"I should have been more sensitive, should have known something serious was troubling you. I should have known. I should have helped you," Sarina said.

"For heaven's sake, don't blame yourself. How could you help me if I wouldn't talk, if I shut you out? And now, I've brought you here, so far from your home, and my behavior has been unforgivable: the things I said, how I said them, and disappearing, going off gambling, and squandering our money. Can you ever forgive me?"

Sarina stroked her husband's dark, thick hair. "There is nothing to forgive. It was my father who sent us away, remember. I thank the gods that you brought me to your people." Her eyes swept the room, and she smiled. "You have been so good to me, all of you, better even than my own family."

She lowered her voice and addressed her husband. "We could stay here, live here. They want us, Zachary. They love us and Sarah."

"I know," he said. "I know." But he made no commitment. And Hannah felt her initial distrust of Zachary spring to life.

What was there to say or do? Silently, slowly, one after the other, they stood and left the room, allowing the couple privacy.

"Will this last, I wonder?" Hannah asked when she and Grace and Amelia were alone.

"Hard to tell. We have to give it time," Grace said. "How does one change? How does one make even a strong motivation last?"

"It seemed too fast, too contrived." Amelia had expressed what they were all feeling. "There's something about Zachary I don't trust or like."

Change in Zachary was neither immediate nor consistent. One day he smiled and spoke in a soft, gentle voice, insisted on clearing the dinner table for Anna and stacking the dishes in the dishwasher; or he could be found sitting on the floor playing with Sarah. Another day, he sulked, was indifferent and unresponsive to his wife and child, ignored the baby, and treated Sarina with discourtesy, not replying when she spoke to him, leaving the house without a word, and returning when he chose, regardless of the hour.

There were times when he treated Hannah with courtesy, and times when he was disputatious and hostile, arguing about every little thing, as where the saltshaker went on the kitchen counter. With Max he was reserved, cautious, and careful; their conversations hovered safely in the arena of ball games and the weather. And there were those few pleasant times when Zachary joined them in the living room after dinner and played Monopoly. When he left the room, he bade them all good night, rather than walking away without a word.

Cajoled by Sarina, Zachary agreed to be counseled by Pastor Denny. He kept the first and failed to keep the next two appointments. As the weeks passed he missed more appointments then he kept. Finally, Denny suggested that he might benefit from someone other than a pastoral counselor and gave him the names of several therapists in Asheville. Sarina found the crumpled paper on the floor near the trash can.

Disappointed and feeling that he had failed Max and Hannah, Denny visited Hannah at her office.

"Zachary rarely came to our appointments. I have terminated my relationship with him. We won't be working together any longer. I am so sorry I was not more effective, could not be of more help."

"I'm sorry," Hannah said. "Don't blame yourself, Denny. Zachary can hardly be called reliable. He's like two people, two personalities. I often wonder who the real Zachary is."

Denny paced Hannah's office, his arms folded across his chest. "I couldn't work with him, even when he showed up. How do you work with a person who stares at the wall behind you, never responds to anything you say, and never shares any information about himself, his wife, his family, nothing?"

Hannah said, "Had Zachary wanted help, I'm sure you could have helped him. Change takes work, and Zachary doesn't want to do the work."

But Denny worried that he was not an adequate counselor. He had failed to reach Zachary, and there had been that dreadful incident with May, which he had handled badly. Had he been a competent counselor, he would have been aware of her growing attachment and nipped it in the bud. What could he have said or done to break through the wall Zachary built around himself? He had not wanted help and had merely yielded to pressure from Sarina and the others. Still, Denny worried that he had failed Sarina, the family, and even Zachary.

Hannah's voice interrupted Denny's musing. "Zachary's a chameleon. He changes color before your eyes. It's scary and disarming. Sometimes he's charming and appears to be devoted to his wife and child. More often he's a self-centered, no-good bum." She rubbed her temples. "Max keeps hoping. Where will this end? I wonder."

She did not have long to wait to find out.

33

The Confrontation

*O*n the day that the two transportation vans pulled into the yard and rounded the house to the barn, and the milk cows began their slow, prodded ascent into the bowels of the huge trucks, Zachary exploded.

He appeared on the scene, paced from barn to van, raged like one gone mad, arms flailing, eyes wild, and screamed obscenities at his father.

"How could you do this to me? This dairy is my birthright, and you're selling it out from under me. Who set you up to this? That g-d woman you married?" He cursed his father. "Damn you, damn you. My mother would never have allowed you to do this to me."

Max had had it! He had tried. Lord knows he had tried. He had promised Hannah to maintain his calm and patience and he had done that. He had ignored his son's inconsistencies, his vacillations and unaccountable, bizarre outbursts, and allowed Zachary space and time to settle in, to adjust. And this was the outcome? How dare he speak to him this way, to curse and embarrass him in front of strangers? The arrogant little punk.

"Who in the h—— do you think you are?" Max bellowed. "When did you ever express an interest in this dairy?

On the contrary, you've made it clear on more than one occasion that you hate my work, my life, this place." Max circled Zachary, assessing the situation, uncertain where this was going or if it would devolve into physical contact.

"I don't know you," Max snarled. "Your mother wouldn't know you. Do you think she'd approve of your gambling, of the way you treat your wife and child?"

Contempt spread across Max's face and sounded in his voice. "You think you can just hop the next ship to another port? It's time, *boy*, to cut the crap and grow the hell up."

The word "boy," and the scorn in Max's voice, inflamed Zachary. Fists clenched, shoulders hunched, Zachary started toward his father.

Max braced, prepared to defend himself. Close behind him, Jose waited, ready to fend off any assault on Max.

Spittle showed at the corners of Zachary's lips; veins throbbed in his neck. He saw Jose, knew he couldn't take them both, and the men with the vans were standing there, arms crossed, staring at him. Zachary stopped and backed away. "You're damned right, I don't want your confounded, lousy dairy or your stinking animals."

Breathing hard, his face flushed, Max's voice came hard and bitter. "What the h——did you come back here for? What the devil do you want?"

Zachary staggered backward. For a moment it seemed he would fall, but he grabbed a post by the barn to steady himself. Then he leaned forward, his eyes steely, and hissed. "Land." He stepped forward. His tone changed to almost pleading. "I want land. Twenty acres, that's all, just twenty acres of your precious land."

Max placed his hands on his hips. "And just what are you going to do with my twenty acres, if I may ask?"

"Build houses, I want to build ten rental houses for in-come."

"Rental houses for income?" Max slapped his thighs and bent, laughing. "So you can sit on your fat lazy butt and collect rent?" He turned to Jose. "You hear that, Jose? My prodigal son returns to turn my hillside into a develop-ment, into another Loring Valley. What does he care about erosion, traffic, or anything else that impacts the environ-ment?"

"Ten houses won't hurt your confounded environment," Zachary said. "You can put whatever restrictions you want on them, size of the houses, their shape, color, the type of roof, whatever you want."

Zachary's bellicosity and his abusive language had un-settled Max. Pulled by the smell and sound of cattle as they moved in melancholy silence from the barn and up the ramp, their hoofs scraping metal before they vanished into the cavernous maw of the van, and by his angry son's de-mands, Max could hardly think clearly. Every swish of tail sounded like the buzzing of bees. He looked about, hand raised as if to ward off a swarm of the furious insects. There were no bees.

He pointed in Zachary's direction and looked at Jose. "He would, if he could, turn our quiet Covington into a noisy, polluted metropolis. Well, over my dead body."

It flashed through Max's mind, then, that Zachary had de-liberately chosen this moment for this confrontation, know-ing that although his father had decided to sell the herd, it saddened him deeply to lose the cattle. Had he hoped to embarrass his father in front of strangers? The thought fur-ther enraged Max.

Land was everything to Max. He had fallen in love with

this land the moment he laid eyes on it, and he loved every square inch of it. He had purchased old man Anson's seven hundred acres at the end of Cove Road for the sole purpose of preventing development and to preserve the quality of life that he and his neighbors enjoyed.

The historical village and the gardens had been afterthoughts. He had used perhaps twenty-five acres of pastureland to create a historical settlement, true to the original settlers, the Covingtons, who had arrived in the late 1800s. Hannah's beautiful gardens occupied a mere five acres. Not a tree had been cut. One single lane meandered across the rolling hillside from Cove Road to the historical site, and that would soon be lined with flowering white dogwoods. Six hundred and seventy-five acres of lush, green, forested hillsides rose one thousand feet above Covington, as pristine as on the day he had purchased them.

To maintain the integrity of Cove Road with its fine old farmhouses, they had saved and restored the old Anson homestead, gutted the interior, and used it as their offices. They had refurbished the exterior of the old, falling-down farmhouse to its original gleaming white clapboard. As they had in the past, rocking chairs on the porch welcomed visitors.

Max saw himself as a preserver in shining armor; he saw his son as Darth Vader, a destroyer. Zachary's plea fell on deaf ears. Twenty acres were to Max as five hundred acres, ten houses the equivalent of a hundred. Father and son were a million miles apart.

Max fixed his eyes on Zachary's heaving chest, on his red, sweaty face, and felt only contempt and dislike. "I've spent my entire life preserving this land from developers, and now you want me to hand it over to you, to bulldozers and graders? Are you insane? The answer is *no*, and that is final."

"You're the fool around here and the crazy one," Zachary screamed. Veins in his neck pulsed. "How can I turn your precious Cove Road into a Loring Valley with twenty acres? You haven't heard a word I've said about my plan, about you setting the rules, and you don't want to. Well, I'll say it again. Ten houses, one house on every two acres, a nice place, perhaps designed as replicas of farmhouses with porches like Bob's place. How come it's all right for the ladies to build not one, but two cottages, for Bob and now for Amelia's so-called family, on their land right here on Cove Road across from you? How come that doesn't desecrate your ideal concept of holding back time, keeping everything as it was fifty years ago?"

Zachary stood before Max. "Look at me, damn it. I said, look at me. Have you ever really looked at me or heard me? No. You don't give a pig's eye about me. You and your land can go to hell." Turning, he stomped toward the house.

Meanwhile, the cows had been secured inside the truck, the ramp retracted, and the huge rear door lowered. Max could hear the shuffling of hoofs. He imagined his animals jammed flank to flank inside, perhaps terrified. He had wanted to touch them as they passed, to silently address this cow or that, cows he had a special fondness for, to apologize, so to speak, hoping that they would sense the loss he felt at their going and understand why he had made this decision. Zachary had taken these special moments away from him, had deprived him of his absolution. He hated his son and wished him gone, out of his sight, forever.

The drivers, embarrassed and uncomfortable at witnessing this raw display of emotion, of venom, hung back near the doors of their cabs waiting for that moment when they might slip clipboards into Max's hands for his signature.

When Zachary, still muttering obscenities, reached the house and entered, slamming the door behind him, the drivers moved forward and handed Max the clipboards. They did not look into one another's eyes. Max signed and returned the clipboards. Moments later the drivers climbed into the cabs and started the engines. Then the huge trunks thundered from the yard.

In the silence that followed, Jose slipped away, and Max, depleted of energy and feeling suddenly desolate, leaned against the side of the barn. It was over! No stomp of hoof, no swish of tail or other movement or sound issued from the bleak, empty barn. His herd, his dairy and its routine, so much a part of his life all these years, a lifetime, were gone. It had been his decision, of course, and it was the right decision, but not like this. No, not like this.

Wearily, Max shoved away from the barn and lumbered toward the house. He entered the kitchen and, heavyhearted, with dragging steps, moved through it into the hall.

What was it to have a child, a son? Certainly it had not turned out as he had hoped, as he expected that day Bella came home from the hospital with the tiny baby. He had been thrilled to have a son. As he started up the stairs, Max stopped and held on to the railing. He remembered standing there looking down at the baby, thinking of all the things they would do together, fish, go to ball games, walk in the woods. He had anticipated teaching his son which berries were safe to eat, which plants were poisonous. He would teach the boy everything he knew.

But it had not turned out that way. Zachary hated fishing and walking in the woods. He was afraid of snakes and reacted adversely to insect bites. He hated ball games. They were too noisy, he said, and the hot dogs gave him a stomachache. Instead of trying to engage his son, take time to discover what it was that Zachary was interested in, he had labeled the boy a sissy and ignored him, and he had resented the many hours Bella spent reading and being with Zachary.

His son had loved books, and his mother was forever sending off for books, especially books on history, mythology, the Arthurian legends. Well, it was too late to do anything about any of that now.

Ahead of him the stairs seemed endless, but finally he reached the top and shuffled down the hall to his bedroom. He needed a shower, but Lord, he was tired. Hannah would be here soon. They were going into Asheville for dinner. They had been alone so seldom lately. But instead of showering, Max fell across his bed and into a deep sleep.

Greatly disturbed at what had transpired and deeply worried about Señor Max, Jose moved swiftly away from the house. Before the trucks turned onto Elk Road, he reached the offices at Bella's Park, where he found Hannah in the Oriental garden with Wayne. They were laying hoses on the ground, shaping, Wayne said, the ponds for the koi and the lilies. He would have liked to ask what koi were, but this was hardly the time.

Immediately, she saw his face, and Hannah's heart constricted. Something terrible had happened, and for a moment she could not move. Was it Max? Had something happened to Max? Was he ill or worse? "What happened?" she asked. "Is Max all right?"

Jose nodded but did not explain. He beckoned with both hands, and before she could question him, turned and ran toward the farmhouse. Without a word, dreading the worse, Hannah dropped the hose and followed him.

34

Aftermath

Max lay there as if he were dead. An icy chill sliced through Hannah when she shook him, and he did not stir. She had taken a CPR class through the Red Cross a long time ago, and now everything she had learned came back to her. Leaning close, she placed two fingers to his neck, hoping to feel a pulse. She did! She rested her cheek against his and felt his warm breath against her cheek. Relief flooded her body, and she collapsed on the bed alongside Max. Then, remembering Jose standing in the doorway, she turned and signaled the terrified man that Max was all right.

Jose nodded and departed, silently shutting the door behind him. Breathing a sigh of relief, he went downstairs to collapse in a chair and tell his anxiously waiting wife all that had transpired that afternoon.

Upstairs, lying next to her sleeping husband, Hannah recalled bits and pieces of the information Jose had imparted to her on their mad dash from the park to the house, mainly that there had been a dreadful verbal encounter between Max and Zachary. Hannah feared that the effect on Max, at his age, could be disastrous. Thank God, he was breathing easily and steadily. He must have been exhausted. She could wring Zachary's neck for doing this to his father. Hannah lay beside Max, her hip pressed to his, her legs covering his, and waited.

Earlier that day, Amelia had driven Sarina and the baby into Asheville for a routine visit to the baby's pediatrician. Afterward they stopped for a bite to eat and returned in the late afternoon. In the driveway of Max's house, Sarina kissed Amelia's cheek and thanked her. She disengaged the sleeping baby from her car seat, hefted Sarah onto one shoulder, and slung the diaper bag on the other. Then, softly humming a lullaby her mother had sung to her and her sisters when they were little, she hurried up the steps, across the porch, and into the house.

Anna beckoned from the kitchen. Sarina set down the diaper bag and went into the kitchen to find a highly agitated Jose sitting at the kitchen table. The look on his and Anna's faces quickly wiped the smile from hers. Anna came to her and took the sleeping baby. Jose pulled out a chair for her at the table.

"Something has happened. What is it?" Sarina looked from one to the other. "Is someone ill? Where is my husband?"

Jose whispered the story of Zachary and Max's confrontation. "The man, he was there, the man come for the cows. It was, how you say, *humillación* for Señor Max. He age twenty years."

Sarina felt cold; anxiety caused her throat to tighten, and she could hardly speak. What had possessed Zachary to behave like that, and on this day with Max giving up his beloved cows? "Where is my husband now?"

Jose shrugged.

"I must find him." Leaving the baby with Anna, Sarina grasped the railing with shaking hands and propelled herself up the stairs two at a time. What could she say to Zack? It was terrible that he should speak to his father with cruel and angry words, but she knew she could not chastise him. He would be seething. His anger was never short-lived. He nursed grudges. He might be waiting for her, their suitcases packed, determined to leave his father's house this very night. What would she say or do? How could she pacify him?

At their bedroom door she stopped for a moment, needing to quiet herself and to stop her teeth from chattering. She would cry, plead, anything but leave this place that she had come to think of as a second home. Bracing for their encounter, Sarina turned the knob. Holding her breath, she opened the door and stepped into their room. It was dark; the shades were pulled down. He's asleep, she thought, and tiptoed to the bed, which to her surprise was vacant, the covers smooth and undisturbed.

"Zack, where are you?" Sarina turned, her eyes moving from wall to wall, corner to corner. She entered the bathroom, also empty, every towel in place. Sarina flung open the closet doors and gasped to see the row of empty hangers. It was then, as she swung about, wide-eyed, searching for a sign of her husband, that she saw the folded sheet of paper half tucked beneath a pillow. Her heart tumbled to the pit of her belly, and for an instant she stood by the closet, too confused to move. Then she ran to the bed and grabbed the letter and sank into the rocking chair by the window. Tentatively, she unfolded the paper and read its message. Then she lowered her head into her hands and wept.

*   *   *

Roused from a deep and dreamless asleep by the sound of someone crying, Hannah was on her feet and in the hall, and followed the sounds to Sarina's bedroom. The door stood ajar. Hannah entered. Asking no questions, she kneeled beside the young woman and cradled her in her arms.

Finally, as the heaving shoulders stilled and the weeping stopped, Hannah asked, "Tell me what has happened. Why are you crying like this?"

Red-rimmed and swollen eyes stared at Hannah, and for a moment they filled with gratitude. Still, it took several minutes before Sarina could compose herself and catch her breath. Then she said in a soft, pained voice, "He's gone. Zachary's gone."

Hannah was not surprised; she was relieved. "Gone? Gone where?"

Sarina handed Hannah the crumpled ball of paper. "I found this on the bed."

Damn Zachary! What had he done now? Slowly, Hannah unfolded the crinkled ball and smoothed it. Zachary's letter was written on Max's dairy stationery.

> *Dear Sarina,*
>
> *Surely by now you realize that I am not fit to be either husband or father. I am leaving. I have no idea where I am going or what I will do. I know you will be cared for in Covington. Should you decide you no longer wish to be married to me and you decide to file for divorce, I will not oppose you. You can send mail to me at Box 99875, San Francisco, CA 99605. Letters will be sent on to me. I have loved you. Never doubt that. I still love you, though I find myself incapable of expressing that love in a healthy manner.*

*I am sorry. I am simply unable to settle down and be
the kind of husband and father you and Sarah need,
or the kind of son my father wants. Forgive me! I am
truly, deeply sorry.*

Love, Zack

As Hannah read, Sarina buried her head in her hands.
Her shoulders shook. Then she lifted her head and the word
"self-reliance" came to mind. Those were the key words in
her mother's advice to all her children.

"Be self-reliant. Learn to stand on your own two feet. Bad
things will come to you in this life, and they will pass, for life
goes on," she would say. "If you can be self-reliant, you will
make it through whatever life hands you."

For a moment, anger raced through Sarina. What did
her mother know? She had led a sheltered life, going
from her father's protection to her husband's home and
protection. What crisis had she survived? But shame soon
replaced her anger. Her mother had buried two stillborn
sons. She had lived in England and longed for India. And
then there was that terrifying night when the mosque had
burned and they had had to flee their home. Her mother
had not been pleased to send her away, only her father
had.

Still, through it all, her mother had been surrounded by
loved ones, strong people like her father and brother. She,
Sarina, had been abandoned by a husband in a land far from
home with a baby to care for. She could not go home to
India. It was intolerable. It was more than she could bear.

When she was able to speak, Sarina said, "I am ashamed.
What will I do, Hannah? Where will I go? I cannot take my
child without her father to my home in India. They will

laugh at me behind my back and inwardly they will scorn me. They will all be thinking, *I told her so.*"

Hannah folded the letter. *Poor child. The dear, poor child. This is like a death for her.* She spoke gently. "Our home is your home. This is not the time to make big decisions or changes. We will tell Max about this; we will show him the letter. Then we will sit quietly and talk. We love you. You and Sarah are welcome to share our home, this home, and my home with the ladies, for as long as you wish to be here." Hannah held Sarina. *How small she is, like a bird, but she's strong of spirit.*

"I am so very sorry," Hannah said. "So very sorry." *Perhaps, if I had been home, I could have stopped the terrible confrontation between Zachary and his father, and this would not have happened.* But then Hannah's anger flared. *Better that he's gone. Sarina should divorce him and make a new life for herself here, with us.* "I am so sorry, Sarina" was all she said.

Calmer now, feeling safe in Hannah's presence, Sarina looked at Hannah. "He was not happy here. Some places are not right for some people. For a long time, I have thought that one day I would wake up and my husband would be gone." Her eyes were pleading now, pleading for understanding of this man she loved, though he had deserted her. "He is not a strong man, Hannah, not strong like you or Max. He did not have the courage to tell me. And you know, Hannah, he could have. I would have understood. I would have kissed him and sent him on his way, and I would have waited for him to return.

"My grandmother told me once that you cannot hold too tightly to something you love, or you will crush it. I would have let him go. But not like this!" For several moments she could not go on, and Hannah waited. Finally, Sarina said, "Zachary could not live in his father's shadow. He could not face him or talk to him in a reasonable manner. I am sorry for what has happened. Jose told me. How terrible to speak to one's father in that way. It is wrong and I am shamed for Zachary." Tears spilled from her eyes, and she wiped them away with the ball of her hand. "Now, he is gone." She raised her hands, as if in supplication to an unseen power, and dropped them back into her lap. "Gone. Just gone." Then she sat straighter. "I will do whatever you want me to do. I will return to India, if you say so."

"I don't say so. I say stay here, Sarina. Didn't your wise grandmother tell you that in times of stress and loss one should never make a major change? You need time to think about all of this." Hannah slipped her palm under Sarina's chin and lifted the young woman's face to hers. "You'll stay right here with us. I love you. Max loves you. You've made a place in our hearts, and we would mourn your going."

Sarina's large, dark eyes looked into Hannah's and behind the tears, Hannah saw both moments of fear and of gratitude. "But . . ."

"Hush, now." Hannah held and rocked her. "We love you. Don't think! Don't do anything but just be here."

Sarina snuggled like a babe against Hannah. In these few minutes, a measure of peace had been restored to her, and she sent a quick prayer of thanks to Krishna. "You have been, you are, a mother to me," she said.

Max awakened with a heavy heart. He lay there and relived the scene at the barn, then shuddered, remembering every word of the angry exchange between Zachary and himself.

When were things ever settled in rage? Could he relive that scene, he would remain calm. He would allow Zachary his anger, and then he would take him aside and talk to him. He would listen to what his son had to say. They would, in time, reach an accommodation.

He remembered something that Zachary had said. Max could determine the size, shape, and color of the few houses his son wanted to build. Max had chosen to ignore those words, which had suggested compromise, and he had reacted in old ways, treating Zachary not as the man he was, but as a strange, unknown quantity of a boy whom Max could never fathom. Did that make Zachary wrong, just because he, George Maxwell, had fathered a son with whom he had not an iota in common? No. It did not.

Max himself had been not at all like his own father, and how disappointed his father had been at his choice of career, agriculture rather than law, and a lifestyle so different from his parents. People were, after all, who they were. He had been hasty and unreasonable with his son, and Max was deeply sorry. Well, today he would sit down with Zachary and they would come to a better conclusion.

Max sat on the side of the bed and, using his toes, fished for his slippers. He drew on a robe and walked with resolute steps to the bathroom. Where was Hannah? Well, first things first. He would find Zachary and apologize. The boy deserved a part of the estate, something more than the trust Bella had arranged to have doled out to him. All these years, Zachary had never once asked for anything. So, he hadn't found his career, his right place in this world. Given time and encouragement, rather than scorn and criticism, he would find his way. Max would aid and abate that search and not be an impediment.

Whistling, feeling much better now that he had sorted it all out, Max showered, dressed, and went downstairs determined to set things right with Zachary, but downstairs he was confronted with a silent, somber household and news that would break his heart.

They sat at the kitchen table and spoke in low voices, as if speaking louder would shatter the fragile air. Again and again, Max read the letter Sarina handed to him, his heart sinking, unwilling to believe its contents.

"This can't be. I wanted to apologize to him, to work things out," he said. No one responded.

Anna rummaged in a drawer and retrieved an iron pot, which she set on top of the stove. The sound of metal on metal jarred the silence. It was followed by the splash of liquid being poured into the pot. "I make soup," she said. The door of the fridge opened. From the crisper, Anna pulled onions and vegetables and set them on a chopping block on the counter. Moments later the *clunk, clunk* of a knife cut deeply into the thickening silence.

The high-pitched yapping of puppies and Grace's voice calling, "Carole, Benji, come back here this minute," echoed from across the road. In her mother's arms, Sarah stirred and howled as if she had been torn from a deep sleep. Her tiny arms and legs flailed. Sarina rose. "I'll take her upstairs and change her."

Max placed both palms on the table and pushed up from his chair. He sighed deeply. "Well, this takes some thinking about. I could hire a detective to try to find him and bring him home, or we can wait and see if we hear from him."

Sarina clutched Sarah to her chest and looked at Hannah.

"We'll talk it over—you, Sarina, and I—and we'll decide together," Hannah said.

Max looked at his wristwatch and nodded. He felt old and weary. "I have to talk to Jose. We were going to go over plans for the restaurant." He turned to Anna. "Your cousin Irena comes this week, eh? You have the place ready for her?"

"Sí, Señor Max." Anna chopped vegetables.

Max stepped outside, closing the door softly behind him. They could hear the crunch of gravel beneath his feet as he circled the barn to Anna and Jose's cottage.

Hannah sat alone at the table fingering a spoon, running her fingers along its edge and pressing her thumb into the smooth roundness of the bowl. Her mind shifted to Zachary and his totally irresponsible behavior, and then to the office and her Oriental garden, delayed due to too much rain and her aching knees. Reaching under the table, she rubbed her knees. The steps in both houses were getting to be too much for her, but saying so would bring the issue to a head. Well, sooner or later she must deal with these confounded knees. She'd discuss it with Grace, ask her to go with her to the orthopedic specialist. Hannah pushed up from the table. She needed to go home and talk to Grace.

"Anna, please tell Sarina I'm over at the other house," Hannah said. "Ask her to bring Sarah over there."

35

Life Goes On

Sitting on the porch step, the puppy, Carole, snuggled against Grace's thigh. Benji lay on his belly, four legs splayed, and gnawed on a bone. The licks from Carole's soft pink tongue were warm and wet against Grace's hand. Hannah said dogs licked you not because they loved you but because they enjoyed the taste of salt or minerals on your skin. What a sad thought! It was far better to think of licks and enthusiastic wagging of a tail as reciprocated affection.

Grace looked down at the puppy. Carole rewarded her with a look Grace was certain was total affection. "Why did I ever wait this long to get a dog?" Grace asked.

Thump, thump, thump went Carole's tail.

"You are so smart," Grace said. "You know I'm talking to you and that I love you."

It was a lovely, honeysuckle-smelling, lazy day. High on the mountains the wind huffed and puffed, scattering puffy white clouds. Grace had forgotten to lower the blinds in her room last night, and the morning sun streaming through her window had awakened her way too early. She had lain in bed awhile thinking of nothing in particular, then decided to get up and do some much-needed mending, until it was time to dress, eat, and take the puppies to the vet.

Grace had carried the sewing basket to the living room along with a skirt that needed hemming, two shirts of Hannah's she had agreed to sew buttons on, and her housedress, whose pockets had holes. This had taken longer than anticipated and when she was done, Grace set the basket aside and headed for the kitchen. She was hungry.

The puppies had been left to run about in the fenced yard off the kitchen, and in her haste to answer the telephone, which was the vet's office changing her appointment to another day, Grace had inadvertently left the gate unhinged, and it took only a minute for Benji to shove it open and race toward Cove Road.

Grace had dashed outside, running so fast she nearly fell on her face when she caught her shoe in a gopher hole. She grabbed both dogs before they reached the road, tucked them one under each arm, and trudged back to the house.

Now she sat with them on the front steps and fanned her face with the newspaper. She would put the dogs in the fenced yard and make sure the gate was secured. Then she would go over and visit Bob. But when she glanced toward Bob's cottage, his car was gone, and she remembered that Bob was at the VA hospital visiting Randy. This was Bob's fourth visit, and a friendship had sprung up between himself and Randy. Randy needed a father figure, and in Grace's opinion, Bob needed what she considered useful involvement with people. She believed that some unspoken law of the universe required people to contribute to what she called the life stream. If you had a skill — be it a learned skill like carpentry or gardening, or an innate skill like being a good listener, or the ability to organize things or do research — it was incumbent on you to use that skill to help others, especially young people. In Grace's mind, chasing a golf ball around a course did not count as useful.

Bob volunteered with the police department, riding with the police occasionally and checking in prisoners' visitors at a local jail. But Grace thought that Bob should be working with young men. He had brushed off every suggestion she made until their visit with Randy at the hospital.

Visiting at the VA hospital was difficult for Grace. There were far too many men in wheelchairs or on crutches. There were too many men with vacant looks in their eyes, and it broke her heart to witness their pain, whether physical or mental. She blessed Bob for spending time with Randy, who, Bob reported, was seeing a counselor and doing much better. Grace knew from a phone call to the boy how much Bob's visits lifted his spirits, and Bob had told her they had discussed Randy's future, and the possibility of his continuing his education with the goal of becoming a history teacher.

It was then that Grace noticed Hannah close Max's door across the street and start down the steps of the porch. Grace watched with increasing concern as Hannah leaned into the railing as she descended the steps, saw how Hannah struggled to hold her shoulders straight and not limp as she crossed the road. Hannah was obviously in pain. This was serious. Hannah must see a doctor about those knees of hers.

Hannah waved at Grace, then walked to where Grace sat, rubbing Benji's belly.

Grace nodded toward the puppies. Carole snuggled in Grace's lap, and Grace stroked her silky hair. "They headed for the road. I nearly fell going after them."

"I saw you running. And you saw me cross the road. Truth is, Grace, I can hardly walk."

"It's time, you know," Grace said.

Hannah nodded. "Yes, you're right, it's time. You'll go with me to see the doctor?"

"Of course."

"I'll call for an appointment," Hannah said.

"Good," Grace said. "That Benji just adores you."

"You think I'm going to argue with you? I admit he adores me," Hannah said. "And I've become quite fond of him. Let's go in and have a cup of tea. I have plenty to tell you." She started up and sat back down. "Lord, I can hardly get up by myself. Give me a boost, will you, Grace?"

"What happens now?" Grace asked, after Hannah told her about Zachary and Max's argument and his missive to Sarina. "What a dreadful thing to do, to just disappear like that without a good-bye. How awful. Sarina must be heart-broken. How can we help her? What can we do?"

"I want her to stay here with us," Hannah said. "And so does Max. I think she will. It's hard for her to consider returning to India. Apparently, Zachary was not much liked by her people, and yet she feels that she would not be welcomed alone with a child. I've come to love her and that baby. I don't want Max to lose his only grand-child."

"Maybe she'll need help, someone to talk to. She must be devastated, and his leaving like that without closure," Grace said.

Hannah tipped her head, looked toward the door, and put a finger to her lips. "I think I hear the front door open-ing. It's probably Sarina and the baby. I left a message for her to come over here."

But it was Amelia, and they told her what had happened.

"That's just dreadful." Amelia shrugged. "But maybe Sarina's better off without him. Zachary never struck me as especially reliable. Once things settle down and she has time to think about all this, Sarina will see he's done her a favor." She looked at the other women. "Is that too cold, too calculating? I'm sure even if you don't say so, you agree with me."

They did.

36

The Trouble with Knees
and Much More

$\mathcal{T}$he doctor sat back in his chair. "The trouble with knees is that they wear out on us." He was a large man and filled the room with his presence. "But in your case, you won't require knee replacements. As I said, what you've got is torn cartilage in both knees. It's an outpatient procedure. You'll come in at eight and be out before noon. We can do both knees at the same time or several months apart."

"How long before I have full mobility?" Hannah asked.

"Couple of months. Differs with everyone. There'll be some physical therapy, but once you get the exercises down pat, you can do them at home." He stood and extended his hand to shake hers. "My receptionist will schedule you, or you can think about it and call back to schedule."

"Thank you, Doctor," Hannah said. "I need to think about whether to do one knee or two. I'll call the office to schedule."

Five minutes later, Hannah and Grace sat in Grace's car in the parking lot. "He made it sound so simple," Grace said.

"He probably does hundreds of knee operations. To him it's simple. I always feel so rushed in a doctor's office. I leave thinking of things I wanted to ask or say. Oh, well, next time. I wonder how long it really takes before you're able to do what you used to."

"Someone must know. We must know someone who's had this surgery. I'll ask Brenda. You ask Velma and anyone else you run into. If you ask five or six people about anything, within no time you have the answer to the question or the contact you need."

Brenda did indeed know two ladies who had had this type of knee surgery, Mary Lyle and Roberta McIntosh. Hannah called them and both agreed to talk to her about their operations. Several days later, as she and Grace drove to Mary Lyle's house, which was located off Main Street in Weaverville, Grace said, "I never meet anyone these days who isn't eager to talk about their operation or other physical ailments. Do we do that?"

"Do what?" a distracted Hannah asked.

"Talk a lot about our ailments. I tell you about my diabetes, how I feel this day or that, or that my feet bother me on this or that day. I went on and on about my kidneys for days, didn't I? Do I go about telling everyone? I hope not. In future, if I do it too much, you'll tell me, won't you? Hannah, are you listening to me?"

Lost in thought, Hannah stared out of the window. "I'm sorry, Grace. I wasn't listening. Ailments, what were you saying about ailments?"

Grace repeated what she had said.

Hannah thought about it. "Well, sometimes you do go on and on about food and diabetes and how you feel when you eat this or that, but we're friends, and we live together. And no, I don't recall you telling other people, not when I'm around, anyway."

"Just tell me when I do it too much, okay?" Grace slowed the car. They had turned off Main Street onto a quiet, well-maintained, tree-lined street of bungalows and cottages dating from the fifties and sixties. "What was that house number?"

Hannah turned a page of her notepad. "Number fifty-nine, there on the left. It's that brown bungalow with the white posts on the porch and those gorgeous flower beds in front. That woman has a green thumb. She's on the porch. Looks like Mary Lyle's waiting for us."

A tall, slightly stooped woman, her white hair pulled back in a bun at the nape of her neck, waved at them as they pulled into the driveway and beckoned them onto the porch. She wore a long-sleeved blue blouse with white polka dots, a dark blue skirt, and sturdy lace-up shoes.

"Y'all come on in. So good to see you." Mary smiled and looked from Hannah to Grace. "Brenda tells me you're gonna have knee surgery, like I had a year ago. Now, which one of you is gonna have surgery?"

"I am." Hannah introduced herself and Grace. "Both knees need fixing, the doctor says, and I don't know whether to do them at the same time or not."

Mary Lyle held the front door open, and they entered the living room. At first glance the room appeared small with its two sofas and a love seat, several armchairs, a beautiful old breakfront filled with lovely china and crystal, and many small tables, from which the faces of family members in gold and silver frames smiled up at them.

"I hope you'll take tea or coffee with me. I made us a crumb cake. The recipe's been in my family for four generations, and everyone just loves it." She smiled. "I've heard so much about you ladies from Brenda. How you ladies just up and moved down here from the North and not knowing anyone. I doubt I'd have the nerve to do anything like that. I was born and raised in Weaverville. My daughter lives over your way. She married a Mars Hill boy, you know, and my granddaughter, Clara Louise, goes to Brenda's school." She studied Grace's face. "I think I've seen you there one time when I went to a school play Clara Louise was in."

They were seated now, Mary in an armchair, Grace and Hannah on the sofa facing the redbrick fireplace. Grace said, "That could be. I volunteer at the school, and I've been to several school plays."

"Well, isn't that nice." Mary folded her hands in her lap. "It's a nice school. I remember when it was an old wood building. The new one's brick and air-conditioned, too. Lord, back when I was in school, it was sure hot in September, and we didn't even have ceiling fans. Children today just don't know how lucky they are, do they?" She stopped. "But I'm going on and on."

They sat in silence for a few moments, then Mary said, "Nice weather we've been having. Spring came early this year, don't you think?"

"It did indeed," Grace said. "You have a beautiful garden. Do you also grow roses?"

"Well, indeed I do, Grace. You're Grace, am I right? I'm sorry. My memory for names isn't what it used to be. Time was, I could remember everyone's name at a party."

Grace nodded. "Same for me. Faces I recall, but can't put the name to the face sometimes."

"Last year my roses—they're out back, where the sun gets them in the morning—they got the blight, and I lost five of my biggest, prettiest bushes. My son-in-law, Hank—you know, from Mars Hill; he's in hardware—he came last week and took out all the old soil and put me in new soil and planted new roses. He's good to me, that Hank."

Hannah cleared her throat. Grace had this small talk down to a science. She, on the other hand, was eager to get the information she'd come for and leave. "When did you have your knee surgery, Mary?"

"About a year and a half ago." Mary pulled up her skirt and rubbed her bare knee. "I have just the tiniest scar here, see?" She turned her knee, and Hannah leaned forward. The inch long scar was pale and thin, hardly visible.

"And you can do everything you did before?"

Mary considered. "Well, Hannah, tell the truth, maybe not quite everything. They do ache a bit, my knees do, and they do swell some if I get down on them and don't cushion them, you know what I mean. If I kneel to weed and forget to put this rubber pad I have under them."

Hannah winced. Half of her life was spent on her knees in her garden at home or in one of the gardens at Bella's Park. "But otherwise, you get around just fine."

"Did you need a cane or a walker after surgery?"

"No, I never did need any of that. I had a brace for a couple of days, one of those lightweight, wraparound things, and then I was fine. Just couldn't straighten it out for a time, but exercise and using it helped." She patted the knee. "I never did have any pain afterward, and I was up and about the very next day. Stretching the leg out full took longer. But then, I admit to you ladies, I wasn't regular with the exercises they gave me. I'd recommend you do them exactly as they tell you to do and be consistent. If they say five times a day, do them five times a day."

Hannah would have preferred to leave then, but courtesy required that they stay for tea and compliment the cake.

Mary told them about her family settling in Weaverville in the mid-1800s. "My family's cemetery's just up the hill behind the big Baptist church on Main Street. The family gathers there in October for a picnic and to clean up the place a bit."

Half an hour later, Hannah and Grace graciously took their leave.

Roberta, whom they visited next, was an old friend of Brenda's. They had grown up together and been roommates at the university in Chapel Hill. Roberta was a no-nonsense kind of person, with whom Hannah connected immediately. There was no chitchat and they got right to the point. She had had both knees operated on at the same time, and recommended that Hannah do the same.

"Get it done and over with," she said. "I was restricted in what I could do for a while and one knee just seemed to get better faster than the other, but I could get around. I was never bedridden. It took a while to get my stride back. I'm a hiker, maybe Brenda told you, and I thought I'd never be off tramping the woods with my hiking club, but see"—she stretched out both legs—"fit as a fiddle. Yesterday I hiked five miles round-trip. That surgery was the best thing I ever did for myself. Without it, I'd have been a cripple. You won't regret it, Hannah, however you decide to do it. The doctor makes the difference, and as far as I'm concerned, you have the best knee man in Asheville."

On returning home, Hannah called and scheduled surgery on both knees. She would get it over with in one fell swoop as Roberta had. As she hung up the phone, it rang. It was Max.

"Hannah, I'm here at the house. Sarina's having a bad time of it. Anna called and since you weren't at work, I thought I'd better get on home."

"I'll be right over." Hannah called to Grace, who had gone upstairs to her bedroom, "Gotta go. Sarina needs me."

Max met Hannah at the door. "What did the doctor say?"

"Tell you later. Did you hear from Zachary?"

"No."

"How is Sarina?"

He nodded toward the living room. "Not good. The reality of what's happened has finally hit, and hit hard. I found her sitting on the floor in a corner clutching the baby, who was yelling her head off, poor little thing. Anna took Sarah to her house."

He led Hannah to Sarina, who was curled up, her knees to her chest, in a corner of the living room couch. The young woman lifted a tear-stained face, then dropped her head onto her knees.

"I want to die, I want to die," Sarina said between moans.

Hannah sat with her and stroked her hair. "My dear child. There have been times in my life when I thought I would never recover from a loss. Long ago, I loved a man with all my heart, and he was killed in a senseless boating accident. It broke my heart. I wanted to die."

Sarina lifted her head. Her voice was strained and raspy from crying. She placed a hand over her heart. "What will make this terrible pain go away? Tell me, Hannah? What shall I do? What did you do?"

Max slipped from the room. Through the living room window Hannah watched him take the steps two at a time

and disappear across the lawn. She could see the humming-
bird feeding station that hung on the porch, see the birds
whizzing up to it, sticking their long bills in to extract the
sweet liquid, then whizzing away. She closed her eyes for a
minute, remembering Dan, then gave her full attention to
Sarina.

"One day, the pain was so enormous that I thought I'd
break apart. I got into my car and drove to the lake where he
had been killed, where he and I had been so often. I stood at
the water's edge. I remember thinking, What is that noise?
Who's screaming like that? The pain gushed up from the
deepest pit of my belly and the sounds I made didn't sound
human, and I didn't try to stop them."

Sarina stared at Hannah, her eyes wide, disbelieving.
"You did that?"

Hannah smoothed the hair from Sarina's face. "Yes, my
dear child, I did that. Too often we want to scream our pain
and we feel we can't."

"And it made you feel better to do that?"

"It made it better. It was like breaking a pot and letting
the contents, the pain, spill out. I'm not saying that was the
end of it. Even today when I think about him, it hurts a
little. That day, I sat on the ground and talked to him. I told
him how angry I was that he had died and left me. I cursed
him for my loneliness and misery. I used language that I
would consider unbecoming and would never use in my
everyday life."

Sarina pulled herself to a more erect position. She dried
her eyes with a big handkerchief Hannah handed her. "You
think I can do that? Is there a lake nearby?"

"It doesn't have to be a lake. It can be anywhere where
you're alone and feel that you can let it all out. Or you could

write your feelings, write letters to Zachary, letters you'll never mail. Tell him how you feel, all of it, your anger, your pain."

"I can do that easier than screaming, I think. I will try the writing first. I will do anything to ease this terrible, terrible pain in my heart." She grabbed Hannah's hand and squeezed it hard. "How could he do this to me, to our baby? He said he loved me. How could he love me and do this to me? What did I do wrong?"

"You did nothing wrong. Zachary brought you here to his home, knowing that there were unresolved issues with his father, issues that went back to his childhood and that have nothing to do with you. It appears that he always stuffed his feelings. Perhaps the trauma of his accident on the mountain triggered old memories and emotions from his childhood.

"The problem was, he exploded at an inappropriate time, with the cows being carried off, and in front of strangers, and Max overreacted. He wishes he had handled Zachary differently, that he had stayed calm and not flown off the handle, but he didn't. Zachary, it appears, did what he's done before. He ran away rather than confront the situation."

"But I am here. He didn't have to run away from me."

"My dear, Zachary's been running away from his problems for a long time. When he first got home, when you were pregnant, did he sit down and talk to his father, talk about his concerns, his work, what he hoped to do and why? No, he chose to disappear, to go off gambling."

Sarina nodded. "Yes, he did not consider how I might worry about him. He is quite self-centered and immature."

Hannah stroked her arm gently. "We make choices as to how we handle life's problems, and who gets through life

without problems? Some people face things head-on. Zachary, I'm afraid, runs away. I'm sure you knew this about him.
You've probably tried to change him."

Sarina nodded.

"You can't change him. No one can change another person. I wish it had been different, that he could have taken
the help offered him." Hannah shrugged. "He wanted land,
not affection or understanding. You could not fix him no
matter how hard you tried."

"Will he come back, do you think?" Sarina asked.

"I don't know."

"What will I do, Hannah?"

"You'll stay with us, focus on your baby, and heal from
this shock."

"It will be all right with Max for me to stay?"

"Sarina, it would break Max's heart if you left. He loves
you. He may not say those words. He's not easy with words,
but he loves you dearly and that baby is the light of his
life."

Briefly, a smile hovered at the corners of Sarina's lips. "I
will stay, then, and I will try not to make a fuss, a scene like
today."

"Make all the scenes you need to make. I'm well aware
of how much this hurts, and it takes time to heal the pain.
We're here to help."

"I will go to Sarah now. I thank you, Hannah, for coming and talking to me and helping me." She threw her arms
about Hannah and for a moment rested against her, and
Hannah held her, wondering that she loved this girl as much
as she loved her own daughters.

37

Hannah's Surgery

*I*n June, Hannah underwent outpatient surgery on her knees. Afterward, she would tell everyone that it was a snap and that the staff had been kinder and more efficient than in any medical facility she had ever been in. Hannah stayed in the guest room downstairs and was up and about the day after surgery, though she moved slowly and carefully. Having given herself permission to take a week off from work, she slept late, caught up on gardening magazines and novels she had been meaning to read.

Max was in and out, and this day he arrived at noon and settled into the glider-rocker, his long legs stretched out before him.

"Medicine has sure come a long way," Hannah said. "If I'd known it would be so easy and this painless, I'd have had this surgery a long time ago."

"You've been walking around in pain for months, and you didn't say anything to me." Max slapped the side of his head. "And I'm such an oaf that I didn't see that? I am really sorry."

She looked at him, her eyes tender. "Don't be sorry, my love. It's not your fault. I'm a stoic, remember, stiff upper lip, that sort of thing. I didn't want anyone to know. I was scared about doing this."

"Well, honey, I'm glad it's over and behind you."

"So am I."

"Soon you'll be climbing mountains." Max grew sober, remembering Zachary and his aborted mountain climb. He wondered where his son was and what he was doing. It was weeks since he had left, and no one had heard from him. He changed the subject. "Sarina seems to be doing better, wouldn't you say?"

"It would seem that way. These things take time. She doesn't spend hours in her room crying anymore," Hannah replied. "She's smart to focus on the baby. Sarina's a good mother." Hannah settled back against the pillows and folded her hands in her lap. "Now, tell me about Jose's restaurant. How is it coming?"

"Well, let's see, it's been four days since we started painting the room. Looks like, with the kitchen area taken out of the space, we'll be able to get six tables for two and eight booths for four. That seems adequate for starters, wouldn't you say?"

"I've always believed in starting small. Maybe because it feels safer. There's less to lose."

"In all the years I've known Jose, I've never seen him so excited and happy," Max said. "He never complained, but with his arthritis, he must have been in pain getting up early in the cold. That's all over with now." Max shifted and tried to fit in the rocker better by sitting taller. "The inspectors were out and approved the electrical and plumbing. The kitchen equipment arrives next Monday."

"I could come to the office and make phone calls." She stretched her arms over her head. "But you know, Max, I don't want to go back to work yet, and I don't feel guilty. Isn't that marvelous?"

"There's no reason in the world to feel guilty, my love." He leaned forward, took her hand, and kissed it. "Give yourself this rest, Hannah. We're fine. Laura's a great help; she's very competent, like you. She handled the inspectors with confidence and authority. You'd have been proud of your daughter. I was."

"I am proud of her. It took her so many years to find herself. Some people take longer to mature."

"Are you suggesting that given enough time, Zachary will find himself?" He shook his head. "Frankly, Hannah, I doubt that. I think his lifestyle precludes happiness. There's a hole in his soul. His hormones landed him in a respectable marriage, but he's not the kind to settle down and be a family man." He sighed. "Sarina's a fine young woman, and I'm glad she's chosen to stay with us."

"Sarina wants to stay, or she'd return to her family in India."

"But what's to become of her? She's a young woman alone with a child." Max shook his head.

"Maybe she won't be alone forever. Haven't you noticed, Max, that our Pastor Denny seems quite taken with Sarina?"

"Sarina needs someone to talk to. He's counseling her."

"I think with him it's more than counseling, but then, what do I know?" Hannah shrugged. "I don't really have a good sense of people."

"I can't imagine Sarina having a romantic interest in Denny," Max said. "Not this soon, anyway, and not knowing if her husband's coming back or what's going to happen."

For a time they were silent. Hannah's eyes strayed to the window and to the hillside beyond where pines rose one above the other. Max broke the silence.

"Did you know that colors like orange, rust, pink, and red in a restaurant stimulate people to eat faster and leave sooner? Blues and greens relax people and they linger longer."

"I didn't know that. So what color is Jose using?"

"Jose decided on an attractive shade of rust-orange, and the booths will be what the salesman calls persimmon and a pleasant shade of yellow. Should be very nice, don't you think?"

She nodded. "Yes, nice. When do you begin to advertise?"

"Next week. I'm going to place ads in the Asheville, Weaverville, and Madison County papers, the *Mountain Xpress*, and *Rapid River* magazine, and an ad, maybe the whole back cover, in that woman's magazine."

"*Western North Carolina Woman's Magazine?* Is that the magazine you're talking about?" she asked. "I intended to suggest that. It's a very good magazine. We ladies all read it every month and enjoy it. Brenda knows the two women who started it, Sandi and Julie. They're hardworking gals. Good people. We ought to place an ad telling folks about the gardens and the historic village, maybe take the entire back cover and run it several times a year, especially during tourist season and the holiday season."

"Good idea. I'll tell Molly to prepare ads, meet with them, and work something out." He rose from the rocker and stretched his back and arms. He ached all over, stiffness that had nothing to do with this rocker, and which he knew would work itself out when he started moving. That was the trick. Moving seemed to oil old arthritic joints. "Well, honey, you rest and don't worry about anything. Wayne's gotten a lot done on the Oriental garden. The aquatic plants arrived and a load of rugged-looking, light-weight boulders. Wayne placed them. He said he thinks they're where you want them. If not, he'll move them. The water in the pond's clear now. I had the man test it the other morning, and the pH is finally what you wanted. All in all, it's going well, and the rain has stopped so the earth's had a chance to dry out."

She raised her hands and beckoned him to her and kissed him on the lips. "Have a good day, a productive day. See you for dinner."

Hannah watched him leave, heard his heavy footsteps on the wood floor, and the front door open and close. Max was right. She needed this rest. But "rest" was hardly a word in her vocabulary. It never had been. She had been a working girl when she met and married Bill Parrish; keeping house for him and their daughters had been tense, anxiety producing, and anything but restful. And then, after she had found the strength to leave him, she had worked hard and long to support her daughters.

What would she do if she didn't work, especially now? She loved every minute of her time at Bella's Park. She could hardly call it work. It was sheer pleasure.

Hannah threw back the covers, eased her legs over the side, and prepared to stand. Hooked over the headboard was a wooden cane Amelia had presented to her when she came home from surgery. Hannah reached for it. Easing herself to her feet, she walked slowly to the kitchen. It was lunchtime, and she was hungry.

Grace had left a pot of stew simmering on the stove and a pretty china bowl and silverware sat on a bright yellow place mat on the kitchen table. Hannah smiled and helped herself to stew. She had just placed the empty soup bowl in the sink when the phone rang. It was Tyler, asking if Grace were there.

"No, I'm afraid not. She'll be back in about an hour, I would imagine. Want to call back, or shall I ask her to phone you?"

"I'll give her a ring," Tyler said, then asked, "Hannah, how you feeling?"

"Pretty good. Bored sitting around by myself all day."

"If you're up to it, I could come over. We're having a kite-flying contest over on the school grounds next week, and I plan to enter and win. Would you like to help me build my kite? It's something special."

"A kite-flying contest?" She thought about that. "Well, why not, Tyler? Come on over and let's see what we can do to get that kite ready for your contest."

"See you in a bit, then."

Hannah set the phone down. What had she gotten herself into? You either related to teenagers or you didn't. She never had. Fifteen-year-old Lucy Banks worked on Saturdays at the gardens and they had never gotten chummy, not the way Grace did with young people. Mainly, she gave Lucy instructions or taught her about some aspect of soil or plants. They had talked briefly about Randy's suicide attempt and how Lucy had been the one who found him. Hannah shuddered. Imagine a teenager finding her brother lying in a bathtub after having slashed his wrists. Listening to Lucy's troubles had been uncomfortable. It seemed incumbent on her to offer words of wisdom, and she felt guilty not doing so. It never occurred to Hannah that listening was enough. She had never had a meaningful conversation with

Tyler. Well, he'd work on his project, she would keep him company, and it would help pass the day.

Tyler arrived with his paraphernalia, which included ripstop nylon and fiberglass rods that fit into one another for the frame. This was very different from the tissue paper and thin sticks Hannah had used for kite building when she was young.

"We're going to do a fiery dragon kite. I ordered the kit on sale for twelve ninety-nine. It's usually sixteen ninety-nine. When it's done, it'll be thirty-eight inches by forty-two inches."

"That's a little over three feet and a little under four feet. Big," Hannah said. "I'm impressed."

"It's diamond shaped." He showed her a picture of the design on the kite, a fire-breathing dragon in brilliant red, gold, and black. "It's an old design, but I like the way these kites handle rather than the more boxy ones. A lot of kids are flying much fancier kites these days. There are different categories of kites, you know. Dragons will fly in six- to ten-mile-an-hour winds."

She didn't know about kites, or wind velocity as it applied to kites. "You mean your kite will be competing against other dragon kites?"

"That's right." Tyler looked at her and smiled.

"Have you always been interested in kites?"

"Not really. Just since I read *The Kite Runner*. Have you read it?"

Hannah shook her head. "What was it about?"

"A boy who lived in Afghanistan and his friend, and they entered kite contests. Kites are popular, and winning a kite contest is important in Afghanistan." He held up the picture of his kite and studied it. He set it down and read from a sheet of paper that had been included in the box.

"Dragons are made up of the parts of nine animals: the head of a camel, the horns of a deer, the eyes of a devil—is a devil an animal, do you think?" He laughed. "The neck of a snake, the stomach of a clam, the scales of a carp, the claws of an eagle, the paws of a tiger, the ears of an ox. Look at this picture." He handed it to her. "Do you see all those things?"

"No, I don't."

"Well, it makes a good story, I guess," Tyler said.

Then, without further ado or conversation, he set about building the dragon kite.

Hannah sat in a chair most of the time, although she walked about to hold this end or that, when he needed her help. When it was done, they stood back and inspected the work.

"It's one pretty kite, isn't it? I'm afraid it takes up so much of your table, you wouldn't be able to eat in your dining room until Dad comes with his SUV and moves it for me. Is that all right?"

"Yes. It's no trouble. We eat in the kitchen unless we're having company."

He walked around the table and studied his creation. "It looks a lot like the one in the picture, don't you think?"

Hannah nodded. It was a striking, fire-breathing dragon as the name on the kit indicated. "It's spectacular. It's huge and looks very sturdy. Once she's up and the wind takes her, she'll be unbeatable."

Tyler grinned ear to ear. "You really think so, Aunt Hannah?"

"I most certainly do. When is the contest?"

"Next Sunday. Maybe you and Uncle Max will come and bring Sarina and the baby."

Hannah stretched her leg. "We just might do that. If I can get about well enough and sit on a folding chair that long. Thanks for asking me to help you. It's been a fascinating experience. I've learned a lot about kites, dragon kites anyway, and I've enjoyed it."

Tyler stopped picking up the bits and pieces left over from kite making. "I enjoyed it too. I never get a chance to talk with you. I've always admired the way you make gardens that are so beautiful. My mother, Amy, would have loved them. If she were alive, I'd bring her over and we'd walk in your gardens, sit on a bench in the shade, and talk about things." His eyes misted and he looked away. "I miss her a lot, still."

"It's hard to lose a loved one, especially your mother. I miss all the people I've ever loved and lost. Sometimes I lie in bed at night and bring a picture of someone I loved into my mind, and I talk to that person. Do you ever do that, talk to your mother?"

He shuffled his feet and was silent for a time.

Hannah worried that this was not a conversation to be having with a teenager. But then Tyler said, "I was so young when my mom died. I don't remember her very well." His eyes sought and held Hannah's. "We have pictures of her. Do you think it would be the same if I talked to her picture?"

"Sure. Some people go to a grave and talk to the person. What you say will come from your heart, and it doesn't matter if you do it in bed at night, walking to school, or anywhere else."

He flushed and was silent for a time. "Would my mother really hear me?" His eyes bore into Hannah's. "I wonder a lot. Is there a heaven? If there is, what's it like? Will my mother be waiting for me when I die?" He shook his head and looked away, and she was spared having to respond to his question when he turned to her and said, "Nah! I don't believe all that heaven stuff. I don't even know if I believe in God. Do you believe in God, Hannah?"

Hannah considered. Over the years, she and God had had an inconsistent and tumultuous relationship. Her mother and grandmother believed in God, and so had she as a child and young adult. They had taken her to church, but not every Sunday. Her father resisted going and joined them only when prodded by her mother on holidays like Christmas. God, as she remembered him, was a grandfatherly man with a long white beard, smiling, sitting on a throne or a huge chair like her father's.

It had seemed to her that Granny Teresa prayed incessantly, her lips moving, and when Hannah had asked what she was saying and to whom, she would cast her eyes skyward and say, "To *him*." When they were out walking, Granny had insisted on visiting every church they passed. She would enter, kneel, and pray way too loudly, which had embarrassed Hannah.

Once, on a Saturday, Granny dragged her into the local synagogue. A service was under way, but they were ushered to seats, and Hannah recalled finding the chanting in another language—Hebrew, her Granny said it was—oddly pleasant and soothing.

"God is everywhere," Granny explained. "And remember, Hannah, he's always watching you, so you be a good girl."

And that left eight-year-old Hannah anxious and worried that a critical or punishing God watched her when she took a bath, when she played with her friends, whatever she did, wherever she did it; and that sense of intrusion into her private moments and thoughts frightened and put Hannah off.

Finally, she had asked her mother about God keeping tabs on her behavior. Her mother pooh-poohed her mother-in-law. "She's a silly old woman. She was born Lutheran. If she would just settle on one church, any church, and meet some women her age, play bingo maybe, do things, go to a movie, instead of all that praying, she'd be a lot happier."

It was a relief to Hannah when she grew older and came under the skeptical and cynical influence of her peers. She stopped attending church and began to think of God as man-made—until a teacher in high school, responding to a student's question about God, said that the belief in someone or something greater than man existed in every culture, in every society, in all parts of the world. They had touched briefly, then, on the religious beliefs of Native Americans, Arabs, East Indians, the Japanese, and for the first time Hannah heard the words Muslim, Hindu, Buddhist, and "ancestor worship."

At some point her father had said, "People make choices and create their own lives." He pointed a long finger upward and rolled his eyes toward the ceiling of their porch. "God's got wars, famine, floods, hurricanes to worry about. He hasn't got time to waste on our day-to-day, petty little troubles."

As Hannah considered Tyler's question, the normal sounds, the hum of the refrigerator, cars passing on Cove Road, even the tapping of her fingers on the table, bypassed

her consciousness. How should she respond to him? How
did she feel about God now, today? God hadn't intervened
to stop Bill's heavy fist from smashing down on her. He
hadn't driven the car when she escaped with two young
children into the cold February night, nor had he fed her
family while she struggled to get enough education to find a
decent job to support them.

But then, that same February night, after Bill found her
at a gas station in Michigan and shot the radiator of her car,
making escape impossible, a burly truck driver had stepped
forward and offered her and the children a ride, and they
had taken it. He had seemed like an angel; perhaps he had
been. She had spent a portion of that long ride from upper
Michigan to New England thanking God.

When Dan, the great love of her life, died, she blamed
God, but when, soon after, she had been contacted by her
daughter Miranda, whom she had not seen in years, she
thanked God and returned east to Pennsylvania. There
Miranda and her husband loaned her funds to open a small
plant nursery, and slowly, working with the earth and living
things, Hannah's spirit had healed.

So what was it all about? God was acknowledged when
things went well and ignored or denied when they did
not? Hannah envied people whose faith led them to simply trust, regardless of how good or bad things were. Still!
Sitting back in her chair, Hannah crossed her arms over
her chest and smiled at Tyler. He was a sweet young man
growing up in a troubled world with issues like terrorists,
fast foods destroying the health of Americans, and global
warming.

"Life is hard. It can be sad and lonely, as you know," she
said. "I believe there is a God, and that we turn to him for

help and comfort, and that no matter when we turn to him, he's there for us."

Tyler leaned across the table, his face animated, his eyes bright. "Yes, you're probably right about God, and as Dad says, there are just some things like Mom's dying that we can't understand. Dad says it's all about love. We have to treasure family and stay true to one another." He blushed and looked away, then back at her. "I consider you and Aunt Amelia, and Granny Grace, of course, my family. So I'm lucky we all live near one another. As for God, I intend to ask him to let this kite win the contest."

And what, Hannah wondered, if he does not win? A great weariness came over her. She was exhausted, had probably been on her feet too long, and wanted to lie down, to be alone. She was relieved when the front door opened and Grace swept into the house, all smiles and carrying a bag of groceries.

"Well, have you heard the news?" Grace set the bag on the kitchen counter. She stopped. "Come over here, Tyler. You're not too big or too old to give me a hug."

He complied, smiling, obviously happy to see her. "Aunt Hannah and I built a grand kite. It's in the dining room. You must see it."

"I will. I will, in a minute. First, I have to tell you and Aunt Hannah the news."

"Out with it, then," Hannah said. "I must lie down. What's the news?"

"That man Ben, from the photo workshop that Amelia and Miriam went to in New Mexico, is coming to visit. He phoned Miriam. He was going to stay at the motel in Mars Hill, but Amelia invited him to stay in our guest room, that is, after you're back upstairs, Hannah."

"And when is he coming?"

"Who are you talking about, Granny Grace?" Tyler asked.

Grace answered Hannah's question first. "He's coming in two weeks."

"Oh, surely I'll be up in my own room by then," Hannah said.

"Who is the man and why is he coming?" Tyler asked.

Grace took Tyler's face in her hands. "The man's name is Ben, and he's coming to visit Miriam. He's a photographer they met in New Mexico."

"Is he Miriam's boyfriend?"

"Heavens, no, Tyler. He's just a friend."

"It's what Amelia was so concerned about," Hannah said. "Well, we'll have to wait to see what he's like and what happens."

"What's going to happen?" Tyler looked from one to the other.

"We don't know, Tyler. Maybe he and Miriam will fall in love and get married, and she'll move away, and maybe they won't and nothing will change," Hannah said.

"I don't think they should get married. They might get divorced like my dad and Emily, and that would hurt Sadie. She's like a cousin to Melissa and me. I wouldn't want her to move away." Tyler looked at the kitchen clock. "I gotta go. Dad's got a business meeting tonight, and I gotta get dinner and watch Melissa this evening. Thanks a million, Hannah. Bye, Granny Grace. Dad'll be by later to pick up the kite, okay?" And he was gone, forgetting to show the kite to Grace and leaving his bag of trash behind him.

38

Grace

Grace was exhausted. She had run errands for herself, for Bob, for the household, and at every turn, traffic had impeded her progress. At one point she smacked the steering wheel with her palm and muttered unkind words under her breath. Red lights held on for what seemed an eternity; drivers in other cars were as impatient as she was. Long lines in stores and young, seemingly indifferent clerks annoyed Grace. Had everyone hired teenagers for the summer, and not bothered to train them? Frustrated, she had tapped her foot impatiently and worried that Hannah was home alone.

What a relief, then, to see Tyler's car in the driveway. He had just turned sixteen, and she fussed when his father bought him a used Chevy. But it checked out well and had not given Tyler any trouble. She had driven with him once and been satisfied that he understood that a car was a dangerous weapon. Of course, you never knew what teenagers would do when other teens egged them on. But Tyler's mother had been killed by a speeding driver, so he was surely more cautious than other teens might be. She could not make herself crazy worrying about everyone.

With Tyler gone, Grace moved between the pantry to the fridge, putting away canned goods, fresh fruit, and vegetables. A can of beans slipped from her hand and rolled beneath the table. Getting down was fine; getting up, well, that was not so easy, but she managed, holding on to the edge of the table and pulling herself to her feet.

"This is crazy," she said. "I need to calm down and leave this unpacking for later. What I could use is a good hot cup of tea out on the porch."

Hannah rose. "I'll make it."

"You said you were tired and needed to lie down."

"Yes, but I can do this, and I'll rest sitting with you on the porch. You sit for a minute now and take a deep breath."

Hannah filled the kettle and turned on the stove, then took two cups and saucers from a shelf above the counter, and the tea canister. When the tea was ready, Grace carried the tray out onto the porch, and they settled into rocking chairs. Hannah raised her leg and placed it on a small stool with a cushion that Grace brought outside.

"Don't rock, now, or you'll drag your leg off and hit the floor." Grace sipped her tea. "This is good. I really needed this." She began to hum, then stopped. "I wonder, is it the tea itself, or taking time out to relax, that makes me feel so much better? Do you remember a commercial about tea, Hannah? I remember a line or two of it." She sang, *"Take tea and see what a difference. Take tea and see.* What brand was that, anyway?"

"I don't recall hearing it, but then, we drank coffee in my house."

"It seems to me that the older I get, the harder it is to stay calm in the face of stress. Why do you think that is?"

"A doctor I went to after Dan's death told me that over time the system in our body that handles stress, the adrenaline system I think he said, loses its ability to return the body to a relaxed condition after we become upset. That day when I heard what Zachary did to his father, how he spoke to Max, I was furious. It took me forever to stop feeling agitated."

"Maybe you and I ought to sign up for yoga or a meditation class, so we can learn how not to get upset in the first place, especially about things over which we have no control," Grace said.

"Lord, but I couldn't get this body into those yoga positions I've seen on television." Hannah laughed.

"They have yoga classes for seniors. The movements are easy and simple. Would you go with me if I found one?" Grace asked. "I could really use something to loosen me up and give me a tool to help when I get upset. Today in that traffic, for example, I could feel my blood pressure shooting sky high, and I kept worrying about you being alone in the house, and here you were just fine, helping Tyler make a kite."

"If you had the cell phone Russell gave you, you could have called me," Hannah said.

"I hate those things. They're way too small. I can hardly see the numbers. My fingers slip and I don't hit the right buttons. I tried to use Bob's before he lost it somewhere, but it's so frustrating."

"Tell you what, Grace. You get another cell phone, and we'll go over it together until you master it, and I'll take a senior yoga class with you."

Grace's rocker slowed. "Will you really, Hannah?"

"I will. I promise."

Grace clapped her hands. "I'll tell Bob to get me a new cell phone. Maybe he can find one with larger buttons. Someone said Verizon makes one for seniors with larger buttons." She was silent a moment. "Shall I ask Amelia if she'd like to take yoga with us?"

Hannah sighed. "Can't this be something just the two of us do?"

"Yes, just the two of us. Of course."

There it was again. No matter how pleasant things seemed between Hannah and Amelia, an underlying tension persisted. Hannah preferred doing things without Amelia. Amelia preferred doing things with Grace without Hannah. Grace preferred having them do things as a three-some. Maybe three was too much of a crowd, as the old saying went.

How, then, had they managed to set aside so many of their differences and live together peacefully most of the time? On some level, they needed one another, less now than they had originally, of course, but they cared for one another and were like sisters. Siblings fussed at one another. Things could change, but Grace liked to think that she, Amelia, and Hannah would grow very old together. And then what? They would all die, of course, and one of them would be left alone. No. They were not alone, not since Amelia had Miriam and Sadie. Grace understood Amelia's concern that Miriam would marry and move away. She had never really imagined what it might be like to grow old without a child. "I'll check the yoga classes in Mars Hill and see what I can come up with," Grace said.

At that moment the sun slipped behind Snowman's Cap. Streaks of flame followed by layers of lavender bowed before the golden hue of a pleasant summer evening.

39

Heartbreak

The FedEx van rolled into Max's driveway and out again. Moments later, Anna placed an envelope in Sarina's hands. "This came for you," she said.

"Zachary?"

Anna raised her eyebrows and nodded. She could see the anxiety in the young woman's eyes.

Sarina slipped the envelope under her arm. "Anna, will you watch Sarah for me, please? She's sleeping, but she could wake up any minute."

"*Sí*, señora."

Gripped by fear and hope, her heart racing, Sarina could hardly breath. "I'm going to walk up on the hill."

She did not think. She could not think. High above the house, she looked down on the red-roofed empty barn and the church steeple. Today she had her weekly appointment with Pastor Denny. He was kind. It helped to talk about Zachary, about her family in India, about things in America that confused her, like the way people spoke to one another with less civility than she was accustomed to. She dreaded and longed to read what Zachary had sent. Finally, she sank to the grass and, hands shaking, opened the envelope. With growing disbelief, anger, and disappointment, she read:

> *Dear Sarina,*
>
> *There are no words to apologize for packing my bags and walking out on you and Sarah, so I will not do so. This letter finds me working on a fishing sloop off of the coast of Peru. The anchovy catch is meager and the boat stinks. I will be leaving here soon for fairer climes and more lucrative occupation. I do miss you and Sarah.*

Liar, she thought. Once a liar, always a liar. She had never told her parents, or Max and Hannah, or anyone else the truth that Zachary was not, as they all believed, an accomplished hiker and mountain climber. Her brother, Sanjay, in reply to her suspicions and pressing questions, had reluctantly admitted that he and Zachary met, not on a Himalayan climb, but in a tavern in Nepal after an aborted mountain climb of Sanjay's. They had awakened from a night of excessive drinking to find themselves on a train bound for India and her family's home, and had concocted a lie, which, over time, Sanjay said, they had come to believe.

And now, after weeks of silence, when she had finally stopped crying herself to sleep at night, he had written this self-centered letter to drive a knife once more into her heart? She would tear it to shreds. She would not subject herself to his lies, his cruelty and lack of compassion. Folding the letter, she held it in both hands, squeezed her eyes shut, and prepared to rip the paper apart. Impossible. Sarina unfolded the letter and continued reading.

I cannot live in one place, settle for some mundane, nine-to-five job. Much as it hurts me to say this, and I know it will hurt you even more to hear it, I cannot return to Covington, nor can I offer you a home anywhere else, not now and possibly never. Believe me, I have loved you and still do and I love our daughter. I hope periodically to visit you both, but that will not be for a long time. I know that you are surrounded by people who love you and will care for you. Divorce me if you wish. You are free to make whatever decision you deem best. If you can, remember me with pleasure, as I remember you.

Zachary

No apology, no "I love you," nothing. Remember him with pleasure? Her throat felt as if a rake had been dragged across it. She pounded her chest with her fist. Cry. Scream. It had been like this when her grandmother died. She had adored her and had been devastated by her death, and had not cried while the entire household wept and wailed.

"You're a freak," her youngest sister shrieked. "Why don't you cry like the rest of us?"

Her mother understood and gave her space. When she finally exploded, she wondered if the tears and sadness would ever end. By all the gods, she needed her mother now.

"Cry," she yelled. "Cry." Unconcerned that insects bit her arms or that a sharp rock jabbed the side of her leg, Sarina rocked back and forth, back and forth. After a time, she struggled to her feet and stumbled down the hillside. In the house, she called to Anna. "Please, watch Sarah. I must find Hannah and Max."

"Sí, señora. I watch *la niña.*"

Sarina ran from the house and out onto the grass along Cove Road. She heard and saw nothing until she collided with Denny Ledbetter, who had just closed the door of the church and started down the walk. They tumbled to the grass in a tangle of arms and legs.

"Goodness me, Sarina. Are you all right?" Denny rolled away from her, pushed to his feet, and offered her his hand. "What has happened?"

Unable to speak or to accept his outstretched hand, she sat where she had fallen, head bent, shoulders hunched. Finally, she managed, "I am so sorry." She shoved the letter at him.

Denny dropped to his knees beside her. Without thinking, he put his arms about her, held her, and rocked her gently. "Bad news?"

She nodded.

"Do you want me to read it?"

Again she nodded, and buried her face in his chest.

Across the road, Alma and her daughter-in-law exited their house and started for Alma's station wagon. They stopped and stared.

"Well, I declare. Our pastor's hugging that Indian woman," Alma said.

The younger woman hurried her to the vehicle. "Come along now, Mother Craine, or we'll be late for your doctor's appointment." Moments later they drove away, but Alma had come upon grist for the gossip mill, and she went on and on about how shocking it was, that Indian woman and the pastor, and how unseemly.

*   *   *

The thin paper made a crinkling sound as Denny slipped it from its envelope. He read slowly, digesting the words, struggling for words of his own with which to comfort Sarina. As he finished the letter and was about to return it to its envelope, he noticed the thumbprint smears and the faint unpleasant odor of fish. His first impulse was to castigate this man who had caused her so much pain. How would that help Sarina?

Sarina righted herself and found her voice. "I will never forgive him." Then, she crumbled and fell sideways on the grass. Was that her wailing? Was it a wolf on the hillside? It didn't sound human.

Feeling helpless, Denny looked around, wishing for Max or Hannah. Silently he prayed for the wisdom to help this young woman. He prayed for guidance, for courage, for self-control, for he knew as he looked down at her, doubled in pain and weeping, that he loved her, and this shocked and left him speechless.

Max appeared, followed closely by Hannah. Without a word, Max bent and scooped Sarina into his arms. As he carried her toward his house, her wails echoed the length and breadth of Cove Road, and Denny was glad that Alma was out of sight and out of hearing.

Hannah touched Denny on the shoulder. He started and looked up at her. "Thank you," she said. "Anna called us. She said there was a letter."

He nodded.

"You read it?"

"Yes." He handed the missive to Hannah.

She nodded toward Max and Sarina, turning into his driveway. "It must have been devastating."

"Yes," Denny said. "Devastating." He could feel heat in his

face, anger roiling in the pit of his belly. "Cruel. He is a totally selfish and unfeeling man. He doesn't deserve Sarina."

"I agree with you, Denny. I'd best get on home. Thank you, again. Thank you for all you've done for Sarina." Hannah hurried away.

Denny's legs quivered. If he tried to stand, he was certain that they would give way beneath him. His confession, though only to himself, confused and unsettled him. It was wrong, just plain wrong. Sarina was a married woman. To love her, to want her, violated the laws of God and betrayed the very core of his being.

Later, after an exhausted Sarina had gone to bed, Hannah and Max sat on the front porch. He reached for her hand and she wound her fingers through his. "Youth is a dreadful time of life. So much angst," Hannah said. "I wouldn't want to be young again."

"Zachary's my son. I can't help but feel in some way responsible for what's happened. But damn it." Max slapped the palm of his free hand on the arm of the rocker. "He picked the worst time to insult me, to make demands." He thought a moment. "Still, if I'd listened to him, sat down, and talked. With all the land we have, what are twenty acres?"

"This goes deeper than Zachary wanting twenty acres to build rental houses. So if you had given him land, for a year or two he would have been busy building houses and renting them. What then? Zachary is possessed by wanderlust. It's like an addiction. He must keep moving, searching for God knows what."

"If I had been a different kind of father, paid more attention to who he was instead of imposing my wants and needs on him."

"You were who you were, Max. You did what you could at that time. Is there a parent who hasn't made mistakes, who if they're honest with themselves wishes they'd done things differently? If Bella were here, don't you think she'd search her soul wondering what she'd done or not done?"

"You're probably right. You do the best you can."

"And if you have several kids, each one of them remembers an event of their childhood differently. You can't win," she said. "I used to berate myself for messing up with my girls, all the things I didn't say or do or said or did wrong. If you're lucky, you have the chance to say you're sorry, and you move on. Hopefully, they're mature enough to accept your apology. I was lucky to have had that opportunity with Miranda and Laura, and they were mature enough, thank God, to accept my apologies.

"I'll make it up to him. I'll take care of Sarina and Sarah."

Hannah took his hand in both of hers. "Dear Max. You're a good man. I know you'll do whatever you can for Sarina and Sarah, not for Zachary and not out of guilt, but because you love them."

His head fell forward. "I do love them, and I hate my son for hurting them."

"Many of us share that feeling."

Across Cove Road, a taxi pulled into the ladies' driveway, its tires scrunching the gravel. A man got out. He paid the driver, slung his backpack over his shoulder, and mounted the front steps of the farmhouse.

"Who's that?" Max asked.

"That must be Ben Mercer, the man Miriam met in New Mexico. He's here to visit her."

The visitor set his backpack on the porch floor. He turned and his gaze traveled to the top of the mountain behind Max's house. He shaded his eyes from the sun.

"What's he doing?" Hannah asked.

"Surveying the scene, I imagine," Max replied.

"Why doesn't he knock on the door?"

"He's probably delaying that. He knows he'll be given the once-over by Amelia and her housemates." Hannah laughed and poked Max's shoulder. "He's a lucky fellow. Grace is home, and she'll give him a royal welcome."

"Doesn't Amelia like him?" Max asked.

"She likes him just fine. She's afraid Miriam will marry him and move away."

"It's that serious, he and Miriam?"

"Amelia seems to think so."

"Hmm. What line of work is he in, do you know?"

"Something with computers," Hannah replied.

"That could be a portable skill," Max said. "If he married Miriam he could relocate here, and Amelia would be happy."

Ben saw them and waved.

Max and Hannah waved. Then Hannah stood and smoothed her slacks. "Come to think of it, maybe no one's home. I better go over and let him in, show him to his room."

Max stood. "I need to get back to the park. See you later. Coming for dinner?"

"Yes. I want to be here for Sarina when she's rested awhile," Hannah replied. She kissed him, stepped past him, and walked swiftly across the grass and across Cove Road. Max watched as she greeted the man, opened the front door, and ushered him inside.

40

The Birth Pangs of a Business

*H*eavyhearted and stiff in every joint, Max walked slowly down the steps and headed for Bella's Park to meet with Jose and the painters. He had forgotten how much work was involved in getting a new business off the ground. He had set Jose up with his own bookkeeper, but after several meetings with Jose, she had asked if Irena or Anna might be better able to grasp debit, credit, and other business concepts. Jose, she said, was wonderful with people but should avoid record keeping.

"He'll make a great maître d', but he seems unable or unwilling to grasp the idea that every pencil he buys, every gallon of gas he uses in service to the restaurant, is deductible. He just won't keep records of his mileage to Mars Hill to Builder's Express for a screwdriver. Slips from his purchases are scrunched into wads, stuck into his pocket, and pulled as sodden globs from the washing machine." Max had scheduled a meeting with her, Anna, and Irena later this afternoon. Now he worried that if Sarina was unable to care for Sarah herself, Anna would not leave them alone in the house and there would be no meeting.

Max stood in the road and looked up at the old farmhouse so carefully renovated to meet their needs. Once the restaurant opened, they would have to sacrifice a part of the lawn to one side of the building for parking, or maybe they could move the parking a bit farther over. They owned the entire cul-de-sac. Yes, he'd rather do that and pave a winding path, something attractive, with an arbor to pass through, perhaps, than lose so much lawn close to the office. He'd discuss it with Hannah.

When he reached the front door of the office, Max leaned against it. He wanted to go home, to fall into bed, and sleep for a week. Why was he so tired lately?

The other day, Hannah suggested that he was grieving the loss of the dairy and his beloved cows. That was ridiculous. He'd made his decision rationally after weeks of deliberation. Then she had said that perhaps that loss, plus the emotional impact of Zachary's verbal attack, followed by his disappearance, added to the stress, and stress could wipe you out. He knew that. And now this confounded cold letter his son had sent Sarina. Max wanted to wring Zachary's neck.

Still, there were nights lately when he awakened in a cold sweat, worrying that at his age, the role of surrogate father to an infant had been thrust upon him. He would probably be dead before Sarah finished elementary school. It didn't seem right.

Odd that Sarina felt she couldn't go home. The belief systems of other cultures had always seemed strange to him, but this was too peculiar, that her parents would not welcome a wonderful girl like Sarina and this beautiful baby. It was their loss. Sarina would always be welcome here.

Raised voices, angry voices, reached him as he entered the reception area of the office. Jose argued in Spanish with someone responding in English. When Jose was upset, his grasp of English drained away, increasing his frustration. Max hastened into the soon-to-be restaurant.

Upturned on the floor, a five-gallon can discharged thick yellow paint onto the drop cloth. Jose grasped one end of the cloth, a soppy mess, sending paint dripping onto the new floor. The painter yelled at him to drop the cloth, saying that he would clean it up, which seemed to further agitate Jose, for he dragged the cloth with its mess, leaving a trail of yellow spots and streaks behind him.

Max put an arm about Jose. "Jose, *mi amigo*. You can let it go now. It's going to be okay." He repeated "okay" several times, until the word sunk into Jose's consciousness, and he allowed the cloth to fall with a swishing sound to the floor.

"Señor Max. I knock it over. I try to fix." He looked with accusing eyes at the painter. "He *no comprende*."

"It's okay." Max nodded at the painter, who threw up his arms and turned away. "He'll take care of it. You come with me." He led Jose, who chattered in Spanish, from the room. Too often, lately, he was called upon to settle disputes. Too big, this whole park thing. Too many people involved. Too darn much work.

Jose was distraught. "I no good at this business, Señor Max. I make big mistake." He was close to tears.

Max led him to a seat in his office and handed Jose a Coke. "Relax. Let's talk about this."

"It bad mistake, restaurant. I miss cows. They do like I tell them, no argue with Jose."

Max ran his fingers through his hair. "I miss the cows too. They were our friends, yours and mine. As you say, they never talked back. Just a friendly moo now and then." He laughed lightly. "It was time for us to let them go, Jose.

We're not young men any longer, much as we hate to admit it. When the restaurant opens, you will greet people, seat them, and inquire if they are satisfied with the service and the food. It will be good. You'll see. You'll be happy you have the restaurant.

"We all have different skills. I'm no good with books. That's why I have a bookkeeper. Hannah's better with plants than people, wouldn't you say?"

Jose smiled and nodded. "She good with plants. *Verde* thumbs. Everything she touch, it grows."

"And if I plant something, it dies," Max said.

They chatted, then, about possible uses for the barn. "Should we tear it down?" Max asked. Seeing it empty pained them. The high walls loomed above as they walked past. Once a shutter came loose and swung back and forth like a finger, as if warning them not to forget the years of service the building had rendered.

"It be a waste to do that, Señor Max. What you think about *cabrones*? They good for eat grass in pasture. No weeds grow. *Los cabrones,* no trouble."

"Goats, eh? That's something to consider, isn't it? They could sleep inside at night and be out of the weather. That lower pasture is fenced, some mending to do on it. Can you get Fortino to help? We could turn the goats out in that pasture every day. It wouldn't have to be on their timetable, and there'd be no milking involved. We could have chickens, too."

"*Sí.* Anna, she want *pollos.*"

"That would give us fresh eggs for the restaurant. Jose, you're brilliant. Our trouble, my friend, is that we are both sad about our cows being gone and the barn sitting there staring at us." Max took long strides about his office. His mind raced. "I'll call the agriculture station and see what's the best kind of goats for our purpose."

Jose's face glowed. Cap in hand, he walked beside Max and spoke rapidly in Spanish. "*Sí*, Señor Max. Good. *Buena idea. Tenemos que conseguir la clase derecha de cabrones. Tenemos pollos también. Bueno.*

"Yes, as you say, we'll get us the right kind of goats, and chickens, too. One rooster is all we'll need, right?

"*Sí*, señor." He held up a finger and stuck out his chest. "*Uno.*"

It was amazing how much Spanish Max had picked up from working with Jose all these years. "And when the restaurant opens, you'll step right in to greet the customers. You'll wear a proper outfit, something a proprietor would wear in his restaurant in Ecuador."

"*Sí. Un traje con colores brillantes y una chaqueta.*"

Now, that I don't understand. Something with bright colors, did you say?"

"*Sí.*" Jose stuck his thumbs under his arms and again puffed out his chest. "Jacket of many colors."

"You get Anna to make it or have it made, and I'll pay for it. My gift to you."

"*Muchas gracias.*" Smiling broadly, Jose left Max's office, ignored the restaurant, where the painter swabbed paint spills, and hurried down Cove Road to report to his wife the good news about goats, chickens, and his fine new outfit.

41

What About Ben?

Covington delighted him.

At thirteen, Ben's life had convulsed in pain and changed forever. On a late-fall afternoon, he had returned from school to find the front yard of his home overrun by strangers. The heat of fire, the fire engines, and firemen dashing about confused and terrified him. Someone strong had grabbed him and whisked him away from the billowing smoke of what had been his home. Shocked and numb, hardly able to speak, a grief-stricken, orphaned boy had been transported from his Vermont village to a Boston suburb, to the apartment of his maternal grandparents.

Whether from the shock and horror of that day, the dislocation from country to city, or life with grandparents who never recovered from the loss of their daughter and son-in-law, Ben, a formerly lively and extroverted boy, became an introverted, somber adolescent. He found a sense of comfort and escape only after being given his first computer.

Now, Covington delighted him.

When he crossed the mountain into North Carolina, the lush green mountains reminded him of Vermont, his first home, his veterinarian father, and his warm and loving artist mother. He pulled into the welcome station, sat in his car, and wept. When he grew calmer, Ben Mercer's heart filled with hope. He had come home, and soon he would be with the woman who had stolen his heart.

Standing on the porch of the farmhouse, he was overcome by a sense of belonging. His eyes traveled from the huge red roses blooming in the garden to the white farmhouses, with their covered porches, that lined the road. They moved on to the small white church with its tall steeple, and on to a sign before a building that said *Bella's Park* and gardens that stretched up the hillside.

The man and woman sitting in rocking chairs on the porch of the house across the road reminded him of his grandparents. They had died two years ago, first his grandfather and then his grandmother, leaving him their house on Travis Lane in Concord.

They had been generous and loving. When he had been so unexpectedly thrust upon them, they had sold their apartment in Boston and moved to a small town in hopes of providing their only grandchild with a semblance of the country, a neighborhood school, and friends. He loved and missed them. They would like this street, this little town, and the couple across the road.

Instinctively, he waved to them, and they waved back. Then the woman rose, walked across the road and up the steps, and introduced herself as Hannah, one of Amelia's housemates. She invited him inside.

The smell of cookies transported Ben to his childhood home and to his mother, with whom he had baked cookies on Saturday afternoons. For a moment he stood silent, missing those days.

The woman in the kitchen did not resemble his tall, slender mother. Grace was short and somewhat stocky. The pattern on her apron was a rampage of red, yellow, and purple flowers. Flour smudged her nose, and he felt as if he had known her forever.

"I hope you brought your camera," Grace said. "It's beautiful here, and there are lots of pretty people." She laughed, stepped forward, and hugged him. "Welcome, Ben Mercer. We're happy to have you in our home. Come now, Hannah, let's show Ben his room."

Ben followed the women. Grace chattered. Hannah was silent as they rounded the staircase and made their way down a short hall to a green room with a large bed and a splendid view of hills and forest. Outside the window a dozen bird feeders attracted a variety of birds.

Grace pointed to the rocker. "I sit and watch the birds. I've left several bird books on the table, if you're interested."

"I don't know much about birds," Ben replied. "But I'm interested. Thank you all so much for allowing me to stay in your home, in this charming room." He wanted to ask where Miriam was and when he would see her.

As if reading his mind, Hannah said, "Miriam teaches, you know. She ought to be by here soon. She's probably stopped to pick up Sadie. Usually Amelia gets her after school, but Amelia's in Asheville setting up a photography exhibit for her partner, Mike. Why don't we leave you to wash up? Make yourself comfortable. We'll be in the kitchen. Join us when you're done." And they were gone.

Ben walked to the window. What was that startlingly blue bird? He could recognize a jay, but this was no jay. It was smaller and a brilliant blue. He knew little of birds or animals in general. He had buried himself in technology. His challenge in going to the workshop in New Mexico had been to open himself to nature. Amelia and Miriam had unwittingly helped him to do this.

He sat on the bed. Firm but not too firm. Four pillows: two foam, two down. He rose and went into the bathroom to shower and shave.

In the kitchen, Hannah said, "Seems like a nice enough chap."

"I can see why Miriam likes him," Grace said. "He's soft-spoken and has such a nice smile." She opened the fridge. "Lord, this is a mess. I'm going to take everything out and give this a good cleaning tomorrow." She closed the door and turned to Hannah.

"By the way, Hannah, I've been meaning to tell you. Randy Banks will be discharged from the hospital on Friday. He's leaving to go to Kentucky to help the family of a boy he befriended who was killed over there.

"Bob hoped he'd work at the golf course and go to college. And he may come back. Randy needs to help that family. The boy was their only child. They're farmers."

"Bob's really taken a liking to Randy," Hannah said.

"It's been wonderful for Randy and for Bob. If anyone needed a father figure, it's Randy Banks. What that boy's been through!" She stood in the middle of the room, hands on hips, scowling. "Most of those young men and women are coming home from Iraq with some type of psychological disorder. How could they not? It's been well over four years now, and the government keeps extending their time or sending them back." Tears filled her eyes. "I can't talk about it. I get so upset. I can't watch the news anymore."

"I don't watch the news," Hannah said.

Just then, Ben walked into the kitchen. "Ladies, is this a bad time?"

"No. Not at all. Come on in and have a cup of coffee, tea, a Coke, and you must try my sugar-free cookies. Freshly baked," Grace said. "Are you hungry? Can I make you a sandwich?" She opened the fridge. "We have several types of cheese, American, Swiss, an Amish cheese I bought at the tailgate market in Mars Hill last Saturday, and very good ham."

"No thanks on the sandwich. I stopped and ate before I got here," Ben said. "A glass of iced tea would be great if it's not too much trouble."

"No trouble at all. Hannah, why don't you take Ben out on the porch? It's a lovely time of day to sit out, and Miriam's sure to be here soon. I'll bring the tea."

Grace stood on tiptoe to reach the iced tea glasses from the cabinet. Ice clinked as she filled them, then crackled as she poured hot tea over the ice. She added fresh mint grown on the windowsill and placed the glasses on a pretty tray along with slices of lemon, sugar, and Splenda for herself, then carried it out to the porch.

Miriam was sitting in a chair, close to Ben.

Grace set the tray on a table. "I'd be glad to get you some tea, Miriam dear."

Miriam shook her head. "Nothing, thank you, Grace."

Perched on the top step, Sadie was intent on scraping bark from a twig with her thumb. Hannah went to sit beside her.

"Sadie, Tyler was here the other day. We built a huge kite with a dragon on it. It's on the dining room table. We're waiting for his dad to come pick it up. Would you like to see it?"

The little girl sprang to her feet. "Oh, yes. Tyler promised I could help him launch it up into the air. I can't wait."

Hannah opened the front door, and she and Sadie disappeared into the house. They circled the table several times. Carefully, the child touched an end of the kite with a fingertip. "It's so angry-looking, the dragon. He looks like he'll eat up all the other dragon kites."

"I picked up a book about kites at the library. Would you like to see it? Kites are interesting. I had no idea there were so many different kinds."

"Oh, yes, please." Sadie clapped her hands.

They sat on the couch in the living room, and Hannah opened the book and began to read.

" 'A farmer lived in a faraway country called China. One day he tied his hat with a string so that the wind would not blow it off his head and away, but the wind was very strong. It caught the hat, lifted it into the air, and took it up and away across the sky. People think that may have been the first kite ever.' "

Sadie giggled. "That's funny, Aunt Hannah." She pointed to a picture of a young Chinese man standing behind a wall, holding the string of a kite. The kite flew high above the wall and a piece of white paper was floating to the ground. A young woman in the field ran to catch the falling paper. "Tell me about that picture, please."

"The young man is sending the girl a message, a letter, and he used the kite to lift it over the wall. See how she's running to snatch it before it hits the ground?" Hannah turned the page.

"Who is that man in those funny clothes with all the horses piled up with stuff?" Sadie asked.

"His name is Marco Polo. He was a traveling salesman, who went from his home in Italy to China, a very long way away. When he returned home, he brought back wonderful things which he sold to people."

"Things like what?"

"Like beautiful silk cloth to make pretty dresses, and rings and bracelets, fine combs and mirrors."

"Did he bring back kites?"

"He probably did. Certainly, he told people in Italy about the kites he'd seen."

"I hope he brought them a dragon kite like Tyler's."

The whirlwind courtship of Miriam and Ben included Sadie, and she came to love Ben and was soon running to him and hugging him. Ben swung her in the air, and she laughed and laughed, her head thrown back, her eyes shining. When, after a week, Miriam and Ben told Sadie that they wanted to be married, if that was okay with her, she jumped up and down and yelled, "Yes. Yes." Then she stopped and asked. "But where will we live?"

"We'll buy a house on the very same street where Tyler and Melissa live," Miriam replied.

There was no pressure to set a date for the wedding. Ben must return to Virginia, find a realtor, and put his home on the market. He must notify his clients and reassure them that he would continue to provide them with the same services they were accustomed to.

There were moments when Miriam was afraid, remembering her first experience of marriage. A chat with Hannah helped.

"It took me too many years before I opened myself to love again," Hannah said. "I have loved two men since I fled Bill, and both were good, kind men. Ben is a good man. He'll be good to you and Sadie."

"Look at Miriam," Grace said to Hannah. "She's so

happy. Remember when she arrived on our doorstep, scared to death of that dreadful ex-husband of hers? She looked so haggard. She and Ben seem so right for one another. They even fit, size-wise."

Hannah looked at Grace. "How do you mean, size-wise?"

"You know, sometimes a tall, skinny man marries a tiny woman, and they never seem to, well, fit right. I always think, if he wants to kiss her he's got to bend over like a pretzel."

"Sometimes you have a weird way of thinking," Hannah replied. Her eyes grew serious. "Grace, on another subject, I'm concerned about Sarina. She's happy for Miriam, of course, but it's got to be tough. So much is happening so fast, before she's had a chance to come to terms with her own situation. It's like a seesaw: one young woman's joyful and celebrating life, the other is devastated, with hardly the energy to get about."

"Sarina will come out of this stronger and with a new direction. I have high hopes for that young woman," Grace said. "She sees a lot of Denny, don't you think? I mean, other than her counseling sessions."

"Don't start that again. It's enough we have that gossip, Alma, going about with stories. Unfortunately, she happened out of her house the moment Sarina ran into Denny. Alma saw them together on the grass and gave it her own narrow-minded interpretation."

"I've explained what really happened to the women at the beauty parlor and anyone who actually asks me about it. You know how rumors spread faster than fire," Grace said.

"She needs someone she trusts to turn to, a listening ear; Denny needs to be helpful, to fix things," Hannah replied.

"Good marriages have been built on less than that,"

Grace said, thinking that passion rarely lasted. A good solid friendship, like hers and Bob's, was the best underpinning for longevity in a relationship or in a marriage.

"It's way too soon for Sarina to be seriously involved with another man," Hannah replied. This conversation was making her cranky. "Well, I have a meeting at Bella's Park. We've got a restaurant opening in mid-July, and it's coming up way too fast. The summer's flying by."

"I'm happy about the restaurant, and for Jose and Anna." Grace's words floated in the air, for Hannah had turned and was walking away.

Ben genuinely loved the area. He rented, on a month-to-month basis, a spacious, furnished studio apartment with a porch and view of the mountains, in Barnardsville. "The housing market in Virginia is hot," he told Amelia. "The realtor says my house would sell if half its roof were missing, and it's in very good shape. I ought to get a great price."

"What about your work?" Amelia asked, still worried that all this might be too good to be true.

"Remember, I'm a consultant; it doesn't matter where I live."

Amelia breathed a sigh of relief.

42

Gossip Mongers

The last time Denny had been this angry was as a young teenager at the orphanage, when he witnessed a bully attacking a smaller boy. Driven by rage, he had clenched his teeth and fists and pummeled the attacker. In the end, he broke the bully's nose and arm and had come out of it black-and-blue with a broken leg. Unhurt, the smaller boy had run off and brought help to stop the fighting, or Denny might have suffered additional damage.

Still, the outcome of that event had frustrated him, since both he and the bully had been reprimanded, as if he, Denny, had been the offender and not the defender. It had been a humbling experience, too humbling, for he felt heroic and had anticipated a pat on the back, a word of credit for his actions. The bully, Denny thought, should have been sent to reform school. The good that came of it, however, was that a lonely Denny and little Billy Hicks became fast friends and still corresponded.

Looking back, he felt that a divine plan had been at work, for William Hicks never forgot that injustice to his defender. He became a lawyer and he specialized in defending the underdog. If he ever married—Sarina flashed into Denny's mind—he would ask Billy to be his best man.

But now his congregation was behaving strangely. There were those sly, knowing looks cast his way, as if they understood the deepest longings of his heart. He worried about it, and it affected his sleep. He especially disliked the way people looked at Sarina when she came to church, not in a kindly, welcoming manner but almost as a challenge, as if they dared her to sit among them. And after the service, they avoided her.

Initially, he had attributed their behavior to Sarina's differences: her looks and speech, the fact that she sometimes wore a sari and covered her head with a gauzy headdress. Or perhaps they were naturally curious about Zachary, who had vanished from their lives without an explanation. Were they owed an explanation? Of course, they were not. Yet Denny had considered initiating his own round of gossip, to let people know that Zachary was a loose cannon, immature and unreliable, that he had been rude to his father and inconsiderate of his wife and child; but Denny's nature would not allow such an action.

And then one afternoon, Charlie walked into his office and asked point-blank if he and Sarina were an item.

"An item?" Denny's mind went blank.

"Yes, you know what I mean, an affair. Is something going on between you two? They all know Zachary, and they're curious why he's not around and she's seeing so much of you. Is he away on business?"

Denny sprung to his feet; inadvertently his chair hit the floor. "An affair? They think I'm so base, so dishonorable?"

"They think you're human, Denny. She's young and alone. It could happen."

Denny felt the warmth spreading up his face. Surely Charlie didn't suspect his true feelings for Sarina. He would never act on them unless Sarina was divorced and free and had had enough time to heal.

"Do you believe such talk?" Spots drifted before Denny's eyes; a vein throbbed in his neck.

"Not really, but I had to ask," Charlie said.

Denny righted his chair and sat. "I'm sorry, Charlie. I'm counseling Sarina. She's been dealt a bitter blow. Zachary's gone for good. He had a terrible altercation with Max just when they were loading his cows into the truck sent to take them away. That was tough on Max, his son acting like a raving lunatic, screaming and cursing at him in front of the truck drivers. Before Max could sit down and discuss Zachary's issues, he'd packed his bags and was gone, no good-bye to his wife and child, nothing. He left a note. No apology, just said that Sarina was on her own, and he was sure that his folks would take care of her and the baby."

Charlie's face fell and he sank into a chair across the desk. "I had no idea. I am so sorry. The poor girl abandoned by her husband in a strange country. The no-good son of a—" He stopped. "Pardon me, Denny, but I'm afraid I'm mad as h———."

"A couple of weeks later, Sarina got a letter from Zachary saying that it's not his nature to settle down and that she's free to do as she likes, return to India, stay here, get divorced, whatever. As you might imagine, she was very upset and was dashing down the road to find Hannah and Max, when she crashed into me in front of the church. We hit the grass together. That, unfortunately, is when Alma walked out of her house. She started this gossip, I'm sure."

Denny leaned forward, elbows on his desk. "I should have realized what was happening, what was being said, unfounded stories that Alma and others have probably spread.

I should have called in a few parishioners and asked what was going on. I assumed that they ignored Sarina because she's different, being East Indian."

Charlie nodded. "Yeh, there could be some of that. The gossip mill's been grinding for weeks."

"I thought I knew these people. How could they be so cruel, so mean-spirited?"

"People are people, Denny, and it doesn't take much to get a story going. When they know what's going on, they'll want to take that poor woman and her child to their bosoms."

The hairs on Denny's arms bristled. "You cannot repeat what I've told you."

"I know that, but I'd like to talk to Max, ask him where his son is. He might tell me. Then it won't be coming from you, and we can nip this thing and put an end to it."

Denny lowered his head on his arms on the desk.

"Hey, Denny. It's gonna be all right. It's better when folks know the truth. It's not knowing that drives gossip."

Denny shook his head. "Pastor Johnson would have handled this so much better than I have."

"I'm not so sure of that. Pastor Johnson and I went back a long way. When he first arrived, folks were gunshy. The pastor before him seemed to have run out on them. They didn't trust any pastor. They didn't know, then, that the man had been fired by the board."

Denny nodded.

"They transferred their anger to Pastor Johnson. I tell you, son, he had a terrible time of it for a while, but he just hung in there. He prayed, and trusted, and it all worked out fine. Looking back, I can't say he did much counseling. He did a lot of work with the women's auxiliary, raising funds, things like that, and he organized activities for the kids. But he didn't counsel anybody ever. I doubt they trained ministers for that when he went to ministerial school. I imagine their idea of counseling was strictly scriptural.

"The congregation likes you, and you've done some good work. You helped May McCorkle out of her mess. She's working at a hospital now and she's even got her a nice boyfriend, I hear. You helped my boy Timmy and his wife when they were so depressed with him being out of work for so long."

"Thanks, Charlie."

Charlie stood. "As chairman of the Church Board it's my duty to stay on top of things, help keep things running smoothly. I'd hate for you to get so mad you left. We need you here." He turned to leave, then stopped, turned again, and looked at Denny. "I'll get back with you." Then Charlie closed the door quietly behind him, leaving Denny with his adrenaline pumping and Sarina very much on his mind.

Charlie's mission was easily accomplished. Max was only too happy to talk about Zachary with an old friend.

"It was a day I hoped never in my life to live through, my son screaming at me like a madman. I didn't hold on to my cool either, and I went ballistic. Zachary stalked off, and I never saw him again, never had a chance to talk about what he wanted and why. I'll regret that to my dying day."

"I sure wish there was some way you could resolve this. It's a doggone shame the way he's left it," Charlie said.

"Worse for Sarina, poor thing. She's in limbo. What's she supposed to do, get a divorce?"

"Maybe she ought to," Charlie replied. "Then she'd be free to make a new life with someone else."

"Someone like Denny Ledbetter? I hear the crap they're

saying about Denny and Sarina. They're wrong, you know. That girl's so full of pain; she's not interested in Denny or anyone else. And even if she was, can you see this congregation accepting a non-Christian foreigner as their minister's wife? Look how they treat her. It's pathetic. They're pathetic."

"Folks don't know where Zachary is: he could be off on business, and she's fooling around behind his back. A lot of them know Zachary from the time he was born. They feel a certain loyalty to him. They haven't a clue what he's turned into."

Max stared at Charlie. "My Lord, Charlie, I hadn't thought about that. You're right, of course. We have to clarify this and set the record right. Got any ideas?"

"What if you said something to the congregation in church next Sunday? I'm not sure how much of this you'd be willing to share with folks, but I think if they hear at least some of it from you, it'll all settle down and things will change for your daughter-in-law." He rested a hand on Max's shoulder. "Hey, Max, I am really sorry. This stinks."

"But you're right, Charlie. Sarina's good name's been smeared. She doesn't deserve that, nor does Denny. He's a good man." Max looked at Charlie. "Thanks, my friend. Thanks a lot."

"Glad to be of help, and by the way, good luck on the restaurant. I stuck my head in there as I came through. Looks great." Charlie smiled and walked from the room.

43

A Time for Truth

A proud and private man, Max reserved business and personal matters to himself and Hannah, but now he could no longer ignore the false rumors and the price Sarina and Denny were paying. For several days, he pondered what he might say and when. Then he squared his shoulders and headed for the church office.

In his office, Denny found it difficult to phrase a talk he planned to give about the dangers of gossip, without naming names.

It was a huge relief when Max walked in and announced, "Denny, I spoke to Charlie. I'd like to talk to the congregation this Sunday. I'm sore as can be and troubled by the vicious gossip about you and my daughter-in-law. It's unconscionable."

Denny stared up at the tall, solid man standing across from him. If there was anyone in Covington whom he respected and trusted, it was George Maxwell.

"Yes, of course. Please sit down, Max. What do you have in mind?"

Max lowered himself into the chair across from the desk. He sighed. "The truth," he said. "The truth about my son. I detest it that innocent people are suffering for the guilty, especially when I am in a position to do something about it. I'm going to tell them the truth about Zachary, who he is, what he's done to that young woman and to his family." His intent made clear, Max rose. "You'll allow me the time to address your congregation?"

"Of course." A huge weight lifted from his shoulders. Denny stood and extended his hand, which vanished into Max's grip. "And thank you."

"The pleasure is all mine," Max said, thinking that he must find Hannah and tell her what he planned to do.

The church bulletin informed parishioners that George Maxwell would speak this Sunday morning, but provided no information as to his topic. As people arrived and took their seats, there was much whispered speculation.

Denny kept the service short, a few hymns, a short reading. Then he announced that Max would speak, waved Max to the pulpit, and stepped aside.

In the front row, Hannah patted Max's hand. He rose and with deliberate steps walked to the pulpit. This is going to be hard, but there's no turning back now, he thought. His hands gripped the edges of the podium, which wobbled in his grasp. Anger churned in his belly. He cleared his throat and began.

"Most of you have known me and Bella, God rest her soul, and our son, Zachary, for many years. We've passed long, hot summers and bitter cold winters together. We've helped rebuild one another's houses after a fire, and plowed snow so we could exit our homes." He paused. *Good Lord, I sound like a preacher. Get on with it.*

"My son, Zachary, was born here. He attended school

with your sons and daughters. He grew up in Covington. After his mother died, he packed a bag and left. What most of you don't know is that he walked away without a word to me or a note to say where he might be going, or when he was returning. He was young, and you can well imagine how I worried and fretted."

He could see heads nodding.

"Over the years, he sent postcards from ports around the world: China, Russia, Iceland, Malaysia, Hawaii, and many more. 'I'm fine,' they would say, or, 'This is an interesting place to visit.' Things like that. Nothing about why he left or when he might return.

"And because life must go on, I did just that. I put my son into the hands of the Lord and stopped lying awake at night worrying about where he might be, if he was well and safe. Many years later, one morning there came a knock at the door, and there he stood with a wife. He'd never sent an invitation to his wedding or even an announcement.

"Immediately he let us know that he was not here to stay. He said he intended to live in India with his wife's family, go into her father's business. My son told me that he always hated the cows and my lifestyle, and a couple of days later, off he goes. Then for a long time, there's no word about how he is or what he's doing."

A woman coughed. People stared at Max, some with their mouths open. His eyes sought Hannah's and she nodded.

This is harder than I imagined it would be. What must they be thinking? Are they thinking I must have been a lousy father that my son ran away from me? Does it matter? I can't let it matter. For Sarina's sake, for Denny's sake, this must be said. The blame must rest where it should and not on the innocent. Max drew a deep breath, lifted his shoulders, and continued.

"A couple of months after Hannah and I were married, the doorbell rang and there was Zachary and Sarina, who was about to have a baby. As many of you know, that lovely little girl was christened Sarah, right here in this church."

Heads nodded again. Some people smiled.

"It seems that there were riots in India, so it was safer to get out of there. Only, coming back to Covington wasn't what Zachary wanted. Still, he had no place else to go. Instead of tending to his wife, comforting her—after all, the girl's separated from her family, her home—he disappears every afternoon. For weeks no one knows where he's off to, what he's doing. Well, Zachary went gambling and gambled away what little money he had."

A murmur of "no's" spreads through the crowd.

Max nodded. "That's right. He gambled. After the baby came, we tried to talk with him, to get some idea of what he wanted to do with his life. Turns out what he wanted was land. My son wanted to hack down trees and build houses for rental income. Income to do what with? Sit on his duff? Gamble and ignore his wife and baby? I said no. Maybe that was a mistake. Maybe I should have given him what he wanted."

Max grasped the podium with both hands. He leaned forward, his eyes raking the congregation. "Well, I didn't." The memory of the day they took away his cows rose before Max. His body trembled, and he planted his feet firmly on the ground.

"The day they took away my cows, Zachary came charging at me, cursing. I thought he was going to strike me, that I'd have to fight him. Luckily, it didn't come to that.

When the truck with the cows left, I went inside to talk to him. But he was nowhere about. He'd vanished, packed a bag and left without a word to his wife or anyone. Until a few days ago, none of us knew where he was or if he was coming back."

His voice rose. "And then, someone saw Sarina on the grass in front of the church and our good pastor had his arm about her. That was the day Sarina had a letter from Zachary saying he wasn't ever coming back, that he wasn't cut out to be a husband or father, and not to count on him. She was frantic, as any of you might have been, and took off running from the house to find Hannah and me. She plowed into Pastor Denny as he was coming from the church. They fell to the ground, and our good pastor put his arm about her shoulders to keep her from falling flat on her face and to comfort her. I'd have done the same under those circumstances, wouldn't you?"

Heads nodded, and Max threw up his arms.

"I'm ashamed for my son. There's nothing I wouldn't do to help my daughter-in-law and grandchild. If she wants to go home to her family, I'll see she gets there. If she chooses to stay and make her home with us, it would please me more than I can tell you. There isn't a sweeter, kinder young woman than Sarina. As for Pastor Denny, we've got a good man here. There isn't a dishonorable bone in his body. Whatever rumors you've heard are wrong, misguided, and cruel. And that's all I have to say."

Max felt as if he were a balloon that someone pricked, and the air was seeping out of him. Slowly, he walked from the pulpit and took his seat beside Hannah in the front pew. The church was silent. Then someone clapped, and the entire congregation began to clap. Only when Denny stepped to the pulpit and raised his hands for the benediction did they stop.

Later, at home, Sarina found Max in the living room watching a ball game. "Excuse me," she said softly.

Max shut off the set. "How you doing, my girl?"

"I want to thank you. I heard all you said at the church. It must have been hard for you to speak about Zachary. I am so sorry." She began to cry.

"Now, now." Max pulled a handkerchief from his pocket and handed it to her. "It had to be done, and now it's over. I don't believe the innocent should suffer for the guilty."

She buried her face in her hands. "I am so ashamed. How will I ever face them?"

"You haven't a thing to be ashamed about."

"They must think I was a very bad wife to drive my husband from me."

"Sarina, I made it very clear who my son is and what he's done. The shame is his, not yours, and as I told them, it would please me very much if you and Sarah made your lives here with us. In time, when you're able to, I suggest you divorce Zachary and make a new life."

She was weeping now, great sobs coming from behind the handkerchief.

Max rose, came to her, and put his arms about her. Sarina collapsed against him. They stood like this for a time, until her crying ceased, and she stepped away.

"Feel a bit better?" He smiled at her.

Sarina nodded. Her eyes were red, her face puffy. "Thank you, Max." She turned and hastened from the room. Max sat in his big chair and clicked on the TV.

Max's action in the church changed Sarina's life. Within a week she was inundated with letters and phone calls. Cards arrived wishing her well. Invitations came to tea, to lunch, to join this or that organization or women's group. But best of all, a young woman, Lucille Binder, who's infant was the same age as Sarah and whose husband was in Iraq, called, and within no time the two became friends.

"It does not take but one friend to make one happy, does it?" Sarina said to Hannah, who agreed.

44

Jose and Anna's Restaurant

*I*t was a festive evening. Music floated the length of Cove Road. Cars lined the road and two busloads from a retirement community to the south of Asheville deposited passengers in front of Bella's Park and drove away to park in the lot at Elk Plaza.

Jose, splendid in his jacket of many colors, welcomed all comers and escorted them to reserved tables. There would be three sittings tonight, with the earliest at four in the afternoon, another at six-thirty, and for those choosing to dine later, a sitting at nine.

The room was warm and welcoming in rust and ocher, rose and orange, with touches of yellow, and people praised the atmosphere. Jose beamed. In the kitchen Irena, Anna, and Irena's son Pedrito cooked, while Pedrito's wife, Lucia, and his daughter Adalena served the diners.

The menu included lemon-marinated shrimp, toasted corn *empanadas* (hot, crispy meat-filled pastries), *llapingachos* (potato-and-cheese pancakes), and *patacones* (squashed, fried green bananas). There was Lorca soup (potato soup with cheese and avocado), and fish-and-vegetable soup (listed on the menu as *chupe de pescado*). Popular dishes, more palatable to Western palates, included *seco de pollo* (stewed chicken over rice with avocado slices), beef-steak smothered with onions, and for the vegetarians, *pollo sin pollo* (all vegetables and no chicken). The offerings were different, and interesting.

Every sitting was filled. Jose, well known to many of the guests, beamed and welcomed all with wide smiles and gestures. At the end of the evening, when the cash was counted in Hannah's office, the celebration continued.

"You have done well, Jose." Max shook his hand.

"I owe much to you, Señor Max. I much grateful all my life." Jose threw his arms about Max and kissed him grandly on both cheeks.

45

The Kite-Flying Contest

On a sunny Sunday afternoon, several weeks after the restaurant opened, the ladies, their menfolk, children, and friends piled into cars and vans and drove to the big open field beyond Caster Elementary School. Wide oaks and tall poplar trees rimmed the area, providing shade for picnic tables and chairs, as well as for those who chose to spread blankets on the ground.

At one end of the field, six steps above the ground, a grandstand with a canvas awning had been erected. Arranged in rows, chairs had been set up from which the judges observed the proceedings.

On the field, twelve boys and girls stood holding their kites. Each had a helper nearby, someone to carry the kite a hundred feet away and hold it high to catch the wind. Tyler's friend Tommy Ullman waited to help him launch his kite.

Running to launch a kite was the hardest way to do it, Tyler had explained to Hannah. The kite might dive and crash before it even got started. Hannah crossed her fingers. Some of the kites were larger than Tyler's and some were smaller, but all were bright and colorful, with exotic dragon designs, though none were as fierce as Tyler's dragon.

A kite-flying contest, Tyler had explained to her, was not like a contest where someone shot off a gun or yelled "Go" and everyone started for a finish line. It was about waiting for the wind, judging its velocity, and catching the wind, then easing out your line, keeping your kite aloft, and seeing that it did not tangle with another kite or in a power line or in a treetop. Kite flying was not a silly game but a serious sport, with clubs and organizations dedicated to this craft and art and with statewide, nationwide, and international contests.

This had all been news to her. When she was a girl, Hannah, her father, and her brother had made kites with tissue paper and thin sticks. They had tied long strands of cloth left over from her mother's sewing box as tails, and run about a field chasing them.

Today, the wind was fickle, one moment stirring among the branches, the next moment still. It didn't take gusts of twenty-five miles an hour to raise the type of kites being flown, but on this fine summer day when wind should be moving among the trees, and flags should be fluttering, the air was stagnant.

Parents and friends waited anxiously, hoping for the slightest stir of wind. In the field, the boys and girls shifted from leg to leg. Under the awning, the judges, binoculars in hand, shifted in their chairs. The tension could be cut with a knife. And still no wind.

And then, as if by some miracle, a breeze rustled the leaves of nearby branches. Hannah felt it touch her face. A hush fell over the field, and everyone rose to their feet in anticipation. The row of boys and girls tensed and moved in unison, handing off their kites to a friend.

Tyler's friend accepted his kite. The line stretched tight

between them as he paced a hundred feet. At a signal from Tyler, Tommy raised the kite with both hands. In an instant, the wind caught the kite and it lifted. Tommy stepped aside, and Tyler reeled in the line to facilitate the kite's climb, ten feet, twenty, higher, then higher, joining the rising kites, their long tails streaming against the deep blue sky.

Hannah found it hard to keep her head bent back, and yet how else but lying flat upon the ground could she see the kites swirl and dip as they climbed up and up? Her heart leaped in her chest when she saw that Tyler's kite was flying too close to the kite of a girl near him, and she watched him take in line and turn his kite away in another direction. Then two kites tangled and their owners walked toward each other. Hannah shaded her eyes and watched as the tangle moved down the line and became undone. A boy lost control of his kite, which dipped, rolled, and dived to earth, eliminating him from the competition. Hannah's heart went out to him.

The wind held steady. Some kites soared higher than others, some dove in a different direction from the others. Kites performed in ways she had never seen. She watched Tyler's kite give a quick spin, a hard flip, and drop fast and sudden before leveling. Later, Tyler explained that it was a free-style competition with few rules and regulations, and the moves she had watched him do included barrel rolls and backflips.

Overall it was lovely to watch, a balancing act between boy, kite, and wind, a dance with gravity. But Hannah's neck ached. Miss Lurina, in a chair nearby, had fallen asleep and was emitting light snores. Her head hung forward on her chest. Grace and Bob had moved farther back into the shade of trees. She wished Amelia would pay more attention to the competition and less to Ben and Miriam. The three of them were whispering together. Hannah turned back to the kites.

Tyler did not, as he had hoped and prayed, win the competition. A girl did. Her kite had outperformed the others in clever movements, Tyler explained, using words like "lazy Susans" and "Jacob's ladder." Lurina, confused by it all and by the heat, kept congratulating Tyler as if he had been the winner. Tyler smiled at her and offered his arm to steady her walk as they left the field. Except for her aching neck, Hannah had enjoyed watching the enthusiasm of the young people, and she was proud that Tyler, a good sport, took his loss in stride.

"Next time," he said. "I'll win it next time."

They gathered for a barbecue in Bob's backyard. He had added a large patio with chairs and tables and a screened pool. Ben had worked his way through graduate school at a fast-food restaurant and had mastered the art of flipping burgers. Sadie ran about delivering special orders, rare, well done, or almost charred.

Miss Lurina settled into a lounge. Her head fell to one side and she dozed. Grace covered her with a light blanket. In an antique shop, Amelia had found an old Victrola and a stack of jazz recordings from the 1950s. Denny asked Sarina to dance. She looked to Hannah for approval, and when Hannah smiled, Sarina handed Sarah to Amelia. Grace was certain that in time something would come of their relationship. Sarina had filed for divorce, and that took a year in North Carolina.

Melissa stood on her father's shoes while he tried to move to the tempo of the music. Russell never had much rhythm. Tyler kept busy serving cold drinks and generally being helpful. The branches of a weeping Japanese cherry tree dipped in the breeze. The Big Dipper emerged, bright against the night sky.

What a grand day this has been, Hannah thought.

"This is what peace feels like, what heaven must be like." Grace tucked her arm through Bob's. "To be among people you love, people you can say anything to and know you will be understood and accepted."

She looked around. Miriam and Ben danced cheek to cheek. Ben had sold his home in Virginia almost immediately and had bought a house here and begun to settle in. There would be a wedding soon.

Grace thought about weddings: Miss Lurina and Old Man, Russell and Emily (though that marriage had not worked out), Max and Hannah, and now Miriam and Ben. Amelia, holding the sleeping baby, sat in a chair near Lurina. She looked radiant. Grace looked at Bob. She loved him, no doubt of that, but she preferred not to marry, and they'd both gotten quite used to things the way they were.

Grace's eye met Hannah's, and they smiled at each other. Life was an endless up-and-down, one thing after another to handle, to fix, to solve, to enjoy, to relish. Grace closed her eyes and silently prayed. *Thank you, God, for this lovely day and night, for the comfort you provide when we most need it, and for all your blessings.*